D0302629

Hidden

WITHDRAWN

D22 212 219 5

Hidden

KATY GARDNER

MICHAEL JOSEPH
an imprint of
PENGUIN BOOKS

MICHAEL JOSEPH

Published by the Penguin Group

Penguin Books Ltd, 80 Strand, London WC2R ORL, England

Penguin Group (USA) Inc., 375 Hudson Street, New York, New York 10014, USA

Penguin Group (Canada), 90 Eglinton Avenue East, Suite 700, Toronto, Ontario, Canada M4P 2Y3
(a division of Pearson Penguin Canada Inc.)

Penguin Ireland, 25 St Stephen's Green, Dublin 2, Ireland
(a division of Penguin Books Ltd)

Penguin Group (Australia), 250 Camberwell Road,
Camberwell, Victoria 3124, Australia (a division of Pearson Australia Group Pty Ltd)

Penguin Books India Pvt Ltd, 11 Community Centre,
Panchsheel Park, New Delhi – 110 017, India

Penguin Group (NZ), cnr Airborne and Rosedale Roads, Albany,
Auckland 1310, New Zealand (a division of Pearson New Zealand Ltd)

Penguin Books (South Africa) (Pty) Ltd, 24 Sturdee Avenue,
Rosebank, Johannesburg 2196, South Africa

Penguin Books Ltd, Registered Offices: 80 Strand, London WC2R ORL, England

www.penguin.com

First published 2006

1

Copyright © Katy Gardner, 2006

The moral right of the author has been asserted

All rights reserved
Without limiting the rights under copyright
reserved above, no part of this publication may be
reproduced, stored in or introduced into a retrieval system,
or transmitted, in any form or by any means (electronic, mechanical,
photocopying, recording or otherwise), without the prior
written permission of both the copyright owner and
the above publisher of this book

Set in 13.5/16pt Monotype Garamond
by Palimpsest Book Production Limited, Polmont, Stirlingshire
Printed in England by Clays Ltd, St Ives plc

A CIP catalogue record for this book is available from the British Library

ISBN-13: 978–0–718–14681–8
ISBN-10: 0–718–14681–6

In memory of my father, Richard Gardner.

DERBY CITY LIBRARIES	
457577	
HJ	18/09/2006
F	£10.99
City Mobile	SP6 8/13

NCP

ALVAS	ALLES	ASRC	BLAG
CENT	CHADD	DERW	MICK
MOBILE	P.TREE	B.G	SINF
2/06			
SPON	SPRW		

Prologue

29 November 2003

Taking a breath and straightening his back, Dave Gosforth paused at the threshold of the flat, his large hammy hands twitching at his side. Despite the contraction of his diaphragm, his gelatinous stomach pressed uncomfortably against his paper suit. Breathing in a second time, he mentally sucked the spare inches in. He had been planning an hour in the gym, but mercifully had been waylaid by the call. Now, as he tugged at his zip, the new fitness regime that only yesterday he had solemnly pledged to follow was thankfully banished into a section of his mind marked 'later'. The call had heralded a new beginning, an as yet unread book that in a matter of seconds he would be opening, scanning the pages for the storyline, perhaps even skipping to the conclusion. He stepped into the hall, surveying the scene.

Behind him the barred front door was hanging slightly ajar: no sign of forced entry here. Moving slowly down the hall he took in the scuffed walls and unopened bills, left in a heap by the mat. There were no pictures on the wall, or hooks on which to hang a coat; the place had a transient, uncared-for feel, like a hostel for the homeless. To the left was the living room: he'd leave that till last. On the right was the kitchen. Pausing by the plywood door, he registered the crater in the middle: a violent kick probably, or a body, falling hard. Stepping past, he looked carefully around the room.

The place was a right mess. The table was overturned, the floor scattered with crockery, and a wooden stool smashed in half. Torn net curtains trailed in the sink, their plastic railing hanging miserably from the pockmarked wall. Someone must have grabbed hold of the flimsy nylon material and brought the whole lot down, either in fury or a futile attempt to resist being pulled away. Between the sink and the capsized table the lino was scratched with a series of skid marks: a woman's heels, dragging backwards, perhaps. Blood was smeared across the wall, sprayed over the freshly kicked-in door, and congealing in pools on the floor. The scene of crime lads had their work cut out.

For the few moments that he looked carefully around the room, Dave allowed himself the small thrill he experienced each time he had a new case. He liked to be the first on the scene, even before the pathologists or photographers had arrived, when everything was still fresh. He was like a dog, catching the scent of the kill: those first, almost sacred moments of inspection, when every sense was tautened and he sniffed the evidence out. You could learn a lot, simply by standing still and looking. Take this kitchen, facing on to a concrete walkway in a mean 1970s block of flats on the outskirts of Margate. The strip lighting was on, so the attack must have taken place last night, or in the dim of the winter morning. The broken bowl and splattered cereal implied it was during breakfast. The pathologists would confirm the exact time of the woman's death, but by the look of the scummy coffee by the sink, it was about twelve hours ago. She'd most likely been alone: there was no evidence of a second mug or cereal bowl. A mobile phone was lying on the table: a little present for the telecom lads. There was no sign of a land line.

From the kitchen a trail of blood led across a stretch of beige carpet towards the squalid living room. Like most people who had the misfortune to live in this part of town, the flat's occupant was down at heel. The ragged nylon carpet was second or even third hand, resting loosely on the concrete floor; the dirty striped wallpaper was peeling at the top. On the wall opposite the kitchen door, older stains had been joined by a reddish handprint. A little further along, a clump of hair hung from a notch in the paper, embedded in bloody glue. Dave proceeded carefully through the door.

Entering the living room, he looked calmly around. The woman's body was slumped over the sagging settee, her head resting on her arms. Were it not for the browning puddle that had gathered underneath her waxy cheek, she might have been having a nap. He gazed at the pale face: the closed, heavily made-up eyes, the half-open mouth, bright pink with lipstick and trickling goo. More blood soaked into the torn foam where she was lying; her black baby-doll dressing gown was virtually shredded, the skin beneath sliced with gashes. It wasn't nice to look at, but his primary emotion was neither shock nor disgust, merely dispassionate interest. He'd seen enough nasties over the years to take this one in his stride: stabbings, bullet wounds, people dismembered by their cars. He didn't like it if a kid was involved, but very little else made him queasy or put him off his dinner.

The state some people lived in, however, never failed to amaze him. To say the room was a tip was something of an understatement. The floor was covered in rubbish: dirty plates, mouldy mugs, takeaway pizza boxes, emptied cans. A broken ashtray lay in pieces at his feet, the fag butts it had once contained sprinkled around the entrance of the room like discoloured confetti. Noting the dent in the wall, Dave guessed it had been thrown at the doorway. The room smelt of stale nicotine, cheap perfume and, with the gas fire hissing all day, the over-powering stench of a violent death. Next to the fireplace a couple of cheap foldaway chairs had been knocked over. Besides these and the settee, the only other pieces of furniture were a huge widescreen TV and fake-walnut stereo units, upon which rested a luminescent lava lamp. The TV was on: EastEnders, burbling inanely, as the dead woman stared into space.

A minute later he was outside on the walkway with the beat bobby who'd found her. They had sealed off the block, instructing the residents to stay put until they'd been questioned. Two floors down, a small crowd had gathered by the yellow tape: kids cruising on bikes, youths in hood-ies, a gaggle of women, craning their necks for the morbid details. It wasn't the first violent incident in the neighbourhood, and it wouldn't be the last. The estate had something of a reputation, to say the least.

'Got a name?'

'Jacqui Jenning. Been here about a year.'

'Got a boyfriend?'

'Not that we know of. From what the lady next door is saying, she had a bit of a reputation.'

'Right . . .'

'"Dirty little tart" were her precise words.'

'You've got this lady here, have you?'

'John's talking to her. She called at six-ten, said she was coming back from work and saw the mess through the kitchen window. Didn't hear anything this morning, though.'

'Okay. Don't let her go anywhere. We'll need a door-to-door on the whole estate. There's been a hell of a fight. Someone must have noticed something.'

Downstairs, the scene of crime lads had arrived. As he heard their boots clumping up the concrete steps, Dave pulled his shoulders back a fraction, gathering his thoughts.

'All righty,' he muttered to himself. 'Let's get going.'

He didn't get away for another four hours. He'd managed to call Karen and warn her he'd be late, so she'd put his dinner on low and told Harvey not to wait up. By the time he'd driven across Margate and returned to Herne Bay, it was nearly midnight. He parked the car in the driveway and sat in the dark for a moment, staring at his lit-up house. Like wiping mud from one's shoes, he needed a moment to sluice off the details of the evening before going inside. He took a pride in not letting his work get to him, but all the same it was unpleasant stuff: a prostitute getting her skull poked in by what looked like a chisel. Closing his eyes he pictured the tatty front room, with the dog-ends and pooling blood. Now the body was photographed and zipped into a mortuary bag, and it was up to him and his lads to find the culprit. It'd either be a domestic: a jealous boyfriend, who didn't like how she made a living, or a crazy john who didn't want to pay for his night of fun. Possibly it'd be drugs.

Opening his eyes he took in the organza curtains of his own front room, drawn against the cold night. Directly above was Harvey's room, with his Ninja curtains, and next to that the master bedroom, emanating the soft glow of Karen's reading light. Levering his heavy frame from the driver's seat, Dave stepped on to the drive with relief.

Forty miles away in the depths of south London a woman lay skewiff across her bed, her small daughter's arm thrown over her back. A well-thumbed edition of Horrid Henry was abandoned beside the pillow; more books littered the floor. The woman had not meant to fall asleep so early and would wake a few hours later, dry mouthed and stiff in her daytime clothes. For now, however, her mouth twitched with a fleeting smile. Another day finally finished, she was alone with her dreams.

As the couple slept, the lights of passing cars threw patterns against the wall. Outside, the city thrummed, a low roar that neither mother nor daughter noticed. They still had almost a month left: over twenty-nine uneventful days before the woman would visit Peckham to value a flat, fall in love with a stranger, and their lives would become inextricably linked to the fate of poor dead Jacqui Jenning.

PART ONE

I

26 February 2005

It's five past four on the last Saturday in February, and we're playing hide and seek. It's Poppy's favourite game, always has been. At fifteen months old she'd stand in the middle of the living room with her chubby fists bunched over her eyes, imagining herself invisible. Later, she learned to crouch behind the door, but when I stepped into the room she'd jump out, giggling. She never let *me* hide, that wasn't the point. What she liked was the delicious anticipation of being caught: that terrifying joy of being swooped upon by giant adult hands that tickled and squeezed. She'd make me find her, over and over again, like a video clip being endlessly replayed.

These days it's more sophisticated. First, I have to hide, but no longer am I allowed to simply hover behind the door. Now it has to be *hard*. She likes a puzzle, does my Pops, and hates to be patronized. '*Mummy!*' she'll shout in irritation if I make it too easy. 'I am *not* six, okay?' Fact is, she's only just turned seven, but six has become a distant and despised land, filled with pink teddies and frilly frocks. 'Before you know it, I'll be a *teenager!*' she announced the other day, making me gawp at her, goggle-eyed at the thought.

So I have to hide somewhere challenging enough for her to feel she's being taken seriously, yet not so obscure that she'll never find me. After my three turns, it's her go. It's

9

always that order, always that number. Currently I'm on hide number two. I have Jo strapped to my chest in one of those complicated strappy slings that takes an age to tie but keeps him snug and warm against my boobs. Bunched up and gently snoring, his wrinkled face puts me in mind of a miniature geriatric. As Poppy counts I lope softly out of the door and into the corridor, my hands clutching the back of the sling so Jo doesn't get jiggled.

In the corridor I pause, deciding where to go. We've been living in the building for nearly eight months, yet still I feel like an interloper. Behind me is the prefab kitchen, tacked to the side of the house like a boil. We're planning to demolish this as soon as the build's complete, but for now Si's set up a temporary sink with plumbing for a washing machine and I'm cooking on a camper gas stove: functional, but not exactly *Homes and Gardens*. Then there's this odd dark tunnel where I'm currently standing, with its concrete floor and damp patches. This connects the kitchenette with the main building, opening out on to the open-plan living area on the ground floor. We've done the most work here: extortionate wooden flooring fitted, new windows on each side so you can see out to the river and fields, and Si's state-of-the-art lighting. Remembering how much it cost still makes my stomach do a little jump. It's an investment, Si keeps saying; it'll be *fine*.

In the middle of the room there's a sunken den, with our three-piece suite and the TV, behind which is the enormous picture window that Si fitted before Christmas. A door on the far side leads to our still unplumbed Fired Earth toilet. At the back are two sets of steps on either side that rise to the gallery at the top. The new wooden stairs are on the right, near the kitchen, and the old metal steps on the left. On the first floor six small rooms, once used for storing hops, lead off the gallery. We've cleared three, making habitation almost feasible, whilst the rest remain ruins. Past these rooms, on the far side of the gallery, is a metal ladder leading to the storeroom at the top. The plan is to fit a fancy spiral staircase and make this a 'penthouse suite' for our B&B guests, with an en-suite bathroom and panoramic views over the estuary. The reality is that half the roof has fallen in and, from the scampering sounds I keep hearing, it's inhabited by rats.

In the kitchen Poppy's reached fifteen. I make for the curtains. It's a bit obvious, but I can't face climbing all those stairs with Jo in his sling. I'll wrap myself up tight, cocooned in the thick white calico, and pray she doesn't spot my trainers. Here she comes. By the time she calls 'Ready or not!' she's already halfway down the corridor. Now I hear her feet, scampering over the wooden planks.

'I'm going to get you, Mummy!' she cries. 'I know where you are!'

Rather than continue towards the curtains, she goes clattering up the metal steps. Jo's wriggling, so I lean over, trying to loosen the sling's corduroy ties. Upstairs, I can hear the slam of our bedroom door. I'm starting to fret about Poppy climbing the rickety ladder to the large loft at the top. I've forbidden her to go up there: the ladder is treacherously steep and on the other side of the padlocked door the floorboards are rotting. Throughout the winter the ceiling has been shedding plastery clumps, flaking away from the rendering like Jo's cradle cap. Worst of all, on the far side of the loft a small door opens on to a rickety platform where a hundred years earlier sacks of wheat or hops were raised from the barges below. The rusted winch is still there, projecting over a sixty-foot drop into the mud. The room is very definitely out of bounds.

Until a short while ago I could hear Si banging about in the room that he uses for painting, but now everything is quiet. I dread him appearing. At my bosom the wriggling is growing more concerted. I place my hand on the fluffy head that's protruding from the sling, but it's too late. Like a cat spoiling for a fight, Jo starts to yowl. Now Poppy's running along the gallery, her feet thudding above me. She stops for a moment, listening, then hurtles down the stairs, a four-foot vortex of triumphant fury, blonde plaits flapping, skinny legs skidding to a halt in front of the curtain which she rips back, like she's proving a point.

'*Mum!* Why do you always have to let Jo spoil it?'

'He's a little baby,' I say, frowning at her as I step from the curtains. 'I can't stop him from crying.'

'You can. You just let him do that so you don't have to play with me.' I feel a heavy lurching in my belly, as if something unpleasant's lodged there.

'I'm *trying*!' I say pleadingly, as if a seven-year-old is interested in my aims and objectives. What she wants is my total, undivided attention. What she wants, she keeps telling me, is to go back to it being just her and me, in our London flat. She doesn't need a daddy or a brother, she says. All she needs is me.

I squat down, releasing Jo from his corduroy bondage and unhooking my maternity bra. Two seconds later he's latched on, his soft lips pulling hard at my nipple. Poppy stands over us, glowering.

'Why don't I skip my last go and you hide?' I say. 'Then it won't matter whether Jo's making a noise.'

'It's still your turn.'

'It'll work much better this way round. Then you can have your tea and we'll go to Pat's.'

'I don't want to go to Pat's!'

I suck at my teeth, wanting to scream.

'Come on, Pops,' I say, trying to be placatory. 'I know you've had a rotten day, but I promise tomorrow will be more fun. Perhaps we can go to that park behind Pat's house. Go and hide and Jo and I will count to twenty, then we'll come and find you.'

She looks at me as if I'm an idiot.

'Jo can't count,' she says, then turns on her heel and strops off.

I count slowly, hoping that Jo will have finished his sucking by the time I get to twenty. As I'm calling out the numbers, I hear a door upstairs open and close. If Poppy was still angry she'd have slammed it, but this is quiet and deliberate, so the game must still be on. At nineteen, I push my little finger into Jo's mouth and gently pull him off my boob. The suction makes a rude sucking sound, like a grotesque kiss, then his head flops back, his eyes woozy. Tying the straps back around my middle, I haul myself up.

'Coming!' I call. 'Ready or not!'

It's then that I hear the car, the distant growl of an engine starting up on the drive. Si must finally have gone out. I'm partly relieved but a bit panicked too. All day I've been waiting for this, and now I need to move quickly. I have to finish the game as quickly as I can, then drag the bags into my car and leave.

'Okay, missus!' I shout. 'Where are you?'

I scout around the living room, knowing she's unlikely to be here. If I find her too quickly there'll be another scene, but I'm horribly impatient. The click of the door seemed to have come from behind me, but whether this means that she's upstairs or in the kitchen, I'm unsure: the building is so large and, as usual, I was distracted by Jo. Checking the bathroom, I haul myself up the steps. Recently she's taken to scooting from one room to the next as I search, making the game last longer. Rocking the sling from side to side to get Jo back to sleep, I push open my bedroom door. The floor is scattered with the overnight clothes that Si discarded before taking his bath. Bending unsteadily, I check that Poppy isn't hiding under the bed. All I can see is the silhouette of a suitcase, crumpled pyjamas and a forgotten paperback. She's not in the wardrobe, either. The room is silent, dust floating in the weak sun that has briefly appeared from behind the drifting clouds. I close the door, moving down the gallery towards her room.

She's not here. For a brief moment I imagine that the rippled mound of her duvet contains her body, but when I pull it back there's just her discarded nightie and Cookie, her blue panda.

I pace down the gallery. Any minute now, Si could return. 'Come on, Poppy,' I call. 'I give up!'

There's no answer. Leaning over the wooden railing I peruse the living room. Not a trace. Could she be in the kitchen? I hurry along the gallery, pushing open the doors of the derelict rooms and glancing quickly inside. It doesn't take long: besides the pots of paint and collapsed slurries of peeled wallpaper, the rooms are empty. When I reach the metal steps that lead to the door at the top my chest clenches at the thought of Poppy climbing so high. Grabbing hold of the railings I start to pull myself up, then stop with relief. The padlock is still hanging from the bolt on the door.

I return down the wooden stairs, still calling Poppy's name. I have been hunting for her for over ten minutes and am teetering on the uncomfortable cusp that divides irritation from unease. The ground floor is too open-plan for effective hiding, so even though I prod the curtains and glance behind doors I've guessed she isn't here. Plodding down the corridor I return to the kitchen, but she isn't under the table or behind the back door. She isn't hiding under the coats that are bundled, collapsed, by the shoe rack, nor is she squatting in the cubby hole where I keep the dustpan and brush. I am beginning to feel rattled.

'Poppy!' I call again. My voice has taken on a different timbre: higher and more fretful. It's almost time for tea, yet any moment Si might return. I'll stop at a garage, I decide, buy some sandwiches.

'Come on, sweetheart!' I call. 'We need to go!'

The building remains silent. I run back into the living room, then freeze, holding my breath so I'll catch the smallest sound. But there's nothing, just Jo's snuffling and the brush of a branch on a window. I've always found her by this stage in the game; she's too young for subterfuge: she laughs or sneezes, or calls out my name.

'Poppy!' I yell once more. 'I give up!'

There is no reply. My emotions are tipping from irritation to something darker: a gathering panic, like a twister spiralling closer. Where the hell *is* she?

'Poppy!'

Biting my lip, I climb back up the stairs. I could move more quickly without Jo in the sling, but am too impatient for the gentle manoeuvrings that releasing him would require. There is no cause for alarm, I tell myself. This is the game. Poppy hides, I seek. Yet as I scuttle along the gallery, throwing open doors and finding nothing, an unformed dread is curling deep inside me. Nearly twenty-five minutes have passed since I heard the door close. I crash back down the stairs and stand by the picture window, trying to remain calm. Behind me the house buzzes with my daughter's absence.

She must be outside. I gaze through the glass at the building site that constitutes our garden: mud, breeze blocks resting against the side wall, tarpaulin covering the abandoned foundations. The yard is empty; as I thought, Si has taken the car and gone. There is nothing for Poppy out here. The weather's bitter; I have been yearning for signs of spring, yet this morning flecks of snow drifted in the air. It's inconceivable that Poppy would have come outside in her thin T-shirt and ra-ra skirt. All the same, I push open the door.

'Poppy!' I shout at the grey afternoon. *'Poppy!'*

Could she have run from the yard along the creek? Imagining the labyrinth of paths that weave through the marsh makes my stomach do a useless flop, like a beached fish trying to return to water. In a short while it will be dark. My daughter is not an adventurer, she will surely get lost in the desolate landscape of decaying boats and mud flats; she could slip, fall into the salty water. I start to move outside, the fear cresting in my chest. In a moment I will find her and this biting panic will be rendered ridiculous: the groundless fears of an over-protective mother.

'Poppy! Where *are* you?'

Clambering around the tarpaulin, I reach the fence that rings the property and peer desperately over. The boatyard stretches behind the warehouse. To the right a muddy lane leads to the Perkins' cottage, followed by a row of garages and Trish's place. To the front, a small path twists through clumps of swaying reeds to the riverside. Beyond that, the marsh sprawls towards the dulling sky. Stumbling towards the creek, I scan the horizon. Six months earlier the view filled me with joy: the vastness of the landscape, the seagulls and abandoned boats, the arching horizon. Now it sickens me.

'Poppy!'

The land is so flat that had she gone along the path I

would surely be able to glimpse her small figure disappearing into the distance. But all I can see is a man with a dog walking fast towards me, his shoulders hunched at the cold. I wave my arms in his direction.

'Have you seen a little girl?' The question makes Poppy's disappearance real, another step towards all-encompassing panic.

'No, love.'

He's in his sixties, buttoned up in a thick rainproof and wearing a bobble hat. His Labrador trots happily behind him.

'We were playing hide and seek,' I say, trailing off as the man stops by the fence. He pulls a face, a gesture from an older generation who believed that children weren't to be fussed over.

'Bit cold for that, isn't it?'

'I can't find her anywhere. I was worried she'd gone off by the river . . .'

'There aren't any little girlies down there, love. There's just gulls and crabs and lots of mud.'

He chuckles and moves on, the dog lifting its leg on the wooden posts of our gate. He's right, of course. Poppy may barricade herself into her room in a sulk or throw herself on to my bed, screaming to be left alone, but these displays are designed to catch my attention, for she hates solitude. With maternal certainty I know she would never go to the river alone.

I start to jog back towards the kitchen, desperately hoping that I will find her there. I'll open the door, and she'll be sitting at the table smirking at me in triumph. But the kitchen is exactly as I left it: the cup of juice and half-chewed biscuit on the table a stabbing testimony to how much I take for granted and how much I have to lose. I gaze numbly at the scene, longing for her with a physical force that clogs my throat. The churning anxiety I experienced the last time I was in the room has now been replaced by something weightier and more certain. According to the kitchen clock, it's ten to five. That means that over forty minutes have passed since I called 'Ready or not!' Poppy has gone. My beloved daughter has gone.

For a moment I am unable to move. I pause on the concrete floor staring uselessly around the room as if it will miraculously yield her up. Forty minutes earlier Poppy went to hide, and now she's gone. This simple statement is so terrifying that my legs buckle.

Jo is beginning to squirm, but I ignore him. Running down the corridor, I hurry to the bottom of the steps that lead to our bedrooms.

'Poppy!'

I am praying for noise: a shuffling of feet or even a faint sob, but none comes. I have checked the upstairs rooms twice. I am sure that she is not in the living room or the kitchen or bathroom. I heard the car, I keep remembering, the movement of tyres down the gravel drive. I am too panicked to let the thought take form.

One faint hope remains. Grabbing my phone from the settee, I press in Trish's number. Her mobile rings twice, then she picks up.

'Hi, Mel! What you up to?'

The normality of her voice makes my eyes well.

'Are you okay?'

'It's Poppy, Trish. I can't find her . . .' My voice is high and shaky, almost out of control.

'What do you mean?'

'We were playing hide and seek . . . she's not come over to you, has she?'

'I'm not at home. I'm just coming back from Tesco's . . .'

'Oh God, Trish . . . Si's gone too!'

Now I've said it, there's no going back. We're no longer playing, no longer edging around the hole that has opened at our feet. Poppy has gone. *And Si's car is no longer in the drive.* Trish pauses. I can sense her draw a breath.

'Hold tight, honey,' she says gently. 'I'm coming over.'

2

I cannot bear to stand here, waiting. I have to take action; anything but remain in the kitchen listening to the echoing silence as my insides swoop like a fairground ride gone wrong. Grabbing my puffa jacket I run to the back door, throwing it open and crashing into the steely dusk.

Jo flinches at the cold, screwing up his little face in disgust. Zipping the jacket around him and placing my hand on his warm head, I stumble over the building site and through the gate, this time turning right towards the cottages at the end of the lane. Only a few days ago Bob hailed us with the news that he and Janice had adopted a baby hedgehog they'd found wandering in the reeds. Perhaps Poppy is with them, I think wildly, feeding it warm milk as she munches on a scone. Yet even as I bang on the door of their neat cottage, I know that I will not find her inside their floral front parlour.

As the door opens, my instincts are confirmed. Bob peers out from behind half-moon specs, a copy of *The Times* folded under his arm. In the background, shapes flicker across the TV, not a kids' show, but a newsreader behind a desk.

'Hello, Melanie. Anything the matter?'

'I've lost Poppy!' The words make my stomach drop even further. I keep falling, yet never seem to hit the ground. 'I thought she might be with you . . .'

He frowns. Janice is hovering behind him, regarding me suspiciously.

'We haven't seen her.' Something tight-lipped and closed

comes into his expression, like he's already made up his mind. In my panic I had forgotten the events of the last forty-eight hours: the things my neighbours have seen and the conclusions they must have drawn. I nod frantically, barely aware of what I'm saying.

'I have to get back, perhaps she's there . . . I mean, I have to call the police . . .'

Then I am back on the lane, hurling across the muddy gravel, my arms gripped tightly around Jo, praying that this will end.

The next thing that I do is dial 999. My fingers tremble as they punch in the number. I am stepping from what could still be perceived as a minor domestic mix-up to the reporting of an official incident. As I wait for my call to be answered I remember DCI Gosforth's card, lurking somewhere in the jumble on the kitchen table. The image of his gloating face makes me feel physically sick. I push it from my mind. There's no connection. There can't be.

'Hello, caller. What service do you require?'

'Police,' I whisper.

Trish arrives first. I have searched each room a third time, paced the garden, and have just finished ringing the parents of Poppy's few friends as she strides through the back door. The response of the two mothers I have spoken to is identical: surprised concern, underlain by a thinly disguised stratum of disapproval. Only careless mothers lose their children, their shocked voices imply; this is not something that could happen to *them*. Elly has been at her ballet class all afternoon, I am informed, and Lily is with her grandparents. There are no more numbers left to call. Gulping back my hysteria, I place the receiver back in its cradle and turn to find Trish closing the door behind her.

The moment I see her face the sharp-edged terror that's been bulking inside me dissolves, becoming hot and viscous, impossible to repress. Trish is holding out her arms, and I fall into them, the hard bundle of her baby pressing into my tummy.

'Jesus, Trish, she's gone!' I sob when I eventually let go of her. 'We were playing hide and seek and she's vanished!'

She steps back, regarding me with her kind brown eyes. We've only been friends for a couple of months, yet as I clutch her hand and gaze into her pretty face she's my only ballast in this sudden tidal wave.

'Tell me what happened.'

We sit together at the cluttered table. As I talk I knead at my wedding ring, the flesh underneath pale and peeling. In his baby bouncer on the floor, Jo burbles happily.

'We were playing hide and seek, and I was looking for her. I mean, I heard her going upstairs . . . And the door closed . . . Then I went up to look and she was gone . . .'

'What about Si?'

'He came back this morning! He's been upstairs all day, working on the top floor . . . Then later I heard this door close behind me and the car drive off . . .'

'And this was before Poppy hid?'

I shake my head, not liking the direction of her questions. 'I don't know!'

'Have you called him? I mean, perhaps there was a mix-up and he thought he was meant to be taking her out or something . . .'

She trails off, watching me thoughtfully. She is so pregnant that she has had to push the chair back from the table and sit astride it, her hands folded over her woolly jumper like an obese diner reclining after a large meal.

'The police have taken his mobile . . .'

I can't continue, for my teeth have started to chatter, like a joke-shop skeleton.

'You're freezing. Put this over you.' Pulling the jumper over her head, she slips it over my shoulders. She's right. Shock has turned me to ice.

'I'll make some tea,' she says, rising.

A few minutes later the police arrive. First the lights of their car sweep up the lane, then I hear the smack of a car door, followed by their boots crunching up the drive. Trish lets them in as I huddle under her maternity jumper. By now I am shaking uncontrollably.

There are two of them: a young man, with a smooth, inexpressive face that reminds me of one of the guys at Don's agency – a lousy salesman who Don caught snorting coke in the toilets and had to sack – and a woman, who stands beside him. She's blonde and pretty in a provincial way, with light blue eyes that impassively scan the untidy kitchen. The policeman offers me a limp hand and tells me his name is Police Constable Johnson.

'We've received a report of a child missing from this address,' he says, turning to Trish. 'Are you the mother?'

'That's *me*.'

I stand, not caring when my trembling legs bump the table and a pile of papers slithers to the floor. PC Johnson has pulled his notebook from the front pocket of his jacket.

'And your name is . . . ?'

'Melanie Stenning.'

He jots it down, not making the connection. With his dead-pan eyes and predatory smile, his manner is significantly different from Dave Gosforth's: a rank and file worker, trained in proper procedures but missing the blooming obvious.

'What's the age of the child?'

'She's seven. Her name's Poppy.'

'Can you give me a description?'

'She's got blonde hair, tied back in plaits, and blue eyes, and . . .' I trail off. How can I describe my child with the bland words that he is waiting to jot down in his pad? She is so beautiful that I could happily cover her from head to toe in kisses, imbibing her smooth ivory skin, her soft pink lips and the silken hair that ripples over my admiring fingers. She is gorgeous, dazzling, an explosion of light. Yet as I gaze dumbly back into the nonplussed face of PC Johnson I have no further words to offer.

'What was she wearing?' he says in a tone edging towards boredom.

'A denim ra-ra skirt and a pink top with love hearts over it, white trainers . . .'

'We'll need a photo, if you've got one.'

'We think her stepdad's taken her,' Trish interjects. 'Mel heard his car leaving just after she'd gone.'

'I'm not sure,' I mutter. 'I don't know why he'd do something like that . . .'

'Okey-dokey. Hold on a minute, ladies; let's take it one thing at a time.'

I bite my lip. I do not want to take it one thing at a time. I want the police to be out in the freezing evening with a helicopter and a fleet of cars, whizzing down every road in the whole damn country, searching for my child. The policeman scribbles in his pad, ignoring the frenzied tapping of my foot.

'And where did you last see your daughter, Melanie?'

'Here, in the house. We were playing hide and seek.'

'And I take it you've thoroughly searched the premises?'

'Of course I have. She's not here.'

'Do you know what time it was when you last saw her?'

'About four? We started playing at about a quarter to. I hid and then it was her turn, then I heard a door close . . .'

'The door to . . . ?'

'I assumed it was somewhere upstairs, or maybe the kitchen, but it could have been anywhere . . . I can't really remember. I mean, Jo was feeding and I wasn't really listening . . .'

He peers ponderously in the direction of the corridor. 'I've looked all over the house,' I finish lamely.

'And there's a possibility that your husband may have taken her out? Do you think he may have forgotten to tell you his plans?'

'No!' I shake my head in irritation. 'It's not like that!'

Trish moves closer, taking my hand and squeezing it. 'We're worried he's not going to bring her back.'

I stare at the unswept floor, taking in the scraps of pasta from lunch, plastic beads from Poppy's hair-braiding kit and my own muddy footprints. I do not want to start crying, not now.

'Or perhaps she's wandered off somewhere . . .' I add weakly.

'Does your husband have a mobile?'

'No.' I stare at him obstinately, refusing to explain why.

'And do you know where he might have gone?'

I shake my head. London? His mother's cold house, with its echoing rooms and mouldy carpets? Anything seems possible, for over the last months Si's normal habits and patterns have become unrecognizable, like racing clouds blown about by the wind.

'I have no idea.'

'Can you describe the vehicle?'

'It's an old white Volkswagen Estate. I don't know the

registration. He borrowed it from his friend this morning.'

'Can you tell us how to contact this friend? We'll need the registration number.'

'His name's Ol. Si was working with him. His mobile number's pinned up on the board over there.'

I point to the cork board that hangs on the far wall, with its load of seven-year-old's paintings, flyers for organic vegetable boxes and letters from the school. In the far corner, Si has scrawled Ol's number on the back of a leaflet advertising takeaway curries, in case of emergencies.

'Righty ho,' says the police constable, nodding. 'Before we go any further I'm going to get these vehicle details and give them to our control unit, then we'll have a quick scoot around the property and make sure she's not still hiding from us, shall we?'

I shrug impatiently. 'Sure. But I've looked upstairs about four times and the door to the top is locked. She's definitely not there.'

Jo has started to complain. Squatting by the bouncy chair I unclick the harness and pull him out, burying my face in his warm body as his dimpled legs kick the air. I still can't believe that Si would take Poppy, but, however much I will it not to be so, she has gone. For the first time the reality of what has happened crashes into me, dragging me down like I'm drowning. I start to sob, rocking poor Jo backwards and forwards as if it were him who needed comforting. This is my fault. I put myself first, didn't listen. And now my daughter has gone.

When I look up, the policewoman is standing by the door, talking into her radio. PC Johnson and Trish have disappeared. From the top of the lane I can hear the high-pitched whoop of a siren, the blue lights of back-up cars flickering through the kitchen blinds.

'You're married to Simon Stenning, Melanie, is that right?' the policewoman asks kindly as she clicks the radio back into her belt. I nod, wiping my cheeks with my sleeve and not meeting her eyes. Jo wants to feed, so I have absent-mindedly given him my little finger to suck.

'He's Poppy's father?'

'Her stepfather,' I mutter. 'And we were just about to leave.'

3

Six months ago I would no more have considered leaving Si than throwing away a winning lottery ticket. I felt like the recipient of a million-pound jackpot: staggered, joyous, my life unexpectedly transformed by this diffident, surprising man. He was hardly my type: an unshaven forty-year-old with a dishevelled flat; a painter who no longer painted; a dreamer, with wrists so thin that when I placed my fingers around them I could feel the bone beneath, sharp and somehow pained. If his details had come up on a computer-dating web page I would have clicked 'next'. I went for blunt, bullish types who were good at sports and drove too fast: men who would have no more discussed their emotions with me than missed watching the Big Match with their mates. None of them had ever made me happy, but they were my default mode, as familiar and predictable as getting drunk.

We met on 28 December 2003. Objectively that's only a short time ago, but to me it feels like for ever: a distant life that's fading fast. It was the tail end of a miserable holiday, the dog days between Christmas and New Year's Eve when the trees drop their needles and the rubbish needs collecting. I was back at work, returning to London from Pat's with relief rather than regret. It had been the worst Christmas that I could recall, probably because I had finally relented to Pat's pressure and taken Poppy to her house in Buckinghamshire. She had tried so hard to do it 'properly', that was what drove me wild-eyed with irritation and self-loathing. She had decorated our room with holly and filled the sitting room with an enormous Norwegian tree garlanded with ornate gold baubles and glass animals that she must have acquired specially, for they had never appeared during my childhood. Around the tree were placed not so much gifts as strategic statements: a set of saucepans and a recipe book for me; a Teeny Tiny Tears doll and pram for Poppy, the sort of traditional toy that in Pat's fantasy her young granddaughter would adore. Every meal was planned with military precision, down to where we were supposed to sit and the games to be played afterwards, and every day filled with outings in which Poppy and myself were paraded triumphantly in front of Pat's friends: her long-lost daughter, finally returned to home and hearth. I had forgotten her neediness and her pretensions; in absentia her desire for me to conform had hardly dented my consciousness, but now, visiting for the first time in three years, I remembered why I had left. 'I've cut out a very interesting article from the *Spectator* about the children of single mothers,' she announced on my arrival, almost before I had taken off my coat. 'About how behind they get at school.' And later, as her elaborate and quite unsuitable meal was finally served to a wriggling Poppy, who regarded her plate of venison and creamed potatoes with disgust: 'I do think that child would benefit from a more settled routine.'

I behaved badly, like I always do. I drank too much, disappeared for too many illicit cigarettes and snapped surly remonstrations when I should have been biting my lip. Pat was lonely and unhappy: retired and widowed at sixty-five, wishing she had more to show for her life. She had wanted a family, but back in the late 1960s IVF was a sci-fi dream. So she ended up with me: another woman's reject, who despite all their entreaties to work harder and take more care had deliberately flunked her A levels, squandered three years on the rave scene, then bunked off to Goa. When Pat and Michael's natural daughter would have got a well-deserved 2:1 in a sensible subject like accountancy or law, I was doing drugs in India. When the proper daughter would have been painstakingly building her career, just as her civil servant father and school teacher mother had so conscientiously done, I was working in a bar and partying in Oz. When the real daughter would have eventually married a sensible young chap and then, a year or so later, produced a well-behaved grandchild, I was getting knocked up by a bartender and bringing up my baby on the other side of the world. They could never understand why I had become a 'dropout', as they termed it. Life was about work and making a contribution to the world, Michael had written to me in India, not a series of 'druggie' parties. In the neat trajectory of their well-trimmed life, I suppose I was their only real failure.

I drove back to London fast, my music cranked up loud as Poppy dozed in the back. Okay, so I was a useless daughter and a useless mother. I didn't *choose* for my life to turn out like this. I had wanted freedom from my adoptive parents and the dull aspirations they represented, but somehow had become ensnared in dreary responsibility. Despite having travelled across the world to escape from suburbia, here I was again, feeling guilty. In Oz I would have been on the beach, drinking stubbies as Poppy played in the surf. As my windscreen wipers sloshed the pouring rain, I couldn't remember why I'd ever returned. Over there, the sun was always shining and no one defined me by what I did or who my parents were. Yet the truth was that I was drifting, taking one meaningless job after the other to pay the rent and moving from one disastrous relationship to the next. By the time Poppy was two, her father had left and I hardly had the energy to get out of bed. I was getting overly fond of the booze, too. Were it not for my little girl, I would have come almost entirely adrift from myself. So I had chosen to come back to Britain, not so much to return home, as to escape the person I was becoming.

The office had an air of mournful neglect. I opened the windows at the sour stench of dog-ends and removed a clutch of empty bottles to the small kitchenette where we made our coffee and, despite strict instructions from head office, smoked our fags. After that I had a stab at rearranging the plastic Christmas tree, which had been knocked over during the last, tipsy day at work, scattering its load of Christmas cards on the acrylic flooring. The usual rush of vendors and buyers would start in the New Year, but Don had insisted we remain open over these in-between days. 'Never miss a deal,' he'd lectured on my first day, his eyes gleaming with missionary zeal. 'Remember, the more we sell, the more we earn!'

I had nodded earnestly at this injunction, but in reality didn't give a monkey's. It was just another job, and today was just another day. Poppy was playing at her friend Jessie's and I was in the kind of mood where I wasn't much bothered what happened. I don't know if you could say I was depressed. Scrutinizing the other blank-eyed faces on the Tube that morning, I felt just like everyone else.

Si's message was on my voicemail.

'Hi.' He sounded harried, as if he was on a mobile, rushing somewhere. 'I want to shift my flat in Queen's Road pronto. If you could call me back, I'd be grateful.' He left a number and the address of his place, which I dutifully noted down as I listened impassively to the handful of remaining messages: a vendor fussing about the results of his survey, a couple of enquiries about a six-bedroom house close to Peckham Rye that required renovation. Such properties are as valuable and as hard to find as ancient gold, shimmering in the murky silt. The young professionals who fifteen years earlier would only consider homes in Dulwich or Herne Hill now pay close to a million for a dump in Brockwell with the roof caving in, rotting windows and a prehistoric kitchen. They want a project, they tell us eagerly, something they can do up and make their own. And they have the cash to do it: installing state-of-the-art kitchen units with Italian taps and marble work surfaces that cost more than the previous owners paid for the entire property back in 1973.

I called Si at noon, hoping that he wouldn't be in and, with the rest of my calls answered, I would be free to lock up the office and go home. Annoyingly, he picked up immediately. He couldn't afford to wait, he announced; was there any chance I could come round today? By two that afternoon therefore I was ringing the bell to his building, an ornate Victorian villa that backed on to Nunhead Cemetery, with an overgrown scramble of bushes in front.

As I waited for my would-be vendor to buzz the door open, I regarded the myriad of estate agents' signs sticking from the front gardens of almost every house on the road, the flags of twenty-first-century capitalism. A hundred years ago these buildings would have been occupied by upwardly mobile clerks and shopkeepers and separated from central London by fields; fifty years later they were lodging houses for young sojourners, newly arrived from the Caribbean, or family residences for down-at-heel Londoners. Today almost all have been converted into flats, their values spiralling out of the grasp of anyone but City types or young, double-income professionals, who knock the rooms through, restore the fireplaces and fill the roads with their four-wheel drives.

The man who opened the door was not, however, what I'd expected. His posh voice and polite impatience had conjured up an out-of-hours businessman, with a gleaming Jag and designer jeans. In contrast, Si was a scruffy mess: his baggy jeans splattered with paint, holes at the elbows of his jumper and dark hair that curled over his shoulders. Pat would have said that he needed a good shave and wash, but I immediately warmed to his appearance of frayed gentility. I liked the way he took my hand, too, shaking it heartily and grinning as he peered short-sightedly into my eyes.

'You're not what I was imagining,' he said, letting me into the communal hall. I laughed, not sure how to respond. He continued to fix me with his gaze, then added, 'The woman from Bonhams was wearing stilettos and this headset phone thing. She kept barking instructions into it, like a pilot. Quite terrifying.'

I glanced down at my jeans, laughing. 'Sorry to have forgotten the power suit. I wasn't expecting any appointments today. My boss would kill me.'

'Well, we'd better not tell him, had we?'

He led me up the stairs to the first-floor landing, where he pushed open the door to his flat. 'Bonhams valued it at three ten. I wanted a second opinion.'

I smiled non-commitally. 'I'll just have a wander around, if that's okay?'

'Sure.'

I edged around the bicycle that blocked the small hall, and walked into the front room, sizing up the large bay windows and high ceiling. Dilute winter sun fell through the smeared glass and on to the floor in pale yellow slabs. The boards were bare – a fashionable plus – but the walls were dingy and scuffed and the furniture shabby. Even worse for a potential sale, the room was crammed with large canvasses, resting on the sagging sofa, piled on the floor and leaning against the walls. I glimpsed swirling landscapes, bright splashes of colour, something abstract with squares of red.

'You're an artist?'

'Was.' He folded his arms. 'The muse abandoned me.'

I smiled back at him. I liked the way that everything he said was tinged with humour, as if he found himself faintly ridiculous.

'At least you had a muse. Some of us spend our entire lives not knowing what to do with ourselves.'

It was too personal a comment for the situation and hardly likely to elicit his business. But I was growing increasingly bored with Don and his agency and, as with my previous jobs, was only too happy to capsize my new career. Si pulled a face that I interpreted as an empathetic grimace. As I turned from the window his fingers brushed my arm.

'Can I see the other rooms?'

He led me into the bedroom, which was covered in discarded clothes and yet more canvasses. I glanced at the jumble of clothes heaped in the far corner; women's things: a lacy skirt, high-heeled boots, a scramble of underwear.

'I'll get this stuff cleared out by the end of the week,' he said, gesturing vaguely at the pile. He seemed suddenly upset, as if confronted by an unpleasant fact that he'd been trying to forget. I grimaced sympathetically. The angry jiggle of his foot against the worn floorboards explained the ill-kempt, empty feel of the place, the gaps on the walls and missing furniture. Almost half of our sales came from the demise of love: homes that were once so hopefully woven together left fraying and ripped when one half of the partnership walks out.

'It would probably be an idea to give the place a tidy before we arrange any viewings . . .'

'Whatever it takes.'

Moving from the bedroom and down the corridor, we entered the kitchen.

'My *God!*'

I was facing a large painting hanging lopsidedly from the wall. I gawped wordlessly, aware of how rude my remark must have appeared. I was struggling desperately to think of something complimentary to add, yet as I took in the angular nude imperiously facing me, her opened legs splayed across the stool where she had been seated, my mind stalled. She was very thin, her clavicles and pelvic bones sticking out alarmingly as she flopped backwards, displaying an unruly mass of black pubes. Untidy curls tumbled down her back. Her expression was both angry and somehow imploring, as if there was something she needed that was being denied. I stared at the image, swallowing hard. On one side of the picture the artist had deliberately smudged her face with a dark, violent smear, making her seem disfigured, as if she had been knocked about. The effect was unsettling, to say the least.

'It's all right, you don't have to say anything,' Si muttered behind me. 'I should have taken it down. It's a piece of shit.'

'It's not that, it's actually very striking, with that blurry effect and . . .'

He was not interested in my fumbling critique. Striding to the wall, he grabbed the edge of the canvas and yanked at it hard until, unbalancing from its hook, it shuddered to the floor. Embarrassed, I glanced hastily around the room, trying to summon up a light-hearted comment about kitchen units or cork tiling. The painting was, after all, not my concern. I was merely an estate agent hoping to flog the guy's flat.

'This room's a good size . . .'

He ignored me. Leaning with his hand against the wall, he glared at the collapsed canvas, muttering quietly to himself. I had the impression he had forgotten I was there. When he finally looked up I was busying myself by peering into his Ikea kitchen units.

'So, what do you think?' he asked abruptly. Something in his face had shifted since our earlier banter, his mouth becoming more set, his forehead creased. For a bizarre moment I imagined that he was expecting me to comment on his angry attack on the painting. I stared at him, my cheeks hot. 'I guess I . . .'

'Speed is the main issue here. I want to release my capital as quickly as possible.'

I almost laughed aloud. Thank God I hadn't blurted out something ludicrous about time being a great healer. 'I wouldn't want to put it on the market at more than two ninety,' I said quickly.

It was both a relief and a disappointment to be back in the safe territory of conveyancy. He nodded, his face relaxing, as if my valuation was what he'd suspected.

'Okay,' he said briskly. 'Well, thanks a lot for coming over. It's always good to get a second opinion.'

We started to move back down the corridor, our business effectively finished. I felt like a fool. Five minutes earlier I had imagined that we were flirting, but now, a boring task completed, I was being summarily dismissed.

*

More policemen have arrived. I am introduced to various people, whose names and job titles I only barely register. They are going to concentrate on tracing the vehicle that Si was driving, I am informed as I slump numbly in his patched-up Parker Knoll. They've looked quickly around the building, inspected the back yard, and for now are assuming that Si has taken her in his car. Outside, it's completely dark. The blackness of the rain-splattered windows fills me with dread. While there was still ebbing light there was hope: Poppy had wandered off somewhere, the game was still on. But now it is night: no unaccompanied child would be out this late. We have moved on to the next stage, the atmosphere solidifying, as if something has been decided. On the floor beside me Jo is leaning over in his bouncy chair, chuckling as he attempts to grab his toes. His jolly expression makes me want to wail. As Trish bends down and tickles him under the arms, a heavy-set man who was introduced a few minutes earlier as a 'police search advisor' squats beside the armchair, his face professionally grave.

'We need to have some of Poppy's property, for forensic evidence,' he says gently. 'If you have a hairbrush, perhaps, or some of her clothing?'

I stare at him with alarm. 'Forensic evidence?'

'It's nothing to be alarmed about at this stage, Melanie. It's just so that we can extract her DNA. We're trying to get the full picture.'

This is hardly reassuring. 'I just want her back,' I whisper feebly.

'That's what we all want. And to help us arrive at a positive outcome we need to get as much evidence as possible. My officers are going to conduct a thorough search of the areas surrounding your property. I've got another team of men on their way from Canterbury and . . .'

'You're wasting your time. She's not anywhere around here. She's been taken by her stepfather!' Trish snaps from behind me. I glance around, glad of her support. She is holding Jo against her shoulder, his face snuggled against her neck. Reaching down, she gives my arm a little squeeze. 'Okay, hon?'

'Just about.'

The police officer straightens up, looking offended. 'I can only reassure you that we're vigorously pursuing all lines of enquiry.'

'You need to find Si's car,' says Trish, giving him a withering look.

*

As I stepped outside Si's building I remembered that Natalie had taken the girls to the flicks. The film was due to end at four-thirty, so I had an hour to kill before picking Poppy up. I turned from Vestry Road into Peckham High Street. It was a gloomy afternoon and the Christmas lights were already on: not the grand displays of central London but a dismal show of illuminated Disney characters stretched over the road. It was the first day of the sales, and the shop windows were plastered with posters announcing the bargains to be had inside. I trudged wearily past, glancing despondently at the offerings – discount pine furniture, factory outlet clothing, Lidl – disposable rubbish for the urban poor. My reflection stared back: a slimmish thirty-something woman in overly tight jeans and ankle boots with curly brown hair that needed cutting and a startled expression on her drawn face, as if she was not expecting to see herself in such a place. I looked tired, I thought, glancing hastily away, almost middle-aged. My gleaming Australian skin had faded to an unhealthy pallor a winter or so earlier, so now I was as pasty as the other south Londoners who jostled beside me. I needed to relax, for the day to be softened at its edges.

I rejected the pub next to the Jamaican greengrocer's, with its piles of yams and dusty chilles, and turned into a small bistro, offering soup and a crusty baguette for £2.50. To be honest I was not much interested in the food. What I wanted was a large glass of wine and a cigarette, succour against the dreary day. Plonking myself down at a table by the window, I stared through the misty glass at the pedestrians and thundering traffic. I had just about had enough of London. Spreading my hands on the paper tablecloth, I silently regarded my chunky silver rings. I had come here to provide Poppy with at least some stability, but I was thinking of moving on: perhaps taking up my friend Josie's offer and joining her in Bali for a month or two, or drifting back to Oz. I felt as light and untethered as spider silk, floating on the breeze; not so much free as aimless, a life without a centre.

'Hello again.'

I glanced up with a start. Si was standing over my table, smirking anxiously.

'Hi!'

Blood swamped my cheeks, a stupid schoolgirl's blush. Plucking the menu from the table, I pretended to busy myself in the choices. He must have left his flat a few minutes after I had and followed me down the road. Had he seen me mooning at myself in the shop windows?

'I'm not stalking you, promise,' he said, with the same apologetic grimace that he'd pulled when I'd been blathering about my non-existent muse. 'Well . . .' He paused, staring directly into my eyes. 'Actually I am.'

I raised my eyebrows. I was trying to suppress a goofy grin.

'I wanted to apologize for being so rude,' he continued. 'You must think I'm some kind of nutcase. All I can say is that I don't usually go around attacking canvasses like that. It's just that I've had a heavy day or so.'

'I wouldn't worry. We see all kinds of interesting behaviour in this job. People can get incredibly stressed about moving.'

39

'But I do worry.'

If I was a different person I would have asked him outright what had happened between him and the nude. He would have sat down and shared my wine and perhaps, in the unexpected intimacy that sometimes occurs between strangers who have no impressions to maintain, he would have told me everything. But I was never so confident or brave. Despite my attempts at escape, I was the product of Pat and Michael's upbringing, an expert in smoothing things over.

'Is this place nice?' I said hastily. 'I skipped breakfast, so I'm starving.'

'Tut, tut.'

'I also really fancied a drink . . .'

'That sounds more up my street.'

I chuckled, surprised at how much I welcomed his company. Away from the grey light of his hall he looked healthier, his face less pale and the darkness around his eyes less pronounced: almost handsome, in a faded, rumpled kind of way.

'I'm going to do a detox for New Year. Or that's what I'm telling myself. I keep meaning to give up the fags too, but it's bloody impossible . . .'

I paused, aware that once again I was drivelling. Si was looking at me almost wistfully, his long fingers clutching the top of the chair opposite.

Sod it, I thought. To hell with Don's *Code of Conduct for Conveyancing*, it's Christmas.

'Why don't you stay and have a drink?' I asked.

I didn't get to Nat's until after six. She had fed Poppy and Jessie pizza and ice-cream, and by the time I arrived they were curled on the sofa in a contented haze, watching a *Blue Peter* Christmas special.

'You look well,' Nat said meaningfully as she let me in. 'Your eyes have gone all sparkly.'

I gave a little yelp of laughter, already too excited to keep it to myself.

'I've just met a *man*!' I whispered.

I pictured Si: his long, thoughtful face, the crease of his eyes when he smiled, the curve of his neck against his surprisingly broad shoulders. He had a gently ironic way of conversing, as if ordinary life were plainly ridiculous and we, naturally, conspired against it.

'Oh my God, Nat, he's *really nice*.'

'And you're pissed.'

'I am so not!'

She laughed. In the two years that Poppy and Jessie had been in the same class we had fallen into an easy routine of reciprocal school pick-ups and sleepovers. I had Jessie on Mondays, and Nat took the girls to ballet on Thursdays; during weekends Jessie often stayed the night with us so that Nat could have her boyfriend over. We were the sole members of the Single Mothers of Buckingham Road Club, non-judgemental support guaranteed. Slipping off my coat, I hung it lopsidedly on the banisters, leaning over and inspecting my face in her hall mirror. It was true that I was a trifle bleary.

'What *are* you like, Mel? You go off to work and end up scoring!'

I stuck out my tongue at her, a gesture garnered from Poppy.

'You're a fine one to talk.'

When we got home the answer-machine was flashing promisingly in the dark. I ran Poppy a bath, squatting by the tub with my hand trailing in the water as we played

I-Spy, then pulled her out into a warm towel and sat her on my lap as I brushed her teeth. 'Wrap me up like a sausage!' she'd cry, and I'd roll the towel around her, so that only a tufty patch of hair appeared at the top. Then I'd tickle her toes until she screamed. After that we'd cuddle up together under my duvet and read stories. She liked the classics best, and I knew them by heart: *The Three Billy Goats Gruff, The Little Gingerbread Man, Little Red Riding Hood.* Then I'd let her snuggle up and go to sleep in my bed. Pat disapproved, of course. By her age she should be sleeping alone, she'd lectured me during our Christmas visit; I was making a rod for my own back.

I wanted to savour the message. After Poppy had gone to sleep I opened a beer and, sitting on the edge of the sofa, pressed 'replay'. It had been a long time since I'd felt so excited, floaty almost. It was like a chink of sun appearing through thick packed cloud.

'Miss Middleton?' his voice sounded more upper class than I remembered. I pictured him sitting opposite me in the café, his tall frame cramped by the narrow chair, the curl of dark hair on his arms, his long fingers fiddling with the cutlery. As he'd inspected the menu he'd placed a pair of wire-framed specs on the end of his nose: a boyish intellectual. I shouldn't let myself feel like this, I told myself; I hardly knew the guy.

'It's me, your untidy vendor from this afternoon. I was wondering if we might arrange a meeting to discuss my sale in more detail. Perhaps sometime tomorrow?' He paused, just long another for my heart to do another dip. 'I think we may have the potential for a promising deal.'

4

I told Don that I had an appointment to view the flat of a Mr Stenning, and met Si outside Nunhead Cemetery, where we spent an hour or so wandering around the crumbling gravestones. It was an unconventional setting for a first date, overlooked as it was by Victorian angels and ivy-covered cherubs. We explored for a while, pushing through thick brambles to find forgotten family mausoleums and, in the middle of the cemetery, a derelict chapel, its walls covered in graffiti, its Gothic windows home to a roost of ravens, which rose, cawing, into the sky. He came here when he needed to think, Si explained as we wandered inside the building. It helped get things in perspective. As he talked I brushed my hand against the freezing stones, glancing at the empty cans of Special Brew that in the brisk winter breeze rolled at our feet. If I had been alone I would have found the place frightening, but, with Si beside me, could sense its tenuous beauty.

'I once spent a whole summer here painting the angels,' he murmured as he stood inside the chapel, gazing up through the jagged roof to the grey sky.

'Wow. I'd love to see them.'

'You can't. They're gone.'

He kicked at the mossy stones, turning abruptly back to the path. My careless words must have hit upon a sore memory, like an aching tooth. When I caught up with him he was leaning against a large stone cross, his hands buried in the pockets of his greatcoat. To my relief he was smiling again, the angels apparently forgotten.

'So, what do you think?'

'Of what?'

'My urban wilderness.'

I blinked at him, sensing that a great deal rested on my reply. 'I love it.'

He licked his lips thoughtfully. 'But?'

'But let's not come here in the dark, okay?'

'Oh, don't be such a wimp! Come on, I'm going to take you to my favourite picnic spot.'

Stretching out his arm, he grasped my hand in his, as natural and easy as if we were already a couple. We wandered down the weedy paths. He'd first broken into the cemetery one summer night about fifteen years ago, he was telling me now. He was a student, studying art at Camberwell and living off a diet of baked beans and overripe fruit that the local greengrocer gave him. That particular evening he'd feasted on a handful of magic mushrooms that he'd picked in Brockwell Park. He couldn't recall how he'd got to Nunhead, only that he had scaled a wall and landed amongst the graves. Lying spreadeagled against a stone cross, he'd imagined himself taking to the air, his greatcoat spread wide as he flew over south London, towards the river. When he woke, chilled and bleary, he found that apart from his underpants, his clothes had vanished. His coat was folded neatly in the grass beside him. He crept back to his Camberwell digs in the dawn mist, chilled and bemused.

'And you've had a thing about graveyards ever since?'

'You could say that, yes.'

Later we huddled on a tombstone, our breath billowing in the winter air. Reaching into his knapsack, Si produced a block of chocolate and a small flask of brandy.

'Tell me more about you,' he said, passing me the flask. 'I know you've got a daughter called . . . Poppy . . .' I nodded at him, pleased he had remembered her name. '. . . and you work as an estate agent and you used to live in Australia, and you've never had a muse, right? But what's your life *like*?'

It may have been an odd way of phrasing the question, but his interest delighted me. The only questions that Pete, Poppy's father, ever asked were to do with where I had tidied his clothes or what time I was going to produce dinner. Before he finally drifted off, most of our communications involved non-committal grunts.

'God, I don't really know. Mostly it's just dull routine.'

He gazed at me, clearly expecting more.

'There's not really much to tell you . . . I work, pick up Poppy from school, look after her, watch TV and go to bed. If I'm lucky I'll get pissed with one of my mates every couple of weeks. It's not exactly how I thought I'd end up spending my life, but there you go.'

I stopped, regretting the bitterness in my voice. I should be making myself sound mysterious, describing my travels perhaps, so that he wouldn't think me dull. But the directness of his question made anything but complete honesty impossible.

'So what happened?'

I took a long swig of the brandy, enjoying the sensation of warmth spreading down my gullet. I did not know where to start. Should it be with my childhood, with Pat and Michael and their bruised disappointment at my inability to conform? Or my squandered youth, bumming around the world? The truth was that I'd never felt that I fitted in: certainly not in the various provincial towns where I'd been brought up, yet not particularly in India or Australia either. Throughout my childhood I had experienced the intangible sense of being a visitor in a place where I did not belong.

Despite the ballet and piano lessons, I was unable to be the daughter Pat wanted. With my dark hair and olive complexion I *looked* so different from my sandy-haired parents, perhaps that was partly why. But I was also obtusely unable to apply myself to the activities that would have brought them pleasure: academic success; an interest in the feminine arts of clothing and cookery; a nice hobby, like horse riding or gymnastics. Instead I stubbornly rejected everything they yearned for me to do, preferring to skulk in my room listening to The Cure or to wander into the woods behind our house to smoke Woodbines. She'd *never* understand me, Pat had yelled in exasperation when, aged about fourteen, she'd caught me rolling a joint with my friend Tracy. Why did nothing *normal* ever make me happy?

Moving to the other side of the world hadn't done it. If I was a foreigner in Surrey, I was one here, too. I had not belonged in provincial England, but in Australia I was, first and foremost, a Pom. I was floating without direction, a rudderless boat on glassy waters, aware that, apart from being a mum to Poppy, my life was taking place at the margins of something I was unable to grasp. And now, as I perched next to Si on the freezing flagstones, explaining how this had happened seemed like a gargantuan task.

'I guess I messed everything up,' I said flatly. 'I let myself drift. I should have gone to university and everything but I ended up a single mum, working in a pointless job.'

'You make it sound as if that's the end of the story,' he said, breaking off a large chunk of the chocolate and popping it into his mouth.

'I guess that's how it feels.'

'Yeah, but it could be just the beginning, couldn't it?'

I shrugged, not sure how to respond. I had grown so used to defeat that the idea of new beginnings made me feel afraid. 'What about you?' I eventually asked. 'What's it like being a painter?'

'I'm not a painter, not any more.'

'You're . . .'

'A "property developer".' He chuckled, presumably at the pomposity of the label. 'I'm planning to use the money from the flat to do up some places in Kent. I'm going to make a heap of money, then retire to Spain and spend my dotage growing olives. What do you think?'

'Fantastic!'

'It's not just a daydream. I'm really going to make it happen. Just watch me.'

I bit my lip at the notion, so casually mentioned, that I might be around to see him realize his plans. 'I'm sure you will,' I said, suddenly too shy to look into his face. 'It sounds wonderful.'

I did not ask about the woman who had been living in his flat.

After I had picked up Poppy from school that afternoon, Si came to tea. As I opened the door to him he greeted me with a gentlemanly kiss, planted on my cheek, then presented me with a packet of Jaffa Cakes and, from the inside pocket of his battered suede jacket, a small sheet of paper covered by a pencil sketch of an angel. As he pressed it shyly into my hand, it seemed loaded with meaning. I leaned the picture self-consciously against the phone, gabbling nonsensically about the weather as my heart pogoed absurdly in my chest. I was mostly anxious about Poppy: either that Si would be put off by the reality of a child in my life or that she would take against him. Since my return to London I had not been in the habit of start-ing relationships with men, far less bringing them home.

As I had told Si in the graveyard, I had resolutely given up on new beginnings.

The presence of a man in my cramped flat made it seem even smaller. For a moment, as Si stepped on to the mat, looking around and nodding at me in apparent approval, my heart tightened with terror. What the hell was I doing, inviting a stranger here? The date was only meant to involve a cup of tea and a biscuit, but already I felt as if we had crossed an invisible line. I took his coat, not meeting his eyes. In the next room I could hear Poppy's footsteps, tramping towards the door. A second later, she flung it open.

'Who are *you*?'

'I'm Simon. Who are you?'

'Poppy.'

'Hello, Poppy. Do you prefer to shake hands or to bow?'

She stared at him in silence, her eyebrows furrowing. I held my breath. Simon held out his hand expectantly.

'Personally I think bowing is rather too formal.'

'What's bowing?'

'This.'

Whipping off his beanie, he bent his long body into a deep, courtly bow. Poppy giggled.

'That makes you look silly.'

'I know, but it's obligatory in the presence of a princess.'

'You're weird.'

But I could tell she was pleased from the way her sparkling eyes followed him along the hall and the small smirk that twitched on her mouth. We trailed into the living room, a small procession led by this tall stranger with his easy humour and bitten nails who already felt so familiar. Then there was me: an awkward flummox of maternal anxiety, fear and swelling excitement. Finally came Poppy, who had folded her arms over her chest and was frowning.

48

'This place is boring,' she announced, raising her eyebrows in a parody of nonchalant sophistication. 'Do you want to see my bedroom?'

I bustled around the kitchen, arranging the cupcakes we'd made in Si's honour on a plate and brewing tea as Poppy solemnly led Si down the hall into her room. It suddenly mattered enormously that she liked him. From down the corridor I could hear laughter. As they returned, still bantering, to the kitchen I silently laid out the food. He had a way of teasing her that I had seldom seen in an adult, least of all a man with no children of his own: not patronizingly, or with a fawning desire to please, but as if she and he were equals in comedy combat.

We squeezed around the table in my tiny kitchen, drinking tea and gobbling the cakes. Si and Poppy had slipped into a long-drawn-out game in which Si was deliberately mispronouncing the names of the characters in *Shrek* until Poppy was wound into a near-hysterical fit of pink-faced squealing. I watched them, smiling at my daughter's pleasure. I was finding it hard to distract myself from the thought of placing my hands around Si's sinewy arms and pulling him towards me. Already I was anticipating how his fingers might feel, brushed against my skin, the half-joking way he might push me back on to the sofa and unbutton my shirt.

Eventually Poppy began to rub her eyes and yawn, her body drooping on to the table. It was past seven by now. Gathering her into my arms, I carried her to the bathroom, where I wiped her face with a flannel and gently brushed her teeth. Then I popped her into bed, kissing her on the cheek as she rolled over, pushing her thumb into her mouth. For a moment I stayed by her pillow, my cheek pressed against hers as I breathed in her smell: soap, Cherryberries toothpaste, the faint hint of hay and something damp. Making her happy and keeping her safe were all that mattered, the rest was just noises offstage.

All the same, my legs were trembling as I walked back towards the kitchen.

*

'Can I ask you some more questions, Melanie?'

I turn, only vaguely aware of where I am. I should be outside, running through the dark rain as I search for my daughter. Yet I have turned to stone, my body literally petrified by what has happened. Poppy has disappeared, and my life has stopped dead.

'Did Poppy have a computer? We can't find one in her room, but perhaps there's a family PC?'

I shake my head. 'You've got the computer. And Poppy never used it.'

'Right . . .' He scribbles in his notebook. 'Is there any reason to believe that she may have run away? Had you had an argument?'

I gaze at my inquisitor: a kind, comfortable face arranged into an expression of trained concern. Has he been on some kind of course, to teach him how to converse with people whose lives are collapsing? When he speaks I catch a faint whiff of garlic, as if he's just had his tea.

'We were always having arguments.' I say numbly. 'She was jealous of her baby brother. But I don't think she would ever run away.'

'What about local friends? Could you tell us about them?'

*

The first time we made love was at Si's flat, about a week after the visit to Nunhead Cemetery. It was one of those crisp winter days of bright blue skies and zero temperatures that make one unaccustomedly clear-headed. I told Don that

I was going to measure up Mr Stenning's flat for the property details that we would shortly be emailing to our clients,
making sure that he noticed me placing the digital camera
and dictaphone into my bag. It was the third time I had
skived off to meet Si on the pretext of some or other
appointment, but even if Don had caught me red-handed
with my illicit assignation I would not have much cared. I
was bored with the estate agency: the greediness of my
clients and colleagues, the endless half-truths and promises
that were required to close a sale. I was in the business of
selling dreams to the gullible, I sensed as I persuaded yet
another couple to mire themselves in vast, engulfing debt
in order to buy an ugly, cramped and shockingly overpriced
house in Camberwell. It was time to move on.

Si must have been waiting for me, for the downstairs door
buzzed open before I had even pressed my finger to the
bell. I trotted up the stairs, my heart banging. I felt as nervous and unprepared as a thirteen-year-old on a first date.
Above me, he was standing on the landing, smiling.

'Hi.'

'Hello there.' He held out his hand, staring. I had taken
more trouble with my appearance than usual: eyes carefully
made-up, my usually unruly hair piled on top of my head.
And rather than my sensible boots and trousers, after much
deliberation I had decided on a tight velvet skirt and heels.

'You look fantastically beautiful.' The teasing in his voice
had gone. He was grave and serious, as if we were standing on the verge of something momentous.

'Can I come in?'

As he stepped aside I entered a transformed flat. The
piled-up canvasses and heaped clothes were gone, the
wooden floor swept; in the grate a fire was blazing.

'You've been busy!'

'I've got a buyer.'

I jerked round, my heart fluttering in my mouth. 'Oh!'

'With Bonhams, I'm afraid. And they're paying the asking price.'

I pulled a face at him, feigning disappointment.

'Well, I'd better go then, hadn't I?'

'Not so fast, Ms Middleton . . .'

He was standing behind me, his hands encircling my waist as he pulled me backwards into his arms. Swivelling around, my lips found his. This was the first time we had touched and I could not bear to wait any longer. As we crumpled ungracefully on to the floor in a tangle of limbs and already discarded clothes, I kissed him back greedily, my hands in his thick hair, his hands fiddling with the zip on my skirt. I wanted to feel his skin against mine, to press him into me, give myself up, feel the world fall away as he became mine.

*

'Mel?'

I look up with a start. Dave Gosforth is standing before me, his arms folded, his face faintly puzzled. I hoped I would never lay eyes on his ugly mug again, with its piggy eyes and red-tipped nose. But here he is, sighing with a little gust of disapproval, as if thoroughly disappointed by my family's wayward behaviour.

'It's me again, I'm afraid.'

I shrug. Hot tears are gathering in the corners of my eyes and I do not trust myself to speak.

'I'm going to be taking over the search for Poppy,' he says slowly, as if communicating with a moron. I still do not respond; too much has already happened for me to ever see him as an ally. 'My colleagues tell me that you heard some-one leave the house just before you started to look for her, is that right?'

'I heard a door close, and then a little bit later a car driving away . . .'

'And when you looked, the car that Simon had borrowed from his friend was no longer in the drive?'

'No, it wasn't.'

He pauses meaningfully. I look into his mournful face, my stomach lurching.

'There's been a sighting,' he says.

'What do you mean?'

'We've been talking to someone who was working in the yard. Apparently he saw a white Volkswagen estate driving fast towards the lane at about quarter past four.'

'But what about Poppy?'

'That's the thing, Melanie. The man clearly remembers seeing a little girl who answers to Poppy's description in the passenger seat. I'm afraid we now have to assume that Simon's taken her.'

I turn and stare into his expressionless face. I know that the words make sense, but they are meaningless, an unintelligible language that I have not been taught.

'But I don't know why he would . . .'

'There are lots of reasons . . .' His hand is hovering over my arm as if he is considering giving it a reassuring squeeze. 'People in distress often do silly things.'

I jerk my arm away from his pudgy fingers. The thought of him touching me is repugnant. 'What about the river? She could have fallen into it . . . And the rest of the houses down the road, have you asked if anyone's seen her?' Yet even as I speak I know how obvious it must seem.

'For the time being we're scaling down our activities in the immediate vicinity,' he says carefully, fingering the radio which has started to crackle at his belt. 'I'm calling a halt to the search of your property and we're putting our resources into tracing Simon's vehicle. We've put out a national alert for the car; a newsflash is going out in the next hour; all the seaports and airports have been alerted. There's every reason to believe that we'll quickly locate the car and get Poppy back to you.'

'But he wouldn't . . .'

It's too late. Tears are sliding down my face, running in rivulets down my nose and over my dry lips. I shake my head, looking angrily away.

5

I was not used to having a regular relationship. There had to be a catch: either Si would have a change of heart and disappear from my life with a puff of emotional smoke, or what had grown so vigorously between us would flower too soon, followed by a sudden and fatal withering of interest. The truth is that I had no idea what to expect. I was thirty-five, but inexperienced in matters of the heart. Yet rather than my usual trajectory of fleeting desire followed by a brief and usually disappointing fling, we seemed to be travelling in the opposite direction: our pleasure increasing with each week that passed.

We slipped into a comfortable routine. Most evenings Si turned up at teatime, just as he had done the afternoon he'd presented me with his angel. As I put Poppy to bed he'd cook, then we'd open a bottle of wine, gobble up whatever vegetarian feast he had concocted and fall into bed like lustful teenagers. He spent every weekend with us too, his quiet, humorous presence so unobtrusive that it was hard to recall what life had been like before. Looking back, something in me seemed to have clicked into place, like a stubborn peg that had finally slipped into its notch. A month previously I had been in a state of depressed inertia, with hardly the energy to take Poppy to the park. Yet with Si at my side I was filled with parental purpose. We showed her the dinosaurs at the Natural History Museum, took her to the zoo, spent a rainy but cheerful weekend in Dorset. Overnight almost, we had become a family.

Poppy treated Si as if he had always been around. After only a few weeks he was virtually living with us, but I don't think she ever felt displaced. Rather, he had an ability to fade into the background whenever it was 'her' time, never once suggesting that we should dump her with a babysitter or engineer a sleepover at Jessie's. He'd brought his battered guitar over by then, as well as a box of books and a mouldy rucksack, stuffed with clothes. As I ran Poppy's bath he'd sprawl in the living room, strumming. She loved watching him play; increasingly she'd eschew my proffered bedtime book for the glamour of sitting at his feet and gazing lovingly up at him as she listened to his rendition of 'Tangled up in Blue'. He had a terrible voice, flat and off-key, but she never seemed to notice. 'Mummy, don't!' she wailed at me, the one time I appeared in the doorway, my shoulders shaking with laughter. 'You're going to make Si feel all sad!'

For his part, he seemed to accept the details of our life without demur. His sole requirement was that by the time we retired to bed Poppy would no longer be there. For a few nights I returned her dutifully to her undisturbed Princess Fiona duvet. On the third night she declared that she no longer wished to sleep in my bed. That was for babies, she declared. Babies, and funny men like Simon.

I was so happy in those early days that it scared me. I did not like to become attached to men: it made me jittery and insecure. On the rare occasions that Si failed to appear I slipped into a gloomy mistrust that darkened what had previously seemed to be composed entirely of light. *This* was the true pattern of my life, I fretted: fleeting attachments, leading to nothing. Si must have discovered my true character and scarpered. What self-respecting man would want to be lumbered with a drifter with no obvious talents, a stroppy five-year-old daughter and a grotty rented flat in Crapsville?

That he had once moved in more elevated circles was obvious from his accent, the occasional, glancing references to the house in Kensington where he had been born and the public school where he had been sent at thirteen. He always insisted that we were alike, and when together I would agree. Yet, when apart, doubts seeped into my thoughts like pollution into a river. He was in a different league, I'd decide. I was used to blunt, non-reflective men, who never expressed their emotions or wanted to 'talk'. I was also used to coming home and finding they had gone. I had never put much effort into these relationships and was rarely surprised or upset at their disappearance: they felt fleeting and inconsequential, like brief sunny days that could only end.

If these affairs were day trips to places where I did not wish to stay, I now felt as if I was exploring an exciting new country, lush with possibility yet somehow deeply resonant, a landscape I had visited in my dreams. I was unprepared for such a journey, perhaps that was the problem. I had departed without a map, or indeed any obvious way home.

6

It was early April, the season of daffodils. Si and I were striding down a series of steep-banked country lanes, knapsacks on our backs, the sun on our faces. So much for winter gloom, the flowers seemed to declare: spring has arrived! In the trees the birds called excitedly. It was a warm morning, and for the first time that year I had discarded my kagoul and looped my sweatshirt around my waist. Yet despite the idyllic morning, I felt oddly downcast. We had started the walk hand in hand, but a mile back had broken apart, falling into a steady silence that could be interpreted in various ways: demonstrating either how relaxed we now were or, as I was increasingly convinced, that something was wrong. It was our first weekend away from Poppy, and I was jangling with nerves. To take so much time for ourselves seemed too big a leap, as if I was asking for too much. Poppy would get sick and I would be recalled to London, I was sure. More disastrously, displaced from our normal setting, Si and I would discover each other to be strangers, our brief sojourn at an end. Since we had left London he had been behaving strangely, too. Despite constantly reassuring myself that everything was normal, I kept turning and finding him watching me, as if gauging my mood. He had an announcement to make, I thought apprehensively. Knowing my luck, it would be bad.

As we reached the bottom of the hill he started to talk about the property he had seen the day before. It was on the outskirts of a small town on the northern coast, and pretty much derelict.

'It's breathtaking, Mel, everything I wanted. I'm sure this is the one.'

I walked quietly beside him. When he reached out his hand I seized it tightly. I felt as if I were watching the scene from afar.

'It's even got planning permission attached,' he went on. 'Apparently they had a buyer last year who went ahead and got the plans drawn up but couldn't get his finances together.'

'Oh.'

'I still can't believe the price they've got it on for. I can't decide whether to just whack in the asking price or try to get them down a bit . . .'

'Try it and see.'

We had reached a corner where the lane branched into a dirt track to the left that was surrounded by water meadows. A lark twittered above us.

'So,' Si said, suddenly swinging me round to face him. 'Why so glum, dear chum? What's up?'

I glanced away from his inquisitive eyes.

'Nothing.'

'Yes, there is. You haven't stopped sighing since we got out of the car.'

I smiled mournfully. I could not remember ever feeling like this: a pain ripping through my chest, as if he were tearing at me with his hands. When Pete had departed all I experienced was faint sadness, underscored by relief.

'Come on, Mel. Don't go all tight-lipped on me.'

I eyed him reluctantly. 'I suppose I'm just thinking about how if you're going to be buying this warehouse and doing it up there won't be much point in you staying in London . . .'

For a moment he simply stared at me. This is it, I thought: the bit where he breaks it off and my life returns to normal.

But rather than sighing in reluctant agreement, Si had started to laugh.

'Oh, you stupid woman!'

Grabbing my waist, he pushed me through the open gate and up against the stone wall that bounded the meadows. I tottered backwards, the rough stones grazing my skin as he kissed me, hard, on the lips.

'Ow!'

'Come here, you daft bat. I thought it was obvious!'

He was pulling up my T-shirt now and rummaging with my jeans, yanking them down as his fingers climbed my thighs.

'Si! Someone will see!'

Peering over his shoulder, I gazed around the field. The cattle that lolled at the other end glanced back disinterestedly.

'So what? Let's give the cows a thrill . . .'

He had my jeans and pants at my knees and, chuckling rudely, was fiddling with his trousers. Pulling him towards me, I helped him out, not minding when my backside knocked against the mossy wall, or even when we slid down together, into the long wet grass.

Afterwards we lay panting and laughing in the mud. The back of my jeans was soaking, and Si's knees were stained green. Sitting up, his face was suddenly serious.

'What on earth makes you think I'm going to leave?' he asked quietly. 'Why can't you trust me?'

His face was puzzled but not unkind. As I looked into it I knew that I would never voice the true reason: I could never trust him because, no matter what he said, I was convinced he couldn't love me.

'I don't know . . .'

Taking my hand, he kneaded it gently between his

calloused palms. 'I was actually thinking about something rather different,' he said quietly. I stared fixedly at the muddy grass, not daring to reply.

'About how we could all go down to Kent together. You and me and Poppy.'

For a moment I thought I must have misheard. I sucked on my lip, afraid that I might start blubbering.

'But where would we live?'

'In the warehouse! After we've made it a bit more habitable, of course.'

'I don't know . . .'

'Duh! For God's sake! You keep saying how much you hate your job and loathe living in London. We both need to start afresh, so let's go for it. Please, Mel, let's at least give it a try.'

'I'm not sure,' I said weakly. 'I'm crap at long-term relationships. You don't know what I'm really like.'

Leaning towards me, he pulled me against his muddy jacket. I could smell wet wool and the furl of tobacco in his pocket.

'What are you talking about, you silly woman? Of course I know what you're like.'

'Do you?'

'Yes, I do! Look, you've got to stop defining yourself by what happened in the past. Isn't that the whole point? Let's move on from all that crap and start again. A double escape act.'

I eyed him doubtfully, thinking that he was probably right. My failure to connect with men or build any kind of future was a self-fulfilling prophecy.

'Is that what you really think?'

'Yes, my lovely. It's what I really, really think.' He hugged me, kissing my forehead. 'This is a new start, for both of us.'

'And you think that's possible, do you?'

'Mel, please, just trust me . . .'

He pulled back, staring intensely into my face. If you had asked me about love three months earlier I would have given a bitter laugh. Not for me, sunshine, I'd have retorted, save that for the movies. But now, as I regarded Si's searching eyes, I could sense the budding hope unfurling.

'Okay,' I said, blinking back tears. 'You're on.'

Events moved quickly. I gave notice on the flat and announced to Don that I was intending to leave the agency. He took the news with a sage smile.

'Thought something was up,' he said, giving my shoulder an avuncular pat. 'What with all the sexy dressing and the way you couldn't stop singing. Shame though, you've made some good sales.'

I grinned, taken aback by the praise. I had never thought that I was good at anything, but now that I had Si, it seemed that anything was possible. My old, uncentred life was gone and a new one about to start in which, together, Si and I conquered the world.

Poppy received the news with a satisfied nod. 'Does that mean Si can be my new dad?' she said after I'd finished telling her how we were going to move to Kent. The question took me aback. I had not considered that Poppy might see Si as a potential father.

'Your dad lives in Australia,' I said carefully. 'He sent you a card for your birthday.'

'But he's not real.'

'Of course he is.'

She scowled. She was right, of course. How could a father she had not seen since the age of two be real?

'Not like Si's real,' she said plaintively. 'You have to make him be my daddy, Mum.'

'It's not quite as simple as that.'

She peered at me crossly. Then her face suddenly cleared, as if she had made up her mind. 'Of course it is!' she laughed. Turning her back on me, she resumed playing with her Sylvanian Cat Family.

The only dissenting voice was Natalie's. Perhaps it was my fault for assuming that she would be as thrilled as me that the membership of the Single Mothers of Buckingham Road Club was to be halved. I told her my news in an incoherent babble of tactless glee, forgetting that only a month earlier she had been dumped by Ned, her gormless on-off boyfriend. We were sitting in her canary yellow kitchen, smoking roll-ups and drinking red wine as Jessie and Poppy rampaged upstairs.

'That's great,' she said flatly, after I had finished raving about the warehouse and Spain and how Si and I were going to wipe our slates clean and start our lives over. 'And have you actually seen this warehouse place?'

'No, but I'm sure it'll be lovely. Si says it's amazing.'

She sipped her wine, not commenting. I charged on, regardless.

'It's such a departure for me, Nat. I mean, all my life I've just muddled along, not really expecting anything out of men and not getting anything. And now, suddenly, this wonderful guy appears, out of the blue, and my whole life is transformed!'

'And you think you know him well enough to go and live in the sticks with him, do you?'

I glanced up, surprised by the sharpness of her tone. She was frowning, her purple nails drumming the table edge. Dear old Nat, with her bright red hair and vast multicoloured cardies. Since Ned, the dreadlocked wannabe guitarist, had run off with a twenty-year-old at a Primal Scream gig, her usual vivacity had been sapped. She looked weary, her usually shining face sagging and lined.

'Yeah, I reckon I do,' I replied, my mettle rising. 'I mean, it isn't necessarily quantity but quality of time. And we *really* connect with each other . . .'

She shrugged sulkily.

'So how much do you know about him?'

'Well, loads, like how he used to be a painter, and how he's got into building and . . .'

I stopped. It was true that there were distinct gaps in my knowledge. After the incident with the painting, Si had never mentioned the woman who had shared his flat, for instance, and I had never probed. For his part he had shown a total disinterest in my previous boyfriends. He did not want to discuss the past, he had announced in the first few days of our meeting. Our relationship was about the present and the future, not what had gone before.

'The point is, it doesn't really matter about the details, does it? What matters is the way you click together. Like a meeting of souls, or whatever . . .' I trailed off, uncomfortably aware that this sounded like tosh. On the other side of the table Nat had squashed her flabby face into a moue of disapproval. No wonder Ned had ditched her, I thought with flashing disloyalty; she could be such a dowdy drag.

'It's just that if it were me I'd want to know everything about him, for Jessie's sake. Like, for example, where does he stay when he's not at your place?'

I could feel my lips pucker. I was growing increasingly irritated.

'In his flat.'

'I thought you said he'd sold it?'

'Well, he has. Or he's about to. God, Nat, I don't know! Does it matter? I can't go over there anyway, can I? With Poppy at home?'

She pulled a face.

'What's that expression meant to mean?'

'Just that you should be careful. He sounds a bit too good to be true.'

For a moment I considered the unkind things I might say back: that Nat was so negative and untrusting it was little wonder she could never keep a man, for example, or that if she wanted to meet someone new she should stop moping around and stuffing her face with chocolate. But instead I managed a tight smile.

'But he is true, Nat,' I said quietly. 'He loves me and I love him. I've spent thirty-five years alone, and I'm not going to turn down the chance of changing that just because he hasn't told me the name of his mother's second cousin once removed.'

Standing up, I pushed back my chair.

'Poppy!' I shouted up the narrow stairs. 'Get your shoes! It's time to go!'

We parted by Nat's bright pink front door, with its rainbow streamers and Free Tibet stickers.

'See you later then,' I said casually, pretending to busy myself with Poppy's coat so that I wouldn't have to kiss her goodbye. 'Take care.'

'Yeah.' She shrugged glumly. 'You too.'

'I'll give you a ring . . .'

But as Poppy and I clomped down the tenement steps, we both knew that I was lying.

7

I am raging around the building, throwing extraneous objects aside as if they might somehow reveal Poppy's whereabouts. The towels lying in a soggy heap on the bathroom floor are chucked violently into the empty bath, the dismembered limbs of a Barbie flung against the wall. If the police knew what I was doing they would rush to stop me. My house has become a 'crime scene', which can only be touched with white gloves, the disorder of Poppy's discarded toys and clothes 'evidence', to be recorded in their notebooks and hauled away in plastic bags. I told them I was going to the loo, but I have escaped to the living room, away from their watchful clusters, the beeping of their phones and endless questions. And now I am finally coming apart. I stagger around the room calling out her name, as if the hide and seek was still on.

But it's not a game. Tears are pouring down my face, my body overtaken by vast, shuddering sobs. I feel as if I have been turned inside out, my heart and innards dragging on the police-trampled floor where my daughter once played. How has this happened, when only a few months ago we were so happy? We were going to move to Spain and start a new life, but now all that has been swept aside, like flood waters crashing through a sedate English village: unexpected and unprepared for, all defences down.

'Mel . . .'

Glancing up, I see a woman standing in the door. She is wearing a homely sort of trouser suit, the kind that a middle-aged middle manager might acquire in Marks and

Spencer, and has short greying hair, cut into a nondescript bob. She reminds me of the teacher Poppy had last year: dull but good-natured, a fan of catalogue shopping and Celine Dion. The woman was introduced to me five minutes ago as Sandra somebody or other, a 'family liaison officer'.

'Shall we go and sit down?'

'No!' I scream. 'I don't want to fucking sit down! I want you to stop pissing around and find my daughter!'

Unfazed, she continues to clatter across the wooden floorboards towards me. I sink to the sofa, weeping; my outburst has shocked me into silence.

'If you want to be left alone, that's fine,' she says placidly as she sits down beside me. She is wearing little pointy boots, I notice, as if making an effort to look younger. My eyes skid off her feet, disgusted at myself for registering such an irrelevant detail.

'But we can't let you lose it like this. You've got your little one to take care of, for a start. Do you want me to get your GP to come over and give you something to help calm you down?'

I shake my head. My face is slimy with tears, my sleeve soaked. Sandra expertly places a wad of tissues into my clenched hands.

'It would help if we could carry on talking,' she continues. 'There's still an awful lot of things we need to find out. For Poppy's sake.'

I nod. I feel exhausted, my chest aching from crying, my limbs weak. 'Okay.'

'Tell me about your relationship with Simon, then. You'd only recently got married?'

'Last summer.'

'And things were going well?'

I stare at her: such a bland question that leads to such complicated answers.

'Not with all you lot coming round and hassling him,' I mutter. Sandra gives me a disappointed look, as if I were a recalcitrant pupil, unable to muster the correct answer. 'And the building was a bloody mess,' I add.

'So you'd been worried about that? You and he were doing it yourselves, is that right?'

'Pretty much. We had builders to start with but then we ran out of money.'

'Right . . .' She is nodding vigorously, soaking it all in.

'But you know all this already. Si told DCI Gosforth and his lackeys about it yesterday or whenever the hell it was.'

'Mel . . .' She takes my limp hand, holding it between her warm palms. 'I know this is a terrible time for you, but you must understand that I'm not the enemy, I'm trying to help.'

I am unable to respond. I can feel the approach of another swell of tears. Pulling my cold fingers away from Sandra's grasp, I stuff them between my thighs.

'Let's talk some more about Simon,' she says, sitting up a little straighter. 'How did he get on with Poppy? Were they close?'

I look up, glowering at her. What the hell is she implying?

'What do you mean, "Were they close"?'

'I mean, what kind of stepdad did he make? I'm trying to build up a picture of their relationship, that's all . . .'

'He was lovely to her.'

'And they spent a lot of time together?'

This is not like me, but I am about to start shouting at her again. My daughter is *missing*, for Christ's sake, and here I am being cross-questioned by British Home Stores Woman about Si's parenting techniques.

'Look,' I snap. 'If you're hoping to find out that he was some kind of paedophile then you're barking up the wrong tree. Sometimes they spent time together, sometimes they didn't. It was all completely normal.'

Sandra chooses to ignore my tone.

'What kinds of things did they do together?' she asks chattily as if we were old friends, having a gossip over a nice cup of tea.

'God, I don't know. He was teaching her to juggle. Or he'd play the guitar and she'd sing along. He hasn't seen her so much lately. He's been away . . .'

'Did he ever lose his temper with her?'

'Why would he do that? If anything it was me . . .'

I stop, looking quickly away as I press my knuckles into my mouth. I cannot bear to think of all the times in the past few months that I have shouted at Poppy. Only last week I grabbed her by the wrists and jerked her furiously backwards, coming closer than ever to hitting her. I was sure that she had deliberately bashed her foot against Jo's chair, transforming his contented gurgling to tomato-faced screeching. I wanted to slap her, to scream that I hated her, and only the terror in her eyes stopped me. Yet Sandra has misunderstood my meaning.

'He was violent towards you?' she asks eagerly.

'No, of course he wasn't! I mean it was me that got angry with Poppy . . .'

'So Simon didn't ever lose his temper with either of you?'

For a while I am silent. How will she respond if I tell her the truth? Everything I say will be taken as evidence of his guilt. She will cluck sympathetically and make little notes in her pad, and I will know for sure that my nightmares have come true.

'No,' I say. 'He never lost his temper.'

She knows that I'm lying. She smiles at me blandly, shifting position as she thinks of another tack.

'So apart from you,' she says, 'who are his main social circle? The people he likes to hang out with?'

'I don't know,' I mumble, aware of how pathetic this sounds. 'He doesn't really have that many friends. We've only been here since August and he's been away in London or wherever for most of that time, so he doesn't really hang out with people down here . . .'

'But what about old friends? His work colleagues?'

I shrug again. Six months ago I felt as if I had known Si forever, but now it feels as if my view of him has been obscured by thick bifocals; where once my vision was clear, now it has blurred into something I no longer recognize.

'There was his mate Ollie, who he was working for in London. I gave that other policeman his number. It's his car that Si's been using.'

Sandra gives a small nod. 'Yes, we're talking to him. Now what about Simon's family?'

Oh God. I gaze at the floor, trying to summon the energy.

'His mother lives near Tunbridge Wells, but I'd be amazed if Si was with her,' I say quietly. 'They don't exactly get on.'

*

We drove down to visit Alicia one stormy Sunday a few weeks after the scene in the cow field. Si had mentioned that he had some business to complete with his mother and was planning a trip the evening before, dropping it as casually into the conversation as if he were simply popping to the shops.

'I thought I'd go and see my mum tomorrow,' he said, contemplatively turning his packet of baccy around in his hands as he sat at the table, watching me cook. I busied myself with an onion, avoiding his gaze. I knew I shouldn't pressurize him, that I should relax and let our relationship take its course. Yet ever since we had agreed that Poppy and I would join him in Kent I yearned for more: some evidence that the relationship was to become permanent. Taking me to meet his mother was one such sign; not taking me would signal the opposite. The silence stretched between us. I *had* to stop being so needy, I resolved as I chopped the onions. I was supposed to be independent, a woman not in need of a man. Yet now that I had tasted love, I was ravenous for more.

'I'll take Poppy swimming then,' I muttered, tipping the onion into my wok.

'Or you could come with me . . .'

He had put down the Old Holborn and was fiddling with a cork. Repressing the broad grin that threatened to engulf my face, I shrugged, as if I didn't much care one way or the other.

'Okay then.'

I turned back to the chopping board, secretly delighted. Later, as I lay beside him in bed, I allowed myself to slip into an idle fantasy in which Alicia was my mother-in-law. We would be the best of friends, I imagined, swapping recipes and homely stories about Si. Perhaps she would take an interest in Poppy and we would spend school holidays staying in what I imagined to be her sumptuous country mansion. Even though I had never managed to have such a relationship with Pat, I held on to the sentimental belief that such things were possible, normal even.

We set out early the next morning. I had arranged for Poppy to go to a friend's, gone through numerous changes of outfits, and spent ten quid on a bouquet of stiff, plastic-wrapped roses from Asda. Si chucked them into the back of the car without comment. He had told me very little about his mother, except that she was divorced from his now-dead father and lived alone.

For the first part of the drive he seemed normal, chatting about the purchase of the warehouse and when we might move in. But as we left the motorway his mood swiftly changed, the way that during an English summer a bank of dark clouds can suddenly overcome the sky. It was the first time I had seen him like this. He hunched gloomily over the steering wheel, his face strained. Every tentative question I asked was answered by a non-communicative grunt. Finally, plainly irritated by my attempts at conversation, he shoved The Clash into the CD player and turned up the volume. I spent the rest of the journey staring out of the window at the waterlogged fields, my fingernails digging into my palms. I was irrationally nervous.

'We're just going to stay an hour or so, okay?' he announced as we'd eventually skidded to a halt on his mother's gravel drive. 'She'll insist on giving us lunch, but it'll be inedible.'

It was an enormous house, enclosed by tall hedges: an ugly slab of Victoriana, with Gothic turrets and large dirty windows. The place had a semi-derelict, neglected feel to it: the curtains of the ground-floor windows were drawn and the windows of the top-storey obscured by ivy. I trudged across the drive behind Si, my heart sinking. When he reached the front door, he visibly took a deep breath, then lifted the knocker and banged it hard. Slipping my arm around his middle, I leaned against him for a moment, feeling for his warm skin under his jacket.

'Don't get stressy,' I whispered, imitating Poppy. 'I'm used to dodgy families, okay?'

For the briefest second he smiled. 'You don't know what she's like,' he muttered, then his face clouded again.

Behind the door came a shuffling sound, followed by the shudder of heavy locks being drawn back. I braced myself, holding out the flowers and forcing my face into a glaze of greeting. The door swung open.

A tall, gaunt woman stood before us. She could have been any age from fifty-five to seventy: her skin was unlined, but her wispy hair white. She had swept this into an untidy bun that was coming down on one side, scattering hairpins and dandruff on to her stained navy jumper. She had a slight stoop, I noticed, as if trying to make herself look smaller. Like Si, she was very thin. Her handsome face was so similar to his that for a bizarre moment it seemed almost as if I were greeting him. My enthusiastic handshake was, however, met with a limp show of fingers, which were quickly withdrawn, then stuffed into the pockets of her cardie.

'Hi!' I gushed. 'It's so lovely to meet you! I'm Mel.'

Alicia took a step back, arching her eyebrows in obvious surprise as she looked me over. Clearly, she was not expecting me.

'You're over an hour late,' she eventually said, addressing Si, who merely shrugged and shuffled past her into the hall.

Still determined, I handed her the roses. She held them loosely, hardly glancing down at them. 'I'm afraid all they smell of is plastic.' I gave her a resolute smile. 'It's so hard to get nice things in our bit of London.'

She nodded, looking me slowly up and down. I had eventually opted for my red leather jacket and a long wool dress. Underneath were stacky black boots that I now regretted. I willed her to look away from my clothes and meet my eyes. It was obvious that Si had not told her about me.

'You're older and less pretty than Rosa,' she said, her tongue working its way around her mouth as if trying to loosen the remnants of breakfast. 'Let's hope this time Simon behaves a bit better.'

For a moment I was unsure that I had heard her correctly. As the words finally made connection with my brain, I swallowed in amazement, too shocked to reply. I could feel my face turn scarlet; even the tips of my ears were burning. 'I'm sure he will,' I murmured.

She gave a fleeting smile, then stepped aside. Behind her, Si had disappeared into the dark house. 'I haven't had time to tart everything up for you, so you'll just have to take me as you find me,' she snapped. 'Come on then, in here!'

Like an obedient spaniel I trotted behind her across the large hall, with its muddy flagstones, dog baskets and fusty portraits of gun-toting ancestors. On the far side, a grand staircase swept upwards. Past this a door opened on to an enormous sitting room, where Si was now standing at the window, gazing out at the grounds.

The room was as dirty and worn as the hall. The once white walls were grey, and the antique furniture sagged. A chaise longue covered in faded yellow silk was pushed under the window, a tear in its seat roughly patched with masking tape. The Persian rug that covered the floorboards was, in places, almost completely worn through; the arms of the sofa by the grand fireplace spilled ancient straw innards on to the floor. I gazed around the room, registering its unhappy decay. The place smelt of wood smoke and dogs.

'Like sherry, do you?' Alicia asked, shoving a smeared glass into my hand. Turning her back on me, she addressed Si. 'What about you? Still drinking yourself silly?' She laughed rudely.

He ignored her. 'What have you done to the yew?' he muttered.

74

'The bloody thing's been dead for years. Had to have it chopped down.'

He did not comment, just raised his eyebrows and turned sulkily back to the window. I stared at his back, feeling stranded. It was as if, on entering the house, he had morphed into a male version of his mother. Even his shoulders were sloping downwards in a way I had not previously noticed.

'It's a beautiful house,' I offered, knowing instantly how gauche I sounded.

'It's a sodding heap,' Alicia replied morosely, pouring a large tumbler of sherry and gulping at it. 'It's falling down around my ears, and I can't afford to get it fixed.'

'Simon's good at building . . .'

At the mention of his name, Si swung around, shooting me a look of such appalling ferocity that I stopped mid-sentence, sucking miserably on my lips.

'He never comes near the place,' Alicia said sourly. She poured more sherry into her glass. 'When he does bother to turn up, it's because he wants money off me.'

'Ma . . .'

She turned on him, her expression oddly collapsed, her wispy hair trailing unhappily down her shoulders.

'Well, isn't that the case?'

I stared fixedly at the greasy carpet. The heavy sweetness of the sherry was making me feel sick. On the other side of the room, Si's expression was grim.

'I thought we'd already discussed this . . .' he said impatiently.

'Anyway you've had a wasted journey. Rosa was here yesterday. I gave everything to her.'

'You *what*?'

'She came down yesterday morning. Took the box off with

her with all the papers. She said you could sign them in London.'

For a terrible moment I thought that Si was about to hit his mother. He took a step towards her, his fists clenched. His puce face transmogrified into someone I did not recognize.

'How could you be so stupid?'

'What on *earth* do you mean?'

'You know exactly what's going on!'

'I most certainly do not! I don't know anything. You never bother to tell me.' From the way she obstinately turned back to the sherry, I could see that whatever it was Alicia had done was deliberate.

'For *fuck*'s sake!'

I had heard enough. Si's behaviour was making me clammy with horror, a sudden swirl of nausea causing the room to tip towards me. Placing my glass carefully on the stained surface of a once-elegant Georgian card table, I looked around for my jacket, which a minute earlier I had placed nervously on the arm of the sofa. Retrieving it, I clasped it resolutely in my arms.

'I'm going,' I said quietly. Then I turned, and walked back towards the front door.

Si caught up with me at the end of the drive. I had heard the crunch of the car's wheels as he manoeuvred it around, but did not glance up until he had drawn alongside me, pushing the opened passenger door into my path. For a moment I considered ignoring him. I could walk to the nearest station – wherever the hell it was – and get a train back to London, I thought wildly. Everything I had dreaded was confirmed. Si was still involved with the woman who had been living with him in Peckham, the spiky nude with her tumbling black hair and splayed legs. All this time I had been constructing fantasies about our future but to him I was just a temporary diversion from his *real* relationship, this *Rosa*, a woman so trenchantly inserted into his life that she could appear at his mother's doorstep and bear away his business papers without question.

'Mel, sweetheart, please get in the car . . .'

He would be sleeping with her too, kissing her breasts and stretching his hands proprietorially over those skinny thighs.

'Piss off.'

'Babe, I'm sorry. My mother's not noted for her tact. I should never have dragged you down here.'

I glanced at him furiously. He was leaning across the car and gazing pleadingly at me, his face a cartoon of agonized apology.

'It's nothing to do with your mother.' I hissed. 'It's you.'

'Please, Mel. You shouldn't have seen me behave like that. It's just —'

'It's just what? You've clearly got another woman on the go.' I could no longer bear to look at him. What was it that Alicia had said? *You're older and less pretty.* The humiliation rose inside me in a hot wave of mortification. How *dare* she? I started to jog along the drive. It was just as Nat had warned. Why on earth would someone like Si ever be interested in me? He was just toying with me, perhaps so he could have somewhere to stay in London. Or maybe it was just the sex: a change of body type, something to break the routine. I was *so* stupid! Behind me I could hear the car door slam and the sound of footsteps on the gravel.

'Mel, please!'

He caught me by the arm, and was tugging me backwards, so that I was forced to turn and look into his pale face. He had *tears* in his eyes, I saw with shock. And, as he gripped my elbow, his hand was shaking.

'It's not how it seems.'

I shook his hand away. 'How is it then?'

'I was living with this woman before I met you, but it's over.'

'So why's she coming down here and taking papers away?'

'Because she's a bitch. She doesn't want me to sell my flat so she's trying to stop me.'

'Why doesn't she want you to sell your flat?'

'She doesn't want me to move on.'

It was exactly what I yearned to hear. I folded my arms. I was still feigning anger, but the hot fury that had propelled me out of the sitting room, across the hall and down the drive was receding.

'Look,' Si continued. 'It was very intense with her at first, but now I'm with you I can see that I never really loved her. It started off as just a sex thing but it got too heavy too quickly, and she wouldn't let go. I finished it at Christmas, and now she's trying to make trouble.'

'So why didn't you tell me about it before?'

'Because I didn't want to think about it any more than was strictly necessary. I wanted to put it behind me.'

'You're not lying to me, are you?'

'Of course not.'

I stared into his distraught face. When I eventually spoke my voice was faint. What I had to say felt momentous: a test that he must, at all costs, pass.

'I really couldn't take it if you were still sleeping with her, Si. I've been messed around too many times by too many arseholes. And I've got Poppy to protect, too. I've got to be a-hundred-per-cent sure that I can trust you.'

'You *can*, I promise. Like I said, I'm not sleeping with her. All I'm doing is trying to get rid of her.'

I glared at him, searching for lies. Anger was making me unusually assertive. 'If I find out that she's still in the picture, then that's it. I'm off.'

'Mel, please, I promise you.' He stood back, gazing imploringly into my face. 'You've got to relax, babe. *You're* the one I choose, okay? She's in the past. Finito. End of story.'

Now he was steering me back towards the car. 'The day's been a complete cock-up. Let's try and forget about it.'

We climbed into the car, and he switched on the ignition. I felt numbed, like I'd taken a hefty dose of painkillers which were starting to work. As Si pushed the car into second we passed the last bend of the drive. When we reached the road, he put his foot down hard, speeding down the winding lanes. I stared at the blurring banks of cowslips and primroses. So, he was involved in a messy break-up. It meant nothing; he was right not to drag me into it.

'You weren't very nice to your mum,' I eventually said.

His face hardened. 'She deserves it.'

We had reached the top of a hill, and through a gap in the trees that lined the road, had a sudden view of the countryside: rolling hills, stretching into apparent eternity; a patchwork of greens and greys. All day a storm had been grumbling in the background, yet despite the bruised clouds nothing had transpired. Now a sudden fork of lightning crackled vivaciously across the horizon, followed by a loud retort of thunder. I stared at the heavy sky, my spirits returning. What had happened made no difference. Like Si said, his relationship with this other woman was over.

Large droplets of rain pockmarked the dusty windscreen; after a little while Si switched on the windscreen wipers. It was raining heavily now, water pounding on to the car's bonnet. I wound down the window a little, breathing in the smell of wet grass and spring blossom. A short while later we joined the motorway.

*

Or did things happen in a different order? I stare at Sandra, the family liason officer, and realize how frayed my memory has become. I remember marching out of Alicia's house and shouting at Si on the drive, but wasn't this after a more prolonged visit, involving a walk around the grounds of her house? Or was that the second time I visited, when Si wasn't there? I gaze at Sandra's kind, round face until it blurs, but the past has been torn apart so violently that I cannot sew it back together. All that is left is this jumble of discon-nected threads that I am sorting so desperately through. Si's hands, stretched tightly around the steering wheel; the veins on his mother's cheeks, raw and pained; the things she said later and the questions I should have, but never dared, ask.

8

It was not the sherry nor even Si's behaviour which made me feel nauseous that day. The next morning I could not finish my morning coffee. Even more strangely, the single ciggie I attempted made me gag. Alcohol was suddenly tasteless, like sipping meths. The weeks slipped past, and I no longer wondered at my symptoms. By the time I did the test I was nine weeks pregnant.

Three weeks later I was lying naked on the crumpled sheets, my damp body pressed into Si's side. He had just returned from Kent and, after a short and friendly tussle on my bed, was lolling on his back, his arms behind his head. As usual he was talking about the warehouse. By now the deal was almost sealed. He'd found a surveyor and got an architect involved. Like a small boy with a new toy, he was obsessively enthused.

'We'll strip everything back to the basics, expose the beams, knock through at the top,' he was saying. 'The roof's a bloody mess though. I'm going to get Ol down to look at it.'

I rolled away from him, lying on one side as I pushed my finger through the soft hairs on his chest. I had already attempted several times to tell him about the blue line that had appeared on the pregnancy testing kit, but, like a pony that having cantered towards a jump rears up in refusal, I always shied away. It was too much too soon. We had discussed living together, but not having a baby. And for some reason the recollection of our unhappy visit to his mother had become entangled with how I feared he might react.

'How's your tummy, anyway?' he said, running his palm over my belly. I stared down. Objectively my stomach was still flat, but to me it seemed to be already swelling, its usual concavity replaced by something hard, pushing out. The prospect made me dizzy.

'It's not really my stomach that's the problem,' I said.

'I thought you said you were feeling sick?'

I sucked at my lips, looking past Si's untroubled face to my small bedroom, with the photos of Poppy in various stages of infancy, the Aborigine painting I'd bought in Alice Springs, and the drab curtains that I'd attempted to dye a warm red but had turned a tepid salmon. When I had told Pete about Poppy's conception, his face had contorted with disgust. For a moment or so he sat wordlessly before me, twisting at a flap of cardboard on his ciggie packet. Then he had stood up, shouted that I was a stupid cow and, giving the table leg a vicious kick, flounced out of the bar.

'I *am* feeling sick, all the time.'

'Shouldn't you go to the doctor?'

I did not reply. My hand dropped quietly off Si's chest. All I had to do was say the words and everything would change. Yet whether this would herald the start of something or its end, I had no idea.

'No, not yet.'

My heart had started to beat very hard.

'What do you mean, "not yet"?'

'Can't you tell?'

Now he was quiet, too. I could feel the sudden tension in his body, the gap between my words and his reply stretching into something inescapably meaningful.

'Tell what?'

My pulse was in my mouth; my palms were sticky. We were going to move in together, so why should I feel afraid?

'I think I might be pregnant.'

His silence was a deep, dark hole into which I was falling. For what seemed like many long minutes we lay next to each other on the bed, neither of us looking at the other or speaking. Finally daring myself to scrutinize his face, I saw that a small dent of what I could only interpret as displeasure had appeared between his eyebrows. After a few moments he took his hand off my belly and folded his arms. My nerves were making me breathless.

'Well?'

'Well what?' He was sitting up now and reaching for his jumper, which he pulled swiftly over his head. I watched him getting dressed in numbed disbelief. The scene was tipping into everything that I'd dreaded.

'Well, what do you think? Why aren't you saying anything?'

'I don't know what to say. Have you done a test?'

'Yes.'

'And it was positive?'

'Yes.'

'Right.'

I had thought that he was different from the others, but now it seemed that I was wrong. He stood up, reaching for his jeans. The bedside clock told me that it was already nearly two. In half an hour I would be collecting Poppy from school and he would be gone.

'I hoped you'd be pleased,' I said quietly.

He turned, finally looking straight at me. His face seemed sorrowful.

'If you really are pregnant then I guess I am pleased,' he said. 'I'm sorry, there's not much more I can really say. I'm not quite in the having babies frame of mind at the moment.'

I swallowed. Like the removal of scenery at the close of a play, my foolish fantasies of building a new life with Si were rapidly collapsing, leaving me half naked and alone in my shabby Brockwell flat.

'Anyway, I thought you were on the pill.'

'I think I must have forgotten to take it . . .'

He did not reply. Grabbing his mobile from the bedside table, he slipped it into his back pocket, then bent to tie up his trainers, his back to me.

'Where are you going?'

'I've got a meeting with some finance people in town. I'll give you a ring.'

Straightening up, he brushed his cold mouth against my cheek. I was biting down so hard on the inside of my cheek that I could taste my own flesh, the beginnings of blood.

'When are you coming back?' My voice had faded to a hoarse whisper; the defiant independent woman I had imagined myself to be vanished.

'It's going to be difficult over the next couple of weeks, hon. I've got to really get going on nailing this deal and getting it all sorted.'

'Are you walking out on me?'

He turned around. His face seemed already to have closed up, his eyes fixing on a spot somewhere above my head.

'Of course I'm not. It's just going to be a bit busy for a while, that's all.'

Then he was gone.

Si's hasty exit from my flat had been so definitive that I was sure he would never return. I cried for the rest of the day: jagged bouts of sobbing, interspersed with periods of barely controlled calm when I fetched Poppy, sat with her over tea and put her to bed. I cried as she watched TV, wiping my face with the back of my hand and turning away so she wouldn't notice. I cried as she splashed in her bath, my hankie stuffed over my mouth as I perched on the edge of the loo. I cried when she was finally asleep, throwing myself on the bed and giving in: great shuddering gasps of grief that made my ribs ache, like I'd been beaten up. It felt so familiar, yet at the same time I was reeling with shock. Si had seemed so sincere and had given me so many assurances that I still could not truly believe his reaction. Could I have completely misjudged his character? I longed now for what, only twelve hours earlier, I had believed him to be: loving, attentive, my entrée to another life. I despised myself, too. I should have learned my bloody lesson, I thought bitterly. I was neither loveable nor loved. Why would anyone want to stay?

The next day I awoke to a headache and a state of dull despondency. I was too proud to call Si, and switched off both my answer-machine and my mobile so as not to hear his resounding silence. Despite all his promises, he had turned tail and fled. He was just like all the other men I'd had the misfortune to meet: full of bullshit. He would almost certainly be back with the nude. Right now, as I shuffled around the kitchen attempting to make breakfast, he was probably fucking her, enjoying the feel of her bones against his. It was hardly surprising, after being stuck for so many frustrating months with my thicker, saggier flesh.

The nausea continued: a heavy queasiness that sploshed unabatingly around, like floating in a dinghy on a choppy sea. The only thing that calmed it was food. As the baby grew fingers and toes I worked my way through mounds of white bread and mashed potato, sucking on crystallized ginger in-between. Some days I imagined the months and years ahead and considered terminating the pregnancy. I would be the single mother of two small children, stuck in the drudgery of full-time work, I thought with despair. I would be trapped in Britain for ever by the need for schools and employment; I would never have enough money to live the way I wanted, and I would always be alone. On other days I felt a little better, pulling down the albums of Poppy's baby pictures to give me strength: her fat little body, buttoned into a white Babygro, toddling on a baby walker, her hair in ringlets. Me, holding her on the beach, the sun in my eyes. Of course I would keep the baby. As always, I would cope.

Another week passed and still Si did not make contact. By now Poppy had started to ask after him. She chirped on about the frilly bridesmaid's dress she planned to wear at our wedding and I could not bring myself to blurt out the truth, which was that Si had disappeared from our lives as swiftly as he had taken them over. The crying was finished now, overtaken by a thick pain, lodged somewhere in my chest. Over the course of a single day I would swerve from stunned disbelief at what had happened, to my habitual mistrust of men, which, like a worn old cardie found in one's wardrobe at the start of a cold autumn, I now slipped into almost with relief. When Nat approached me in the playground I found myself taking her arm and strolling home with her as if we had never quarrelled. Ned had tried to return, she said, snorting derisively. The floozie had dumped him and he'd come round in tears, begging for forgiveness. She told him to sod off, she finished, chuckling with triumph. Men: who needed 'em?

She did not ask about Si.

Then, late one Friday night as I slumped in front of the telly, the doorbell rang. It was three weeks after Si had walked out and I had convinced myself that I would never see him again, yet as I stumbled blearily into the hall, my heart was crashing at my ribs like a wild animal trying to escape.

'Who is it?'

'Me.'

I flung open the door. Si was standing in front of me smiling sheepishly. He looked thinner and tanned, as if he had been travelling somewhere exotic. I was damned if he should know, but the sight of him made my insides swoop with joy.

'Can I come in?'

I shrugged and stepped aside. I wanted to appear haughty and indifferent, but it was impossible to keep up the pretence. I longed for him so desperately that I was fighting hard to stop myself reaching out and grabbing hold of his lapels. He followed me into the small kitchen, watching as I put on the kettle. My hands were shaking so crazily that I could barely operate the switch.

'How *are* you?'

'Sick as a dog.'

'Mel, darling . . .'

I glanced around. He was slouched against the Formica cupboards, looking pleadingly across the narrow kitchen. His face was so downcast that for an absurd moment I almost burst out laughing: he looked like a scruffy dog begging for chocolate. 'I'm so sorry,' he said slowly. 'I've behaved like a total shit. I love you. I want us to be together for ever.'

'I didn't get pregnant deliberately, if that was what you were thinking,' I said coldly, turning my back on him again.

'Of course you didn't. And even if you had, it wouldn't have mattered. It's not that I don't want a baby, it's just that it was so unexpected. It freaked me out.'

87

I stopped fiddling with the plug, a little tug of anger pulling inside me.

'Have you been with her?'

'With who?' His voice was ominously quiet.

'That *woman*.'

He flinched, stretching his face into a grimace of disgust. 'Like I told you, it's *over*!'

I stared at him, shocked by his vehemence. Then suddenly his expression crumpled; he looked down at the floor, as if trying to control himself, then up at me, his eyes mournful, almost pleading.

'This isn't about her, I promise. I've finished it for good. She's never going to get in the way again.'

'What is it about then?'

'It's just me, being in a mess and getting scared.'

I folded my arms. I so badly wanted to believe him.

'And how do you think it made *me* feel when you suddenly disappeared like that?'

'I'm sorry.' He was speaking with deliberate slowness, his voice placatory and contrite, as if this was a speech he'd prepared. 'I've behaved appallingly. I know there's no excuse.' He paused, perhaps expecting me to question him further. When I didn't, he said, 'Look, I want you to have this.'

He was fumbling in his jacket pocket. I watched him, my mouth hanging open. Eventually he produced a small black box, which he handed tremulously to me.

'What is it?'

'Open it and see.'

I pulled at the gold catch on the box, hardly daring to breathe. Inside was a plain gold band with a single ruby set in the middle.

'Let's put everything behind us,' Si whispered. 'Marry me, Mel. It'll be a brand-new start.'

Finally I allowed myself to smile. I wanted to cry, and scream with laughter, and collapse into his arms, and dance hysterically around the room, all at the same time.

'And you've really finished with this Rosa woman?'

'Like I told you before, it's history. One hundred per cent.'

'You haven't been with her, have you?'

He seemed to hesitate. I stared into his tanned, anxious face, willing him to say what I wanted to hear. The seconds ticked past, my impatience quickly superseded by terror. Then suddenly his face crumpled.

'Please, Mel. You have to trust me. I will never, ever, betray you, I promise . . .'

Stepping decisively across the kitchen, he pulled me into his arms. My face was buried in his chest, my hands grasping his middle. I breathed in the fuggy smell of sweat and tobacco. From the shuddering of his shoulders, I gathered that he was crying. When I finally pulled away, his eyes were red.

'So will you marry me?' he whispered. 'Please, say you will.'

I gazed back at him, my stupid heart still bashing at my ribs. Of course I was going to marry him. It felt like my last stab at happiness in a life that so far had yielded only disappointment. Why would I choose to remain alone?

'Okay then.'

'Thank God!'

He was gripping me so hard that my tummy was getting squashed. I pushed him gently away.

'What about the baby?'

For a moment he seemed confused. Or perhaps he was simply trying to work out how to respond. Falling to his knees, he pushed up my jumper and placed the side of his face against my tiny, tightening bump.

'I can't wait to meet him,' he breathed.

I couldn't stop myself. I was grinning so widely it felt as if my face might split. 'Or her,' I said, punching him lightly on the shoulders.

*

I give my head a little shake, looking around the room in confusion. Although nothing has outwardly changed, it looks indefinably different, as if it is less the objects that fill a space and more the activities that take place within it which give it character. Stripped of our rumbustious domestic disorder – Poppy's gymnastics on the sofa, her figure skating on the wooden floor, Jo's nappies and clothes strewn around – it has become a place I only vaguely recognize: formal and hard, with too many edges. Even the furniture, chosen for its functional modernity, seems unfriendly: the metallic chairs and uncarpeted floor are unforgiving, the open-plan nature of the room too cold. How could we have believed we might make this place our home?

I don't know how long I have been sitting here, my chilled hands held inside Sandra's fleshy palms. I blink at her, as if surfacing from a dream.

'Where's Jo?' I say, jumping up. 'I need my baby!'

'It's okay, love. He's fine. Your friend's put him down in his cot.'

Her proficient hands are around my shoulders, pulling me back down.

'But where's *Poppy*?' I wail.

'We're doing everything that we possibly can to get her back, Mel. There's just been a newsflash on the evening news and it's gone out on the radio, too. Every force in the country has been alerted. The whole nation is looking for the car.'

I ogle her, trying to force meaning into the words. How

can it be that Si, with his gentle brown eyes and encyclopaedic knowledge of Bob Dylan, has suddenly become Britain's Most Wanted Man? He loved Poppy. He thought she was hilarious. Despite everything that's happened, why would he want to hurt *her*? Nothing makes any sense. All I know is that I yearn for my daughter with a physical force that makes me gasp. I want her here, *now*. I want to feel her solid weight in my lap, to run my fingers down her smooth, plump arms, to bury my face in her thick flaxen hair. Yet she is not here. She has been plucked from me, spirited away by a monster.

'He didn't take her!' I whisper. 'Si wouldn't do that!'

'There's an awful lot of evidence that points in his direction, Mel. That's why we're putting so much energy into finding his car.'

'But you don't know him! He'd never put her in danger!'

Sandra does not reply. She sits opposite me, nodding and holding my hands as if she were my best friend, but her mind is made up. I am, in her view, a wife in denial. She must have seen it countless times in the relatives of the accused: the fevered refutation of what to the police is obvious, the dogged repetition of their loved one's innocence, and finally the gradual encroachment on their impassioned defence by objective fact.

'Poppy was having these nightmares!' I blurt. 'She said there was someone in the warehouse!'

'Uhuh . . .'

'There were letters, too! It had nothing to do with Si!'

'What letters, Melanie?'

'I don't know. We thought they were from a friend, but she wouldn't let us see them. And she kept saying there was a ghost wandering about upstairs . . .'

I am crying again, my cheeks slick. Sniffing, I accept the wad of tissues she is proffering.

'We kept telling her there wasn't anyone there . . .'

I close my eyes, squeezing out more hot tears. Poppy, sitting up in bed, screaming herself hoarse; my bleary reassurances, half asleep, not really concentrating; Poppy appearing in our bedroom, crying in a way I had rarely seen: deep sobs, her whole body shaking. Her eyes, as the lights were finally turned on, darting around her room, searching for something. There was a bad person standing on the gallery, she whispered. They were going to come back and get her.

'A lot of children have nightmares,' Sandra says quietly. 'Perhaps she was worrying about school?'

I slump against the sofa, too exhausted to continue. Sandra is right. I am clutching at straws. I have to face the facts. I have not forgotten them, though I wish I could. This is not the first time that my home has been filled with police, you see. Only yesterday Dave Gosforth was here in a different guise, his white-suited men carrying away our belongings in carefully recorded plastic bags, as he leaned against his car, regarding me without sympathy. He'd done this a hundred times before, his bored eyes proclaimed, dealt with hundreds of hostile women twittering uselessly about the mess his boys were making. He was nearing his quarry, sniffing the scent of the kill, why should he care two hoots about my ruined dreams?

Yes, I have to face facts. Less than thirty-six hours ago, Detective Chief Inspector Gosforth was discreetly steering Si into the kitchen, one practised hand on his elbow, as I stared fixedly from our picture windows at the low grey sky. A little while later I saw them walk across the drive. Such an odd couple: the detective chief inspector, with his expensive leather jacket and neatly ironed jeans, and the suspect, with his long hair, his battered carpenter's fingers and fraying clothes. Si slipped into the back of the unmarked car without even glancing back to see if I was watching. It was as if in the course of that devastating exchange in the kitchen all life had been bleached away, turning him from human being into ghost.

And now they're here again, with their careful questions and forensic procedures. Yet what no one has yet said out loud is that only yesterday morning my husband, Simon Stenning, was arrested on suspicion of murder.

9

26 February 2005
8.25 p.m.

*Dave Gosforth leaned against the breeze block wall of the Stennings'
kitchen, cupping his hands against the wind. Christ, it was freezing.
Blinking away the fragments of ice that were blowing into his face,
he huddled over his lighter, willing it into life. Finally, after three or
four tries, he produced a shivering flame. Sucking on his fag, he breathed
out, relaxing a fraction as he stared grumpily across the marsh. The
last hour had been one of frenetic activity, in which they had done
everything in their power to trace Simon Stenning's car. There was a
national newsflash, and the vehicle's registration had been circulated to
every force in the country. All over Britain patrol cars were cruising,
ready to spot him. The airports were on alert, too, although it was
unlikely he'd be heading abroad. They'd confiscated Stenning's passport with the pile of personal effects that they'd taken from his house
yesterday.*

*Yet despite all this, Dave was as close to panic as he had ever been
in twenty years of service. The moment the call had come that afternoon, summoning him back to the warehouse, he'd been tight with
anxiety, an overwound clock that couldn't stop ticking. The stupid prat
had taken the little girl! This was not something he had anticipated,
the worst outcome imaginable. What he dreaded was a hostage situation, or something even nastier. Now he needed a minute or two alone,
so he could think it through.*

*It was a dramatic turn of events, that was for sure. If he'd so much
as considered that Stenning would play a trick like this, he'd have*

applied to the magistrate and held him for another forty-eight hours. By then the forensic results would have been in and, if luck was on their side, they could have charged him. The bloke was obviously as guilty as sin. Dave had been edging towards that way of thinking when they'd arrested him the day before. Now he was 99.9 per cent certain. The stupid pillock had panicked and done a runner, taking the kid with him.

The wind was making his cigarette burn down fast. He took another drag, then flicked the stub towards the creek in disgust. Karen would have his guts for garters if she smelt the tobacco on him, so perhaps it was just as well that he wouldn't be going home. He'd been trying to give up for months. Patches, hypnotism, aversion therapy, he had tried them all. Yet rather than becoming the newly healthy and invigorated DCI Gosforth of his fantasies, with a firm stomach and chiselled upper body, his lack of smokes had turned him into an irritable pig. He should've been at the gym, but instead had been lazing on the settee, or in his car, gorging himself on junk food and wine gums. A week ago he had caved in and snapped open a new packet of Benson & Hedges. Karen still hadn't guessed. It was bad, bad, bad.

Reaching for his mobile, he punched in his home number, picturing the phone ringing in their comfy living room, with its new wool carpet and nice bright prints. Karen would be watching TV, most likely, perhaps nibbling on some chocs. She was always moaning about her weight, but to him she was perfect: voluptuous, as he put it, nice and curvy; not like the scrawny woman on the other side of the breeze block wall whose life Simon Stenning was in the process of wrecking, with her uncombed curls and bony hands. He appreciated that Mel Stenning was attractive, but she was too brittle. He'd clocked the way she looked him up and down, too; the snotty judgements, putting him in his place.

'Hello?'

'It's me.'

'Hi, honey!'

'I'm going to be late.'

'Aw!'

If Karen minded about his unpredictable absences, she never showed it. That was what being married to a copper was like, she'd say if he started to apologize for yet another cancelled outing or ruined dinner. It was his job. He was her big hero, going out and catching all those baddies; she wouldn't change a thing. Now, just hearing her voice was making him feel better, like warm hands spread over an aching back.

'Things have taken a bit of a turn for the worse, love. I don't know when I'm going to get home.'

He wouldn't tell her about the little girl; it would only upset her. In some cases she knew all the details, in others he'd gloss them over: they were simply too horrible and he felt the need to protect her. She was a big softie, always weeping over stories of kids with cancer on the evening news, or donkey abuse in the Third World. She wouldn't want to hear about what had happened to little Poppy Stenning.

'Okay, lovey.'

'You won't wait up for me, will you?'

'Not unless you make it worth my while.'

'I only wish I could.'

She chuckled rudely. 'You take care of yourself.'

'I'll ring you later . . .'

Slipping the mobile into his pocket, he turned back to the ware-house. Why did posh, arty people choose to live in places like this? It wasn't his idea of a nice home, stuck out here in the bogs with its draughty spaces and eerie echoes. What did they call it? Open-Plan Living. More like Bloody Freezing Living. Shuddering, he stepped into the kitchen.

IO

High summer, and life seemed perfect. Si had returned, his sudden disappearance a blip that we did not allude to. This time he was going to stay. I forced myself to forget about Rosa: Si had made his promise and I had chosen to believe him. Now, as London wilted under the smoggy July heat, I could barely take my hands off him. I luxuriated in his presence: my beautiful ragged man, sprawled at the table rolling his cigs as I cooked; my artist, who covered Poppy's drawing pads with bizarre goggle-eyed monsters or little pencilled portraits yet claimed he could no longer paint; my lover, who in bed never selfishly galloped towards his goal but was careful and assured, as if I was to be cherished. I had spent so long alone that I had forgotten what it was to have the regular comfort of another person's body. Five, six, seven months into our relationship and still it thrilled me to see him lolling on my pillows. I would never take him for granted or succumb to boredom, I was sure, for the old Mel was fading away, her droopy defeatism defeated by joy. Despite all my fears, our future seemed secure. These days the creeds that had once dominated my life seemed ridiculous. Why had I given up on men? There had been a few disappointments, but my belief that men could only mete out pain was surely based on foolish superstition. I was like someone who, having spent her formative years in a convent, gains the courage to blow a raspberry at 'Our Lord'. Or perhaps it was the other way: perhaps I had finally found God.

Si radiated happiness. He was away in Kent for much of the time, but when he returned his cheerful energy gusted warmly through the flat. He would wander from room to room, singing loud and excruciatingly bad renditions of 1980s pop songs and joshing with Poppy, or whoosh us out for a surprise treat: pizzas or the cinema, or a visit to the lido at Brockwell Park. He could not wait to be a father, he declared. He delighted in the baby's growth, resting his hand proprietorially over my stomach. It was he who pulled my pregnancy books from the stack of old paperbacks under my bed, pouring over the diagrams of developing foetuses with an enthusiasm that eluded me; he who ogled baby clothes in Mothercare, and he who assiduously drew up lists of names.

We talked about the future, not the past. He knew a little about my childhood, but showed scant interest in learning more. We had visited Pat for lunch shortly after I had agreed to marry him, and perhaps that had said it all. Over soup, roast ham and apple crumble she had subjected him to a rigorous interview about his schooling, his training in fine art and his subsequent career prospects. He refused to play the game, dodging her questions with the foggy vagueness that sometimes beset him when probed too deeply. Oh, you know, he'd murmured in response to her questions concerning exactly which public school he'd attended, one of those places you'd rather not remember. Can one make proper money as an artist? Well, sometimes one can, and sometimes one can't. He glanced over the table at me, pulling a face. It was clear that he and Pat would not be friends.

On the subject of his own background he would rarely be drawn. Like the story of his nocturnal visit to Nunhead Cemetery, he'd sometimes recount anecdotes about his student days at Camberwell but made no reference to friends or lovers. Many of his stories involved experiments with drugs, or escapades into the edgier parts of London: a night spent breaking into a deserted Docklands factory, for example, where he'd taken a tab of LSD, or the time he'd slept on a pavement in Soho, just for the experience. None of these accounts involved anyone else; if there were girl-friends, they were edited out. For a year he had lived alone in a caravan in the Scottish Highlands, painting. There was also a long spell hitch-hiking across Europe. He did not seem to require to company of others.

As the months went by I learned that there were areas of his life that he refused to discuss. If I enquired about his childhood, for instance, his face would harden and he'd curtly change the subject. Questions involving the recent past elicited a similar response. Why did I want to know about that shit, he'd snap as, flushing, I bit my lip. The only thing that mattered was our future. Then he'd start discussing the warehouse, or how in Spain we might keep goats, whilst I stared down at my hands. It was a strange experience, like swimming in tropical waters and hitting unexpected eddies of cold.

At other times his silence was more comfortable, a shared peace that I had learned not to interrupt. We often sat together in the evenings, his arm around my shoulders but saying very little. By now I had grown used to his quietness. He was not a chatterer, someone who needed to fill in the spaces. He had a stillness to him, I told myself. The new, calm centre to my life.

In August we were married in a shabby south London registry office, with Pops as my bridesmaid and a small gaggle of friends to witness the event. It was a muggy London morning, the heat spread thick under the polluted skies, covering us with a layer of slime. I wore a cream silk dress that stuck sweatily to my protruding belly, and white irises in my hair that after only a short while inside the sweltering Marriage Suite drooped with exhaustion. We repeated the vows, signed the book, and emerged onto the municipal steps, breathing in the marginally fresher air with relief. Jessie and Nat threw a handful of confetti at us, Ollie kissed me on the cheek and Pat took us to lunch at an Italian restaurant in Streatham. I was unsure of her views on my changed circumstances. From the corner of my eye I noticed her gazing at me with the same expression she had once assumed when I was a rebellious teenager, piercing my nose and staying out all night: confused concern, unsure how to react. Yet when I looked at her directly she smiled brightly back.

Whatever Pat, or indeed Nat, thought of our hurried wedding was immaterial. I was groggy with pleasure. I sat squeezed against Si's side throughout the meal, my dress soggy, the baby fluttering inside me like a trapped butterfly. Watching Si do a balancing trick with Poppy's breadsticks, I felt a swirl of exhilaration at my good fortune: it was as if I had fallen by accident into someone else's life. It was other women, not me, who enjoyed these things. For years I had heard them refer to their lives with the careless abandon of those who have never been alone, professing irritation at where their husbands dumped their dirty socks, or crowing about how they craved time to themselves. Each time I had shrunk inside a little, knowing I would never be included in the Smug Wives Club. But now I was married. My daughter had a father, and would soon have a baby brother. My fairy godmother had waved her magic wand.

After the meal Poppy went back to Pat's, and Si and I blew three hundred quid on a room at the Ritz. The expense did not matter, Si insisted, for we were currently flush. There had been some kind of business deal involving Ollie about which he remained vague, and I did not press for details. I should stop fussing, I told myself, allow someone else to take decisions for a change. The opulence of our room was overwhelming: heavy velvet drapes, a vast bathtub with a jacuzzi, and a bed only slightly smaller than my living room. We sat on its brocade edge, giggling like school children. Si had already opened the complimentary champagne, glugging at the bottle as he inspected the contents of the fridge. I sipped at my glass, knowing I wouldn't finish it: the bubbles gave me indigestion and already my face felt heavy, sleep extinguishing me as irrefutably as a fire curtain. Leaning over, Si removed my satin pumps. Brushing the back of his hand against my cheek, he pulled the irises from my hair.

'Your face is all sprinkled with flower dust,' he muttered. I sagged against him, lifting up my arms like a child as he pulled the dress over my head. When he placed his head between my sore, swollen breasts I buried my hands in his thick hair, bending down and kissing his rough face, his long, elegant ears and soft lips.

'I love you.'

I had said it to Poppy, but never to a man. The words sounded strange: too intimate and innocent for such a swanky setting, with the roar of Piccadilly outside and muffled footsteps in the corridor beyond.

'I love you too, babe.'

Tears clogged my throat. I stared down at Si's head, my hands exploring the smooth skin underneath the back of his shirt. I had known him for less than a year, but his body felt like familiar territory; home, almost, the place where I finally belonged. Inside me, Jo was doing somersaults.

'This is the way it's always going to be,' Si continued

huskily. 'You and me and Poppy and the baby, for ever and ever.'

The warehouse was ready to move into a week after the wedding. I had not seen it since June: a dull, damp day that had filled me with a gloom that, by the time we returned to Brockwell, I had convinced myself was hormonal.

'You have to remember that what we're looking at is potential,' Simon had kept repeating as he'd parked the car on the verge. 'It's in a bit of a state at the moment.'

We were on the edge of the town, the creek that led through the marshes to the River Swale a little way ahead. We walked past a row of cottages and along a muddy path that led into a boatyard. The building loomed at us through the misty drizzle of a disappointing summer morning: a large Victorian warehouse that had once serviced barges and coasters from London and Rotterdam. Following Si past the deserted boats and beached yachts, I trudged towards the three-storey slab of industrial real estate, my spirits rapidly deflating.

The interior of the building was derelict. There was no running water, no electricity and virtually no roof. We clambered over the rubble, gazing at the echoing expanse.

'So? What do you think?' Si spread out his arms, grinning. I stared around the place, trying not to shudder. It smelt of old piss and damp.

'It's going to be a challenge.'

'Yeah, but imagine what it'll be like when it's fixed up. Properties like this sell for a small fortune, especially so close to London.'

I nodded, trying to appear cheerful. In the rafters above a rowdy flock of starlings swooped and squawked like affronted revellers whose party had been crashed. My nausea was rising to a queasy peak; every swerve of movement bothered me and almost every smell. The movement of the birds and musty stink of the building had me heaving.

'You go ahead,' I gasped. 'I'm going to wait outside.'

I spent the remaining hour squatting on the banks of the river, staring across the muddy water at the flat fields and leaden sky as Si showed the surveyor around. It did not matter about the state of the building, I told myself. Like Si said, I should see it as an opportunity.

Six weeks later, Si assured me that there had been radical changes. The building was connected with electricity and water, and an ad hoc room built on to the back where we planned to cook until the kitchen was fitted in the main building. The rest of the summer was to be spent in a mobile home in the back yard. By Christmas, Si promised, the place would be habitable.

We therefore spent the days immediately after our night at the Ritz packing up our possessions. Si had sold his furniture along with his flat, and during my few years living in London I had accumulated remarkably few possessions. Besides the beds, my futon and some tables and chairs, all I had were a few boxes of kitchen equipment, several suitcases of clothes and another carton or so of books. Poppy's contribution was more considerable. She had four boxes of toys, a large bag of dressing-up clothes, a tricycle that she had long grown out of but refused to leave, a bike, three doll's prams, a pair of roller skates and Bertie, her hamster. When removal day arrived we spent the morning cramming all of this into the van that Si had hired. By midday we were ready to go. Si sat at the wheel with Poppy beside him, Bertie's cage on her lap. Behind the van I squashed into my beaten-up Fiat, filled to bursting with suitcases and bags. We would travel in convoy.

There was no send-off party, no wistful farewells from neighbours or nostalgic tears. Poppy and I had said good-bye to Nat and Jessie the day before, with hearty assurances that we would stay in touch.

'You take care of yourself, yeah?' Nat had whispered as we finally parted. Her plump fingers, with their psychedelic glass rings and bitten nails, clutched my arm, her beady eyes peering closely into my face. I flashed her a cheery smile, not wanting to be drawn in. Why did she always have to be so cautious?

'Of course I will!'

Now she was at Camden Market, where she had a stall selling joss sticks and scented candles, and Jessie was with her childminder. As my car pulled away from the kerb of the tatty, busy street where we had lived for the last two years all I felt was a pure rush of excitement, like snorting a line of high-quality coke.

The roads were surprisingly quiet. There were no queues through south London, the A2 was clear, and in under an hour we had turned off the dual carriageway and were progressing through Sittingbourne towards the coast, past acres of orchard and vineyards, towards the marshland that was to become our home. I was nervous, I admit, an excited fear fluttering low in my belly. Steering the car down the pretty Georgian lane that led through the town, I followed the van's bumping backside. Taking a smaller road, we passed the cottages and garages, and were at the water's side. And suddenly there it was: the place where our dreams were centred. In the hot sunlight the place appeared transformed, rising majestically from behind the boatyard, the rusty winch that swung above the water glowing in the sun, a gang of seagulls yabbering cheerfully on the peaked roof. As I gazed up at it, the warehouse seemed full of welcome and possibility: our escape-route to another life.

Lurching over the potholed road, we passed the boats and drew up in the front yard. The air smelt of the sea: salt and fish, like the Norfolk beaches of childhood holidays. Ahead of me, Si was lifting Poppy from the van.

'Welcome home, darling.'

She peered doubtfully around.

'What do you think?'

'Are we going to live on a boat?'

'No, you silly sausage, we're going to live there!' He pointed at the warehouse, grinning. Poppy frowned.

'What, in a factory?'

'Sort of. But it's going to be a lovely house, too.'

'Are there chocolate-making machines inside?'

Si laughed, stretching. I wandered nervously across the dried mud, looking up at the bleak walls of the building. A great deal had changed since my first visit: trucks and diggers were parked in the front yard, the roof had been mended and the temporary breeze-block kitchen completed. A skip filled with rubble had appeared, and scaffolding supported the riverside wall. Parked behind the warehouse was our mobile home, which Si had spent the last few days preparing. Around us, boat masts clinked in the breeze like wind chimes. Over the water a heron was lifting into the air, its long legs trailing languorously as it flapped across the water.

'Come on, Pops,' I said, holding out my hand. 'Let's go and explore.'

'What about Bertie?'

'He'll be all right in the van. We can find a nice place for his cage later.'

We followed Si into the warehouse. Here, too, much had

changed: the rubble slumped on the ground floor had been cleared away, the walls partly plastered and the space for the picture window that Si had designed knocked through. Gaping wide and covered with blue plastic sheeting, it looked like a badly dressed wound. Beside me, Poppy groped for my arm.

'Is this where I'm going to sleep?'

'No, darling. We're going to make you a lovely bedroom upstairs.'

'Will there be ghosts?'

I squatted beside her, holding her soft hands in mine. Her lovely face frowned back, her bottom lip quivering. Over the last few weeks I had been too preoccupied to prepare her properly for the move, I thought with a jab of reproach. We should have brought her down before, shown her the plans.

'No, my most gorgeous and wonderful girl, there won't be ghosts. It's going to be a lovely house, with masses of room for your toys and all our stuff, so we aren't tripping over things any more. You're going to have the prettiest bedroom you can imagine. We'll paint it your favourite colour and Si will do a mural for you, of animals or fairies. Would you like that?'

She stared solemnly back. It was indeed hard to imagine.

'And then upstairs,' I continued, 'we're going to make rooms for guests to come and stay, so we can make pots and pots of money. Right now Si's fixing it all up nice for us, so until then we're going to live in a sweet little house in the garden. Won't that be fun?'

'Are we going to be living in a shed?'

'No, my love, it's called a mobile home. Shall we go and see?'

She did not respond. Pulling her hand from mine, she

gazed at the raw bricks and gently flapping sheets. Her expression was like a shadow, a sudden chill that I was not expecting. In retrospect I should have seen the darkness reflected in her eyes. Grasping everything that was to come, I should have swept her into my arms and hurried away from this godforsaken building, out into the bright sunlight, then back, past the empty marshland and swaying boats, towards the town. But instead I chose to ignore her. Stepping around her small, unhappy body, I walked across the floor and inspected the new wooden staircase that led to the upstairs rooms.

Later I strolled with Poppy along the edge of the creek, the path snaking along the muddy banks towards the mouth of the river where the brown swirled outwards, towards the Isle of Sheppey. The air was less sticky here than in London, but I was weighed down by the heat, sweat pouring down my back and between my breasts. It was the baby. As I puffed along the path, he flopped cumbersomely inside me, my belly twitching.

The sky stretched above us, already fading into the deep indigo of an August evening. From the fields I could hear the cry of larks; above the water a flock of swallows darted and dipped. Back at the warehouse Si was cooking Poppy's tea. When she'd finished eating we would take her to the Portakabin and pop her under the dribbling shower. Then I would settle her in the boxy room where we had unpacked her toys and placed Bertie's cage in the corner. Since those first shaky minutes inside the warehouse, her mood had lifted. She had loved the mobile home, with its fold-out beds and secret cupboards, and was running ahead, her hand trailing through the long grasses that swayed across the path. Suddenly she halted, swinging around to face me.

'Mummy?'

'Yes?'

'When are we going home?'

I stopped, resting my hands on my bump.

'This is our home now, darling.'

'No, it's not. We live in Buckingham Road, next to Jessie.'

'Honey, we've moved. This is where we're going to live.'

'But what about my *school*?'

I took a deep breath of the muggy air. I felt as if I was melting, my skin slowly sloughing off to join the slushy bog. A month earlier we had walked out of Poppy's school playground for the last time. It was the final day of the summer term, and all around us mums were making arrangements for the holidays. I had stepped past them with few regrets. I had always felt excluded by their cheery bustle, with their cake making and arts and crafts for the school fair; even if they had asked for a contribution, I was no good at baking. Like me, Poppy too had demonstrated considerable insouciance about leaving. Since she had been at the school she had made friends only with Jessie, whom she had been remarkably unsentimental about leaving. Uprooting her was going to be easy, I'd decided.

'You're going to be starting a new school, here in Kent. Do you want to walk there tomorrow and have a peek through the railings?'

Her face dropped. 'No.'

'I bet there'll be some really nice girls. And you're going to be in Year Two!'

But she wasn't listening: she was scampering ahead, her skinny legs bashing the reeds as she skipped away from the boatyard, towards the marshes, where the curlews dipped and swaggered in the glistening mud.

I I

August passed swiftly, a succession of seemingly identical hot, dry days interspersed by dramatic downpours during which we huddled in the mobile home, laughing as bullets of rain ricocheted off the metal roof. A few hours later the puddles would be reduced to cracked craters, the water instantly absorbed by the parched earth. It was the hottest summer for thirty years, the papers declared: a right scorcher. As I sit here shivering beside Sandra, it seems as distant and fractured as a half remembered dream.

Poppy and I slipped into a seamless routine in which very little happened or got done, each day as empty and aimless as the last. Around us was frenzied activity, with Si rising at dawn to attack the upstairs beams with his sander, and the builders arriving a few hours later, obliterating the early morning peace with their bawdy jokes and oaths. They were working on the roof, swarming over the rafters like ants as their backs turned scarlet in the sun. I grew accustomed to their cheery, leery presence: the chipped mugs bunched in the sink, the din of their radios and mobiles and the constant crashing of their tools. By four they roared off in their vans, allowing the cry of curlews and the lapping water to fill the sudden silence.

Yet whilst I am able to remember these details, I can barely recall how Poppy and I spent our time. We had picnics on the bank of the creek, and played hide and seek amongst the boats. Sometimes we whiled away the afternoons with felt tips and stickers in the cool of the breeze block kitchen, or

Poppy would play alone, arranging her Sylvanian Families mice in the long grass that had survived the onslaught of the builders' trucks, while I dozed in the sun. Like a picture chalked on a well-trodden pavement, very few details remain. Perhaps it was my pregnancy which made me so fuggy and forgetful. I was curling deep into myself, swooning in the late summer warmth, a cocoon from which Jo would soon burst.

There was one afternoon that I do remember, however. By now it was nearly September and the air had assumed a soft haziness, the horizon smudged by the dust of distant harvests. The blackberries that all summer had been ripening along the riverside path were finally dark and juicy, the evenings dipping more quickly into dusk. In less than a week, Poppy would start her new school. For a final holiday treat she was staying with Jessie and Nat for the weekend, so Si and I were alone. The warehouse was empty too, the builders having knocked off for the weekend. Unaccustomed to the silence, we wandered through the dim shadows of the ground floor, then up the steep metal steps that led to the top rooms, where honeyed sun radiated from the musty Victorian windows. Up at the top was the loft space we were planning to convert into a suite of rooms for bed and breakfast guests. One day there would be bathrooms up here, with power showers, porthole views across the creek, and bedrooms built into the rafters, all stunning blonde wood and whitewashed walls. Today, however, the eastern wall was held in place with a metal joist and the creaking wooden boards gave way to alarming gaps through which one could glimpse segments of the rooms below. In one corner lay an old pile of sacks and in another ancient clumps of straw and plaster that had tumbled from the rotting wall. Starling droppings splattered the floors.

We climbed the ladder, the light drawing us upwards. The works to the roof finally completed, four large skylights now opened on to the blue sky. As we emerged from the gloom of the currently windowless lower floor, it felt as if we had entered another world: heaven, perhaps, where golden sun splashed on to our upturned faces. We stood for a moment in silence, peeking out of the opened windows at the view of the glistening creek as it snaked across the marshes. After that came the flat stretch of fields, and, far in the distance, the industrial cranes and cooling towers of Sheppey. The vast sky, with its wisps of herringbone cloud, left me breathless.

'Come and lie down.'

Si was spreading an old duvet on to the dusty floor. I sank down with a huff, the warm light bathing my face. I was over six months pregnant and no longer recognized my body. My face had turned into that of a jolly nursemaid, round and chunky with a cap of springy brown hair; my normally thin thighs mutated into thick trunks and my breasts and belly so swollen that they might have been mistaken for balloons, stuffed up my dress. Yet Si could not stop touching me. Placing his hands on my shoulders, he pulled me towards him, hooking one bony leg over my thigh, the only form of embrace I could currently endure.

'Happy?'

'Of course.'

His hands were roving over my skimpy vest, pulling it up as his fingers gently probed the insides of my maternity bra.

'Ow!'

'Sorry.'

He was pressing too heavily on my stomach. Gasping for breath, I pushed him backwards, then straddled him with my lumpy legs, the bump resting on his narrow hips like a pillow as I fumbled inside his baggy jeans.

'Perhaps we should try it like this.'

'Perhaps we should . . .'

He may have been about to say more, but it was too late. He gave a little sigh, as if some burden had been lifted from him, then his eyes went hazy. As for me, I was already lost. Beneath us the swallows were calling to each other as they swooped across the water, but I was not listening. I was tumbling headlong into the surging sweetness, my body rocking against his hips, my eyes tight shut, blinded by the light.

Afterwards we lay in a sweaty heap, my arm wedged under his back, our legs scrambled. My head was resting on his chest, his fingers entangled in my hair. He was so quiet and his breathing so steady that, imagining he had fallen asleep, I started to nod off, lulled by the heat. When he eventually spoke his words seemed distant.

'Do you love me?'

'What?'

Blinking, I rolled off him, supporting my bulk with my elbow. Perhaps it was the play of light and shade on his face, but he looked older than his forty years, his skin more lined, his brow indented with deep creases.

'Do you love me?' he asked intently. 'I mean, *really* love me?'

His pale face peered into mine with what seemed like trepidation, as if he had seen some unexpected shadow cross my eyes. I gazed back uncomprehendingly. The anxiety with which he had asked the question made it feel like a non sequitur, an intrusion from another world. Certainly, it could have nothing to do with what had just transpired between us.

'Of course I do, you plonker! Why are you asking me that?'

He shook his head, as if he was trying to dislodge an unpleasant thought.

'I need to know if I can be honest with you. I mean, really share things.'

'What kind of things?'

'Things that happened in the past . . . I mean, with previous relationships . . .'

I frowned, momentarily irritated by his unexpected intensity pulling me so roughly from my dozy bliss. I did not want to talk about previous relationships, especially not Rosa, whose name I had almost succeeded in banishing from my thoughts. I wanted to lie with him here for ever, not talking, just staring up at the sky. I thought that was what we'd agreed: the past was gone; what mattered was the future.

'Of course you can,' I said vaguely. 'You know that.'

'I mean, supposing there's stuff that's happened to one of us that the other should know about? We could, you know . . . wipe the slate clean . . .'

He stopped, pulling his fingers from my hair and sitting up. He was not usually so hesitant in his choice of words. Placing my hand on his back, I ran my fingers over the bumps of his spine. Until now he had always veered away from such discussions. Now, just when I was content to do as he wanted, living only for the present, he had decided to dredge everything up.

'There isn't anything to tell you,' I said wearily. 'Like I told you, I've been involved with some twats. It doesn't make any difference to how I feel about you.'

'But maybe you've made mistakes . . .'

I felt chilly. Moving away, I retrieved my crumpled dress from the floor and pulled it over my head. Why the hell was he cross-questioning me like this?

'I still don't see what difference it makes.'

'I just want us to be honest with each other. I mean, about mistakes we've made.'

'Okay then,' I said, taking a breath. 'I've probably made more mistakes than you've had hot dinners. I got knocked up by a useless plonker in Australia who I thought was deep because he never said anything. Trouble was, he was as thick as two short planks. Since then, what few pathetic little flings I've had have been a disaster. Until, of course, I met you. Okay? Is there anything else you want to know?'

Si was silent, his expression mournful. I did not want to think about Pete; our unhappy relationship was an episode from another life, which I'd been happy to escape. Thinking now of my dog-like dependency on his occasional morsels of love made me ashamed. I should have asserted myself more defiantly, but I was too needy and he had easily seized the upper hand. By the time I had Poppy the affair was doomed, yet we struggled on for two miserable years, with me stupidly pretending I could make it work whilst he enjoyed serial flings with other women. I had turned into what I most despised, I slowly saw. Okay, so I was in Australia rather than Britain, but here I was, living in the 'burbs, acting like a put-upon housewife. A few weeks after this realization, I packed my things, and Poppy and I moved out.

'They were all just dope-heads who sold me a pack of lies and screwed around. You're completely different and that's why I love you in a way I could never, ever, have loved them. Okay?'

Si turned, peering morosely across the room. Something was wrong: it was in his eyes, in the way he had turned his back on me, and in this sudden coldness that made me shudder with apprehension. For a long moment I thought he was about to speak. I clutched my arms around my belly, trying to pretend that nothing was happening. Yet with every second that passed he seemed to be moving further away, turning into someone I did not know. In the end, I could bear it no longer.

'I've never loved anyone before you,' I whispered, standing and placing a tentative hand on his slim, strong forearm. 'We don't have to wipe the slate clean. There isn't anything to say.'

When he eventually replied his voice was so low that I barely heard it.

'But what if *I'd* done something terrible? Would you still love me then?'

God, what a fool I was. If I could, I'd go clattering up that rickety ladder, throw the door open and scream at myself, standing in the sunshine in all my glorious, pregnant naivety, my hands clutched over my eyes and ears like two of the little monkeys. 'Listen to him!' I'd yell. 'Ask him what he means!'

But if Si had something to tell me, I was desperate not to hear.

'What could you do?' I said lightly. 'You promised you'd never betray me and I trust you. What more do we need to say?'

PART TWO

12

22 August 2004

It was bloody sweltering. Dave wiped his grassy hands on his shorts and glanced around his newly tidied garden in satisfaction. Beside him lay a large pile of grass clippings: Karen had been nagging at him to cut the lawn for weeks, and finally he had relented. After that there was Harvey's bike to mend and some scheme she had involving trellises, which were to be put up on the back wall. None of these activities were his idea of how to spend such a glorious afternoon. They should be at the beach, or at a nice open-air pool where Harvey could work off a bit of energy, not stuck at home doing chores with Karen's mum about to arrive for Sunday dinner.

Next door were having a barbie. As he regarded the compost, trails of smoke drifted over the fence; a little way down the garden he could hear the fizz of opening lagers. If he got a chance he'd pop over and join Barry and Maureen after dinner, he thought. He'd stack the dishwasher, then drift as unobtrusively as possible out of the house, across the drive and through their gate. Meanwhile, back in his own garden, his mother-in-law would be spreading her hefty legs over the sun lounger which he would have been commissioned to place in exactly the right shady spot, whilst complaining about her constipation.

If it weren't that, it would be her palpitations, or the shocking cost of an item spotted in one of Karen's catalogues. As Dave pushed the lawnmower back into the shed, he registered the depressingly familiar signs of her arrival: the faint plink of the doorbell, then a flicker of movement through the sliding living-room doors. Karen's patience with her mother's endless complaints was saintly. They'd moved her here from Hastings a year earlier so that she could be closer, and as far as Dave was concerned she'd been a pain in the bum ever since. 'She's my mum, love,' Karen would say if he objected to her by now obligatory appearance at their house for Sunday dinner. 'I can't have her spending all weekend alone, can I?'

'Harvey, go inside and say hello to your grandma.'

His son ignored him. Dave stood by the shed, vacillating between irritation and comradeship. The boy had been kicking a ball against the back wall for the past hour: bony-kneed in his Man U kit, muttering what was probably a burbled sports commentary under his breath.

'I said, go inside and say hello . . .'

'What?'

'Go inside and say hello!'

Harvey's mouth was hanging slightly open, his feet twitching at the ball.

'Earth to Planet Harvey . . .'

Striding across the grass, Dave picked up the ball, frowning in mock anger at the eight-year-old, who was now squinting dumbly up at him.

'I'm sure she'll want to hear all about your match on Thursday. You know how much Grandma loves football.' He winked, conspiratorially.

'Aw, Dad!'

'Come on now, Harv. It's time to go inside and face the music.'

Putting his heavy hands around the boy's skinny shoulders, he led him inside.

The meal was as dreary as he'd anticipated. He'd concentrated on Karen's roast, trying not to pay attention to the rambling accounts of his mother-in-law's latest foray to the shopping mall with her friend Ivy, or how George from down the road was going to the Isle of Wight for his holidays. As she droned on, he downed two and then three glasses of wine, deliberately ignoring the disapproving glint in Karen's eye. It was all right for Harvey, who could bolt down his food then slip off his seat and back into the garden, where his beloved football awaited. Dave had to sit politely through two long courses, plus coffee, by the end of which he was twitching with impatience at the way the old woman chewed her food, her habit of running her tongue around her false teeth, searching for bits of meat that were stuck. He had started to find the manner in which she replied, 'Oh, I don't know about that, dear,' to everything Karen suggested, even if it was the second helping of trifle or third glass of lager, for which she was obviously gagging, unbearably annoying. When she said it in response to the box of Black Magic that Karen had now opened, Dave wanted to reach out across the table and punch her wizened face. Put it like this: his mother-in-law's presence in their home helped him understand why criminals turned to murder. He exhaled sharply, a gesture that he knew Karen had clocked. He was yearning for a fag.

There was no denying it: he was in a filthy mood. It had been building all week, a culmination of small incidents which, taken alone, would not have unbalanced his normal good humour, but, coming together, had left him feeling unusually bleak. Most weeks, he'd approach Monday with purpose and energy. There'd be leads to follow, interviews to conduct. It was often routine work, but always spiced with the constant hope of a breakthrough, a sudden unravelling of the knotty problem they'd been worrying at: the flashes of pure excitement and adrenalin that kept him in the job. Yet today he did not anticipate the start of the working week with an ounce of relish. The previous week had gone unusually badly. First there'd been a critical article in the Kent Enquirer, a two-page spread of local unsolved crimes which hinted strongly at police incompetence, and which put Jacqui Jenning's case at the centre. Then he'd had a less than enthusiastic chat with his superintendent about his chances for promotion. Not a snowball's hope in hell, seemed to be the verdict: his performance over the last year simply hadn't been up to it. And finally, to top it all, on the Friday, there'd been an angry visit from Jacqui Jenning's mother.

Mrs Audrey Jenning wasn't the kind of mum you'd expect for what the law still referred to as a 'common prostitute'. Instead, she was a respectable lady in her fifties, who, sitting primly on the edge of the battered seat he'd offered, virtually spat blood at him.

She simply couldn't understand why the police still hadn't caught her daughter's murderer, she'd snarled. They'd surely got enough evidence from her flat, they'd held the body for the post mortem for months, they must have had enough time. What the hell were they playing at? Was it that they didn't really give a damn? Didn't they bother about working girls? Perhaps they assumed that their families didn't care? Jacqueline hadn't always been living in that way, that was one thing she wanted him to know. She was a lovely girl, good at everything. The woman's shaking hands had produced a photo from her handbag: a pretty teenager in school uniform, smiling for the camera. She had got ten GCSEs. She should be at university. It was those blasted drugs. The hellish state society was in.

By the time the woman had finished, Dave had wanted to bang his head on the table, anything to stop her from venting more of her terrible grief on him. Instead he had had to act professionally, reciting each avenue they'd explored, outlining the number of hours, days and weeks they'd spent on door-to-door enquiries, checking every tiny lead, and eventually explaining that some crimes were simply never solved, no matter how hard the police worked. He hated to say it, but it was an unpalatable fact of his profession. Some nasty villain would commit a murder, then he'd simply disappear, leaving no trace behind. He'd get off scot-free.

As Karen ushered her mother into the garden, Dave cleared the table. He should try to stop brooding about Jacqui Jenning, he told himself as he slotted the greasy plates into the dishwasher. It wasn't his fault they'd not found a single significant lead; they'd done everything they could. In his considerable experience, homicides involving prostitutes were particularly difficult to crack. Not of course that you could predict how any case would go. Some investigations virtually solved themselves.

People panicked or were stupid: they'd leave prints or say the wrong thing and within a matter of days the team would have a nice tidy file, ready to go to the CPS. Once he'd even found the perpetrator sitting by the body of the young girl he'd killed. His clothes were soaked with blood and the knife rested beside him, but his face was as guileless as if he were taking a tea break from a boring chore. Getting that particular young man put away was oddly dissatisfying, like passing an exam in which the cribbed answers were written up your sleeve. In contrast to this were the other cases, the ones that would persistently refuse to fall into place. No matter how hard his lads worked they'd accumulate only a few tattered shreds of evidence. It was like digging at stone with plastic forks.

These were the cases that kept him awake. He'd lie on his back in the early hours, listening to the steady rhythm of Karen's snoring, as the disparate facts they'd gathered gnawed at his thoughts like bad-tempered mice. It was like having a puzzle with the crucial pieces missing. And if there was one thing he hated, it was leaving things uncompleted.

Plainly, Jacqui Jenning's case was in the latter category. Somewhere, the lunatic who'd punctured her skin with over thirty stab wounds then gouged out a sizeable part of her brain was strutting around, enjoying his freedom. Dave couldn't help but see it as a personal failure, an affront to his professionalism. The case was still officially open, but after nearly nine months of door-to-door enquiries, interminable checks on her regular clients and detailed interviews with her few friends, he had serious doubts they'd ever find who killed her. They had plenty of forensic material from her flat, but none of it helped. The bloodstains matched only Jacqui's DNA; frustratingly, too, all but one of the prints they'd found belonged to her. The only real lead was some semen, staining the sheets of her dishevelled bed. But, short of demanding that every man in the country donate a sample, this led nowhere. The national DNA computer base produced nothing. All they could tell was that the man was white. There was no boyfriend, ex-husband or pimp.

Dave was pretty sure that the perpetrator was a client, perhaps someone spending the weekend by the sea. Jacqui had worked for a while in a rundown brothel on the other side of town but more recently had been trawling for custom in the Starlite night club, where she'd been the night before her murder. A bouncer remembered seeing her leave at about two in the morning with a tallish, white man. CCTV film showed a drunken couple meandering across the shopping precinct at 2.23 a.m., heading towards the taxi rank, but the cameras had only caught the blurred image of their backs. None of the local minicab drivers remembered giving them a lift.

It would be the usual story. She'd picked up a stranger, had sex with him, then he'd killed her. By now he could be anywhere. Dave didn't feel particularly sympathetic: most prostitutes led chaotic and violent lives which, if they were unlucky, ended abruptly. It was a shame that young girls had to get involved with drugs and the sex trade, but he couldn't take on the world's problems. His job was simple: to catch villains. The rest was for politicians and social workers. What irritated him was that it should be so easy for someone to commit murder then melt back into their normal life. He was neither a political nor a religious man, but what he believed with all his heart was that justice should be done.

He wandered outside, hearing the whine of his mother-in-law's voice, which was like an irritating insect that one wanted to swat, followed by the softer, conciliatory replies of his wife. He had to stop thinking about the Jacqui Jenning case. They would continue to follow every new lead; the enquiry would remain open. Yet the likelihood was that her murderer would never be caught.

Much later, after he had driven his mother-in-law home and they had put Harvey to bed, watched the late news and locked up the house for the night, Dave clambered upstairs. Karen was already in bed, reading one of her magazines — Chat, *or* Closer, *or whatever they were called — filled with diet plans and photos of celebrities with* cellulite. As he joined her, she placed her reading matter carefully on the floor.

'All right, love?'

'Yeah.'

'Bit down in the dumps today, aren't you?'

She had her arms around him, was snuggling down, her head nestling against his chest as her fingers gently kneaded his spare tyre.

'Nah, I'm fine.'

'You sure about that?'

She had rolled on to her back, her hands moving into his hair as she pulled him on top of her. He loved the feel of her satin nightie against his skin, the warmth of her skin beneath. Stretching up, she kissed the end of his nose, almost as if he were a child.

'I may need a little therapy, I s'pose . . .' he said huskily.

Reaching down, her expert fingers smoothed out around him, pulling tighter, until he gasped. He'd stopped thinking about work now. He was moving on waves, closer and closer towards his wife in whose soft-ness he would soon be engulfed; the final, thankful release of his burden, a way of coming home.

13

Autumn. Clouds rolled over the flats, bringing estuary mists, northern winds and driving rain that the sun was no longer able to vanquish. The grasses that edged the creek-side path stiffened and died; the blackberries turned sour. The swallows that in late August had perched in chirping rows on the telegraph wires were gone too; the colour drained from the landscape like old clothes that had been washed too often. Grey, brown, dark green. In the wings, winter waited.

Poppy started school. I took her in the first week of September, holding her hand tight as we edged through the throng of children and mums. They were a different lot than the London crowd: women in four-wheel drives with the comfortable appearance of the prosperous Home Counties: no clothes from Asda here, no multiple piercings or rows of gold hoops strung through sagging earlobes. And no brown or olive faces, either. For the first time since we left Buckingham Road, I missed Nat.

'I don't want to go.'

She whimpered it so quietly that, had it not been for the fierce manner in which she now gripped my arm, I might not have noticed.

'Come on, sweetie. It's going to be fine. You're going to meet lots of new friends.'

'But they aren't my friends!'

Squatting down, I pulled her into my arms. Around us, a

group of little girls who would surely be in Poppy's class were calling excitedly to each other.

'Elly! Have you got your Tamagotchi?'

'Look at my new coat!'

Blonde plaits, sparkly silver anoraks, bobby socks and pink leggings: a gaggle of girlie girls, types that in London Jessie and Poppy had despised.

'But they will be, once you've got to know them. Come on, Pops. You've got to be brave.'

She pulled away, standing angrily before me in the alien playground, my lovely tomboy, with her jeans and trainers, her practical bob and the sweater that Pat had knitted her for Christmas. Out of the corner of my eye I could sense the other girls staring.

'I don't want to be brave!'

'Come on, love. Look, all the others are getting into line. There's your teacher . . .'

With considerable effort, I straightened up. The bending had made my womb tighten into a fake contraction, a gentle squeezing that in two months would turn to ferocious labour. I wanted at all costs to avoid a confrontation.

'She's waving at you, darling!'

Pulling her by the hand, I frogmarched her to the front of the line. Miss Graves, a pretty young woman that Si and I had briefly met in June, was smiling at us reassuringly.

'Hello, Poppy! Are you going to come inside with me?'

She had no choice but to nod, yet her eyes were watery. Slowly, reluctantly, she released my hand. 'And then we'll find some nice girls to look after you, okay?'

'Okay.'

Defeated, she followed her teacher across the playground and into the school building. Head drooping, shoulders bunched, she looked so small and lost that I couldn't bear to watch. Turning quickly away, I pushed swiftly past the milling mums and out of the gate.

Back at the warehouse, there was nothing to do. The floor was being fitted downstairs, and upstairs the bedrooms were being replastered. Si was up every morning at six, working in the loft, where we had made love in the sunshine. We wanted to have at least part of the building habitable by the time the baby arrived. Regarding the naked gaps where the kitchen was supposed to be fitted, the raw brickwork and trailing cables, I wondered if it would ever happen.

I took to meandering through the boatyard, taking the path along the side of the creek until I had progressed so far into the marshes that the warehouse had shrunk to the size of my fingernail. However far I walked, I could still hear the scream of Si's sander. Eventually I would wander back, hoping he'd agree to take a break, unaccustomed to boredom.

I got to know our neighbours. Bob Perkins introduced himself to me in the boatyard after Ronnie, his Labrador, jumped up with such enthusiasm that, like an unbalanced skittle, I was nearly knocked over. I'd already noticed him walking the dog along the riverside path: a retired chap in a mountaineering fleece and thick glasses who was now eagerly telling me how he and his wife had been living in their cottage for nineteen years.

'Doing up the warehouse, are you?'

I winced apologetically. 'Sorry about the noise.'

He shrugged.

'It's about time somebody tried to do something with the place. It's a white elephant, been left to rot for years. You might as well try to live there.'

Refusing to be discouraged, I gave him a bright, determined smile.

'We're hoping to open as a B&B when it's finished. It's such a pretty spot.'

He looked around doubtfully. In front of the warehouse a large dredger was rusting into the water. Further down the creek an old barge lay sunken and forgotten, its roof peppered with holes. The working yard, where boats were repaired and docked for the winter, was behind us. This was the graveyard: where the corpses of abandoned boats were left to decay in the mud, a place of maritime ghosts.

'I suppose you might get some people that were interested . . .'

Other characters slowly came into focus: Richard, the owner of the boatyard, who accepted a beer as Si showed him around; Janice, Bob's wife, whose manner was faintly disapproving, as if we had already inadvertently offended her. Perhaps it was the noise of our builders, or the churned-up lane. I started chatting to the lady in the chemist's, who sold me Gaviscon by the bucketful and asked matronly questions about my due date; another lady, who walked her dog by the creek, now nodded hello.

I would never have admitted it – not to Si, Poppy or myself – but I missed Don and his sales team, and Nat and the hurly-burly of London, like a limb that had been ripped off at the joint.

Poppy continued to trail to school reluctantly, gripping at me as we entered the playground and glancing back forlornly as Miss Graves led her inside. Each afternoon that I waited for her in the playground, my anxiety would rise a notch. I longed for her to come skipping from her classroom like the other girls, waving their paintings and books like trophies and being swooped up by their respectable mummies in happy, girlie gangs, off to Brownies, or back to someone's house for tea. In contrast, Poppy was always alone. I had given up asking who she played with. My gauche questions were invariably answered by a scowl.

'It's none of your business!' she'd cry, marching ahead. Or: 'If you care so much, why did you take me away from Jessie?'

I, too, suffered from new-girl solitude. At Buckingham Road Infant School I had rarely had the time to linger in the playground. Either Nat picked up the girls, or I would arrive in a tearing hurry, having double-parked the Fiat or dumped it on a double yellow line. In the mornings Poppy would leap from the car and rush through the gates alone. Unlike the stay-at-homers I was unable to hang around and chat. I had appointments that started at 9 a.m. There were properties to be valued, prospective buyers to meet. I could not afford to lose my job.

But now I had joined the other side. Once I had completed my pregnancy yoga routine, tidied the remains of breakfast and made tea for the builders, my day was empty of meaningful activity. Yet whilst Poppy remained unattached to their children, I had no entrée to the groups of mums who waited so companionably in the playground. How had they become so close? As I hovered on the edge of the playground they clustered together in cliques, ignor-ing me. It was reminiscent of being nine once more and back at my own primary school, where, on the instruc-tions of a plump girl called Josephine, I was summarily blanked. Unlike the other children I had never figured out how to negotiate the complex rules of engagement of pre-pubescent girls. For them, friendship seemed to occur naturally. Yet for me it was constantly elusive, slipping intangibly out of my grasp. It was as if they all knew something I had never been told, I sensed; a secret that remained hidden.

Back at the warehouse the build was going badly. The team that Si had employed had done a good job of tearing out the decrepit interior and mending the roof, but now that the riverside wall was about to be rendered, a malevolent rot had been discovered in the brickwork that the cheapskate surveyor had overlooked. The whole lot would have to come down, Si muttered gloomily. It would add another fifteen or twenty grand to the bill. Pipes were a problem, too. The plumber who over the summer had connected the waterworks for the new kitchen had messed up. Three months earlier Si had been drinking with him in the Anchor Inn by the brewery. Now he declared that the man was a cowboy, a dodgy contact of Ollie's, who should never have been given the gig. The whole job would have to be redone.

He took it hard. Each problem sapped at his previously gung-ho optimism until what remained was a weary gloom, which swirled around us, as dampening to the spirits as fog. Even worse, the builders suddenly disappeared. If their rowdy presence had been vaguely irritating over the summer, their autumn absence was infuriating. They had taken on another job, I learned, there was some problem with payment. Si refused to discuss the details. Withdrawing to the top of the building, he spent long afternoons bashing at the rotten plaster with a pickaxe, reappearing grim-faced and fatigued, perspiration running from his lined face like a fever.

I wanted to help him, but in my encumbered state there was little I could do. The kitchen units were ordered, the flooring and paint colours chosen. Until the far wall was rendered and replastered, we could progress no further. And even if there had been work for me, I had little energy for it. The baby weighed me down, pushing into my oesopha-gus and bringing burning indigestion that no amount of Gaviscon could soothe.

The days passed sluggishly. I slumped around, contribut-ing nothing and trying to remain conscious. For weeks I had been unable to sleep, the fold-out beds of the mobile home proving both too narrow and too hard. As the baby punched and squirmed, I lay awake, listening to the wind rattling at the roof and dreading the exhaustion of the approaching day.

Then, some time in October, Poppy made a friend.

'Mummy!' she shouted happily as she met me at the gate. 'Can Megan come back and play?'

She shoved her bag into my hand and was beaming up at me excitedly as she hopped from foot to foot. Next to her stood one of the girls from her class, a sharp-faced child with brown pigtails and a silvery anorak.

'What, now?'

'Yes! Oh, please say yes! Please, please, please, please!'

'Okay, if Megan's mum agrees.'

'Yes!' Poppy cried in triumph, punching the air. I winked at her, pleased to finally have my daughter back on form. 'Which one's your mum, Megan?' I asked, turning to her new friend.

The girl pointed to a woman standing in the centre of a gaggle of mothers. She was nodding exaggeratedly at some-thing then suddenly barked with laughter, her voice rising above the playground din. I had noticed her before: a heavy-set woman in slacks and high-heeled boots, who drove one of the showiest of the bull-barred trucks, into which she seemed continually to be herding large groups of children. On the first day of term I had attempted a smile as we had passed by the netball hoops, but she had gazed past me, as if I wasn't there. Steeling myself, I grasped Poppy's hand. We walked resolutely across the tarmac towards Megan's mother.

'Hello,' I said, smiling broadly. 'I'm Mel, Poppy's mum. We were wondering if Megan would like to come back for tea.'

The woman blinked back at me politely. Clearly, she had never heard of Poppy. Taking in her polished nails, her jolly striped jumper and the prim set of her mouth, I was suddenly aware of my own straggly appearance: the men's jeans that sagged beneath my bump, my paint-speckled baseball boots and hennaed hair.

'Unfortunately Megan has ballet,' she said, smirking slightly. Beside me, I could sense Poppy deflate. '*Please*, Mum,' she hissed, tugging on my sleeve.

It was clearly of utmost importance that I nail this date.

'What about tomorrow?' I persisted brightly. 'We can bring her home, if it's a problem.'

Megan's mother gave me a tight, unfriendly smile. 'Tomorrow shouldn't be a problem,' she said. 'Isn't that nice, Megan?'

But Megan had run off and was giggling with the other girls.

I had strict instructions from Poppy concerning preparations for the tea. I was to supply Jammie Dodgers, crisps, peanut butter sandwiches and chocolate milkshakes. I should tidy up the mobile home beforehand, and not ask Megan embarrassing questions. I must neither dance nor sing. On no account was Si allowed to appear with his guitar. Her vehemence on this last point surprised me. A few months earlier his performances were the high point of our evenings.

Now, with new friends, a Bob Dylan-warbling stepfather, with unravelling jumpers and sawdust in his hair, was obviously not cool.

After I met them at the school gates the girls ran ahead as I waddled behind. They seemed to be plotting. Arms around each other's shoulders, they paced down the lane and through the boatyard, yabbering secrets. I watched them with relief. Clearly, I should not have been so impatient. Poppy was perfectly able to forge new friendships without my interventions; she had, after all, only been at the school a few weeks. As Si kept telling me, I should learn to trust.

Yet by the time the girls sat down for tea, the atmosphere had shifted. Unlike the happy chatter I had anticipated, they guzzled their food in silence, then disappeared solemnly into Poppy's small room. After so many afternoons spent in the jocular company of Jessie, who was as loud and bumptious as Poppy, I had been taken aback by Megan's formality. Sitting with a straight back at the tea table, she referred to me as 'Mrs Stenning', a title that made me blanch, frowned at Poppy's suggestion of blowing down her straw into her milk and suggested they play with the toy make-up that Megan had produced, packed into a pink plastic purse, from her school bag. Closing the door to Poppy's room firmly behind them, they did not reappear for another hour. I left them alone, listening hopefully for the sounds of laughter as I fidgeted in the small kitchenette.

When the door finally opened, my hopes capsized. Poppy appeared first, slamming it behind her. She pushed past me, her pointy face pink with anger.

'Please can Megan go home now? I don't want to play with her any more.'

Megan appeared behind her, smirking. As I glanced at her

face it occurred to me that her eyes had a vindictive, almost gloating glint.

'Oh, come on, girls! Megan's only been here a short while. Why don't we show Megan the river, Pops? There might still be some blackberries by the path.'

'I don't want to go to the horrid river.'

'Actually, nor do I, Mrs Stenning.'

They remained intransigent. Whatever fragile bonds had existed before tea had been snapped apart as definitely as a broken twig. Folding her arms, Megan sat stiffly on the fold-down sofa in the small living area as Poppy stomped back to her room. Ten minutes later Megan's mother arrived in her four-by-four.

'Never mind!' She flashed me an icy smile, glancing curiously at the mess strewn around the yard. A tremor of shock registered on her face; nothing too obvious, just the slight batting of her lids at the chaos of builders' tools, boxes of tiles, paint pots and other miscellaneous rubbish. We were clearly trailer trash; Poppy's friendship with her daughter was not a relationship to be encouraged.

'Girls will be girls!'

Two minutes later they had disappeared, roaring back up the lane to their neo-Georgian show home.

When I gingerly pushed open the door to Poppy's room I found her lying on the bed, the covers pulled over her head. Hair bobbles, star-shaped clips and baby pots of nail varnish were scattered across the floor, rejected birthday presents that had previously been shoved at the back of her drawers and only reinstated for Megan's entertainment.

'What went wrong?' I asked gently.

'Nothing!' her muffled voice wailed from under her Princess Fiona cover. 'Go *away* Mummy! I *hate* you!'

My stomach felt as if it were filled with rocks. I sat down

heavily on her bed, fiddling with the edge of her cover. 'Why do you hate me?'

'Because it's all your fault!'

'Why's it all my fault? I was trying to make things nice for you, honey.'

She sat up. With her tangled hair hanging over her face and cheeks smeared with tears, her face was contorted with misery.

'Because it was you who made me come here! I never wanted to live in this horrible place!'

'I thought you'd be happy here. When the warehouse is finished we'll have lots of room, and it's so beautiful . . .'

'Megan said it was *weird*! She said only losers live in caravans!'

I sucked at my lips, wincing. All the time that the little madam had been having her tea, she had been storing up her nasty narrow judgements.

'But this isn't how it's always going to be, sweetheart,' I said, trying to remain calm. 'We're going to make the warehouse really nice and then we're going to move in there. And anyway, this isn't a caravan, it's a mobile home.'

But Poppy merely stared back at me, blank-faced. 'Why can't we live like a normal family?'

'But we do live like a normal family!'

'No we don't! Why are you always lying to me? Megan said that if your mum's husband isn't your real dad that makes your mum all slutty!'

My mouth dropped open. I was literally winded: how did seven-year-old girls learn to belittle people like this? Whilst I had been serving her cakes and pink milk, Megan's prudery had come crashing into our home like a boulder, with the words 'Middle England' carved into it.

'That is total, utter nonsense.'

Poppy jerked away from my outstretched hand, pulling her cover back over her head.

'Go away! I really hate you, Mummy!'

I trailed back to the kitchenette, feeling as if I were filled with the bags of cement slumped outside on the drive. Poppy was right. I loathed the moralities of Megan and her ilk, but I had been unable to provide my daughter with a conventional family, or even a conventional home. And now, like me, she was an oddball, not allowed to fit into this small-minded setting. If I were a better mother I would be able to comfort her, to teach her to laugh at nasty little prigs like Megan; she'd be surrounded by friends. Yet I had no idea how to achieve social success. I was as adrift as her. As a child we had moved house according to the vagaries of Michael's career: a spell in Reading, then Milton Keynes, then Swansea. My teenage years were spent mostly in Surrey. I had never felt that I belonged.

I started to clear away the tea, sniffing disconsolately. Since meeting Si my feelings of inadequacy had been pushed aside, but now they were back and biting hard. How could I have a second child when I was such a failure with the first? It was yet another example of my foolishness. I was unversed in the proper techniques of motherhood. Everyone else made it appear so easy, but, however hard I tried, I remained a learner, who kept endlessly failing her test.

14

As Si worked with increasing fervour on the building, I sank ever deeper into antenatal lethargy. The time that we spent together dried up almost completely. He couldn't afford to pause for long lunches or laze with me in the late autumn sunshine, and he'd snap if I attempted to entice him away. Even if the builders had upped tools and left us in the lurch, he was damned if he was going to stop work. I knew he was right: in order to keep our debts at bay we had to get the building ready for paying guests. Yet I found it hard not to take the rejection personally. When he was not crashing around in the rafters, he was in London. There was 'business' to see to, he retorted in response to my feeble questions. I knew better than to question him more closely. From the outset he had resisted my attempts to probe his affairs. 'Don't worry about it, babe,' he'd say, his expression suddenly impenetrable. 'Everything's fine.'

This was not how I had imagined our new life. I had had a bellyful of being alone; it was why I had married him. I'd assumed we would work on the warehouse together, breaking off for companionable walks or sharing a sandwich by the creek. At the very least, I had not expected to spend most evenings in our cramped mobile home alone as he zoomed off in his van for endless 'meetings' with architects and contractors. He was busy, I kept telling myself, that was why we no longer talked; when the build was finished our intimacy would return. After all, now that we had the security of being married we did not have to glue ourselves so assiduously together through 'quality time'. And I was so heavily pregnant, too. Perhaps my lump was putting him off. 'After the baby comes' and 'after the build is finished' became my mantras, endlessly chanted at the altar of my neuroses. They did not necessarily work. Sometimes, as I lay fretting beside him, listening to his soft snores, after another evening of non-communication consummated only by a peck on the cheek, I feared that our relationship was already over.

I had other worries, too. My due date approached with merciless speed. What only a few months earlier I had thought of in abstract terms was now vividly real. Poppy's birth had been a forty-eight-hour ordeal in which I had been convinced I was going to die. When her waxy body finally emerged from mine I was so stunned that I was still alive and, even more shockingly, that this perfectly formed baby had just appeared from between my legs, that I spent the first few hours unable to utter a word. That my body would undergo this event for a second time both terrified and dumbfounded me. It simply could not be that the squirming lump which now inhabited my tummy would, in a month or so, fight his way out. The more I brooded, the more impossible it seemed.

And yet there he was. I lay on the bed, prodding what I imagined to be his bottom with my fingers. Each day he was growing larger until, inescapably, he would have to be born.

'Are you okay?'

I looked up with a start. Si was standing in the door of our bedroom, squinting at me in the late morning light.

'I've been looking everywhere for you.'

'I'm just having a rest.'

He wandered into the room, absent-mindedly setting

down the hammer that he had been holding in his battered hands on the pillow as he sat down.

'How's the baby?'

'Fine.'

Laying his hand tenderly on my naked belly, he leaned over and kissed it.

'So what's the matter?' Rising, he took my hand and nuzzled at my knuckles.

'I don't know. I . . .'

A wave of hormonal misery rose inside me. Unable to continue, I stared at the cotton counterpane. I was concentrating hard on not weeping.

'I'm just being pathetic . . .'

'Are you worrying about the birth again?'

I stared into his dusty face. Since moving to Kent his hair had grown so long that he had taken to tying it back with a rubber band. He had grown fitter, too; his London stringiness turned muscular. Pulling my hand away from his mouth, I stretched my fingers around his biceps. Now that he was beside me, peering into my face with such gentle concern, my fears were melting away like morning mist.

'I'm just being stupid.'

'It's not stupid to be scared, hon. I'm just trying to imagine what it must be like . . .'

I didn't reply. The truth was that until the birth there was little he could do to reassure me. I was moving into an altered, liminal state, in which my body and the baby took over. Even if we both survived the birth, I had started to conclude that I would never be able to give the baby what he needed. Pat had not provided me with a template; where other mums seemed automatically to know what to do, I had always felt as if I was floundering, lurching from one crisis to the next.

'I'm just feeling bad for Poppy,' I eventually whispered. 'I mean, how am I going to cope when there's two of them?'

'You'll cope fine. And it'll be great for Poppy to have a little brother.'

I glanced up at him. I had not told him what Megan had said to Poppy. 'I suppose it's that having another baby makes me think about my own mother,' I added, dabbing at my eyes. Until the words were out of my mouth I had not realized that this was what underlay my depression.

'Oh, come on. Pat's not that bad. She's just a bit stiff.'

'I don't mean her. I mean my real mother.'

He frowned, leaning over and fingering a strand of my hair. I had told him I was adopted, but not much more. As with his own childhood, he had always made it clear that he believed that our less-than-happy backgrounds and families were best forgotten.

'You mean it makes you think about being adopted?'

'Yeah. And the fact that now that I'm an adult she still doesn't want to know.'

There was a long pause. I kneaded at my fingers.

'Have you met her?' Si asked quietly.

I nodded, feeling the weight of grief rise inside me. It was the first time I had told anyone.

'It was when I came back from Australia. I got into this thing about Poppy needing to meet her real grandmother. I wanted Britain to be a place where she had proper blood connections. So I went back to the agency that had placed me, in the West Country.'

Si continued to stroke my hair, looking carefully into my face.

'It was amazingly easy. They had a number so I rang it up and spoke to this old lady, who I realized later must have been my grandmother. She said her daughter had moved out of the area ages ago. She'd got married, apparently. The old lady seemed to assume that I was something to do with the social services. She gave me the address without even asking who I was.'

I had left Poppy at Pat's for the night and driven to the address that my trembling hand had scrawled down. A narrow street in Bristol: small terraced houses with scrappy front gardens and cars continually banging over the road humps that were supposed to slow them down. I was in a kind of daze. I imagined a homely woman opening the door, who would instantly open her arms in welcome and explain how she'd been forced to give me up. I thought she would be everything that Pat wasn't. Her name was Sally Arkwright.

But rather than my long-lost mother appearing, the door was opened by a man, a slobby looking bloke, with a large belly that flopped over the belt of his jeans and a grey beard that was tied into a little plait at its straggling ends. He looked like a biker. When I asked for Sally he glared at me suspiciously, then turned on his heel, leaving me standing on the step, my heart pounding so hard I could barely breathe.

A few seconds later she came to the door. I gawped at her, for a moment too suffocated by my own emotions to be able to speak. She was utterly different from how I had pictured her: permed hair peroxided blonde, sequinned jeans that were cut too tight for her middle-aged body, hard eyes set into a lined face. She looked exactly how I might appear in sixteen or seventeen years' time, were my character completely changed.

'If you've come about Darren, he can piss off as far as I'm concerned,' she said, folding her arms.

'No, it's not that.'

'What is it then?'

'My name's Melanie,' I said in a rush. 'I was born in a

home for teenage mothers near Cheltenham in 1969. I was given your mother's address, as a contact . . .'

My mother's eyelids fluttered a few times, but apart from that her expression did not change. Instead, it seemed to harden, solidifying into something impenetrable.

'I don't know what you're talking about.'

'You are Sally Arkwright, aren't you?'

Perhaps I'm fooling myself, but a tremor of something softer passed across her face. Then she placed her bony fingers around the door handle.

'Drop it, love,' she said. 'It's never going to go anywhere.'

She closed the door in my face.

'So, what happened?' asked Si.

I gazed back at him, imagining a crane shot of the scene in Bristol, the camera panning up and away from my dejected back and the closing door as if these were the final sequences of some corny film. It did not matter that she had shut the door in my face. I had my own family. As Si would say, what was past was passed.

'Like I said, she didn't want to know. It was a total disaster.'

His hand cupped the side of my face. 'Poor darling Mel.'

'It doesn't matter now. I never think about her any more.'

For a while Si stared at me, chewing on his lip. I wished I had never brought the subject up.

'Why were you looking for me, anyway?' I said, rolling off the bed and easing my feet into my slippers.

'I've just had a call from Ol.'

'Oh yeah?'

'He's having a bit of trouble on this conversion job. I'm going to go up to London for a couple of days and help him out. You don't mind, do you?'

I stiffened. Turning away from Si, I walked towards the

143

window and stared down at the muddy river. Outside it was spitting with rain.

'Okay.' I had tried to keep the complaint from my voice, but the phrase sounded tight and forced.

'It won't be for more than a day or so. And I can't get anything more done on upstairs until the oak's delivered.'

I shrugged, willing myself to turn around and smile. 'Really, it's not a problem.'

'I thought I'd go straight down there this afternoon. I mean, we could do with the money. And you're not due for another month or so . . .'

'Si, don't worry. Poppy and I will be *fine*.'

But after he had gone I went back to bed. He was lying, I thought darkly. He had had enough of me and was seizing any excuse to get away. Perhaps there was another woman involved. I had promised to trust him, but now tiny doubts began to bite into me, like an infestation of weevils. It would explain so much: the frequent outings, his new disinterest in sex. I was such a bad-tempered blob, why would he ever want to stay?

Forty-eight hours later I leaned against the front door as Si jumped out of the van on to the forecourt. I was both yearning to see him and dreading the signs of infidelity that in my increasingly paranoid state I was sure to find plastered over his face.

'Hi, honey!'

Leaping over a puddle, he landed neatly at my feet, gathering me into his arms into a great squashy hug. 'I've missed you.'

I did not return his embrace, just stood with my arms hanging loosely by my sides. Si pulled back, scrutinizing my face.

'Are you feeling better?'

'Better in what way?'

He frowned. 'Okay, let's start again. Are you feeling more *cheerful*?'

'I'm doing my best.'

I sounded bad tempered and resentful, the kind of woman that any man in his right mind would wish to escape from. Reflected in the front window of his van, I glancingly caught sight of myself: arms folded over massing belly, face crumpled with childish pique; I was barely recognizable. Was it hormones that were making me so suspicious? For a moment my mind cleared: I was pregnant, happily married to a caring man who had simply gone to London to do some work. Then I remembered Rosa, and the studied nonchalance with which Si had told me he was leaving, and my paranoia pushed my good sense aside.

'You haven't been with some other woman, have you?' I blurted. Slowly, almost wearily, Si shook his head. I was sure that I saw something dark pass over his eyes.

'Honestly, Mel, chill out! Of course I haven't.'

Then, surely too hastily, he brushed past me and into the warehouse.

*

And now it all fits sickeningly together, like the handcuffs that DI Simmons clicked with such bored competence around Si's wrists the day before yesterday. *Supposing I did something terrible?* he'd asked and, fool that I was, I assumed he was talking hypothetically. But even then, when I was pregnant with Jo, it now seems that I was correct and he *was* still seeing Rosa. Yet why would he take Poppy? Something is missing in the story that the police have down so pat. It *cannot* be true; Si would never put Poppy in danger, whatever mess he was in. He wouldn't do this to me, he just wouldn't.

But the facts remain. I was playing hide and seek with Poppy, and I heard a door close behind me. A few minutes later, Si drove away. I continued to search for Poppy, but she had vanished. The police must be right. They're the professionals, experts in the unravelling of personal tragedy. Poppy has gone, and Si, who I once believed to be my saviour, has taken her.

I am sitting on the sofa, rocking. When I open my eyes, I see that Sandra has positioned herself at the other end of the sunken cushions. There she sits, quietly watching. I cannot recall how long I have been here, or when she joined me. Outside the night has taken over. As we sit under the electric light the picture window throws back our reflection. It is not the usual tableau that the casual passer-by might see, glancing into our home as they take the dog for an evening stroll. Framed by the window, they might notice a woman with a little girl on her lap, watching TV. On another evening the girl might be curled up alone, perusing a comic; in the background her mother bustles contentedly around, a baby strapped to her chest. Later, a couple might appear, apparently happy in their domestic disarray as they cuddle on the cushions. Taking in the scene, the passer-by might experience a series of fleeting emotions: satisfaction, perhaps, at the sight of happy family life, disapproval of the squalor, or maybe surprise that the occupants have not bothered to put up blinds. Whatever they thought or saw, it would be unexceptional, not worthy of note.

But today the scene has changed. At one end of the sofa a neatly dressed woman perches, her legs drawn up to one side as if she wishes to protect herself from the chaos. If it were not for the radio that she has clipped to the waistband of her sensible slacks, she might be a bored passenger at an airport, waiting to board her flight. At the other end slumps a younger woman. Perhaps she has been crying, for her face has a raw appearance, as if something has been stripped away. Her untidy dark hair is plastered unflatteringly around her face; at the back, it sticks up in unhappy tufts, as if she has been pulling at it. She must be experiencing some kind of breakdown, for she is rocking backwards and forwards like a loony, her hands clasped around her knees. If the onlooker were to step closer to the glass and peer inside more closely, he or she would see that her reddened eyes were empty of expression.

'There's some news, Mel,' Sandra says quietly.

I stare at her, my stomach plummeting. For a second or so something blocks my throat. From the way she is looking at me, I know it's bad.

'What kind of news?'

'There's been another sighting of the car – a member of the public in response to the newsflash.'

'And?'

'He remembers spotting a vehicle which sounds similar to Simon's car. It was about four-thirty, on the Sittingbourne road.'

I swallow, feeling the weight of this news sink into me. 'What does that mean?'

'We're not sure yet, but it's an important lead. The reason the man remembers the car so clearly is that he almost crashed into it. He was driving towards the town centre, and Simon's vehicle was travelling very fast in the opposite direction. As it approached, it overtook a slower vehicle and our witness had to swerve into the verge to avoid a collision.'

'Right.'

Sandra pauses. I am clutching my hands so tightly that my fingernails almost break the skin.

'The man also noticed a little girl sitting in the passenger seat.'

'You mean he saw Poppy?'

'That's what we're assuming, yes.'

In the background I can hear the shuffle of policemen's boots on the stairs. From the kitchen comes a hubbub of voices and the sudden beep of a mobile phone. Upstairs, Jo has started to cry. I can hear Trish soothing him in her sing-song voice. After a second or so, the wailing stops.

'I just don't understand why he'd take her . . .'

'It's the kind of thing that people sometimes do when they're under extreme stress,' Sandra says sadly.

My bowels are starting to loosen. I feel nauseous, sweat prickling my skin.

'We think he's panicked,' Sandra continues, placing a cool hand on my shoulder. I do not respond. All I can think is that it must be some kind of ghastly mistake. Si's a careful driver, a loving stepdad. This *can't* be him.

'We're afraid he might be planning something silly.'

'Something silly?'

Sandra bites her lip. 'We can't of course predict the eventual outcome, but we're worried that he may be experiencing suicidal thoughts. We're very gravely concerned for Poppy's safety.'

It's as much her expression as her words that make my belly do another sickening flop. I gaze back at her face, unable to reply.

'What I can tell you at this stage is that we're doing everything we can to trace the car,' she continues. 'We've circulated the details nationally, there's going to be an item on the local TV news, we're . . .'

I do not hear the rest. Jumping up, I dash to the toilet.

*

148

There are arms around me, soft bodies to lean against. I am being propelled across the living room and seated back on the sofa. Someone has draped a duvet around my shoulders; Trish is fussing around with a coffee table and a steaming mug. I still can't hold the drink, for I am shaking uncontrollably, like I did after my waters broke with Jo. In an odd way it is a relief to allow my body to take over. All I am is skin and bones, physical impulses and reactions. It's chemistry that causes these muscular spasms, that's all anything is.

'Have some of the tea, sweetheart,' Trish is saying. 'It'll help warm you up.'

She's handing me the mug, but I push it away.

'I want Jo,' I whisper. 'Bring me Jo.'

He's placed in my arms. He's beginning to stir from his nap, his arms stretching upwards, his eyelashes fluttering against his pearly skin. I clasp his bundled body, my trembling fingers automatically pulling up my jumper and reaching for the hook of my maternity bra. Despite the turmoil, my breasts are hard and sore. Now, as I bring his head towards my nipple, my bra soaks with the sudden let-down of milk. Jo sucks greedily, snuffling contentedly as his hand curls around my outstretched finger. With his warmth against my belly, I feel a little better.

'Is there anything else I can get you?' Trish says, leaning over and touching me lightly on the hand. I take in her lovely concerned face and the swell of her own baby, stretching her woollen dress.

'I'm fine,' I say. 'You should get a sit-down, too.'

'The police are doing their best . . .' She stops, glancing with a hopeless shrug across the room, presumably in the direction of the various officers that remain in the building.

'Yes,' I say. 'I know.'

'Do you want me to sit with you?'

'Actually, would you mind if you left me alone for a little?' I give her hand a squeeze, showing it's nothing personal.

'Cool. If you need me, I'll be in the kitchen.'

I nod, watching her sway gracefully across the cluttered room. Perhaps she's going to talk to Sandra, or DCI Gosforth will bombard her with questions about our family life. They won't find anything out, not by talking to her, or to any of the neighbours. As I pull Jo off my right breast and swivel him round so that he empties the left, I know that neither Sandra's careful questions nor the multitude of procedures that the police are bringing to bear upon the situation will bring Poppy back. Jo slurps and smacks his lips, oblivious to his sister's plight. As I watch him I know what I have to do. I have to stop panicking and start focusing. It's no good weeping and wailing and being so passive: I'm the one who has the answers.

What I have to do is remember everything that happened.

15

Jo arrived at the end of November. It was a short, agoniz-
ing labour, slamming into me with the force and fury of
a hurricane. Like a photo that's been left too long in the
sun, my memory curls and fades around the harsher details.
To my shock my waters broke in the shower, just before
I went to bed. Si heaped towels around my shoulders and
I rested for a while on the puddled floor until the shaking
subsided. He was almost as agitated as me, clattering up
and down the stairs in an attempt to locate the phone,
changing his mind and going to get a hot-water bottle, then
forgetting where he'd put the maternity ward's number. I
waited on the bathroom floor, worrying about Poppy. This
was not meant to happen until December, when Pat had
agreed to come and look after her. What were we going
to do now?

Then came the contractions, erasing all thought. How can
the human brain recall that level of pain? I don't remember how it felt, just that the only possible position was standing, my arms draped around the sink, my bottom waving in
the air. There is no dignity in childbirth. By the time Si had
persuaded the hospital to send an ambulance, I was squatting by the newly installed bath, mooing like a cow. Jo arrived
after a few tortured pushes, just after the midwife had come
clumping up the stairs.

Despite my fears, I was still alive and the baby was
perfect. He didn't cry, just lay in my arms blinking. Ten

tiny fingers and ten tiny toes, long skinny legs, vernix still covering his bald scalp in waxy patches: our little son. Si was ecstatic, bounding around the place like an over-excited puppy as he made tea for the midwife, tried unsuccessfully to locate a bottle of champagne and helped to tidy up. When he cradled Jo in his arms, his face was softer than I'd ever seen.

'I can't believe it,' he whispered, his eyes filling with tears.

How could I have doubted him? In the days that followed, the formless anxieties that had beset me over the last months of my pregnancy vanished without trace. It must have been my hormones that made me so paranoid, I decided. It was ridiculous to imagine that Si was anything but the most devoted of partners. Here he was, making me lunch as I fed Jo, or sweeping him away to change his nappy as he belted out one of the nonsensical nursery rhymes that he had taken to composing. Gone was the tight-lipped silence of the autumn, when he had shut himself upstairs, doing God knows what to the loft. Gone was his habit of dodging outside to make calls on his mobile, as if he didn't want me to hear. Gone too was the distance in his eyes, which had made me feel so chilled. The man I had fallen for in London was back. He had never been happier, he declared one morning as he covered my face with kisses. Having me and Jo and Poppy was like a dream come true.

Work on the warehouse ground to a halt, but Si no longer seemed to care. The builders would reappear in a couple of weeks to install the new kitchen, he insisted. Until then, there was little to do. We had moved from the mobile home into the warehouse a few weeks earlier, and welcomed the change. The building was unusually quiet, filled only with the sounds of Jo's crying or the clatter of our footsteps, hurrying over the wooden floors. If previously the boatyard had resonated with the screech of drills or crash of hammers, now all we could hear were the yowl of the wind, the flapping of canvasses, and the constant chink of nylon ropes against masts, like cowbells. Winter was here, turning the marshland wild.

Si returned to his painting. He set up his materials in one of the bedrooms-to-be along the gallery, transforming it into a makeshift studio and working late into the night while Jo and I dozed in front of the TV. It was because he was finally at peace that he could paint again, he muttered, shyly producing a landscape of the creek, with the gas towers of Sheppey rising in the distance. A week later he completed a series of charcoal sketches of me lying on the sofa with Jo. They were so good that I tried to persuade him to take them to a local gallery. Predictably, he refused. He wasn't ready, he said; he needed more time to recover. Distracted by a ratty baby and a pile of washing, I did not ask what he meant.

In December, everything suddenly changed. He had received a call from Ollie, Si announced one blustery afternoon as the wind screeched across the marsh. He was having a work crisis, there was some kind of deadline. We were in the bathroom at the time, Si hovering by the door as I bent over the changing mat, arranging Jo's nappy. To be honest I was barely listening. Kissing Jo's freshly powdered bottom, I glanced vaguely in Si's direction.

'Oh dear . . .'

Now he was telling me in detail about a contractor having let them down; something to do with deliveries of tiles and a restaurant that had to be open by Christmas. He would have to go up to London and give Ol a hand, he concluded; his old mate was in an almighty panic. Wrapping Jo in his nappy, I picked him up. All I registered was that Si was being unusually verbose. It was another side of our freshly invigorated intimacy; now that everything was finally working out so well, he was starting to relax and let me in.

He went to bed early and left for London before I had woken up.

It was almost dark when he returned the next afternoon: 4 p.m. on a dull winter's day. When I noticed the headlights of his van moving down the lane I hurried to the front door to greet him, happily surprised that he was back so early. Yet as he climbed from the van and I saw his face, I felt myself grow cold.

He looked terrible. In the twenty-four hours since I had seen him he seemed to have aged about ten years. His face was pallid and his shoulders stooped, even his straggly hair seemed to have acquired a tinge of grey. Jumping on to the muddy yard and slamming the van door with a crash, he did not even glance at me.

'What's the matter? Are you ill?'

'I'm fine.'

As he glanced up I saw with a shock that his lower lip was swollen and bloody, as if he had been punched.

'What happened to your lip?'

'Oh, that.' He put his fingers to his mouth, wincing. 'I was hammering in this skirting board and my hand slipped.'

I grimaced, trying to imagine the scene.

'Smacked myself on the choppers with the bloody hammer.' He gave me a ghostly smile.

'Have you put some antiseptic on it? Shall I get some?'

As he stepped into the porch I attempted to put my arms

154

around his shoulder, scrutinizing his messy lip, but he pushed me gently away.

'Nah, it doesn't need it.'

He moved away from me into the cavernous ground floor, still not meeting my eyes.

'Has something happened?'

'Huh?'

'Has something happened?'

He wasn't listening. He peered vaguely in my direction, shaking his head as if he had barely heard the question. Wandering around the room, he fiddled with some cables in the kitchen area, picked up a loose floorboard that still had to be fitted, and leaned it against the wall, then started to push the sliding windows open and closed. The last time I had seen him like this, when he had failed to meet my eyes or answer my questions, was just after I had told him I was pregnant. As I watched him finally slip away from me and up the stairs, I felt as chilled as the winter air that blasted through the opened windows.

Over the next few weeks Si retreated into himself, as non-communicative as a crab drawing into his shell. He was not bad tempered, or unpleasant. He continued to bounce Jo on his knee whilst I cooked dinner, and helped rock him to sleep at night. He sometimes picked Poppy up from school or did the shopping; he continued to work on the refurbishment. But although physically present, something else was absent. He seemed continually distracted, as if pondering some great problem that was too weighty to share. If I tried to discuss anything other than domestic details, his face would assume a hazy, unfocused quality, as if he was only pretending to listen. In the evenings he would go upstairs and paint, whilst I watched TV. He did not want me to see what he was working on at this stage, he muttered in response to my increasingly persistent enquiries; it was kind of private.

Since his trip to London we had barely touched, let alone made love.

16

Jo developed colic. The early peaceful weeks of his life became a distant country, only dimly remembered. Now, my days were dominated by his crying. I spent my evenings jigging him on my shoulder as he bawled. I rarely finished a meal, for every time I attempted to eat he'd start screaming again. Mornings consisted of jagged breastfeeding sessions, in which he'd suck for a few minutes, then go rigid and pull furiously away from my aching breasts. In the afternoons I took him on brisk walks around the back streets of the town, my speed increasing with the level of yowls that emanated from the buggy. If I was lucky, he would sleep for a few hours after I picked Poppy up from school. Then the evening ordeal would begin.

I bordered on hysteria. Poppy had never been like this. She had fed and slept, occasionally rousing to stare dreamily around. The health visitor said I should try a bottle, but he rejected it. We gave him Infacol, tried a homeopathic remedy, attempted desperately to burp him. None of it worked. My life was reduced to a grim round of breastfeeding, rocking and hastily snatched sleep. I was nauseous with exhaustion, my head ached continually, my senses muffled as if I had been wrapped in cotton wool. As the warehouse descended further into chaos, my relationship with Si comprised grunted exchanges of vital information. He tried to help, but every time he took Jo from my arms the level of screaming increased tenfold. Accepting defeat, he returned upstairs.

Poppy was left largely to her own devices. It sounds

callous, but I had little choice. After school, she'd watch TV. If we were lucky, Jo would sleep during her tea and bath. After that I barely had the energy to read her a story, far less sit by her bed chatting like we used to. During the weekends she tended to play by herself or was occasionally invited out by the few girls she had finally befriended in her class. Si sometimes took her swimming, or we'd go for muddy walks, Jo strapped around my chest as we tramped across the marsh. It was nearly Christmas now, and Si had strung fairy lights around the warehouse.

It was after we'd returned from one of these walks, the day dimming as the peewits called across the marsh, that Poppy discovered the first letter. It was lying on the door-mat, and when she saw it her face lit up.

'Ooh look, Poppy!' I cried as we pushed open the front door. 'You've got a Christmas card!'

Grabbing the envelope, she started to rip it apart.

'Who's it from?'

Putting his hand on her shoulder, Si peered down at the scrap of paper she was holding tightly between her fingers.

'Is it from somebody at school?'

'None of your business!'

Scrumpling it into a ball, she ran across the ground floor and up the stairs. A few seconds later we heard the slam of her door.

Si and I exchanged glances.

'What was that all about?'

'Search me.'

I was unwinding Jo from the sling, concentrating hard on keeping him asleep.

'Can you give me a hand with this? Oh sod it, he's waking up!'

He cried for the next two hours, refusing my breast and

only calming as I paced around the building. By the time I managed to ascend the stairs and talk to Poppy, Si had fed and bathed her and she was asleep.

We hunkered into something roughly resembling a routine. Jo became marginally calmer, and would lie on his play mat long enough to allow me to get dressed before he started to fuss. Now that he could hold his head upright, I was able to pop him in his bouncy chair, where he watched with interest as I scurried around the room, trying hopelessly to tidy. As the health visitor had insisted, the colic was just a phase. Yet despite this gradual improvement, I felt more exhausted than ever. He was growing hungrier, and had taken to waking me three or four times a night to feed.

Befuddled with fatigue, I kept losing things and forgetting appointments. When Sally Travis, the mother of one of Poppy's few friends at school, bounded up to me in the playground, all set to whisk Poppy off to a play date with Lily, I stared at her blankly, my memory of the arrangement deleted. As I was feeding Jo a few evenings later, I remembered that I was due to attend the school's parents' evening in ten minutes' time. Arriving in a red-cheeked flurry twenty minutes later, I found the school gates locked, the classrooms in darkness. It had been the week *before*, I now recalled. Even worse, the week after Jo's birth I had lost my house keys, dropped, presumably from the handle of the pram, where I'd taken to slinging them.

Now my bag disappeared, too. It was the first week of January, a whole year since I had valued Si's flat. We'd had a quiet, happy Christmas, just the four of us, with a roasted goose, some good red wine and a huge trifle. Despite our perilous finances, we'd scraped together enough money to give Poppy a bike and Jo a Happy Tot Touch and Play Centre.

For Si, I had bought oil paints and brushes. In return he presented me with a silver charm bracelet, something so beautiful that for a moment, as I pulled away the soft tissue paper, I was unable to speak. Despite his silences and general air of distraction, he still loved me. Everything was going to be all right. The weather was quiet and grey, the soft winter light that fell across the marshes during the mornings dipping quickly to dusk in the afternoons. The boatyard was unusually silent, too: no building works, no screeching winds, just the cry of seagulls and the occasional splash of plovers diving in the creek. We went for walks, built fires in the new wood burner, played Mousetrap with Poppy. It finally felt as if we were a family.

But that morning the fridge was empty, I had run out of potatoes and Jo was down to his last nappy. Reaching for my credit cards at the end of the supermarket shop, I realized that the leather satchel in which I carried my purse, Jo's nappies, my mobile and a myriad of small plastic toys had disappeared.

'Damn it!'

I began to search frantically through the carrier bags, scrabbling past tin cans, toilet rolls and cartons of juice, but finding no satchel. On the other side of the checkout, the rotund cashier was pursing her lips disapprovingly. She had already sighed pointedly as Poppy swung on the trolley whilst I loaded my purchases on to the conveyor belt. Now she folded her arms, watching unsympathetically as I trotted out the little dance of panic, patting my shoulders lest the bag was hanging there, unnoticed, peering underneath the trolley, then down the queue of increasingly impatient customers that bulged behind me. Could I have left the bloody thing in the car?

'Sorry,' I croaked. 'I can't find my bag.'

The woman at the till sniffed. If she were one of the waiting customers rather than checkout personnel with 'Jenny. So Pleased to Help' emblazoned on her tunic, she would have given a little tut, perhaps raising her eyebrows heavenwards for added effect.

'Do you want to leave your groceries here and come back for them later?'

I nodded mutely. In his sling, Jo had started to whinge. I had to get him back to the car and feed him, otherwise he would start yelling and my misery would be complete.

'Poppy!' I shouted. She had squirmed her way past the queue of trolleys and was milling hopefully in the sweets and snacks aisle. 'We have to go home and get some money!'

I drove home in a fury. How could I have trailed around the supermarket for over an hour and not noticed that my bag was missing? It was the last straw. I was fed up with the mess. The house was a permanent building site: jumbles of trash lay everywhere; all the surfaces were covered in dust, the laundry was forever unsorted, so that getting dressed involved a lucky dip into the bulging mound of un-ironed clothes. Each letter that Poppy's school sent became lost in the heap of mail that slithered across the kitchen table, so I never knew if she was going on a school trip or what events I was expected to attend. Now, once again, I would have to replace my mobile, get new house keys cut and cancel my credit cards. I had also lost about thirty pounds in cash. Perhaps the bag had been stolen. More likely, I had simply allowed it to fall off the trolley. My incompetence made me bash my hands so hard against the steering wheel that I bruised my knuckles. In his car seat, Jo was screaming once more.

'Shut it!' I yelled.

*

Back at the warehouse, Si was loading the van. As my Fiat bumped down the muddy lane, I could see his long figure bent over the heavy plastic cases that stored his tools, lifting, arranging, then returning to the building for more. There was something melancholic in his stance, I noticed fleetingly, that had not been present when we first met. Drawing up beside him, I drew down my window.

'I've lost my bloody bag.'

He stared at me uncomprehendingly. I had the impression that for a sliver of a second he had forgotten who I was. 'Oh, God,' he said vaguely.

'Can you come back to Tesco and pay for the shopping? I don't have any cards.'

He stood on the drive, blinking at me. It was a freezing January morning, in which flecks of ice drifted half-heartedly around the boats, yet he was only wearing a T-shirt. I stared at his goose-pimpled skin. His hands were encrusted with paint.

'I don't have any cards,' he said.

'What do you mean you don't have any cards?'

'I think I must have left them at Ol's . . .'

I gawped at him.

'When I was there the other week,' he finished lamely. He looked mutely down at his battered work boots, his jaws grinding. It was true that our Christmas purchases had been made from my own account: money I had painfully saved from my estate agency job. At the time I had hardly noticed; now that we were married, what difference could it make? And Si, of course, had poured so much of his money into the warehouse. As I'd passed my card over in Toys R Us, I'd experienced a tinge of pride that I was in some small way able to redress the balance. But how could he have been so absent-minded as to leave them at Ol's and only now seem to notice?

'But that was *ages* ago!'

'I know, I . . .' He trailed off, his gaze flicking away from my face.

'So are you going to get them back?'

'Of course. Ol's keeping them for me . . .'

'And until then how are we supposed to eat?'

'I've got some cash.'

Reaching into his jeans pocket, he produced a wad of notes, presumably payment for one of his jobs. 'Have this. It'll tide you over . . .'

I glanced at his face in sudden trepidation. Why was he talking about 'you' rather than 'we'? And why was he packing up the van? When I spoke my voice was glazed with ice, like the puddles that lay around us.

'Where are you going?'

'London.'

'You're going to work for Ollie again?'

He stared at me sullenly. We were married, for heaven's sake. Was I not allowed to question him about his movements?

'Kind of,' he muttered, kicking at the dirt. 'I've taken on a job.'

'And in the meantime, what am I supposed to do about money?'

'That little lot should last you a while.' He nodded at the roll of notes. 'By the time it's run out the bank will have sent you a replacement card. We'll just have to get overdrawn for a bit.'

'Mummy!' Poppy trilled behind me. 'When are we getting out?'

Leaning back, I unclicked her seatbelt.

'Go inside and watch TV.'

Grinning at Si, she skipped past him and into the building. Jo, thankfully, had dozed off. I gazed at the top of his head, so innocently covered in blond fluff. I had a sick feeling in my stomach.

'What kind of job is it?'

'It's a mate of Ol's. He's taken on a big refurbishment in Kennington. They need some carpentry doing.' He paused, obviously choosing his words carefully. 'It's going to take a couple of months.'

I stared at my hands, still clutched around the steering wheel as if it were I who was about to depart. My fingers were cracked and wrinkled, my nails torn, the digits of an old hag. 'A couple of months?'

'We need the money, Mel. I can't afford not to take this up.'

'So you're going to be gone for ages?'

He attempted a smile. 'It might not be so long. And I'll come home at weekends . . .'

'Where are you going to stay?'

His eyes went foggy. Everything he said made sense. We could not continue with the building until we had more cash. He was an experienced carpenter; he had worked wonders on the loft. If anything, this was a lucky break. Yet inside my head a snide voice hissed that he was lying.

'And you're going now?'

'I'm just going for the night, to dump my tools in Ol's lock-up and size the place up. I'll be back tomorrow afternoon. We can discuss it more then.'

I slumped in my seat. Why was he only telling me about this now, when he was about to go? 'Fine. I'd better move the car round then.'

'Mel?'

He was squatting by the car window, pushing his face

close to mine. I could smell coffee on his breath, the faint trace of sweat.

'I love you, babe, okay?'

Blinking back my tears, I pushed the car into reverse.

17

That night Poppy had her first nightmare. I awoke with a jolt to the sound of screaming, staring in momentary confusion around the darkened room. The noise was terrible: not the familiar low-pitched wailing of a half-asleep child, but sharp bursts of yelling, as if she was being cornered by a monster. Next to me, Jo was fast asleep. *Poppy!* Leaping out of bed, I pattered down the corridor to her room.

'What is it?'

Peering around her room, I tried to make out her shape in the dull orange glow of her night light. At the sound of my voice the screaming had changed tempo, slowing into a low animal moan. As my eyes grew accustomed to the dark, I saw that she was cowering in the far corner of her bed, the covers pulled up over her head.

'Darling, what's happened?'

Stumbling across the room, I took her in my arms. She clung to me, wiping her snotty tears on my T-shirt.

'There was a person outside my room! They were walking past. I saw them going down the stairs!'

'It was a nightmare –'

'No, it wasn't! They were out there, I saw them!'

She pointed to the gallery, in the direction of Si's painting room, the steps to the loft and the metal stairs that led to the ground floor. Could she have spotted a burglar? Stepping out of her room, I listened for sounds from the rooms below, my heart pattering in my mouth. But there was nothing, just the whisper of wind and the tapping of boat masts outside. The image of an intruder creeping around downstairs was too horrible to countenance.

'There's no one there, promise.'

Walking back across the room, I flicked on the light. The contents of Poppy's room revealed themselves: her chest of drawers, covered with drawings and boxes and felt-tip pens; her clothes, heaped over the small wooden rocking chair that Pat had given her for her sixth birthday; a muddle of toys, pushed into a plastic crate.

'Who would want to burgle us? All they'd get is a sack of rubble. You dreamt it.'

'They must have run away . . .'

Tears were still spilling down her cheeks. Standing up on the bed, she put out her arms to be picked up, the way she did when she was a toddler.

'Poppy go in bed with Mummy,' she murmured.

The muscles in my face tightened. We had been having this fight ever since Jo's birth. During the days she seemed fine; a bit quiet perhaps, but generally co-operative. But at nights she had started clamouring to come into bed with me, alternately using her baby voice or shrieking angrily that I no longer loved her. The night before, she had flung her Shrek doll at me, only missing because I had ducked.

'Honey,' I said, trying to keep the tension from my voice. 'There isn't room. Jo's in there. I don't want him to get squashed.'

'Poppy go with Mummy!'

I swayed blearily by the door, prevaricating. I wasn't strong enough for the fight that was brewing. Relenting, I padded across the floor and let her cling to me for a while, her strong legs crossed determinedly around my back. She was too heavy, and after Jo's tiny floppy head, her skull felt like an oversized boulder against my shoulder.

'I'm going to put you back to bed now,' I eventually said.
'Poppy sleep with Mummy!'

But I had made up my mind. 'Stop talking like a baby,' I said tersely, putting her down. 'You're seven years old, not two. Now go back to sleep.'

'Poppy wants *Mummy*!' she yelled.

I did not stay to hear the rest. Closing her door firmly behind me, I hurried back to my own bed, made so huge by Si's absence, and the tiny figure of Jo, stretched out on his back. After a while Poppy stopped yelling. I, however, was hopelessly awake. I turned on to my back, then rolled on to my side, arranging and rearranging the pillow. Soon the light would seep under the curtains and Jo would start grizzling for his morning feed. Then there would be no return: Poppy would rouse, and all day I would be seasick with fatigue. I recalled her tantrum the day before, the way that Shrek had whizzed past my ear and slapped into the wall. Her punishment was to be sent, howling, to her room. She was jealous of Jo, uprooted from her life in London, with so many changes to adapt to. Yet I was unable to provide the time or comfort that she required. I should pay her more attention, I decided miserably as I trawled through a hundred similar incidents in which I had shouted at her whilst cuddling Jo, or refused to read a story because I was feeding him or changing his nappy. Of *course* she was going to be traumatized. The combination of guilt and exhaustion made me weepy. I should be more caring towards her, I thought despairingly. No matter what Si or the health visitor said, I was a terrible mother.

Outside, a bird started to chirrup. I lay on my back, cursing. If I were more attentive, I would have carried Poppy back into our bed, evicting Jo to the empty cot that waited on the other side of our room. Why was I so hard on her? She had screamed that there was a malevolent presence outside her room, a stranger who wanted to do her harm. Wouldn't an analyst label this 'projection'? I had sentimentally assumed that she would adore her baby brother, yet all he had done so far was to displace her from my affections. As a second horribly merry bird joined the first, I replayed the scene in my mind. I had experienced similar nightmares as a child, imagining bogeymen under the bed, their skeletal hands shooting out and grabbing my ankles. A bad person had been standing at the top of the stairs, Poppy had cried. And then, when I arrived, she had regressed four or five years. It was such an obvious cry for attention. Yet, once again, I had refused to listen.

*

I am outside, breathing hard. Rain is driving into me, covering my dark hair with a fine sheen. I tip my head at the wind, listening to the flap of plastic sheeting around the building. I want to be cold. I want my clothes to be soaked, the freezing water beating on my skin. How can I sit inside in the warmth, sipping tea, when my daughter is lost? I want to be punished for everything that I failed to see and everything I failed to do.

Splashing past Sandra's maroon saloon, I make it to the edge of the boatyard, gazing past the rocking masts to the black emptiness that stretches beyond. Is Poppy out there, lying cold and afraid in the mud? I start to stumble towards the wooden bridge that leads to the marsh. Poppy and I must have tramped down it a hundred times, laughing as it swayed unsteadily above the sludge. Now it seems to mock me, filled with memories, yet leading nowhere. As the racing clouds unveil the moon, my surroundings are suddenly illuminated: ghostly boats bobbing in the water, banks of mud glistening in silver light, then endless bog. In the distance an animal is shrieking.

'Mel, what are you *doing*?'

I feel hands on my shoulders, pulling me back. Turning, I see Trish's face looming over me.

'I have to look in the marsh . . .'

'Poppy isn't going to be out there, hon.'

'Where the hell *is* she then?'

'Si's got her.'

My legs give way. I flop against the bulk of Trish's body, dragging at her shoulders. I am making a strange keening sound.

'But why would he take her?'

She shrugs disgustedly. 'He's lost the plot, I suppose.'

'Do *you* think he murdered those women?'

She starts to lead me back to the warehouse. Right now, I would give anything to be in her position: expecting her first child, safe and unentangled. That I once pitied her seems ludicrous.

'I think most men are capable of anything.'

I stop, staring into her face. I feel hollowed out, as if everything I once believed has been scooped from inside me. A good man, family life, stability: that was all I wanted. I thought it was built with bricks, but my house was made of straw; one puff from the wolf and it has collapsed around me. Placing her arm firmly around my shoulders, Trish leads me inside the kitchen. The police have gone, leaving their cleaned mugs draining neatly by the sink. From the living room I can hear Sandra talking quietly on her mobile.

'I should have listened to Poppy,' I moan, sinking into the chair that Trish has placed proficiently behind me. 'I never listened!'

'You've got to stop beating yourself up, Mel. None of this is your fault.'

'But she was getting those letters! And the nightmares . . . maybe it's connected?'

Trish gazes back at me. She looks tired. Lines have appeared on her forehead that I have not noticed before, and her eyes are bloodshot. Her due date is only a few weeks away; she should be tucked up in her cottage resting, not becoming ensnared in my crisis. Yet the prospect of dealing with the police alone fills me with terror; she is my sole support, the only friend I have left.

'There was never anyone prowling around the warehouse,' she says quietly. 'It was just . . .'

I am not listening. My mind can't settle on anything long enough to carry out a normal conversation.

'What's the time?' I say, jerking upright.

'Eight-fifteen.'

'Oh, Jesus,' I wail. 'She's been gone for nearly four hours!'

As she pauses by the table, Trish takes a sudden breath. She is about to say something, I am sure. Perhaps she has had enough of my hysterical ramblings and wants to snap at me to shut up. At the very least, she must be thinking what a fool I've been. She *told* me to leave Si, but I ignored her. Yet, whatever she was going to say, the moment passes and her face softens.

'Shall I make another cup of tea?' she asks.

18

I was in the third storeroom along the gallery, the one we were planning to convert into a bedroom for Jo. Previously this had been the most decrepit part of the warehouse, the walls sagging with damp, the window frames crumbling. After the re-rendering and roof building that had annihilated most of our cash during the summer, the builders had spent September plastering the walls and installing new windows. In December Si had fitted a new wooden floor. Now, as Jo slept, I was finally decorating.

I was growing accustomed to Si's absence. In an odd way I was calmer without him. There were no signs of disenchantment to brood over, no impatient exchanges or incomplete explanations that I might interpret as lies. If anything, he was more affectionate. He rang every night, texted that he loved me and returned at weekends tired and thin, but with another roll of cash in his pocket. As he said, this was a temporary phase in which he earned enough money to finish off the building. Not wanting to provoke an argument, I did not mention the strange loss of his credit cards. As with the last months of my pregnancy, I felt that I was waiting for our real life to commence, my refrain of 'after the baby is born' morphing into 'after we get more money'. It was my solve-it-all phrase, absolving me from the need for further analysis. Jo was more settled, too. At seven weeks old, he had clicked into a predictable routine of naps, feeding and happy sessions spent kicking his legs under his play centre. I had not spent an entire evening jiggling a screaming baby for weeks, I realized; perhaps I wasn't such a failure after all. The image of our new life, in which, like the other mothers in the playground, I had built a contented, loving and normal family, flickered constantly on the horizon, like the mirage of water along a desert road.

One morning, as I was slopping magnolia paint on to the plaster, I heard a crash downstairs. It was loud enough to make me start; not the dim rattling of wind or creak of boats, but something definite and deliberate. Placing my paintbrush back in the tray, I walked cautiously to the top of the stairs. A few feet along the gallery, Jo was asleep in his pram.

'Hello?'

I felt like a fool, calling out to the empty building. Perhaps it was a dog or fox, investigating our bins. Walking gingerly down the stairs, I stepped across the half-laid floor. Through the high windows I could see the motionless sails of the boats that were beached in the yard. I waited for perhaps five or six seconds, breathing quietly as I tried to discern the direction from which the sound had come. Then I heard a noise that turned me cold: the soft click of the latch.

Spinning around, I scurried towards the back door. Was there someone in the house? A builder, perhaps, returned without warning? Or *Si*? I had not heard a vehicle on the drive, but perhaps he had parked in the lane.

'Si? Is that you?'

Flinging open the back door, I ran around the side of the building. The drive was empty. In the far distance I could see a donkey-jacketed man pottering around a yacht. In the other direction, Bob was tramping down the creek-side path. I must have imagined the noise, I told myself as I returned through the front door. All the same, as I carefully locked the doors my hands were trembling.

That night I took no chances. Rather than confront another of Poppy's nightmares, I tucked her directly into my bed. It was not that I believed in the ghost that she still swore she had seen on the gallery and who she now claimed had 'climbed into her dreams', the bed-sharing was simply for a treat. Nor was I being overly twitchy if, for the third time that evening, I checked that the doors and the windows of the warehouse were locked. When Si came home he could chortle at my precautions. But he didn't know how it felt to be a woman, alone.

Like the riverine sludge that flowed down the creek, one week ran into the next. During the days I would decorate the bedrooms, or tuck Jo into his pram for long, meandering expeditions to the shops. After school Poppy watched TV as I cooked her tea. Had she not been so changed, it would have been like the old days in London. But in small, barely perceptible ways, she was a different child. She had become quiet, sullen almost. She no longer wanted to cuddle, or for me to roll her into the towel after her bath, and nor did she skip into school, singing. Instead, she trailed behind me, tutting crossly if I tried to take her hand. Perhaps it was that she was growing up, already at seven moving intangibly out of my reach. Or maybe there had been too many changes. Like me she was adjusting to this new, isolated life.

'She's had a lot going on,' Sally Travis concluded one afternoon as she perched on the sofa, waiting for Lily and Poppy to appear from upstairs. 'I'm sure it's just a phase.'

I sipped my tea, wishing I had not brought the subject

up. Lily was the youngest of four and Sally radiated maternal confidence, taking any upset from her kids with a wry shrug of her rounded shoulders. A year earlier I could never have imagined myself sharing confidences with a woman like this: a full-time homemaker, famous for her prodigious fund-raising abilities at school bazaars and cake sales, a reader of the *Daily Mail* whose life revolved unquestioningly around her husband and children. Yet, as I glanced at her contented face, I suddenly wished I could be like her. What, after all, did I have to show for my so-called unconventionality? I had wasted most of my adult life avoiding what she represented, yet all I had encountered were loneliness and uncertainty.

'I know she needs more attention,' I said. 'But it's really hard to give it with Jo around . . .'

'And didn't you say she was having nightmares?'

'It's really awful. She's waking me almost every night.'

For a moment I imagined telling Sally everything: how Poppy's nightmares left me jangling with half-formed fears, the odd sounds I now imagined emanating from the un-inhabited parts of the warehouse, the day the door had closed behind me. I stared at her pale blue eyes and padded cheeks, teetering on the edge of exposure. She was nodding sympathetically, but as she sighed and ran her manicured hands through her middle-aged bob, I knew that I would never be able to confide in her.

'Oh dear,' she said, raising her eyes heavenwards, as if Poppy's behaviour was a run-of-the-mill irritation, one of those annoying little blips that all mothers must endure. 'Is there something up at school, do you think?'

'I don't know. It all seems fine. She never really talks about it.'

'Is she part of Megan's crowd?'

I looked up sharply. 'She was for about a week, but not any more.'

'Ah . . .'

She seemed on the brink of saying more, but must have decided against it, for suddenly she gave herself a little shake, placing down her mug.

'I ought to be getting along. I've got Harry to pick up from football.'

Ten minutes later, Poppy and I stood by the front door, watching the Range Rover reverse down the drive.

'Do you like Lily, then?' I asked, brushing my fingers against her golden hair.

'Mmm.'

'It's great that you're making some friends at school.'

It was the wrong thing to say, in this new relationship where I had to choose my words carefully. She jerked angrily away. 'Mummy! Why do you always have to keep going on about friends?'

I found it increasingly difficult to sleep. With Si by my side I plunged into oblivion as soon as the light went out. Now, in my too-large bed, I lay awake for hours, listening to the squeaks and groans of the building. Sometimes it was one or two in the morning when I finally slipped into unconsciousness. Turning over, or re-plumping my pillows, I'd notice that my fists were clenched, my brow furrowed with tension. I lay on my back, trying to relax. Being alone had never bothered me in London, but the warehouse was so large, and its position by the boatyard was so far from other houses, that every faint bump or distant scrape set my pulse racing. I woke throughout the night, too, scudding the surface of sleep but never truly relaxing. This new, cowering woman jarred with how I had previously seen myself. I used to take a pride in my independence, my ability to be alone. Yet here I was, cringing at every creak and longing for the sky to lighten and for the birds to start singing so that I could finally fall asleep.

When a few hours later the alarm clock dragged me into wakefulness, I would stumble blearily from my bed to the bathroom and, if I was unlucky and had forgotten to compose my expression, would catch the shocking sight of myself in the cabinet mirror: dark bruises of exhaustion around my eyes, drawn face furrowed with complaint, dull hair swirled into a bird's nest, I hardly recognized myself. It was in those scattered moments, between Jo's cries and Poppy's shouting for breakfast, that I faced the question that over the last months had been building inside me, a gnawing puzzle that I did not yet dare answer: *What is happening to me?*

19

It was during this period of dull days and uneasy nights that I met Trish. We'd caught sight of each other several times before we actually spoke, in the shopping precinct or passing with a slight smile in the boatyard. I was not in the habit of eyeing up strangers, but in Trish I had instantly recognized a potential pal. It was partly the way she was dressed, her long parka, cropped hair and cowboy boots signalling a boho chic that was unlikely to have originated in provincial Kent. She was pregnant, I clocked as she smilingly made way for Jo's buggy one morning by the creek. I suspected that she was alone, too. Perhaps it was that she seemed to be as keenly aware of my presence as I was of hers, unlikely behaviour for someone enjoying cosy coupledom. I could sense her eyes on me as I wandered along the cobbled street that led past Woolies and Boots; when we passed for the third time in as many days, by the side of the river, she gave me a shy nod. I decided that she must be the person who had moved into the empty cottage at the end of the lane. Only that week I had noticed blinds on the windows, and discarded packing cases in the front garden. I had not yet spoken to her but instinctively knew we would be friends.

Jo enabled us to finally introduce ourselves. He'd been whingeing all morning, and now, as we made our way up the lane, I was fussing around the pram, trying to pull his woolly hat back over his head just as Trish appeared from her front door.

'Someone's not happy!'

She grinned at me cheerfully. Reaching the pram, she peered inside. 'Poor little thing. Is he hungry?'

'He's got a cold.'

'Ah . . .'

For a moment she gazed at him, slack jawed. He had quietened now, and was fixing on her face with total concentration. A minute earlier I had been tight with irritation. Now I was gooey with maternal pride.

'Isn't he beautiful?' she whispered.

'I don't know. Is he?'

Straightening up, she threw back her head, showing off her long neck as she laughed. 'Of course he is. Just look at those eyes! How old?'

'Nine weeks.'

'And is it easy? Or just back-breaking? You have to tell me! I mean, how do you begin to manage with it all? I don't even know how to change a nappy!'

Her eyes twinkled merrily. She didn't have a wedding ring, I noticed. But in her nose she wore a tiny diamond. Her easy smile and breathless questions, which, had they not been so charming, were almost gauche, made me want to grip her arm and tell her everything.

'Oh, God. I don't know what to say!'

'You've got a little girl too, haven't you? I've seen you taking her to school. How do you cope with *two* of them? I just can't imagine it. I can barely look after myself, let alone someone else!' She laughed again, but panic flashed in her eyes. She was about eight months pregnant, I calculated, glancing surreptitiously at her belly.

'I just muddle along, I suppose.'

For a moment she was silent. We stood on the pavement, smiling inanely at each other. From inside the pram, Jo had started to mew.

179

'I'm Trish, by the way,' she suddenly said, shooting out her hand. 'Sorry, you must think I'm mad, accosting you on the street like this.'

'Mel. I live in the boatyard, in that wreck of a warehouse.'

'I know. I've seen you.'

'Have you just moved in?' I nodded at the cottage. She'd put a wind chime by the front door and cleared the packing boxes away.

'Two weeks ago.'

'Where've you moved from?'

'London. It was kind of a lifestyle decision. You know, for the baby . . .' She grimaced.

'Have you met Bob and Janice yet?'

'Yeah. Janice baked me a cake. Isn't that sweet?'

The mewing was growing in intensity. Placing my fingers around the pram handle, I gave it a little shake.

'Look, I have to get him home and feed him. Do you want to come and have a coffee? If you don't mind the place being a bit of a state . . .'

She laughed again. From the faint glow of her cheeks I could tell that she was pleased.

'You should see what it's like in my place, and I haven't even got any kids.'

She stayed the whole morning, putting her feet up on Poppy's sticky, jam-smeared stool as I pottered around the kitchen. She had not blanched at the mess, just picked up the pile of Jo's Babygros and miscellaneous undies that had been draped over the chair, and dumped them unceremoniously in the laundry basket.

'It's a bit of a pit, I'm afraid,' I said, watching her glance around the room. 'What with the building and everything, there doesn't seem much point in cleaning it up. We're hoping to move out of this room and into our new kitchen by the end of spring.'

She shrugged. Unlike Janice or Sally, I had the impression that she hardly noticed the domestic squalor, let alone passed judgement. 'That's a great angel,' she said, nodding at the sketch that Si had given me in London. I'd had it framed and it now hung above the sink, an icon of our new life.

'Yeah, my husband did it for me. We had our first date in Nunhead Cemetery and there were all these stone angels there. He's an artist . . .'

'How romantic.'

I handed her a mug of tea, registering the irony in her voice. Why should she care about my love affairs?

'Tell me about *you*,' I said hastily. 'Like, why have you moved down here?'

She was an out-of-work actress, she said, surviving off the odd advert. She'd done a couple of police serials last year, and had made a minor appearance on *EastEnders*. I eyed her as she sipped at the tea. I did indeed vaguely recognize her. She'd moved down to Kent to escape the pollution, she continued. And of course property prices down here were so much cheaper. Having the baby was obviously going to make an acting career difficult, so she was considering a change of direction. Maybe she'd write a novel. And yes, she was single, her boyfriend having dumped her when she refused to terminate the pregnancy.

'What an arsehole, eh?' she finished. 'But then I just thought, sod it, I'll show him.'

'Good for you.'

'Yeah, well, you can't let the bastards beat you, can you? Since we had that particular little discussion I've discovered that he was also screwing some other tart on the side . . .'

She paused, her lips quivering wickedly. 'So I'm pondering my revenge.'

'What, you mean like cutting up his suits?'

'That kind of thing, yeah.' She laughed wickedly. 'Don't look at me like that! The stupid sod needs to be taught a lesson!'

As I mushed up a banana for Jo's lunch, I found myself telling her about Pete. Or rather, I gave an edited account, leaving out my desperate, pathetic terror at being alone, and centring around his various infidelities, refusal to pay the bills and inability to look after Poppy for more than half an hour at a stretch.

'Men, eh? Who needs them?' Trish finally concluded. I grinned at her, only feeling slightly disloyal.

'Well, this one's dad isn't so bad . . .'

'Uhuh.'

'To tell the truth, I'd pretty much given up on men before I met him,' I continued in a gush. 'But now everything's changed. I've never been so happy in my life. It just goes to show, sometimes Prince Charming really can come along, even if he is a bit frayed at the edges!'

'In what way is he frayed?' she asked, smirking humorously.

'Well, he's been around a bit, I suppose. And he can be a bit absent-minded. He's a painter, so he has a tendency to disappear upstairs and not come down again until midnight. But I'd rather he was doing that than off with someone else!'

If I was being insensitive, Trish did not show it. 'What kinds of pictures does he paint?' she asked, still smiling.

'Oh, you know, landscapes and stuff. As a matter of fact I'm not actually allowed to see what he's working on at the moment. He's incredibly secretive . . . I guess that's just artists for you!'

I stopped, embarrassed by how much I'd revealed. I had, after all, only just met the woman. She looked slightly bored, staring out of the window at a sparrow that was pecking at something on the sill. I had been tactless, I realized, boasting about how perfect my life was when she was alone.

'So,' I said quickly. 'Do you know if you're having a boy or a girl?'

20

February, the drabbest month. South-east England was stuck under high pressure, bringing still grey days in which nothing seemed to change. How can one feel joyous when the sky is the colour of puddles and everything covered by mud? In the few patches of grass that remained in our back yard, snowdrops were appearing, but the memory of how the creek could glisten in the sun like a string of diamonds, or the call of the summer swifts, was too distant to grasp. Inside the warehouse the floor was still only partially laid. The kitchen remained unfitted and the loft was uninhabitable. Perhaps Bob Perkins was right, I thought dourly. Perhaps the place *was* a white elephant.

Poppy still woke at night, only sleeping through when I allowed her into my bed. There were more letters, too. They usually appeared on the mat at weekends, but she always got to them before me, bearing the envelopes silently to her room without comment. One morning, when she was at school, I finally gave in to my curiosity and searched her room. I found nothing: not under her bed, or stuffed to the back of her drawers or folded beneath her mattress, just fluff, forgotten toys and pink pyjamas that no longer fitted. Yet I was sure she was keeping secrets. She was turning away from me, closing up like the petals of a flower denied light.

I continued to sleep badly. I kept dreaming that someone was trying to get into the building. I'd go running down the stairs, flinging myself at the front door to fasten it before their dark shape appeared through the frosted glass. I was always too late. I'd grasp the handle, desperately trying to turn the key, and feel the pressure of another, stronger hand, pushing on the other side. Awaking with a gasp, I'd lie panting in bed. Beneath me, I could hear the slap of water against the boats, the ancient creak of timbers.

It was around this time that I received an odd phone call. I was in the bedroom dozing with Jo when the shrill bleep of the phone dragged me into bleary wakefulness. Grabbing the receiver, I hauled myself up, trying not to squash Jo's somnolent body. My mouth tasted sour.

'Hello?'

It was a man's voice, brusque and slightly slurred, as if its owner had been drinking.

'Stenning there?'

'No, he's not,' I snapped, already affronted. 'Who's calling?'

The caller chuckled unpleasantly. 'Don't worry who I am, darling. Coming in later, is he?'

I sniffed huffily, on the brink of retorting that Si's movements were none of his damn business. 'He's away at the moment,' I said stiffly. 'Can I take a message?'

More sleazy laughter. I pictured a fat, pink man, with hairy arms and tattoos; a builder, no doubt.

'Sure can, love. Tell him Boz called and that I'm getting a teeny bit fed up.'

Then he rang off.

'Si?'

'Yeah?'

'It's me. Where are you?'

'On site. I'm just measuring up these banisters.'

'There's been a man calling for you.'

'Uhuh . . .'

'Called Boz. He was very rude.'

Silence. My fingers flicked at the mattress. I could feel the tension ratcheting up my responses.

'He said he was getting fed up.'

'Right.'

'Who the hell is he?'

A longer silence. I started to dig into the flesh of my palms with my nails, almost enjoying the pain.

'Aren't you going to answer?' I had not intended to sound so plaintive, yet my voice was small and whiney, like Poppy's when she was being denied more biscuits or TV.

'He isn't anyone. Look, I'm right in the middle of something, babe. I'll call you back, okay?'

For the second time that afternoon, my line went dead.

Later that evening, Poppy appeared by my side as I was bobbing Jo in the baby bath. Her face was dreamy, her finger trailing slowly along the untiled wall as she muttered to herself. She had changed from her school clothes into a floaty white ballet dress and gold spangled sandals and had tied her hair into a tufty plait. For a while she simply stood beside me, gazing down at my suddy arms as I squeezed water from the sponge on to Jo's tummy. It was a new game, and he loved it, throwing back his fat arms and giggling in delight as the water splashed on to his skin.

'Look at Joey,' I murmured. 'He likes being tickled.'

She was not listening. She knelt beside me, putting her hands around my knees and staring moonily out of the window.

'Mum?' she suddenly said.

'Yes, poppet?'

'Is there still a ghost in this house?'

I stopped squeezing the sponge, my hands hanging motionlessly above the bath. What felt like a large block of ice was sinking deep inside me.

'Of course not, sweetheart!' I said brightly. 'Why do you say that?'

'There's this big fat person creeping along the gallery. I saw them coming out of that room where Si paints all his pictures.'

'What?!'

Throwing down the sponge, I spun around, staring at her in horror. The hairs on my arms were bristling like those of a frightened cat. Poppy blinked back at me, the corners of her mouth twitching with what appeared to be humour.

'Are you telling fibs, Poppy?'

'No!'

Grabbing Jo from the bath, I wrapped his streaming body in a towel, then bundled him on the changing mat, fastening his nappy tightly around his tummy with an angry tug. I should not be reacting with such irritation. If I were a good mother I would be calmly asking her for details, trying to discover why she was making up such stories. But I was too tired for empathy, my nerves rubbed raw.

'I don't believe you! How can there be someone wandering around upstairs? How on earth would they have got inside the building?'

I was shouting at her now. Bending her head, she started to snivel.

'I'm just telling you what I saw. Why do you always tell me off?'

'Oh Jesus, this is all I need!'

Picking up Jo, I marched out of the room. Poppy trotted beside me, sniffing noisily. 'Come on then, show me this ghost!'

We climbed the stairs to the gallery. There was no one wandering around up here; there couldn't be: I had taken care to lock all the doors to the building when we returned from school. As we reached the steps that led to the loft, we stopped, gazing up. As usual the small hatch door was fastened with a large metal padlock.

'You haven't been playing up there, have you?'

'It's locked!'

'You know how dangerous it is —'

'*I haven't been up there!* Why do you always think I'm doing bad things?'

She was howling now, her reddened face scrunched with misery. Softening, I put my free hand on her shoulder and gave it a little rub. If I had not been holding Jo, I would have pulled her into my arms and kissed her slimy face.

'All right, honey. I shouldn't have been cross. It's just that the idea of you going up there gives me the willies. Now are you going to come with me and help find this ghost?'

'No!'

'Then let's put Jo on your bed. You can look after him while I go upstairs.' Moving into her room, I placed Jo on her duvet, bolstering his body with pillows. 'You can watch him for me. Just stay there, okay?'

She nodded silently, placing her hand gently on his tummy. Leaning over him, she started to croon a lullaby in his ear. As I reached the door, she stopped singing.

'It's a bad person,' she said. 'They want to hurt us.'

Ignoring this, I stalked back along the gallery and down the stairs. It was dark down here; the only source of light was the soundless glimmer of the TV; deserted by viewers in the centre of the den, the images flickered meaninglessly across the screen. Walking towards it, I squatted down and switched it off. Straightening up, I now stood motionlessly on the floorboards, listening. The building was silent, an unnatural hush, as if someone was holding their breath. Around me, dim shapes loomed: the bulk of the sofa; a heap of something on the floor that could almost have been a prostrated body; the hulk of unpacked boxes, behind which the man might be hiding.

No. I was not going to feel afraid. This tale of an intruder was merely one of Poppy's stories, a ruse to grab my attention. Striding purposefully across the room, I flicked on the light, glancing around the littered space in relief. The shapes on the floor had been formed by a large pile of cuddly toys that yesterday Nurse Poppy had been operating on; the boxes revealed no lurking figures. Trotting down the corridor, I glanced quickly around the kitchen. The refuse of supper lay in the sink; the floor was scattered with the debris of fish fingers and mashed potato. The door was locked; the windows closed. There was no one here.

Returning to the living room, I climbed the stairs to the gallery.

'Pops!' I called. 'Are you and Jo okay?'

Taking her lack of response as affirmation, I moved along the gallery to the metal steps that led to the locked door at the top. There would be nothing up there, I was sure. I would take a quick look around, then, after securing the padlock, come straight down. All the same, as I started to climb, my pulse jumped skittishly.

The padlock was the sort that was released by a security number rather than a key. Twisting the components into the correct code, I pulled it apart and pushed open the door, which swung back with a crash against the crumbling wall. We hadn't rewired up here yet, so there was no light. For a short while I stood on the threshold of the room, gazing into its dark interior as the roof beams and lumpy walls came into focus. Through the skylight the cloudy evening sky dimly radiated. As I stepped on to the broken floorboards I tried to make out the shapes that skulked in the corners. Dust sheets, folded in a pile; Si's work bench, which he used for sawing; an old CD player, splattered with paint. When I opened my mouth to speak, my breath puffed white in the frigid air.

'Is anyone there?'

The question was ludicrous. How could there possibly be anyone hiding up here? Glancing at the old hatch that housed the rusting pulleys, I turned sharply away. In August I had lain under hot sun in this very spot, my head resting on Si's naked chest. Now everything had changed. Si was gone, and the building that had once promised us a happy future remained derelict, its echoing rooms empty and dark. For a couple of seconds I hovered by the door, gazing around the room as a crest of tears rose, hot and pathetic, in my eyes. Giving myself an angry shake, I closed the door, clicked the padlock back into place and climbed hurriedly down the steps.

Now I paced along the gallery, opening the doors of the storage rooms and peering inside. There was no one hiding here, just rubble, broken boards and crumbling walls. Moving on, I turned to the last room, closest to Jo's nursery, which Si had been using for painting. I had not been in here for almost a month. Stepping inside, I gazed around the small space, my skin puckering at the cold. The usual muddle of paints and rags was strewn about the place, an easel leaning against the paintings of the marsh that I had hoped Si would one day exhibit. In the corner was a stack of the charcoal sketches of me, asleep with Jo.

But it was not these that attracted my attention. Directly opposite the door, leaning against the window, was a huge canvas that I had not yet seen. Walking across the room, I peered into the gloom. I had started to feel very tense. The picture was of a woman, a vast painting of a nude, with the same angular bones and jutting hips as the one I had seen in Si's London kitchen. At her sharp breasts was what must have been a tiny infant, but looked more like a wound: an indistinguishable scrawl of reds and pinks. The woman's head was turned away, her features blurred, as if they were irrelevant. The background was splattered with what appeared to be splotches of blood.

The picture exuded a violence that made me blanch. I stared at it for a moment or two, the heat rising in my cheeks. Was this what Si really felt about me and Jo? No wonder he had not wished me to see his latest work. It made me feel as soiled and humiliated as if I had discovered a cache of hard-core porn under our marital bed. Turning hastily away, I walked quickly across the floorboards, slamming the door behind me. Now, as I paused on the gallery, I heard a sudden thump.

'Poppy?'

From her bedroom, Jo was shrieking vigorously.

'What the hell's going on?'

Bursting into the room, I saw Jo wriggling on the floorboards, his face puce.

'What the hell have you done to him?'

Scooping him up, I cradled his rigid body. There were no obvious bumps, just a red mark on the side of his cheek where presumably he had hit the floor. In the corner of the room, Poppy squatted over a box of Lego. Her face had the set nonchalance of a guilty person pretending to be innocent. As I turned furiously towards her, she jumped up, placing her hands over her ears.

'I don't want to hear your shouting! He just fell off!'

'You were meant to be watching him!'

'I couldn't, could I? The ghost was outside, running away!'

I had finally had enough. Yanking her up by her sleeve, I pulled her to her feet, then grabbed her wrist, my fingers digging roughly into her skin.

'Will you stop lying?'

'I'm not lying!'

We stood in the middle of the room, eyeballing each other. I wanted to slap her, to shake out a confession, anything but continue to play this eerie game. Suddenly she flopped backwards, crumpling into a flouncy heap of ballerina dress, her golden hair falling across her face.

'You don't love me any more!'

'Oh honey, I do!'

And now I was sobbing too, holding Jo with one arm and Poppy with the other, my too-large face buried in her shoulder: a soggy bundle of need and regret.

When Si finally called I was asleep. Surfacing from uneasy dreams, I reached groggily for the phone.

'Hello?'

'It's me.'

From the hubbub of voices in the background, he was obviously in a bar. Glancing at my clock, I saw that it was nearly eleven. I pictured him huddled in some south London pub with Ollie and the lads from the build. They were probably on their third or fourth pint, lounging on stained leatherette benches in a nicotine fug.

'I'm asleep.'

He paused, catching the accusation in my tone.

'Why didn't you call back earlier?' I added.

'Sorry, but I've had a hard day.'

I was spark awake now, my anger rekindling into bright,

shooting flames. If he thought that measuring and cutting up bits of wood was hard he should try a day alone with Jo and Poppy in a semi-derelict warehouse booby-trapped with power saws, broken floorboards and suspected prowlers.

'Well, so have I,' I retorted. 'Jo fell off the bed and bumped his head, and Poppy thought she saw someone wandering along the gallery again.'

'But there wasn't anyone there?'

'Of course there wasn't. She's just making things up to get attention.'

'Well, that's all right then, isn't it?'

I did not reply. In the background I could hear the chink of glasses and a sudden burst of laughter. Four or five seconds passed in silence. We had never had such a hostile phone conversation; it was making me feel tight and aggrieved. I should have backed down, apologized and asked him caringly about his day. But as I shivered in the chilly dark I could focus only on how deserted I felt.

'And who the hell is Boz?' I demanded. 'It's not very nice, you know, answering the phone to some crook who's after your husband.'

The bitterness and self-pity in my voice was repellent.

'He's not a crook,' Si said evenly. 'He's a tiler. He's fed up because we're behind on the job.'

'So why's he ringing me in Kent?'

'Because he's a prize prat.'

Another long pause. 'When are you coming home?' I mumbled.

'I don't know.'

'But I miss you so much!'

'I know, babe. I miss you too.' He sounded defeated. 'But we've got to go with the flow until this job's finished. We're

193

working flat out to meet the deadline.' He paused. 'Ol's actually talking about doing a big push over the weekend.'

I stared across the dim room. Something, a rat, probably, was scuffling in the beams above. I did not feel I could bear for Si to be away a single night longer.

'Fine.'

'Don't guilt-trip me, Mel —'

'I'm not guilt-tripping you, I'm just tired. I'm sorry if I've been grumpy but I've had a difficult day and I need to go back to sleep. Goodnight.'

Without waiting for his reply, I switched off the phone.

21

A few days later, Trish dropped by to pick up a bag of Jo's newborn baby clothes. Since that first morning in our kitchen, when we had talked with such intensity about men and life, we now met most days. We were both lonely and both biding our time, and, unlike Nat, who had sometimes bored me with her gloomy end-of-the-world predictions and earnest admonishments to adopt homeopathic medicine or vegetarianism, Trish was witty and sophisticated. She'd been brought up in a series of alternative schools whilst her rich and bohemian parents gadded around the world, she told me as we progressed from tea to wine one afternoon. After that she'd spent time at art school, in an alternative community on the Isle of Skye, and had eked out a living selling second-hand clothes at Portobello Road market. She thought of herself as a misfit, but didn't care. Thank God she'd found me, she declared with a hoot of laughter as I described the mothers in Poppy's playground. How else would she survive the coffee mornings?

Now, as she rummaged through the bag, I was trying to explain why I felt so angry with Si.

'I mean, I know he has to work. It's just that I'm so fed up with dealing with everything alone.'

I stopped. She had pulled out a tiny blue Babygro and was holding it adoringly to the light.

'Oh God, I should shut up about dealing with things alone, shouldn't I?'

She shook her head, laughing. 'Don't *worry*! I'm completely fine with being a single mother. Saves a lot of hassle, if you ask me.'

Folding the Babygro, she placed it carefully back in the bag. Despite the dark rings around her almond-shaped eyes, she was looking particularly beautiful, with her high cheekbones and graceful neck. Next to her, I felt stubby and unstylish in my ubiquitous jeans and baggy jumper.

'I can't exactly imagine you being single for long.'

'But I will be! I'm finished with men. Don't look at me like that, Mel! It's the way I want it.'

'Really?'

'Well, take you, for example. I know you love Si, etcetera, etcetera, but does he *really* make you happy? I mean, tell me to sod off and mind my own business, but from the outside it seems like all you do is fret and get upset because he's not here.'

I bit my lip, feeling myself flush. Was this really the impression I had given?

'You're worried that he's playing away, right?' she continued. I stared into her concerned face. I had been skirting around the idea for months, but she was right. The real reason why I did not like Si working in London was that, despite all my surface justifications, I was unable to quell my paranoia about Rosa's continued presence in his life.

'That's how I was always feeling, too,' Trish continued. 'It drives you mad, doesn't it? Eats into you so you can't stop thinking about it.'

'It's not quite as bad as that . . .'

'No?' She eyed me sceptically. 'Personally I'd rather not have that kind of hassle.'

'I mean, Si's a really lovely man. I'm sure he wouldn't do anything to jeopardize what we've got.'

196

She gave a low chuckle. 'Yeah, well, in my experience men are all pain, no gain.'

'He really loves me,' I said, feeling the colour rising in my cheeks. 'I know he does. Okay, so things have been going a bit pear-shaped lately. But once he finishes this job and we've got the money side of things sorted, it's going to be fine.'

When I looked up, Trish's eyes were upon me. She looked melancholy, as if she had a more realistic hunch than my own about how things would work out.

'I really hope they do, for your sake,' she said sadly. 'It's just that, in my experience, when men start suddenly having to be away all the time, it means trouble. I guess I'm a bit biased.' She shrugged, smiling kindly, so that her eyes crinkled up at the edges. 'Maybe your bloke's different,' she added lightly. 'I hear there *are* some nice men out there.'

'He *is* different! I mean, I know all you've heard so far is me whingeing on about things, but wait until you meet him. He's lovely. And he really adores Jo and Poppy. It's just the money problem that's making things difficult.'

She nodded, but said nothing. The conversation was filling me with dislocated dread.

'Ooh look,' I said brightly, turning towards the window with a fake cheer that would surely fool no one. 'It's gone all misty!'

Fog rolled in. From the plate-glass windows I could discern the tips of the boat masts protruding through the murk, but the creek and surrounding marshes had vanished. Swaddling Jo in blankets, I tramped up the muddy lane to collect Poppy from school, returning half an hour later with my damp hair flopping over my forehead and Poppy dragging so far behind that I feared she would grow disorientated and topple into the river.

As we plodded past the boats, I noticed a large van appearing through the mist. It was parked almost bumper to bumper behind my car, an unusual spot for someone merely visiting the yard. I was not expecting a visitor, and as we approached the drive my skin prickled with unease: the fog was so thick and the yard deserted. Glancing behind, I hoped to catch sight of Richard or one of his workmen, but all I could see was the mist, closing around us. Gripping the handle of the buggy I passed the van's tail lights, noticing that the engine was running. It must be someone with work in the boatyard who, in the fog, had mistakenly parked in our drive. Or perhaps it was a delivery of fittings for the new kitchen. Yet as I glanced through the windscreen, what I saw made my guts contract.

Slumped inside the van was a thick-set man, his large hands clutching the wheel, his eyes staring fixedly ahead. He had the overblown, blotchy appearance of a heavy drinker, his nose purple, his complexion bilious. He was either completely bald, or he had shaven his head, skinhead style. He appeared to be sneering, but whether this was with actual contempt or simply his natural expression, it was impossible to say. As he registered my presence he turned and stared at me, his gaze moving slowly up and down my body and then towards Poppy, who had finally caught up and now silently placed her hand in mine. For a ghastly second or so, he grinned. I stared back, my face flickering into a faint smile. Then, gravel spraying from under his wheels, the man reversed the van down the drive and disappeared into the mist.

Beside me, Poppy was tugging at my hand.

'What was that man doing, Mummy?'

'I don't know. Perhaps he was lost.'

'He looked really horrible.'

'Well, he's gone now.'

*

I spent the rest of the afternoon watching kids' TV with Poppy. Then I cooked her some tea and ran her bath. I fed Jo until his eyes rolled back in his head and he went limp with sleep, read Pops a story and tucked her into my bed. Besides Trish, I hadn't spoken to another adult for days. It was dark now, the fog impenetrable. Despite the bustle of the evening's activities, I could not stop thinking about the man in the silver van. I sat in the kitchen, supping a glass of wine and trying to forget about him. It seemed as if the warehouse was floating in calm waters, the vessel abandoned, its direction lost. There was nothing beyond the windows, just a mist so thick it was suffocating.

I drained a second glass of Merlot, my senses sufficiently numbed. In a short while I would stumble up the stairs and crawl into bed. Then finally I could blank out. The driver of the van must have been taking a break, I told myself. Perhaps he had turned in the wrong direction at the bottom of the lane and was trying to get his bearings. Standing wobbly, I began to clear the clutter, lifting plates to the sink in a half-drunken muddle. When I heard a crash from the yard outside, I gave a little gasp, almost dropping the pan that I was about to dunk in the greasy water. Now the handle of the kitchen door was being rattled and turned, and through the frosted glass I could see a figure, pressed up against the door. I stood frozen by the sink, my heart stalling.

It was Si. Dropping his bag on the floor, he pulled off his wire specs and blinked at me tiredly. He had lost weight since last week, his threadbare clothes hanging off his thin frame, his long hair hanging lankly over his face.

'You gave me a start!'

I bounded across the kitchen, my arms out to hug him. 'I thought you were a burglar,' I whispered as I buried my face in his thick overcoat. 'Why didn't you ring and tell me you were coming?'

His hand hovered over my hair. Then he pulled it suddenly away.

'It was a snap decision,' he said flatly. 'There's an unexpected delay on the flooring, so there isn't anything to do.'

It sounded too pat, like something he had rehearsed. I glanced up at him, about to ask more, but the terseness of his voice and lines around his mouth stopped me. He seemed terribly tired, standing lifelessly in the middle of the breeze block kitchen as I clasped my arms around his waist.

'That's great!' I said, slipping my arms inside the coat and squeezing his skinny waist. Yet, rather than pulling me closer, Si shuddered slightly and broke away.

'It's been a pig of journey,' he muttered. 'Thick fog all the way down the M2.'

'God, poor you. Come and sit down. I'll get you something to eat.'

I was propelling him across the floor, willing him to take off the coat and let me cook for him, like in the early days of our relationship when he would sit at the table, doodling and regaling funny stories as we shared a bottle of wine. It *could* be like that again. I would plug up my insecurities and ask him about the Kennington refurbishment. I would not refer to Boz, or to the lurking unease that now gathered in so many unexpected corners. Instead, I would chat happily about my new pal Trish, or report upon how Jo was taking to his bottle. Then we would retire upstairs. Yet as Si stood woodenly by the table, not sitting down, but gazing unhappily at the mound of mail that had accumulated there, the disjunction between how we used to be and how we now were made these simple aspirations appear as impossible as trying to walk when one's legs are broken.

'More bloody bills . . .'

Money and the warehouse were subjects hemmed in with difficulty. Stroking his arm, I tried to divert his attention.

'Have you eaten, honey?'

He didn't reply, just turned away from the table and gazed in a befuddled way across the kitchen as if not completely sure where he was.

'Are you all right?'

For a moment, as he glanced around, I thought he was on the verge of saying something, but then his mobile started to bleep.

'It'll just be Ol or someone from the build. Why don't you leave it?'

He shook his head in irritation, reaching into his pocket for the phone. As he pulled it out I noticed with a jab of shock that his hands were shaking, his face pinched. Snapping open the phone, he pressed it to his ear, then walked rapidly out of the kitchen, taking care to kick the door shut behind him.

I remained at the table, fiddling with my glass. The sharp frown Si had pulled on seeing the caller's number had made my insides plunge. Why was he always so secretive? We were meant to be partners, yet whenever I asked about his affairs a door would be slammed in my face, often literally. Ten, fifteen minutes passed. I glugged a third glass. He was clearly not going to return to the kitchen. Chucking the bitty remains of the wine into the sink, I wandered groggily through the door and down the dark corridor that led into the warehouse.

The ground floor was in darkness. Fumbling up the stairs, I began to make my way along the gallery. Perhaps I would find Si soaking in the bath, his mood more relaxed and expansive. I would join him, stepping into the steaming water as he pensively fingered my thighs. Then later he would tell me who had called and the tension would ease, like an untied knot. I was bleary with alcohol, but determined that we should not end the day so estranged.

He was not in the bathroom, but lying on the bed, gazing up at the ceiling.

'Poppy was here,' he said as I pushed open the door. 'I've put her back in her bed.'

'She keeps having her nightmares so I've been letting her sleep with me.'

Sitting down, I tentatively stroked his hand. It remained limp, his fingers not returning my touch. 'Are you all right?'

'I'm fine.'

'Who was on the phone?'

His eyes flicked away, fixing on a point somewhere above my head.

'Just someone about the build.'

'What's the matter?'

He winced in irritation. 'Nothing. I've got a headache, that's all.'

'Something's happened, hasn't it?'

If only he would reply. As I stared, agonized, at his set expression, I could feel the reality of how alienated we had become, sinking cold and hard inside me.

'Tell me what it is!'

Sighing, he finally turned to look at me. 'For God's sake, Mel, stop going on at me. It's just more crap about money. I'll tell you all about it later, okay?'

My mouth was dry. I swallowed, trying to remain calm. It suddenly seemed imperative that we be reconciled.

'You've lost so much weight,' I said, shuffling closer and

placing my head on his chest. 'Ol's been working you too hard.'

Sliding my hand over the hair that fuzzed around his stomach, I pushed my fingers downwards, reaching inside the warmth of his underpants.

'It's been too long,' I whispered. 'Come and give me a kiss.'

As I lifted my face upwards, his mouth found mine. He kissed me hard, his teeth knocking against my lips. I began to relax, leaning against him as my body started to melt. Everything was going to be all right, after all. Like he said, it was just something boring to do with money. As my fingers stroked his penis, I could feel it swell, rising hotly in my hands. Pulling my face away, I started to nuzzle at the soft skin behind his ear. It was so simple. Sex was all that was required to pump the intimacy back into our marriage. We had not made love for so long; that was why things were so strained. Si was sighing now, his fingers digging into my shoulder. Traversing his neck and chest, my mouth moved downwards. For a moment his grip loosened, his hands fell, fluttering by his sides as he breathed in small, almost pained gasps.

Then suddenly he sat up, his hands pushing me away.

'No, Mel, I can't . . .'

Falling back against the pillows, I gawped at him in mortification.

'Why the hell not?'

'I'm knackered,' he said shortly. 'And I've got a splitting headache.'

My cheeks were on fire. I dabbed at them with my fingers, temporarily unable to speak.

'We haven't done it since the autumn . . .'

'Well, you've been having a baby, haven't you?'

'But I'm not having a baby now!'

He did not reply, just sighed, as if I was nagging him to perform some disagreeable chore.

'You don't love me any more,' I murmured. It was the wrong thing to say, but I had drunk nearly an entire bottle of Merlot and his sudden refusal had unravelled my good sense. In the summer he would have pulled me into his arms, kissing the top of my head and telling me to stop talking nonsense. But the summer was long past. These were the dead months, and everything had changed.

'For God's sake, don't start on that,' he said wearily. Swinging his legs over the edge of the bed, he stood up. 'I'm sorry to be unfriendly, babe. I've got flu coming on or something. I feel like shit.'

'Where are you going?'

'If it's okay with you, I'm going to sleep on the sofa. I really need to get a good night's sleep and, you know, what with Jo and Poppy coming in and everything . . .'

He stopped, his hand resting lamely on the handle. I gazed at him, taking in the details: a lanky man, with bitten finger-nails and ears that had once been pierced. His eyes were sad, as if he was grieving something he could not share. As I took in his dishevelled appearance, which once I had found so charming, I felt as if a boulder of grief were lodged in my chest. He was a stranger, really. I had believed we were close, but it turned out that the threads that connected us were as tenuous as gossamer.

'Okay,' I said. 'Goodnight.'

When I woke, the fog was gone. I lay for a while on my back, listening to Jo's even breathing as the weak winter sun fell in patches across the bed. It was seven in the morning and Jo's last feed had been at midnight. For the first time since November I had slept for seven glorious hours without interruption. Now, as I rose on to my elbows and gazed at his plump face, I felt unaccustomedly well rested. Poppy had not woken either. My head was clear, like a smeared mirror that had been polished; rather than the queasy exhaustion that normally swilled around each heavy movement, my limbs tingled with the urge to leap out of bed. It was a new day, the sun was finally shining, and I was filled with purpose.

Swinging my feet energetically on to the floor, I walked across the room and pulled up the blinds to the north-facing window, gazing out at the creek. A milky mist furled softly over the water, lapping mildly at the boats, then dissolving as it rose into hazy pink sunlight. Further away, the marshes had been transformed into fairyland: the swirling white vapours twisting around the silhouetted trees before giving way to the sun. Pushing open the window, I breathed in the cold air. From now on, everything would improve. Jo was going to sleep through the night, Poppy's nightmares would cease, and whatever schism had taken place in my marriage would be healed. All that was required were mutual goodwill and effort. Si and I needed to share a meal together, discussing anything but the building or our finances, or go for a walk. Then, later, we would go upstairs, remove each other's clothes and, our sex life finally restored, everything would return to normal. What was the term? *Quality time.*

Turning from the view, I wandered towards the small port-hole on the far side of the room which faced west, across the drive and towards the boat sheds. I thought I had heard the sound of a car's engine, moving down the lane. Now, as I wiped my hand across the grimy glass, I heard the distinct clunk of a car door being shut. I peered down at the drive, my heart jolting. Si's van had gone, I saw. In its place was a police car, its uniformed inhabitant at that very moment stepping around the puddles and approaching the front door.

22

'Good morning!'

The police officer gave me a perfunctory smile, cupping his identification badge in his palm. I glanced at it unseeingly, then up at his smooth-cheeked, youthful face. His uniformed presence, here on my doorstep, with his thick boots and the business-like truncheon that hung from his belt, was causing my pulse to skitter with alarm.

'Am I speaking to Mrs Stenning?'

'Yes?'

Si was dead. He'd decided to go back to London and crashed the van on the icy motorway. It was like a scene in the soap operas I'd taken to watching. This was the bit where the policeman asked if he might step inside. Then, as he imparted his news, I would collapse against the wall moaning with grief, my hand clamped over my mouth.

'Is your husband by any chance at home?'

My first reaction was relief, hot viscous stuff that pumped into my arteries, making me light-headed.

'I don't know,' I said faintly. 'His van isn't here. I'll go and have a look.'

Turning, I glanced around the living room. A folded duvet was heaped on the end of the sofa, but there was no sign of Si's clothes. Despite the story about the undelivered flooring, he must have risen early and returned to London without bothering to tell us he was going. Feeling the disappointment fur my mouth, I hurried across the living room and down the corridor, hastily surveying the empty kitchen.

After what had happened last night, his sudden departure smarted like a slap.

'He's already left,' I announced, returning to the front door. Upstairs I could hear Poppy's feet pattering along the gallery. In a minute or so she would be scampering down the staircase. Once she was in the living room she'd turn on the TV and jump on to the sofa, waiting for me to produce breakfast. It was our morning routine, as fixed and predictable as Monday following Sunday.

'Could you tell me where he is?'

'Up in London, working on this renovation.'

I scrutinized the policeman's bland, business-like expression. Now that my initial panic had subsided, a new emotion was developing: curiosity, mixed with blurry unease. 'Is it something urgent?'

He ignored the question. 'When are you expecting him back?'

'I'm not sure . . .'

'Do you have a number where we can contact him? Or the address where he's working?'

'Not exactly the address. It's just some building site where they're refurbishing this house. I mean, there's no need for me to ever go there . . .' I trailed off, embarrassed at my ignorance. 'You can always call him on his mobile.'

He nodded. 'Yes, we'll try that later. In the meantime, may I come inside for a moment? It won't take long.'

'Sure.' I stepped aside, pulling my dressing gown nervously around my waist. What the hell was going on?

'Mummy!' Poppy called from the living room. 'Who are you talking to?'

'No one!'

The policeman stepped into the untidy lobby, where crusty boots jostled for space with bikes and buggies.

'Do you have any idea who these people are?'

He had produced a photograph from his pocket. I stared at the picture, my insides clenching. It was not the original photograph, but a copy on hard-backed paper, blown up and covered with a thick plastic coating, as if the police anticipated a horde of witnesses thumbing it over. It showed a grinning couple relaxing on the deck of a boat. Behind them the sea was turquoise. The man was directly facing the camera, his arm flung casually over the woman's shoulders. I couldn't clearly make out her features, but it was clear that she was beautiful. Her head was turned towards her lover, her eyes gazing at him. It must have been windy, for tumbling black curls flicked across her cheeks and into the corners of her laughing mouth.

It was Si and the woman whose nude portrait I had seen hanging in his London kitchen. My husband in another, happier life: his body less hunched and thin, his skin tanned and hair bleached from the sun. A good-looking man, clutching a beautiful girl who adored him. *Rosa.* The image winded me; everything I had longed that my marriage should be had been turned into a mockery by the couple's confident joy. What was it that his loathsome mother had said? *You're not as young and pretty as Rosa.* Thrusting the picture back into the policeman's hands, I folded my arms defensively.

'It's my husband. He looks a lot younger so it must have been taken a while ago. The woman's his ex-girlfriend.'

The policeman licked his lips; a little flick of pink, like a lizard. 'Does the name Rosa Montague mean anything to you?'

'Yes. That's her.'

I glared back at him, bracing myself. I was getting the chilly, numbing sensation that spreads through one's insides on hearing unpleasant news. Only later, when the details have sunk in, does the real pain begin.

'We're conducting a missing person's investigation,' he continued blandly. 'Ms Montague has been missing since before Christmas. We found this picture by her bedside. We were curious about the identity of her friend.'

'She used to live with my husband in London,' I muttered. 'I don't know anything about her. When I met him the relationship was over.'

'And that was when?'

'The Christmas before last. He'd finished with her sometime before that though.'

'So you met him in December 2003?'

I nodded.

'Right.' Taking out his notepad, the policeman scribbled something down. 'Thank you. That's helpful.'

He was almost turning towards the door, almost bringing the interview to a close. Just because Si's ex-girlfriend kept a photograph of him, it meant nothing. So, she had disappeared. This did not mean that Si was involved. The police were simply checking out everyone who knew her. I could return undisturbed to Poppy's breakfast, feed Jo and get them to school on time. There was nothing whatsoever to worry about. But the policeman's boot was still on the step.

'There's just one other thing . . .'

'Yes?'

I released my fists, trying to breathe normally. I did not want him to see how nervous I was.

'It's just that we found your husband's credit cards in Rosa Montague's property,' he added casually. 'Were you aware that they were missing?'

My face swamped crimson. I spread my hands over my

cheeks, trying to hide my confusion. *Si had said he'd left the card at Ol's in London!* For a moment I felt as if I were suffocating, the shock sharp and malevolent, pressing down over my mouth and nose like a smothering hand. I took a deep breath, trying to steady myself.

'He lost them . . .' My heart was beating so fiercely he must surely hear. 'I think he must have had them replaced by now.'

'I see . . .'

He gazed thoughtfully at me, perhaps hoping for further revelations. Was he aware of the devastation that his question had caused? For him, it was everyday police procedure. For me, he might as well have crashed a cast-iron breaker's ball through the side of our home. Even if I had more to say, I would not have been able to speak. The policeman smirked, pushing the pad back into his pocket.

'Here's a card with the number of the enquiry room,' he said chattily. 'If you could get your husband to contact us when he comes in, I'd be grateful.'

'What about his mobile?'

'We've already got the number. Thank you for your time.'

I gazed after him. He was turning now, about to step through the door. Did they really have enquiry rooms for every person that went missing? And how had they got hold of Si's mobile number?

'Try not to worry, Mrs Stenning,' he said, smiling perfunctorily. 'All we want to do at this stage is to eliminate your husband from our enquiries.'

Nodding at me, he walked across the drive and opened the door to his car. I closed the front door, my mind stalling. I could hear the car starting up, the crunch of gravel under its wheels. For a moment, before I girdled in my panic and returned to Poppy and Jo and the preparations for their breakfast, I sagged against the closed door. All the time I thought Si was with Ollie, he was with *her*!

PART THREE

23

The cottage was in the middle of thick woodland, its crooked chimney rising from the trees like the witch's house in Hansel and Gretel. *Dave tutted as he pushed the car into second. He had not been expecting such a remote or muddy track and hated to think about the puddles splashing over the car's normally gleaming bodywork, let alone what the potholes were doing to its suspension. Navigating the car around the final bend, the front wheel hit the deepest hole yet, bumping his belly into the steering wheel. Inwardly cursing Clive Jenkins, the DI whose call had interrupted a cosy morning with his paperwork, Dave changed gear again. As he'd said on the phone, Clive had better have something interesting.*

After five minutes of navigating the looping track, the car finally reached the bottom of the dell. Now he could see the property in its entirety: a small wooden-fronted house surrounded by the weedy remains of what might once have been a pretty cottage garden. The place had, however, been left to rack and ruin. The sweet peas had bolted from their broken canes, the cabbage patch was covered with bindweed, and the grasses of what might once have been a pretty lawn were invaded by thistles and sycamore saplings. Pulling up on the verge, Dave climbed from his car.

The place looked like a slum. If he had a cottage like this, he'd turn it into a little palace. If it weren't for the trees crowding so oppressively around, it was the kind of home that he and Karen dreamt of. It wouldn't take much to fix the crumbling chimney and retile the roof. Then he'd set to work in the garden. His old dad had kept an allotment, so he'd learnt all he'd need to know about vege-tables from him. There'd be plenty of flowers, too: busy Lizzies and geraniums, maybe a rose bed or two, not these wild grasses that were so long they could be turned into hay. Harvey of course would have a ball. As he picked his way through the puddles, Dave pictured his son roaming the woods with a band of friends, just as back in the '70s he'd spent his summer holidays in rural Kent: the good old days, when boys were out all day, building camps or playing with their bikes. Banishing the fantasy, he stepped past the rotting gate and walked up the path.

The front door was open, and he could hear voices coming from inside. Striding into the narrow hall, he peered quickly around, his brain sift-ing the scene for obvious evidence. In contrast to the dishevelled appear-ance of the outside, the inside of the cottage was surprisingly well kept. He took in a neat front parlour, filled with china knick-knacks and battered, yet obviously classy, antique furniture. It was probably the home of an elderly person, most likely a woman. The kitchen was a relic from the 1960s, or even earlier: worn blue lino, an old-fashioned gas cooker, and chipped Formica cabinets in a style that to his amaze-ment he had seen in Karen's Ikea catalogue under the heading 'Retro'. Despite the aged feeling of the room, and the smell of damp, it was notably spotless. Whoever had last been here had swept the floor, polished the draining board and taken out the bins. Two laundered tea towels were even arranged symmetrically on the work surface, their corners folded back fancily, like the sheets in the posh Maldives resort where he and Karen had spent their honeymoon. It was an odd touch.

'Dave!'

Turning from the kitchen door, he saw Clive Jenkins approaching from the bottom of the narrow stairs. The two men shook hands. They'd worked on a firearms case in Ramsgate a year back, and had achieved a highly satisfactory result: a narcotics gang busted with four convictions. The memory produced a pleasant glowing sensation in Dave that spilled into a wide smile for his more junior colleague.

'What have we got, then?'

'A young woman who's gone missing.'

Dave pursed his lips, raising his eyebrows in a way that implied that Jenkins had better not be wasting his time.

'Looks to me like she's just gone on her holidays.'

Holding up his hand as if to tell him to wait for the whole story, Jenkins continued. 'It's not that straightforward. The lady that owns the place, Mrs Montague, rings us on Monday. She's concerned about her niece, who's been living here.'

'Right . . .'

'Apparently the niece hasn't been in contact since Christmas. The aunt's tried to call her, but she doesn't pick up the phone. It was the aunt's birthday last week and the niece had promised to come and see her in London, but she didn't show up. The old lady's getting on a bit and can't come down here herself, so she calls us. She's very worried: it's not like her niece to forget her birthday, she says, she can't understand what's happened.'

'So you come down here and have a look around . . .'

Dave folded his arms. He was thinking of the mud on his car and the hour or more it would take him to return to Herne Bay. He'd told Karen he'd pick Harvey up from his karate club, but now he'd be too late. It was as he'd suspected: a wild goose chase.

'And what we find is that the place is all shut up, as you can see. Everything's clean and tidy, letters on the mat date from December, there's no food left rotting, no obvious evidence of a sudden disappearance. There's some personal effects that we've been checking out, including a man's credit cards that we found in her kitchen drawer, but to be honest we're not too concerned. Looks like you said. The young lady's just gone away —'

'— and forgotten to tell her aunt.'

'Exactly. But wait a sec before you start bawling me out. This morning we find something rather more interesting . . .'

Gesturing towards the front room, Jenkins led Dave across the hall, ducking through the small door frame then standing aside as the larger man entered.

'Have a look in here. See if you can spot it.'

Dave peered around the small room. It was decorated with the frayed gentility of the English upper-middle classes, a style which he instinctively understood that Karen's chintzy curtains, studded leather settee and fake Georgian fireplace emulated. The decor brought to mind a vicar's front parlour, or elderly ladies with yapping dogs who lived in places like Whitstable. The Persian carpet was worn but clearly valuable; the china figurines could have featured on The Antiques Road Show. The paintings that hung in gilded frames from the walls looked like originals. And now, as he scrutinized the room, Dave suddenly experienced the tingling sensation that ran down his spine whenever he noticed something significant. His mouth, which had previously been twisted into a bored scowl, started to twitch at the corners.

'The curtain on the left's had a little wash,' he said slowly. 'But the one on the right hasn't. It's darker.'

'Yup. There's more, too.'

He peered at the wall next to the curtains. He was beginning to feel excited.

'Yeah, I see it. The wall on this side's been repainted. It's a different shade . . .'

'And if you look closely . . .'

The men crossed the room together, peering at the paintwork. It was a hasty job: white emulsion slopped over one section of the wall, the older paint that surrounded it duller and darker.

'Someone's been doing a spot of decorating.'

Now that he was close up he could clearly see an area of tiny brown spots that had been missed by the paintbrush. Dotted around the window ledge and over the skirting board, at least thirty flecks were clearly discernible.

'Forensics are going to have fun with this.'

'We've found more marks in the downstairs toilet. There're also some areas on the carpet where someone's had a go with a scrubbing brush.'

Glancing down, Dave followed Jenkin's finger, taking in the lighter patches on the carpet where it had been cleaned. Moving away from the wall, he nodded at him in approval: no geese to be chased here, then.

'Very interesting. What do we know about the missing woman?'

'She's called Rosa Montague. Lived here for about a year. Not married, but had a boyfriend who was away a lot. The aunt hasn't met him, but we've got his details off his credit cards. I got the impression that the niece had a private income. There's a photo we can use.'

'Have you contacted the boyfriend?'

'My boys are on it today.'

'Any other family or friends?'

Before Jenkins could answer, there was a sharp cry from the garden. Glancing through the leaded panes of the small sitting-room window, Dave saw a uniformed officer, running across the garden.

'Over here!' he was shouting.

24

How does it feel when the surface on which you're tread-
ing gives way? Until those dreadful five minutes with the
policeman on my doorstep, I still believed the ground
beneath me to be solid. There were bumps and potholes to
be negotiated, it was true, and at times my legs felt tired.
But I never seriously doubted the terrain. Yet now the landscape was revealed as illusion. Unable to get a foothold, I
tumbled fast and furious into a strange, scarred territory that
I did not recognize. That moment, when the ground began
to shudder and I could discern the fractures, was almost
worse than what was to come. Suddenly everything I thought
real was gone, a joke almost. After that, there was only the
rushing of air in my ears.

So, Si was still involved with his ex-girlfriend. Or rather,
his ex-ex-girlfriend. *Rosa.* She had long dark hair and a model's
body, and her elegant hands were draped around his shoulders as if this was their natural resting place, conferring an
ownership I still only hesitantly assumed. And no wonder.
From the very beginning he had been deceiving me. He had
promised that the relationship was over, yet he was still visiting her, their intimacy sufficiently intact for her to keep his
photo displayed on her wall. Now, as I brooded over every
twist and turn of my marriage, Rosa's slanting shadow fell
across my view. Nat had been right, damn her. When Si was
not with me in Brockwell, he was with her. *She* was the reason
why he had taken such fright at the news of my pregnancy;
it was to *her* place that he had scarpered. What had caused

his sudden reappearance? A temporary lover's tiff? The thought of his hands on her body, and hers on his, made my stomach turn. As I pushed Jo back from the school, I had to clutch at the buggy handles to stop myself from keeling over. I walked fast, tears streaming down my face. I felt as if my life had fallen apart, my worst fears finally confirmed.

Back home, I gave in to despair, curling foetally on the sofa and snivelling as Jo chewed on his teething ring. I felt such a fool. All the time that I had been immersed in my cosy fantasy of family life, Si had remained involved with Rosa. Conceivably, he had only married me out of pity. Or perhaps, after a week or so of reflection, he had decided that he did, after all, fancy having a child, and I was merely a conduit for his paternity. Whatever the reasons, he did not love me enough to relinquish the stunning Rosa, in whose house he had only a few short months ago left his credit cards and whose calls he was obviously still receiving. He had been talking to *her* on his mobile last night, I now realized. She had probably been whispering about her desire for him, bringing him to climax as he touched himself in the privacy of the bedroom. That was why later he had not wanted to have sex with me.

Perhaps the territory was not so strange after all. Dragging myself off the sofa to change Jo's nappy, I realized that many of the landmarks were deeply familiar. Men were shits, betrayal the norm. Unsurprisingly, given my inability to inspire love, I was alone. For a few short months I had been wandering in a world where I did not belong, of happy-clappy families, nights in the Ritz and irises tucked behind my ears. But ultimately I could never fit into fairyland. I was too heavy with need, too saggy with insecurity. Inevitably I had crashed through the thin skein that had temporarily separated me from reality: single parenthood, a thickening, ageing body, and a life set apart.

Rosa, of course, would be different. As I brooded, I tried to imagine the home from where she had gone missing. She would have a little mews house, somewhere smart like Chelsea, or Notting Hill. It would be feminine and artistic, with fresh flowers and crisp white linen, which she and Si would leave stained from their ardent encounters. Before I could control my rampaging imagination I pictured them in bed together. She would be passionate and fierce with him, a welcome respite from my dull performances. Recalling his bloodied lip back in December, my heart snagged on a barb of jealousy so sharp I felt it might tear me in two.

Or was I over-dramatizing? As the day wore on, I convinced myself that things were not so bad. Perhaps Si had business affairs with this Rosa that needed sorting out. The papers, for instance, that she had taken from his mother: he would have needed to retrieve them. *That* was why he had been back in her house. It was a one-off, not worth mentioning. If, many weeks later, she had disappeared, leaving Si's photo by her bed, it had nothing to do with him. As the policeman had said, they merely wanted to eliminate Si from their enquiries. He'd be bound to have an alibi, and that would be that. Si had said he was no longer involved with her. As he had insisted, I should trust him.

But just as I was starting to believe this benign version of events, I recalled the other dreadful phrase that the policeman had used. *At this stage.*

I summoned the courage to call Si on his mobile. By now it was after lunch and the bright promise of the day had faded. As I cradled the phone in my lap, I gazed from the windows at the brown water that flowed sedately past. Spring was almost here. Already the riverbank was sprinkled with snowdrops and the birds were calling to each other with a new, hopeful note. The change of seasons could not come soon enough. If only the sun would burn more brightly and the earth revolve more quickly, then we would leave this unrelenting grey chill and return to the long light days of the summer, when Si still loved me.

My trembling fingers dialled the number. It was not rational, but I believed that his response would decide everything. He picked up almost immediately.

'Hi!'

I could not speak. I had not expected such warmth in his voice, and tears clogged my throat. In the background I could hear the unmistakable crash of hammers.

'What's up?'

'I . . . I didn't know where you'd gone!'

'I'm sorry, hon. I was going to call you, but we've been rushed off our feet. Ol texted me last night to say that the flooring guys had fast-tracked the order and were delivering first thing this morning. If we keep going at this rate we'll . . .'

I did not hear the rest.

'The police have been here!' I wailed. 'They want to talk to you!'

There was a long silence. Finally, Si said, 'Hang on, I'm going outside.' Around him I could hear the uproar of a happily occupied building site. When he next came on the line his voice was muffled, as if he was cupping his hand over his mouth.

'What do you mean, the police want to talk to me?'

'A policeman was here this morning. They've found your credit cards.'

I pressed the receiver hard against my ear, willing him to

produce an obvious explanation, some miraculous truth that would absolve him. But as the silence lengthened, my fragile hopes spun hopelessly apart.

'My credit cards?' Si finally echoed. He sounded scared.

'Yes. They found them in your girlfriend's house.'

Another long pause. My heart was plummeting at his failure to deny that Rosa Montague was his girlfriend. Then: 'So why do they want to talk to me?'

'Why do *you* think?'

'I have absolutely no idea.'

'They said she's gone missing.'

He was silent. Perhaps he was working out what to say.

'Are they coming back?' he eventually asked.

'I don't know. There's a number for you to ring.'

If only I could see his face, then I would know the truth.

'You're still seeing her, aren't you?'

'No!'

'So how come your cards were at her house?'

'I had to go and see her to get the deeds back. I left them there. She's been playing these games with me —'

'But that was ages ago!'

'I know, but I had to go and sort some other things out with her. I swear this isn't how it looks, Mel.'

'Isn't it?'

Squeezing my eyes shut, I blinked away more tears. Had he any idea how I was feeling?

'Mel?'

'What?' From the kitchen, Jo had suddenly started to cry.

'You do believe me, don't you?'

I glanced down the corridor, instinctively distracted by the wails, which were rising to a sharp crescendo. 'What did you say?'

'You do believe me?'

He started to say something else, but with the din of screaming in the background, I could barely hear it. Now, as I sit hunched on the sofa, with my life crashing around me, I realize that a part of me did not want to hear. It was obvious that he was lying, yet I remained too terrified to hear the truth.

'I have to go,' I muttered. 'We'll talk later.'

Putting down the phone, I hurried towards Jo.

I was supposed to be meeting Trish later that afternoon, but I told her I was coming down with flu. Fifteen minutes later she was standing at the front door, her hands on her hips in a parody of bossiness.

'Come on, give me that baby! You're going to have a couple of hours' kip before Poppy gets back.'

'Are you sure?'

'Of course I'm sure! I wouldn't offer if I wasn't, would I? Anyway, I need the practice.'

'You're an angel . . .'

As soon as they had gone I started to rummage through the papers piled on the kitchen table. I had over three unencumbered hours in which to search the house. I trawled through shopping receipts, builders' invoices and letters from the bank, unsure what I was looking for. Upstairs I went through Si's clothes, convinced that each time I plunged my fingers into the crummy seams of his pockets I would pull out a black thong, or a silver-foiled condom.

There was nothing. If he had been deceiving me, surely I would discover the snail's traces of his infidelity? Or was he an expert in subterfuge? I continued to search, working my way through clothes, bills, and crumpled envelopes covered with his doodles. In his painting room I deliberately ignored the canvas of the woman with the baby-like wound and progressed to a pile of papers, shoved into a corner. On top was a catalogue for sliding windows, lying above a plan of the garden we had hoped to build. I studied the yellowing diagram sorrowfully, recalling how Si had sketched it one warm September evening. He had been a little stoned from the joint that he was smoking, and we strolled, hand in hand, around our small plot, pointing out places for a tree house, a site for the vegetables. Would the garden ever be grown? As I stared at the faded paper, it seemed unlikely.

Underneath the plan was a postcard from Nat that I had barely bothered to read. It showed a collage of a goldfish, which the artist had stuck on top of an old-fashioned bicycle, its fins flapping comically over the handles. The caption read: A WOMAN NEEDS A MAN LIKE A FISH NEEDS A BICYCLE. On the back, Nat had written: *How's true love ever after? Thinking of you. Hoping everything's* okay!!! She had underlined 'okay' three times, each stroke of her pen indicating the strength of her doubt. I gave a sour laugh, dropping it on to the floor. Nat had never been one for subtlety. Finally, languishing under more catalogues for garden furniture and a chart of paint colours, was a statement from Si's bank. It was for December to January of this year. I pulled it from the envelope, my pulse romping.

To start with, there was all the usual stuff: Unwins, for a crate of 'winter warmer' wines; supermarket bills; a jewellery firm in London that I assumed had supplied my bracelet. Then, suddenly, from 15 December, I no longer recognized the creditors. There was a petrol bill from a garage in Hayward's Heath, followed, after a long interval, by a bill for £80 from the hairdresser Molton Brown's in South Molton Street, followed by £325 from a boutique in Bond Street on 29 December. After that was a list of cash withdrawals, until the statement abruptly stopped at the end of January. I stared at the blurring figures, trying to remember when I had lost my bag at Tesco's. It was the first week of January, I was sure. That meant that when I was struggling to pay for my groceries, someone else – Rosa Montague presumably – had already spent most of Si's money in the sales. Was this his Christmas treat to her, to make up for his absence? The thought of my rival spending Si's money on her appearance, when I had been cutting my hair in the mirror and living in jeans and charity-shop jumpers, made me so furious that I crushed the statement into a tight ball and flung it across the room. Later I would retrieve it, smooth out the creases and fold it into my back pocket.

That evening Poppy was particularly quiet. As I tidied away supper she sat sucking on her thumbnail as she drew with her crayons. I busied myself with the washing-up, sensing that I was being observed. Each time I glanced in her direction I found her big blue eyes trained ponderously on me, as if she was trying to work something out.

'What's the matter, Mummy?'

I glanced up. I had made a supreme effort to disguise my distress. Before collecting her from Lily's house, where she had been playing after school, I had washed my face, tidied my hair, even smeared lipstick over my cracked lips. By the time I was ringing the bell to her friend's house I had arranged my face into a glaze of polite neutrality. I had even managed to respond cheerfully to Sally's chatter about next week's school trip to Hever Castle. Yes, I would be giving lifts, I assured her with a jolly laugh. It would be great fun.

'Nothing's the matter!' I brightly replied. 'Why should there be?'

'It's just that you look all cryie.'

I frowned, pretending to be perplexed. 'Well, I'm not. I'm perfectly fine.'

'Why are your eyes so red then?'

'I'm tired, that's all.'

Wandering across the room to where she was sitting, I put my arm around her shoulders and kissed the top of her head, inhaling the sweet smell of her hair.

'What are you drawing?'

'It's just a picture of that ghost that I saw by the stairs.'

I stared at the paper, first turning cold, then very hot. As I had been washing up, Poppy had produced a picture of the warehouse. She had made it very tall and narrow, with lots of boxy little windows facing out. On one side was the river, curving blue, on the other blobby trees and flowers, coloured pink. Standing in front of the building were three stick people of descending sizes, holding hands. It was not these who attracted my attention, however: it was what she had drawn at the top. In the pointed roof she had depicted the dormer windows as a large rectangle. In the middle, staring out, was a purple face: a large head, with round eyes, a stick nose, and a big O for its mouth.

'Who's that?'

'It's the ghost.'

I did not know what to say. I cleared my throat, trying to remain calm.

'Who are those people at the bottom?' I eventually asked.

'That's you and me and Jo.'

'What about Si?'

She started to slide off her seat, grabbing my hand as she pulled me away.

'He doesn't live here any more.'

25

When Si returned, the children were asleep and I was painting the downstairs cloakroom. The physical activity was
surprisingly therapeutic. With every swipe of the roller I was
obliterating the ugly, scuffed surface of the wall and turning it into a vibrant canary yellow that defied melancholy.
If only I could wipe out the events of the last twenty-four
hours so easily. I dabbed at the ceiling, the paint sprinkling
my hair. Now that the truth had begun to seep out, it
threatened to destroy everything: the floorboards would
begin warping, the plasterwork crumbling. Eventually the
whole building would sag into the bog, collapsing under the
weight of Si's lies.

I finished the ceiling and moved on to the adjacent wall.
I was feeling increasingly fatalistic. When Si appeared I would
listen to whatever he had to say. Then I would know one
way or the other whether he had betrayed me. When I heard
the sound of the van pulling up in the drive, I placed the
roller back in the tray, wiped my hands and pulled off my
overall. Then I walked into the living room, where I stood
by the darkened windows, waiting for him.

The door swung open. The weather had turned windy,
and the wooden handle crashed loudly against the lobby
wall. Dropping his bag by Jo's buggy, Si strode into the living
room. Unlike the evening before, when he had hardly
seemed to register my presence, his eyes were fixed on my
face. Placing his arms around my waist, he pulled me hard
towards him. I stood motionlessly in his grip, my hands

hanging by my sides. So much had changed since the evening before, and now I could hardly bear for him to touch me. Finally he gave up, releasing me as he took a step backwards, staring intently into my face. Batting my eyes away, I stared at the floor. His performance seemed staged.

'I know what you're thinking,' he finally said. He looked exhausted, his face sagging, his forehead riven by deep creases. If I had passed him in the street, I would have thought he was in his fifties.

'Do you?'

'The police showed you that photograph . . . they rang me about it this afternoon. Apparently you provided an identification.'

I nodded, still not making eye contact. 'I wasn't going to lie, was I?'

'Look, Mel,' he went on, grabbing at my arm imploringly. 'I can imagine how this appears, but you've got to believe what I've always told you. Rosa and I are finished.'

I shook his fingers angrily from my wrist. 'Oh yeah? Then why do you keep popping in to see her?'

I glared at him. His grim expression, which seemed to confirm all my fears, blasted me with hot, swelling panic. Trish was right: he had been 'playing away', and now, when confronted with the evidence of his infidelity, was not even going to bother denying it. The way he was looking at me, with his mouth turned down and eyes moist, made my knees go weak. It felt as if, after weeks drifting in the doldrums, the wind had unexpectedly picked up and we were whizzing furiously towards the end of our journey.

'What were you doing at her house?' I whispered.

If only he would look me in the eyes. He tried to smile, his eyes darting across the room and fixing on the table. Taking a step away, he fingered its waxed covering.

'It's like I said, there was some business stuff to sort out. I'd hoped I'd seen the last of her, but she managed to get our number off Ol and was hassling me about various things so I had to go over there. Honestly, Mel, I wish you'd just relax and trust me . . .'

'It all sounds a bit odd to me.'

'Well, that's because *she's* odd. To be honest I'm completely sick of her games.'

'So why didn't you tell me you were going to see her?'

'Because I didn't want to burden you with it all . . .'

It was a lame excuse. Folding my arms, I sighed angrily. 'Why the hell not?'

'Because it was too complicated . . .'

'For God's sake, stop fobbing me off! In what way was it too complicated?'

He shook his head, his face paling with rage. I pictured the painting of the woman with the baby: a portrait, presumably, of me and Jo. The menace and violence that it exuded made me feel physically sick.

'*It doesn't matter!*'

Crimson spots had appeared on his cheekbones. I remained silent, shocked by his vehemence. 'Look,' he said more gently. 'If I could have just walked away and never laid eyes on Rosa again, I would have been overjoyed. But things were more than a bit messy. The only thing that really matters is that it's *you* I love. I promise you, Mel . . .'

He was lying. Pulling the bank statement from my jeans pocket, I handed it over.

'If you wanted to get rid of her so much, why did you let her keep using your cards?'

He slowly unfolded the paper. For a couple of moments he made a show of glancing down the list of withdrawals, yet the speed with which he did this indicated that he was already familiar with the statement. I watched him impatiently. I could feel a hot flush rising on my cheeks.

'I don't know what you're talking about,' he murmured.

I could bear it no longer. With a roar of fury I hurled myself at him, my fists pummelling his chest, my slippered feet ineffectively kicking his shins.

'You're lying, you shit! You promised me you'd never, ever do that!'

He was so much stronger than me. Grabbing my arms, he pinioned them behind my back, forcing me to stagger backwards on to the dusty floorboards. Suddenly he was on top of me, his knee parting my legs as he pressed his mouth hard against mine. As my head knocked against wood his fingers were in my hair, his lips moving over my face as he covered it with kisses.

'Why can't you just believe me?' he whispered. 'For God's sake . . .'

Closing my eyes, I began to kiss him back. For that short moment, everything fell away. *This* was the sum of things, the driving force; nothing else mattered. Extracting my twisted arm from the floor, I brought my fingers to his face. Above me his body was rigid, filled with an anger I did not understand. Grabbing my hand he started to knead it, crushing my fingers inside his.

'I love you!' he groaned. 'Please, you've got to trust me, Mel . . .'

My fingers hovered around his bent head. With one small movement, I might change everything. I could stroke his hair, whispering my absolution, or pull his face up, so that my kisses exonerated him. Yet as I lay on the dusty floor, listening to the creak of old beams and the rhythmic chink of boat masts from the yard, it no longer felt possible. He started to tussle with my clothes, pulling them down and spreading his hands over my flesh as if nothing had changed. How many times hadn't he touched me in this way? Reaching inside my pants with his fingers, his mouth moved over my neck. Only a few short weeks ago that same touch had brought me alive, confirming everything I wanted to believe. Now as I lay beneath him I was overcome by revulsion. He was obviously deceiving me. And apparently I was expected to lie back and play the role of the trusting little wife.

'Get off, you shit!'

Pushing him off with a furious shove, I rolled over, effectively shielding myself from his touch.

'Honey, please, don't be like this . . .'

'I'm not in the mood.' Pulling my jumper down, I sat up. From the floor above, I could hear a thin wail.

'Then let's talk some more . . .'

'Jo's crying,' I said, standing. 'He needs his feed.'

I ran upstairs. I was relieved to get away.

*

Should I have foreseen the direction in which we were heading? If I were a different woman, less needy perhaps, with a tighter grasp upon reality, would I have already packed my bags, strapped my children into the back of the car and departed? As I pick over these last terrible days, I'm searching for clues, but everything is muddied by my conflicting emotions. The evening that Si came back from London and pushed me on to the floorboards, I still wanted to love him. He was the father of my baby, the man I believed had transformed my life. Was it really so foolhardy?

Trish has brought me a piece of toast. She has placed the plate on the arm of the sofa, giving my shoulder a sympathetic squeeze before tiptoeing back towards the kitchen. I'm grateful for her sensitivity. I do not want to talk to her, or to anyone. I need to sit quietly by myself, concentrating.

Something is bothering me, a buzzing at the back of my mind that refuses to hush. There's so much other noise that I can't hear it properly: every time I try to concentrate I picture Poppy, flopped in the front seat of the Volkswagen as Si careers towards disaster, or the expression on her face when she pulled back the calico curtains and found me hiding there with Jo. But if I force my mind to focus, recalling every detail of the last few days, I realize that what I'm hearing is a distant bell, ringing in some forgotten corner. At first the sound was so faint and I was so panicked that I hardly noticed. But with every hour that Poppy's gone it's growing louder: the clanging of an alarm in a place I still can't name, somewhere we haven't thought of yet, somewhere completely unexpected.

26

Draining his polystyrene cup, Dave took a final glug of coffee, then, smashing the beaker in his hands, lobbed it into the bin by the door. Bingo! He'd been using the bin as target practice all morning, and this was his first direct hit. The scrumpled evidence of his many misses scattered the floor: memos concerning race equality training; a monthly newsletter issued by the Met, an unreadable document concerning some working party's deliberations on the government's new flexitime directives.

He had a good feeling about Simon Stenning, a very good feeling. He was, as he had informed his superintendent the day before, 'an important lead'. Not only were his fingerprints all over Rosa Montague's house, but the joker's grinning photos were plastered over the wall above her bed. To top it off they had found his credit cards in the kitchen drawer. Dave's hunch was that Rosa was Stenning's kept woman, a nice bit on the side that his current wife knew nothing about. Rosa was almost certainly dead, and in cases where women suddenly disappeared it was more than often their boyfriends or husbands who had killed them. She definitely hadn't planned to go away. Her clothes were hanging in her wardrobe, and her passport, plus a pile of other personal effects, remained in her aunt's fancy little bureau. More important was the matter of her blood sprayed around the window sill. Whoever had cleaned it up probably considered they'd done a thorough job. They'd even painted over sections of the stains. But they'd left a total of fifteen tiny patches, barely discernible to the naked eye, both on the sill and the carpet. Rosa's medical records confirmed that it was her blood.

But it was not this alone that had excited Dave, it was what they'd found in her garden. It was one of those God-given gifts, a discovery which could almost have you back in church on Sundays, one of the finest break-throughs of his career. A week earlier the Jacqui Jenning case was as dead as a dodo, but now they were back in business. He took in the bustling investigation room with satisfaction. The scene of crime photos, which for fourteen long months had been furling around the edges on the board, no longer depressed him; the place had a new vim and vigour to it, an energy that made him sit up straighter, smile rather than scowl at his colleagues, and miss his fags just a little less. He had even been to the gym. They were going to crack this one, and when they did, the bubbling feeling in his chest told him that it was going to be big.

'Clive! Come and sit down.'

Removing his feet from his desk, he gestured to the chair opposite. Perching on the edge, Clive Jenkins nodded at him good humouredly. He was such a skinny bastard, Dave thought enviously as he eyed his colleague's slim frame. They'd played squash a couple of years ago and Clive had smashed him.

'All ready for our little trip?'

'All ready and willing. You sure you want to come?'

'Yeah, it'll be interesting to have a little look at what we've got. They're living in some old warehouse, right?'

'Apparently it's a wreck.'

'So we're going to go in there, keep it nice and simple. See how he reacts.'

'Come on, then.'

Clive was already on his feet, glancing at his watch.

'Lips sealed over Jacqui, right?'

'Of course!'

Pulling on their coats, they walked across the busy room.

The morning after Si's return the police were back. I had dropped Poppy off at school and caught sight of their car as I turned into the lane. It was an unmarked blue saloon, too gleaming to be owned by one of Si's building chums, and too free of booster seats or 'baby on board' stickers for another mum. As I wheeled Jo up the drive, I saw that Si was opening the door to two men. The leather coat of the first and dun-coloured puffa jacket of the second, worn over chinos, told me all I needed to know: they were plain-clothed policemen, returned to interrogate Si. They stepped quickly inside, the door slamming behind them.

Overnight the wind had worked itself into a fury. It howled across the yard, the boat sails flapping frantically as they rocked from side to side, the water on the creek ruffled into sudden splashing squalls. Ahead of me the warehouse loomed into the bruised, stormy sky. I shuddered, pulling my coat tighter. I had woken with a dull ache in the pit of my stomach. Now, as I hurried through the boatyard, the pain sharpened, digging into my intestines and making me weak with dread.

I entered the building through the kitchen door, closing it quietly behind me. Pulling Jo from the buggy, I crept along the corridor, holding his body tight against my chest to muffle his crooning. Through the connecting door, I could hear the men talking.

'What if I refuse?' Si was saying. 'You can't force me.'

The high-pitched, panicky timbre of his voice caused my throat to contract. I swallowed hard, straining to hear what was said in reply. One of the policemen must have been standing on the far side of the room, for with the clatter of the wind around the building I could only hear a dim trace of his words. Then, very clearly, what I now know to be Dave Gosforth's voice said, 'It's up to you, Simon. We can either do it here, nice and relaxed without any fuss, or we can bring you in and do it at the station.' He had a strong estuary twang, the guttural gobbiness of a man at ease with his power.

Si said something in reply, but I was unable to catch what. Now I could hear footsteps clumping across the wooden floor and the skid of what sounded like furniture being moved. Summoning up my courage, I pushed open the door.

I gazed around the room in confusion. Si was sprawled on the sofa, which had been pushed back a little, perhaps by the force of his collapse. Squatting next to him was the man in the puffa jacket. In his plastic-bagged hand he held a swab, which he was pushing into Si's opened mouth. As he did this, the man in the leather jacket was sidling up to the coffee table and examining the photograph of Poppy holding a newborn Jo, which I had framed and placed there. At the approach of my footsteps he spun around, smiling facetiously.

'Melanie?' He stretched out his large paw. For a second I allowed his fingers to brush against mine, then I pulled my hand away. He was a large, baggy man, with too-small features that were crowded into the centre of his pallid face as if forced there by the pressure of accumulated fat. His cheeks had the raw, slightly bloodied appearance of a recent shave, and the end of his sharp nose glistened with moisture. His eyes were rimmed red, as if he had a bad cold.

'Detective Chief Inspector David Gosforth, Kent CID . . . And this is little . . . ?'

'Jo.' I clutched his warm head a little more tightly to my bosom, not wanting this odious man, with his dripping nose, to infect my son. 'What are you doing?'

'Your husband has very kindly agreed to give us a DNA sample.'

There was clearly nothing kind about it. Inspector Puffa Jacket had finished now, and was placing the swab into a plastic bag. Si remained seated, staring morosely at the floor.

'What for?'

Gosforth grinned broadly. He was playing a game, I thought, horrified at the familiarity with which his eyes roamed around the room. What clues was he expecting to find in the clutter? And why was Si just sitting there, saying nothing?

'Your husband is, as we say, "helping us with our enquiries",' he said, clearly enjoying the effect he was having on me. 'We've just been having a little chat about Rosa Montague, this young lady who's gone missing.'

'What about her? Like he's told you, he's not with her any more. He's married to me.'

To my amazement, Gosforth chuckled nastily. 'I'm sure he is,' he said.

On the other side of the room Si still stared fixedly at the floor.

'We'll be in touch, Si,' Gosforth was saying. Giving me a wink, he padded across the room towards the front door, his lackey following behind. He was wearing smart new brogues, I noticed, as conventional and uninspired as his ironed jeans.

'Don't worry, we'll show ourselves out!' he called over his shoulder. As we heard the door slam, Si sagged forwards, his head dropping into his hands. I stood for a while, watching him as I jiggled Jo.

'Are you going to tell me what's going on?'

When he looked up, his face was lifeless, as if he'd pulled a plastic mask over his features. He rested his nose against his folded palms, as if praying. For a moment he seemed to be on the verge of saying something. Then suddenly he stood up.

'I'm sorry, hon, I . . .'

His voice broke, his pink eyes glazing. If he had stayed like that for just a second longer I would have gone to him and put my arms around his shoulders and perhaps everything would have changed. But presumably he did not want me to see him crying, for he turned hastily away.

'I'm going upstairs,' he said.

27

Five minutes later I had strapped Jo into his baby seat and driven to the top of the lane, where the car was out of view of the warehouse. Once I'd parked, my shaking fingers punched Alicia Stenning's number into my mobile. For what felt like many long minutes the phone rang without answer. I imagined the empty house, with its cavernous, echoing hall and worn carpets. Clutching the phone, I willed Jo not to start crying. Suddenly there was a click, and Alicia's voice came on the line.

'Hello?' She sounded older and more frail than I remembered. I pictured her standing over the hall table in her navy cardigan, the dandruff sprinkling her shoulders. I was so tense that it was an effort to speak.

'Alicia?'

'Yes?'

'It's Mel . . . Simon's wife?'

A long pause. For a terrible moment I feared that we had forgotten to tell her about the wedding. Then I recalled the note she had sent, written in spidery italics on an old-fashioned card with her address embossed at the top: *To Simon and his new wife, from Alicia.* If there was supposed to be a present attached, we never discovered it.

'Yes?' she said again. 'What do you want?'

'I need to see you . . . I mean, if that's okay . . . ?'

The line crackled. Placing my hand on Jo's warm tummy, I rocked him a little, until his face creased with smiles.

'Simon's in trouble,' I said, more emphatically. 'I can't talk about it over the phone.'

'I don't know. I . . .' Her voice quavered with uncertainty. 'Please?'

'When do you want to come?'

'Now? If it's at all possible?'

'All right,' she finally said. 'But for goodness sake, don't drag me into another of Simon's messes.'

An hour later I drew up in front of the house. She must have been watching out for the car, for as I pulled on the brake the battered front door opened and she stepped on to the gravel drive, regarding us silently as I pulled Jo from his seat. This morning she was dressed in slacks and a black polo neck that revealed her figure as surprisingly youthful. Her long white hair was untied, the wind causing it to whip savagely around her face. With her straight nose and high cheekbones, she was strangely beautiful. Yet whilst my eyes were on her, she was not looking at me but Jo, with an expression almost of longing. This was the first time she had seen her grandson, I realized with shame. No matter what bad blood had passed between her and Si, it was unforgivable. We hurried across the drive, the wind buffeting us.

'This is Jo,' I said, holding him out. 'I'm sorry it's taken me so long to bring him over.'

For a few seconds she gazed at him, her face softening. Then suddenly she frowned.

'For God's sake, girl, come in out of the weather,' she barked. 'You'll give the poor child pneumonia if you keep waving him around like that.'

We stepped into the chilly hall, where she plucked Jo out of my arms, holding him up and examining him as if he were a pedigree puppy.

'Just like his father,' she said, her jaw working in the way that I remembered from the spring. 'It takes me back.'

'He's a bit of a pickle sometimes,' I mumbled.

'Well, that's the same too, then!'

Marching across the hall and into the sitting room, she competently propped Jo's small body between two large velvet cushions on the sofa, then sat beside him, clasping his tiny fingers in her hand. He gazed across the room at me, his bottom lip quivering.

'He's a bit clingy at the moment . . .' I started.

'Oh, what nonsense! We're not having that, are we, young man? Not with your grandmama? Look, you can play with these keys.'

Scooping up the car keys that I had placed on the card table next to the sofa, she dropped them in his lap. I held my breath. For a moment Jo simply stared at them, undecided. Then his clumsy fingers reached down and brought them happily to his dribbly mouth. I breathed out in relief.

'So why have you come?' Alicia said, turning to me. 'I gather this isn't merely a social call.'

The rebuke in her voice made me flush. 'No. I'm sorry to have just landed on you like this. I really have been meaning to come over. But, you know, what with Jo's birth and everything . . .' She peered at me suspiciously. 'And Si's been away, you see, working on this refurbishment . . .'

'He's not trying to be a great artist any more, then?'

'We need the money.'

She raised her eyebrows, glancing towards the empty grate with what appeared to be anger. The rawness in her eyes filled me with sorrow. What had happened to cause such alienation between mother and son? I stared down at my reddened knuckles, wishing we could be friends.

'The thing is,' I mumbled. 'I mean, the reason why I came

over . . .' My heart had started to thump. It felt as if the words would strangle me. 'I wanted to know about Rosa,' I blurted.

To my surprise she winced, as if the name caused her pain. For a while she seemed to have decided not to respond. She sat stiffly by the fireplace, her blue-veined hands planted firmly on her knees as her eyes went hazy. Then suddenly her face contorted into an ugly smile. She looked up, glaring at me.

'What do you want to know?'

I should get it over and done with. Steeling myself, I managed to look into her watery blue eyes. 'The papers she took from your house, that day we came over . . . What were they about?'

'They were the deeds to her flat.'

'To *her* flat?'

'As far as I'm aware.'

'So why did you have them?'

'I was keeping them safe for her,' she said, frowning. 'She was afraid of Simon taking them, poor girl.'

I swallowed. By now my cheeks were burning. 'So he didn't own the flat?'

There was a long, unpleasant silence. 'I can't explain the exact ins and outs of it,' she eventually said. 'They fought a lot, I'm afraid, and poor Rosa used to come to me for advice. She told me the flat belonged to her, so one can only assume that it did. Since Simon never tells me anything I've obviously only heard her side of the story.'

I tried to arrange my face into an expression of dispassionate interest, but produced only a warped grimace. I felt as if I were shrivelling up, turning into something small and dead. 'I see.'

'Of course her family were terribly well-to-do. According

to her that was always a big draw for Simon.' She stopped, looking at me in perplexity. What did she see? A cheap slapper, not a patch on her precious Rosa?

'I can't imagine him behaving like that,' I murmured.

She ignored my comment. 'I was so thrilled when he first brought her home, you see. She was such a lovely girl. She had a knack of really making one feel appreciated. She used to send me little presents, things she'd seen in the shops that she thought I'd like. Nobody's ever done anything like that for me before, so I was obviously very taken with her. But then, just as I was getting accustomed to it all, Simon started behaving badly and upsetting her and then, suddenly, she called and told me that it was over.' She gave her head a little shake. 'Sometimes I really despair.'

'What happened?' My voice was so faint that for a moment I assumed she hadn't heard. She stared in my direction for a while, looking me over disdainfully as if she had only just noticed my presence. No wonder she despised me. Compared with Rosa's brilliant plumage, I was as common and plain as a suburban sparrow. Now she was starting to chuckle, her mouth turning down into what I could only interpret as an unpleasant smirk.

'Well, obviously she left him. Why would a lovely girl like her put up with that kind of treatment?'

I stared back at her, my face fixed. I think I was nodding, or even trying to smile politely, as if we were discussing gardening or the baking of cakes, but my brain had stalled. *Rosa had left Si!* All this time I had assumed that he had finished the relationship, not the other way around. But now, as Alicia leaned forward, placing her bony fingers on my knee, I realized that this changed everything.

'What kind of treatment?'

'I'm afraid he hit her, dear. He was very jealous, apparently. There were heaps of fights. Poor Rosa used to put up here when it got very bad. She needed someone to stand up for her.' She stopped, regarding me thoughtfully. 'You ought to be careful of him. He can be very changeable.'

'I . . . don't . . .'

She was grinning now, the claws digging harder into my knees. Was she trying to be kind? I blinked at her, remembering Si's sudden anger at my questions, the way his mood would unexpectedly shift, like the darkening of the sky.

'So what's this trouble he's in?' she said abruptly, pulling her hand away from my knee. 'Run out of money again?'

'It's nothing really,' I said, standing. I had been considering telling her about Rosa's disappearance, but now it seemed impossible. Having been drawn so closely to her truths, I needed to pull back before they scalded me. Plucking Jo from his nest of cushions I pushed my face into his belly for a moment, breathing in the rancid smell of his dribbled-upon jumper. I had to get out of the house, before she saw me cry.

'Look, I'm sorry, I need to go. I've just noticed the time.'

Swinging him on to my hip, I pretended to busy myself with searching for my coat.

'But you've only just arrived!'

Alicia was on her feet, too. Placing her hand on my arm, she halted my progress towards the chair where I had flung the nappy bag.

'What's going on?'

'I don't know . . .'

'What don't you know? Why won't you let me help you?'

Gripping Jo's fat legs, I tried to move past her, but she was in the way, her anguished face peering into mine. What would happen if I told her the truth? For a moment I imagined confiding everything: Rosa's mysterious disappearance, the visits of the police, Si's 'lost' credit cards. Could I also share my gnawing fear that my short marriage was doomed?

'Well?'

She folded her arms, waiting. Stepping away from her, I stared through the large bay windows at the tossing trees. A branch from an overhanging sycamore was clicking impatiently on the glass, as if trying to get in.

'It's just that we've run a bit short of money,' I said, trying to sound breezy. 'I was trying to get to the bottom of what papers Rosa had got. I think the mortgage was a bit complicated, so we're trying to work it out, that's all.'

'What was complicated about it? As I told you, the flat belonged to Rosa.'

With the utmost effort, I managed a tight smile. 'Oh, I don't know. Perhaps Si and I have had a miscommunication. He's been away in London, so I've been dealing with all the admin.'

Retrieving my bag, I started to move across the floor towards the door, my arms clamped around my waist. It was such an obvious lie that Alicia did not bother to respond.

'I'm sorry, I really have to go,' I burbled. 'I'm meant to be picking Poppy up early from school. There's tons of roadworks on the motorway, so I should get going before the traffic builds up . . .'

She followed me wordlessly to the hall, tugging open the front door. Outside we could hear the rustle of dead leaves in the wind. As I stepped into the gale, the leaves that had accumulated in the drive gusted around my feet in swirling eddies. Alicia gripped my arm.

'You can go in a minute,' she said. 'But first there's something I want to show you.'

Hooking her fingers around my elbow, she led me down the side of the house, past old garages and neglected herb beds, to the back. The grounds were enormous, far larger than was apparent from the drawing-room windows. Bracing ourselves against the blustering wind, we stood on the mossy lawns, regarding the elegant box hedge that swirled in a semi-circle around the grass, the rose gardens and, at the bottom of the slope, the ornamental pond. Tall firs divided the garden from the ploughed fields beyond.

'You see over there?' Alicia gestured to a wooded area to the east of the lawns. Following her finger, I focused on a giant oak that billowed blowsily in the gusty air. In its branches were the remains of what looked like a tree house, the derelict structure rocking so violently that it seemed to be in danger of imminent collapse.

'Simon made it with his father when he was eleven,' she said. 'He did a lot of it himself. He was always very talented with his hands.'

'It's certainly lasted a long time . . .' I murmured. Pressing Jo to my chest, I glanced towards the house, anxious to get away. The last thing I wanted was for Alicia to insist on some misjudged horticultural tour.

'He used to spend all his time in it,' she went on, ignoring me. 'In the summer he put up a camp bed and slept out here. I'd hardly even see him. He never wanted to play with other boys. He just wanted to build things, and draw. His father was an artist too, you see . . .'

'I didn't know that.'

She laughed bitterly. 'Well, I don't suppose he bothered to tell you, did he? He never mentions poor Leo if he can help it.'

I did not know what to say. Like so many areas of his life, any tentative questions that I put to Si on the subject of his family led to monosyllabic mumbling, his face closing as firmly as a security shutter. I stared at the tree, trying to imagine Si up there, aged eleven. He'd have had shaggy hair like some kids did in the 1970s, and his schoolboy's hands would have been perpetually stained with paint or ink. Like now, he'd have been a dreamer, planning inventions and contraptions as he camped up in the trees. If he'd met me, aged five or six, he'd have been kind and helped me up the ladder to his secret house, pointing out squirrels and telling me the names of birds.

'Never made any money out of it, of course,' Alicia went on. 'And drank like a fish. If it hadn't been for my family we'd have been out on the street.'

'That must have been difficult.'

She glanced around at me, one eyebrow arched. It was a lame comment, but her abrupt confidences were wrong-footing me for I had no reference point, nothing to compare her to. With their middle-England morality, in which you did as you would be done by, endured unpleasantness with disapprovingly sealed lips and kept conversation as neutral as possible, my adoptive parents were as different from Alicia as supermarket Chardonnay is to a bottle of dusty and possibly sour vintage wine.

'In the end the stupid bugger hung himself,' she added, deadpan.

I stared at her in shock, but her face remained unchanged. *Si's father had committed suicide!* 'In the woods over there,' she said evenly. 'Si found him.'

I gasped, my hand fluttering over my mouth in horror. 'Oh, my God!'

Alicia did not respond, just shuddered slightly, pulling her

249

jacket a little more closely around herself. I stared into the dense trees, picturing the discoloured, swinging body. The thought of what Si must have suffered, and how little he had shared with me, clogged my throat.

'How old was he?'

'Twelve or thirteen, I couldn't exactly say.'

Her tongue worked its way around her mouth. She was frowning hard, as if attempting to prevent any emotion from seeping out. 'He never forgave me. Said it was my fault.'

'But that's terrible!'

Involuntarily, I had gripped her arm. Glancing down at my hand, she allowed her fingers to brush against mine. 'Yes, I suppose it is,' she said softly. 'I daresay we mishandled the whole thing. These days there's so much therapy and counselling and so forth. But back then one was supposed to get on with things. So Simon was sent off to school just after the funeral, and not a great deal more was said. It was only when he was older that the difficulties started.'

I nodded, still clutching her arm. 'I'm sure it's not your fault . . .'

For a moment a flimsy intimacy had existed between us. At this clumsy comment, however, Alicia stepped smartly backwards, grabbing at the tendrils of hair that flapped around her face. 'Of course it's my bloody fault.'

Turning, she tramped back over the grass towards the drive. Shifting Jo on to my hip, I followed her miserably. I had clearly angered her. She had wanted to explain her son to me, but my reaction had been thoughtlessly mundane. And despite the veneer of intimacy that marriage and shared parenthood had brought, I was beginning to learn how little I knew about him. As I joined her on the gravel she was gazing up at the tossing trees, her hands clutched behind her back like a sentry man.

'I should be going,' I said quietly. 'Thanks so much for . . .'

She shook her head dismissively. 'I've been a terrible mother, Melanie,' she said. 'I can see that with you it comes naturally, but I've never really had a clue about children. When Si was a teenager, I pretty much left him to his own devices. I simply wasn't able to show him I loved him. That's why he hates me. I only wish I could start the whole damn thing again.'

A dark flush had risen on her cheeks. She gave her head a sharp, angry shake. 'You're a good girl, I can tell that. Love him as much as you can.'

I nodded slowly. 'I'm trying.' My voice was wobbling perilously. I had anticipated subdued hostility from her, or the frigid politeness of the English gentry, not this drench-ing outpour of intimacy. It left me tongue-tied.

Putting out her hand, she placed it around Jo's soft cheek. 'Will you do one thing for me?'

'Of course.'

'Will you bring this little one to see me again?'

'I'd love to.'

Leaning towards her, I kissed her papery cheek. We were oddly alike, I thought as, pulling away, I gazed back at her weather-beaten face. For a second or so her fingers squeezed mine.

'He used to be such a good boy,' she whispered.

I kissed her again, awkwardly, but not without feeling. Then I walked with Jo to my car.

'Bye!' I yelled over the wind. Alicia stood on the drive, watching me but not responding. As I opened the car door a gust snatched it from my fingers, slamming it hard against the metal chassis. For a while I tussled with it, my eyes streaming at the cold air. By the time I had fastened Jo into the baby seat and succeeded in shutting the car doors, she had gone.

28

I drove home fast, swerving around fallen branches and splashing through the grey puddles that pooled in the country roads. What Alicia had told me explained a great deal about Si's moodiness and reticence to talk about his past. Yet rather than dwell on this, my thoughts returned mercilessly to Rosa. Perhaps I was becoming obsessed, for every time my mind cleared, her image would flood into the empty space. I churned relentlessly over what Alicia had said. If she was correct and Rosa had finished with Si, then the entire story I had constructed around our relationship was as false as the gemstones set into Poppy's plastic tiara. The old doubts, held off since the birth of Jo, returned with a vengeance. Now that I had heard of Si's jealousy and desperation to hold on to Rosa our own relationship zoomed into focus, as sharp as broken glass. He had not chosen me in preference to Rosa, but on the rebound from a love that he had lost. She had evicted him from *her* flat, not the other way around: that was why he had torn her portrait from the wall. Perhaps he only took up with me because he needed a place to stay. And when he returned to me in the spring with his proposal of marriage, it was because she had rejected him once more. He had said she was a bitch, but he was obviously still seeing her: he had left his credit cards in her house and had done nothing to stop her from using them. She even kept his picture by her bed.

Pushing into top gear, I grimly accelerated along a stretch of open road that cut through acres of orchards, the stumpy fruit trees rocking in the wind. The car skittered along the road like a marble. So, Si had once been a good boy, but now he 'can be very changeable'; I should 'take care'. So, Rosa had finished with Si. So, she was missing. Surely it did not mean that Si was involved? His mother had said he was violent, but he had never hurt me, had he? Recalling the way he had pushed me on to the floor, my chest tightened. The police had taken a sample of his DNA. What stains had they found in Rosa's house that they wanted to match?

I could not stand these thoughts a moment longer. Jabbing at the radio, I switched to a local station, trying to concentrate on the anodyne tone of the presenter. An exhibition of steam trains was taking place at the weekend, he droned. There was to be a phone-in concerning the provision of local care homes for the elderly. Taut with impatience, I jabbed at the button.

The next station was playing rap, far too grating and violent for my mood. Radio One was broadcasting saccharine pop. Punching at the dial, I caught the tail end of the local news. We were coming to the outskirts of the town; as I approached the traffic lights, I changed down to third gear.

'Some breaking news, just in,' the newsreader announced as perkily as if she were broadcasting news of a bring and buy sale. 'Kent police have confirmed that the weapon they believe may have killed murder victim Jacqui Jenning has been discovered in the gardens of local missing woman Rosa Montague.'

I nearly hit the car ahead of me. With a little shriek I rammed my foot on the brake, narrowly missing its tail lights.

'Police are reported to be gravely concerned about Rosa Montague, who has not been seen since Christmas,' the newsreader went on. 'Police checks at her home near Canterbury have revealed bloodstains in the property, which apparently has been empty since the end of December. Today, in an unexpected twist to the case, a chisel that was discovered in her garden is believed to match the weapon used to murder Jacqui Jenning, who fifteen months ago was discovered dead in a property in Margate . . .'

The lights turned green. I grasped the steering wheel, gawping as they juddered to and fro in the high winds. The newsreader moved to traffic congestion on the M25, but I was no longer listening. *A chisel that was discovered.* The vehicle behind me was sounding its horn, but my car didn't budge. All I could register were those words, tangling up in my head until they no longer made sense. *Believed to match the weapon used to murder Jacqui Jenning.* On the pavement, life continued. A woman pushing a buggy; a group of raucous kids shoving each other; crisp packets, chip papers, yesterday's *Sun*, all whirling senselessly down the road, flapping into the side of a postbox and against people's legs. Despite all his guff about trust and truth, Si had lied to me. He was still seeing Rosa. And now a chisel, believed to be the same weapon that had murdered some other poor woman, had been discovered in her garden.

'Get a move on, ya stupid cow!'

I jerked the car forwards, my teeth chattering with shock. What kind of injuries would a chisel cause? Puncture wounds, splitting soft flesh? Eyes gouged? Skulls pierced and spiked, like chestnuts on a skewer? For a moment the road ahead blurred. Could Si do such a thing? Shaking myself, I peered through the windscreen, trying to push the images away.

'Calm down,' I whispered, as if soothing a small child. 'Just calm down.'

The chisel was nothing to do with Si. There was no hard evidence against him. It would be someone else, a violent lunatic that Rosa had picked up, perhaps. Or a serial killer who stalked single women, the kind of thing one read about in the paper. Horrific, but nothing to do with me. The chisel could not possibly belong to my husband. It was out of the question.

I reached the top of the lane. As the car splashed through the puddles, I could see the tops of the boats swaying on the scuffled water. I passed Trish's place, then the garages, and finally Bob and Janice's dinky little cottage, where I waved overly cheerfully at Janice, who was standing in the doorway. She did not wave back.

Outside the warehouse Si's van was in the drive. Parking the Fiat, I slipped quietly from the driver's seat on to the mud, taking care not to wake Jo, who was lolling happily in the back. Glancing up at the warehouse to check that I was not being observed from a window, I tiptoed to the back of the van. The wind screeched across the boatyard, the masts clicking frantically, but I hardly registered the cacophony, for everything was muffled by the booming of my heart. Praying that they would not be locked, I pushed at the doors. They swung open, flapping on their hinges. Hitching my leg over the back, I climbed inside.

Like most of Si's belongings, the van was in a mess. I burrowed past heaped dust covers, a stepladder, mugs coated with tannin and discarded music magazines. Any minute now Si would wander outside and I would have to explain what I was doing in his van. Delving more deeply into the back, I finally saw what I was searching for. I lugged the toolbox into the light and opened it up.

Everything was there: the tray for nails, bolts and nuts springing out first, covering up a second layer filled with tacks and screws. The next tray was piled with screwdrivers of various sizes, plus a special compartment filled with attachments for drills. I had seen Si use them a hundred times or more, but never before had I examined the screwdrivers. Now I pulled out the familiar tools with their scuffed yellow handles, weighing them in my hand. These were innocent domestic implements, used for erecting flat-pack furniture, not murdering women. The idea that the toolbox contained grisly secrets seemed increasingly ridiculous. Pushing the tray back, I turned to the bottom layer of the box, where Si kept his miscellaneous tools. I had started to forget what I was looking for. The battered appearance of the various hammers and pliers was increasingly reassuring: speckled with paint and chipped by years of handiwork, they waited patiently for the next assignment. There was no gore-splattered weapon here.

But when I reached the bottom of the box I felt myself grow cold. Nestling amongst a collection of small yellow-handled spanners was a new chisel with a smart red handle. I yanked it out, feeling dizzy. It even had the price tag attached, for God's sake.

'What are you doing?'

Twirling around, I found Si standing behind me.

'Hi!' My voice was high and hysterical, like a silly trilling bird. Dropping the chisel back in the box, I jumped clumsily from the van, banging my knee hard on the edge.

'I need to wake Jo up. He's been asleep for ages!' I cried. But as I scurried towards my car, Si stopped me, his hand on my arm.

'What were you doing in the van?'

'Looking for a screwdriver . . . the wing mirror's coming loose . . .'

It was blatantly untrue. He stared at me, as if through a

fog. His grey face was drawn, his eyes bloodshot. He had cut himself shaving, I noticed, and had stemmed the blood with a scrap of toilet paper, which now stuck to his chin like a tiny white flag. Raising his eyebrows, he walked over to the van and gently closed the back doors.

'Where've you been?'

'Just for a drive.'

Opening my car door, I unstrapped Jo and heaved him out. When I turned around, Si was standing in the same spot, still gazing at me. As my eyes caught his, he looked away, biting his lip. From the careful manner in which his eyes now studied the gravel, I could tell that he knew I was lying. He knew about the chisel, too, I was sure.

'Let me have him for a bit,' he said. 'It's ages since I've had a cuddle.'

I gripped Jo more tightly. 'He's smelly,' I mumbled. 'I need to change him.'

'I'll do it. You go and pick up Pops.'

'Nah, it's okay. There's plenty of time.'

Pushing past him, I hurried inside.

We spent the rest of the day apart. As I watched cartoons with Poppy, fed her pasta and put her to bed, I could hear Si's drill upstairs, a high-pitched screech that made my head throb. When the sound finally stopped and his footsteps clumped down the stairs, I made sure that I was too busily engrossed in the children to look up or speak to him. I only registered his thin figure loping across the ground floor after he had passed, head down and eyes averted. He appeared twice, once to get a beer from the fridge, the second time to retrieve his mobile. We did not exchange so much as a glance.

*

258

'Mummy, what's the matter with Si?'

'Nothing, honey. He's just busy.'

'Why doesn't he come and sing to me any more?'

'I'm sure he will later, once all this building is over.'

'Can I come in your bed tonight?'

I paused, regarding Poppy's eager face. With her body wedged next to mine, Si could not touch me. And if I was asleep before he came upstairs, we could delay the inevitable exchange that I was so desperate to avoid.

'All right then. In fact I'm so pooped I think I'll come to bed with you now.'

'Yes!'

She punched the air in triumph, having just scored a rare and unexpected treat. After tucking Jo into his sleeping bag and switching on his Sleep-A-Bye lullaby tape, I quickly brushed my teeth and slipped into bed beside her.

'Mummy?'

'Uhuh?'

'That ghost isn't coming in the house any more . . .'

'Good!'

Enveloping her body in my arms, I kissed her silky hair. She was getting so big, her long bony legs knocking into mine, her hand no longer fitting so snugly into my palm. I had neglected her in the last few months, I thought sadly. Sighing, she rested her head on the pillow.

'I love you, Mummy.'

'I love you, too.'

Her eyes closed. Within seconds her breathing thickened, becoming slow and rhythmic. I lay beside her, listening to the wind bashing around the building and watching her lovely face. I think I was in shock, for my brain was refusing to work properly, sticking on specific details, then sliding off in another direction, like melting snow. I recalled

Alicia standing in the doorway of her battered house and the terrible things she had told me. *Why would a lovely girl like her put up with treatment like that?* He had hit her, had become obsessively jealous, she said. *He can be very changeable.* And now Si was linked to this poor woman whose name I had never even heard before. How did the pathologists know she'd been murdered by the chisel? Were there marks on her skull, or was it from DNA or some other forensic clue? As Poppy sighed and flopped over, I recalled the scene in the drive. Si *knew* what I was looking for inside his van. And there it was, nestling so innocently amongst his yellow-handled tools: a new red chisel, the price tag still stuck to its base. Over and over the images churned. It was like being caught in a blizzard, with no idea of where to turn.

I don't know how long I lay next to Poppy, staring into the dark. By the time I heard Si's footsteps approaching the door, I had started to plan our escape. We would go to Pat's, I decided. Even if I had to put up with months of her pursed lips and reproachful sighs, I could not bear to stay another night in the same house with this stranger whose presence now made my heart dip, not with excited desire, but fear. His mother had said I should try to love him, but after everything I now knew, it no longer seemed possible.

He was in the bedroom now, padding around the bed and lifting the covers. I held my breath as he climbed inside. Surely he would assume that I was asleep?

'Mel?'

I lay rigidly under the covers, willing him into silence.

'Are you awake?'

Rolling over, I pulled the pillow over my head in a masquerade of exhaustion. 'Mmph . . .'

'I'm not involved with Rosa Montague going missing, you

know that, don't you?' His voice was thin and faltering, as if close to tears. 'Mel?'

I did not reply.

We were woken the next morning at dawn. Outside the wind had dropped, leaving the sky pale and lifeless, as if exhausted by the exertions of the previous day. I opened my eyes, gazing through the blinds at the sky. Downstairs someone was banging at the door.

We both knew who it was. Jumping up, Si threw on his clothes. His face was grey, and as he fumbled with the buttons of his shirt, his hands trembled. In the bed Poppy curled up tighter, gathering the covers around her.

'Who is it, Mummy?'

'No one. Go back to sleep.'

I hurried after Si, arriving at the top of the stairs just as he opened the door. As the policemen spoke to him he glanced back at me, his eyes panicked. The night before I had hated and feared him, but now my heart turned over with pity. Swallowing hard, I returned the glance with a tiny smile.

On the ground floor the two men were stepping inside: Dave Gosforth, with his leather jacket and brogues, and the younger man, this time wearing jeans. I could not hear what they were saying, but their faces were grave. I did not like their posture, either: it was too stiff and tense for another routine visit. Clattering down the steps, I arrived by Si's side just in time to hear Gosforth say, '. . . you do not have to say anything, but it may harm your defence if you do not mention when questioned something which you later rely on in court. Anything you do say may be given in evidence.'

'You're arresting him!'

Gosforth turned to me, nodding sadly. 'I'm afraid we are,

Melanie. We also have a warrant to search these premises, so you may want to be somewhere else for the day.'

'But he hasn't done anything!'

I could hold it back no longer. The lump in my chest was forcing its way out, making me paw uselessly at Si's arms, my knees sagging.

'You didn't kill that woman, did you?'

He bit his lip, not looking at me.

'For God's sake, what have you done?'

He just shook his head. Gosforth was cradling his elbow with his hand, propelling him towards the door. Feeling the other man's fingers on my arm, I shook them angrily away.

'Try and calm down, Mel,' he said gently.

'Don't tell me to fucking calm down!'

I fell back against the wall, watching aghast as Si was led out of the warehouse and into the back of Gosforth's blue saloon. There was a police van parked beside it, I noticed with shock. As Gosforth reversed his car around the builders' rubble, a second group of uniformed officers were making their way towards me. One of them had a sheaf of papers in his hands. He started to introduce himself, explaining politely about the search warrant and the need to impound Si's van, but I hardly heard. All I could focus on was Si, disappearing up the lane in the back of the unmarked car. Not once had he looked around at me. Instead, he was staring straight ahead, his face set, as if all along this was what he had been expecting.

29

Si was arrested on suspicion of the murder of Jacqui Jenning and the abduction of Rosa Montague. The police had had a breakthrough in the case, but the search team refused to tell me what it was. They trudged inside, not making eye contact as they swarmed through the building. The search of the premises would take all day, I was told. They would be grateful if I could provide a statement, too. I watched, dazed, as the insides of my kitchen drawers were pulled out, the cutlery removed. How could our home, with its kiddie pictures on the walls and toy-strewn rooms, become the scene of a criminal investigation? In the living room they were pulling up floorboards, poking around the dead spaces where the kitchen had still to be fitted. They'd need full access to all the outbuildings and storerooms, they said. Could I come straight back after dropping Poppy at school? They planned to take me to a police 'suite' where they'd be taking the statement.

I bundled Poppy and Jo outside, feeling sick. In the drive Si's van was being loaded on to a truck. I hurried up the lane, picturing his toolbox and the brand-new chisel. When we passed Bob and Janice peering curiously from their front garden at the commotion in the boatyard, I took care to look in the other direction.

Poppy ran into school without a word. As we'd hurried up the lane I'd told her that a lady had gone missing and the police were trying to find out where she had gone. She nodded soberly, her eyes wide.

'Those policemen won't find that lady,' she suddenly announced as we reached the top of the lane.

'What do you mean, honey?'

''Cos she's in heaven. Si's turned her into an angel.'

I spun around, goggling at her.

'What?'

'He painted a picture of her. She was wearing a white frilly dress and had wings. I saw him burning her up.'

'What on earth do you mean?'

She was tripping merrily beside me, her eyes flashing mischievously.

'He said he didn't want to look at her any more.'

'Poppy!' Grabbing her by her wrist, I yanked her backwards so that she was forced to turn and face me. I felt as if I might burst. 'Are you winding me up, madam?'

'No!'

But her eyes sparkled. Looking away, she stuffed her hand over her mouth.

'Then what do you mean he burnt her up?'

'He burnt up her picture.'

'When? Which picture are you talking about?'

I had started to shout. On the other side of the road a woman with two little boys frowned disapprovingly.

'I'm not telling you, Mummy!' Poppy hissed. 'Stop pinching, you're hurting me!'

Wrenching her arm away, she glared at me furiously. 'I *hate* you!'

We walked the rest of the way to school in silence.

After dropping Poppy off, I trailed back along the dreary streets, past rows of turn-of-the century red-bricks, with their neat privet hedges and Ikea furniture. Inside, women were bustling around, tidying up the breakfast things, or getting their toddlers ready for a trip to the swings. Other houses were empty, their occupants squashed on to trains or already packed into their multi-storey offices. Once I had pretended to despise such normal lives. I wanted travel and excitement, to be different. But now, as I glanced into the almost identical front rooms, I yearned to have what their owners enjoyed. Solid, well-worn marriages, with a couple of children to love. A nice garden, plans for home improvement, regular holidays in the sun. Was that not what most people aspired to? Decent, ordinary lives, unblemished by lies. This was what I had tried to have. It was why I had married Si, and why I had moved to Kent. Yet now I knew I would never get it. For rather than returning to my so-called 'home' for a morning of domestic chores or to prepare for a visit to the park, I was going to spend my morning being questioned by the police about the whereabouts of my husband's mistress. Meanwhile the building in which I was supposed to be discovering the joys of conjugal life was being pulled apart as the police searched for her body.

I started to jog along the pavement, my head down as Jo's buggy bumped over the paving slabs. All the way to school I had reined myself in, but now I gave in to great hiccupping sobs, not caring about the strange looks I attracted. How could the man I had loved so intensely, who had fathered my precious baby, stand accused of *murder*? It was surreal, like buying a ticket for a romantic comedy and slowly realizing that one was instead watching a horror flick.

When I got back to the warehouse, a car was waiting for me. I stood in the drive, watching in dismay as Si's plastic-bagged clothes were loaded into the police van. The computer was gone too, I noticed as I stumbled around the living room trying to locate Jo's nappy bag. In the brief half hour that I had been gone, the place had been ripped away from my tentative ownership, reduced to the sum of these previously unimagined parts: a newly laid floor, underneath which a corpse might be crammed, a wardrobe where a weapon could be hidden, my old sheets, in which my husband might have wrapped his girlfriend's body. Clothes, revealing stains; computers that might open, like windows, on to our secrets. Plank by plank, the police were dismembering our life.

I was driven to Sittingbourne, where, in a quiet cul-de-sac, I was shown into a Barrett-like home. It was a special suite, where they conducted the more sensitive interviews, the plain-clothed policewoman who appeared from the back of the house pleasantly informed me. They couldn't haul a breastfeeding mum and her little baby off to the police station, could they? They would be recording the interview, she went on; amongst other devices the room into which I was shown was equipped with a video camera. The place reminded me of Pat: pastel colours, beige curtains, stripy wallpaper, a salmon-coloured sofa. On the floor was a large plastic crate, filled with second-hand toys; if there had been dog-eared magazines rather than a large glass ashtray on the coffee table, it could have been a doctors' surgery. I was given a cup of muddy-coloured tea, but couldn't drink it. I breastfed Jo to sleep, trying not to weep at his innocence. Then the video was turned on and I was interviewed.

I sat in the comfy chair facing my interrogator, too horrified to process what was happening. Each line of questioning provoked a fresh spurt of alarm, like electric currents pumped through my veins. Had my husband ever talked about his relationship with Rosa Montague, the policewoman asked, smiling politely. No, I mumbled, he never told me anything. Was I aware that he had been seeing her in December? Perhaps there was some reason why he had visited her cottage before Christmas? Would I know what it was? They were particularly interested in his movements during December. Could I account for them? Or perhaps there were unexplained absences? I gazed back at her, unable to think clearly. Only later would the correct answers come to me, like after an exam. I'd need to look at the calendar, I muttered; it was all a bit of a fog. Did Simon ever borrow my car, the woman suddenly asked. Could I explain why he'd apparently scrubbed the passenger seat of his van? At this information I clutched at Jo, feeling as if I were falling. In my experience Simon never cleaned *anything*, especially not the inside of his van.

And then there was the building work. What exactly were we doing to the warehouse? Stumblingly, I started to explain our plans, aware only of the woman's sceptical expression. What was Simon doing in the loft? I didn't exactly know. Was she correct that a new floor had been laid in the living room? Did Simon do this work alone, or with someone else? Where else had floorboards been put down? What about walls or other features? Could I explain exactly what work had been completed since December? I stared at the print on the wall behind the woman's head, a Monet that was presumably supposed to relax the interviewees. My mind felt overloaded, as if a fuse might blow. There had been no substantial work on the warehouse since Jo's birth in November, I replied in a monotone. Si was sanding down the beams in the loft and painting it. The living-room floor was laid in September. The only digging that had taken place had been for drains and carried out by the builders; I couldn't recall when.

The questions went on for hours, circling around Si's whereabouts and the building, returning again and again to the same topics, like a prowling cat about to pounce. Then suddenly the interview was over. If I could wait for a short while, they'd prepare a statement for me to read over and sign, I was informed. After that I was free to go. It was 12 p.m., the middle of what I thought must be the worst day in my life. What I know now, of course, is that it was only the beginning.

30

The police car dropped me at the top of the lane. They'd be searching the premises until at least six or seven that evening, the policewoman told me. If I could spend the rest of the day with a friend it would be helpful. Helpful or not, it was inconceivable that I return to the warehouse whilst the police remained inside. Barging through Trish's gate, I hammered at her door. As she opened it, I virtually fell into her arms.

'Thank God you're in!'

'Blimey, Mel. What on earth's going on? There's police everywhere!'

'I have to talk to you.'

Taking Jo from my arms, she led me inside her cosy kitchen. In here, with her scrubbed slate tiles and terracotta walls, it was hard to believe that only a short distance away forensic experts were sifting through the insides of the warehouse. I slumped by the Aga, wiping at my face with the back of my hand as Trish clicked on the kettle. It was the first time I had been inside the cottage: she had been decorating, so we had got into the habit of meeting at the warehouse. I gazed around, taking in my surroundings. The warmth and brightness of the room instantly soothed me. Over the window she had strung up a length of Rajastani fabric embroidered with tiny mirrors and bells; on the whitewashed table was an artful arrangement of pebbles and driftwood. On the wall she had hung an old-fashioned railway clock; underneath it the butler's sink gleamed. It was a shame we couldn't sit in the sunny sitting room, she'd mentioned as she showed me inside, but she'd just started painting in there.

'It's perfect in here,' I mumbled as she handed me my mug. 'You're so creative.'

She shrugged, as impatient with small talk as ever.

'God, Trish,' I burst out. 'Everything's in such a mess!'

'Tell me.'

Squatting down, she brushed her fingers against my cheek. I gazed into her eyes, longing to confide in her, yet not sure where to start.

'Si's been arrested. They think he's killed this woman . . .'

'Jesus!'

Shock, but not the voyeuristic curiosity I had feared, registered on her face. Taking my hand in hers, she placed an arm around my shoulders.

'How horrendous!'

For a while I flopped against her, unable to continue. Then, very slowly, I told her everything. My story was like patching a quilt of rags, filled with fraying gaps and odd fragments that did not fit, but she kept holding my hand and nodding as if it all made perfect sense. I had trusted Si, I blubbed; I had truly believed that he loved me. Or rather, I was so desperate not to be alone that I had wilfully closed my eyes to any evidence to the contrary, beguiled by his passionate insistence that we could start our lives anew. But from the very beginning he had been lying. He had lied about Rosa, lied about the flat and lied about his credit cards. And now, as the neighbours peered from their upstairs windows, the police were trawling through our possessions whilst Si was being interrogated by the police over the murder of one woman and the abduction of another.

'It's not exactly your average marital breakdown, is it?' I finished mournfully.

Trish's pale face gazed back into mine, her eyebrows raising into little arches of amazement.

'Not exactly, no.'

I tried to smile, but my face was wobbling again. 'I'm so pathetic! I know I ought to just grab the kids and leave him, but a bit of me still wants to believe that he hasn't got anything to do with these murders. I mean, suppose he didn't do it?'

Trish regarded me gravely, her knuckles pressed to her mouth.

'One minute I'm thinking about that chisel and what it must have done to that poor woman in Margate and I'm completely terrified of him. Then the next I remember what he used to be like and how much I loved him and I can't believe this is happening to us . . .'

'But it *is* . . .'

'Like, back in the spring he told me Rosa was this clingy bitch he couldn't shake off.'

Trish frowned, almost wincing.

'Are you okay?'

'Yeah, it's just another Braxton Hicks.' She put her hand on her belly, waiting for the tightening to pass. 'Sorry, hon, I'm still listening.'

'I mean, I really believed him,' I continued. 'It made sense. He'd had this horrendous relationship, he said, but he'd finished it. Yet now it's like everything's been turned upside down, what with his mother saying that *Rosa* ended it and he was devastated. So why does he keep telling me he can't stand the sight of her?'

'Maybe he's angry that she dumped him. Some people can't stand being rejected.'

'You mean enough to bump her off?'

In his buggy Jo had started to grumble. Rising, I pulled him from his harness, then flopped down again with him on my lap. 'I believed everything he said!' I wailed. 'I mean, he seemed so keen to move on. And he told me I was the only woman he'd ever loved! He said with this Rosa woman it was just about sex. But now it turns out he was still seeing her . . .'

Trish looked at me sadly. Standing, she started to clear away the mugs. 'I think you should leave him,' she said flatly.

'I *believed* him.'

'Of course you did. We always believe what we want to hear.'

'I don't want to leave him . . .' I was starting to cry again. Moving quickly back to my side, Trish gave me another hug.

'But you have to. I mean, what about the kids? Supposing you're putting them in danger?'

'Si would never hurt the kids!'

The expression on her face told me what she thought.

I spent the rest of the afternoon at Trish's cottage, leaving only to fetch Poppy from school. We did not return to the warehouse until after six. As we walked through the boat-yard, I could see the police loading various bagged items into their vehicle. Other men were pulling off their white overalls and rubber gloves, chatting and laughing with the relaxed air of workers who had just clocked off. I wheeled the buggy stonily over the drive, filled with an irrational loathing for their sanctimonious smirks. They were taking the computer, a goofy-toothed officer informed me, plus our mobile phones, all of Si's clothes and all of his shoes. I was given a form to sign, releasing the items for further investigation, then they were gone.

Inside, everything felt disjointed and displaced. I shuffled around the ground floor, picking things up then placing them down again, as if I wasn't sure what they were for. It was not that the police had made a mess of our possessions. Rather, the happy chaos of our lives had been tidied into neat piles and no longer seemed to be ours. As Poppy splashed in the bath and Jo squirmed on his play mat, I wandered around the place, feeling numb. I hated it here, I decided as I kicked at the loosened planks. However hard we tried to wrench it into our possession, the building would always remain an industrial warehouse: cold, draughty and damp. As I clanked up the steps to bring Poppy a towel for her bath I recalled the first time I'd visited, and the ominous feelings the place had evoked. I should have taken my cue from the starlings that flapped in the rafters seeking an escape. The place was malevolent, full of ghosts. It was being here that had ruined us.

Later that night I packed our bags. It was Saturday tomorrow, and I planned to leave for Pat's first thing. When the phone rang I ignored it, sure it was Si.

31

25 February 2005

So. They had the murder weapon, with traces of Jacqui Jenning's DNA smeared over it. They had Rosa Montague's blood sprinkled in tiny patches on the walls of her cottage. And, most promisingly of all, they had a very interesting DNA match to the semen stain found on Jacqui Jenning's sheets. It had been a particularly sweet moment when the result of that little test had come in; no wonder Stenning had been so jittery about having his mouth swabbed. They still didn't have enough evidence for a conviction, but Dave had high hopes that by the end of the week they'd be charging him with double murder. It was true that so far their evidence was wholly circumstantial. Even if he was the man who had left the Starlite night club with Jacqui fifteen months earlier, it didn't prove that he had killed her. And, disappointingly, the search of his property had failed to yield a body. But at least they'd got the van. In a day or so they'd get the results of the DNA tests of those interesting patches on the passenger seat. Dave would put money on a direct match with Rosa Montague's DNA.

There was also the hope that he'd simply cave in and confess. They were going to press him as hard as was legally permissible, they'd decided, really make him wriggle and squirm. At the moment he was saying nothing, asserting total innocence, his arms folded and his face haughty, but after twelve or so hours of their questioning Dave was reasonably confident he'd start to cave. Men of his sort often got weepy: the posh ones, who weren't used to the hard treatment. They'd realize that they couldn't get out of it, and then turn on the waterworks, like little boys.

Chomping at the last piece of pizza, he wiped his mouth with the back of his hand and stood up. Once again he was eating his dinner on the hoof. He didn't know when he'd next get home; when they got this close to cracking a case he liked to push on and on until they got a result. They planned to grill Stenning for another hour or so. Then they'd give him a little break and start again. It would probably go on all night.

I slept fitfully, waking every hour or so from uneasy dreams in which men forced their way into the building or chased me through claggy mud. In the bed beside me Poppy kicked like a donkey, whilst her baby brother yowled at regular intervals for a feed. By dawn I finally collapsed into deep slumber, waking with a start to find that it was nearly ten. Sitting up, I looked around the room in bemusement. They had snuggled in my bed all night, but now Poppy and Jo had vanished.

Pulling on my clothes, I stumbled along the gallery. What I saw on the floor below left me temporarily speechless. Lounging on the sofa, one arm around Poppy, the other supporting Jo on his knee, was Si. Jo was squealing with laughter, his arms thrown back in ecstasy as Si tickled his tummy. As she watched them, Poppy was beaming.

'Do it to me!' she pleaded. 'It's my turn now!'

I walked slowly down the stairs, the colour draining from my face. The scene was identical to so many others in which I had watched Si play with the kids: an unremarkably happy picture of family life. Now it was part of another world, like finding the ghosts of long-dead relatives sitting around one's table.

'Hi,' Si said turning around and smiling at me as I reached the bottom of the stairs. 'I've given them their breakfast. I didn't want to wake you.'

I swallowed. He looked painfully thin, the sleeves of his jumper hanging from his bony wrists, his drawn face anxious. His left eye was twitching slightly, as if he was more nervous than he wished to admit. I walked slowly across the floor towards him. So much had changed that I did not know what to say.

'Mummy! Si says that as soon as he finishes making those rooms at the top, we're going to Spain!'

Leaping from the sofa, Poppy skidded over the floorboards and into my legs. Reaching down, I fingered her hair. I could not take my eyes from Si.

'They let you out, then,' I eventually murmured.

'They released me without charge. They don't have any real evidence.' He attempted to smile, his face crinkling unnaturally at the edges.

'How did you get back here?'

He blinked at me. 'I got Ol to come over. He's lent me one of his bangers. I dropped him at the station on the way back.'

'That's kind of him.'

'He's a very old friend.'

We fell silent, simultaneously glancing away from each other. We were like ill-matched partners on a blind date, struggling hopelessly for conversation.

'Have you done Jo's nappy?'

'Yup.'

'And he's had his bottle?'

'That too.'

'And now everything's going to be fine and dandy, is it?'

'So long as we think positive.'

His eye went into spasm. Reaching up to his father's face with his chubby arms, Jo pushed his tiny fingers inside his mouth.

'Watch out, sausage, or I'll bite you! Grr!'

Jo pealed with laughter. Placing him gently on the mat, Si walked towards me, holding out his hands.

'But first we need to talk.'

I put a video on for Poppy and we filed into the ramshackle kitchen, where I silently prepared the coffee. When it was ready I handed Si his mug and sat down at the table, staring at my pale hands. If I glanced up and saw his face I knew that the resolve of the previous day would dissolve, like ice held over a fire.

'I didn't do it, Mel,' he said quietly. 'I swear to you.'

I studied my rings. I could not have spoken even if I had wanted to.

'But there is some stuff I have to tell you about.' He took a breath, as if steadying himself. Glancing up, I stared at his pale face.

'I spent the night with Jacqui Jenning the night before she was killed,' he said quietly. 'The police have matched my DNA to stains they found on her sheets. That's why they arrested me yesterday. I was the last person to see her alive, so it's not surprising they wanted to talk to me. But I didn't bloody kill her; you've got to believe me. And I'm not in the habit of picking up women in crummy night clubs, either. It was an idiotic thing to do, but I'd just finished with Rosa and I was very drunk and very angry.'

He stopped, placing his fingers around his mug. They were trembling so violently that coffee dribbled over the rim. 'I have no idea what's happened to Rosa,' he finished. Something in his voice was wrong, too insistent and definite, as if it was a lie he had repeated many times over. When I managed to reply, my voice was hoarse. 'Where's she got to, then?'

'I don't know. The last time I saw her was before Christmas. Like I told you, I had to go and see her to sort out some stuff. After that I have absolutely no idea what happened to her. As far as I was concerned I was never going to see her again.'

I stared at my coffee. The milk had curdled slightly and now rose to the surface in greasy blobs. All I could think was that he was lying. He'd obviously returned to Rosa for sex. After being stuck for so long with me and my neuroses, he was gagging for a different body, toned and young, an attractive change from my post-natal sag.

'So what was all this stuff you had to sort out with her?' I said coldly. 'You've never actually explained to me what it was.'

'Oh, God . . .' He half stood, then sat down again, running his hands through his greasy hair. 'It doesn't really matter, babe. It's all in the past . . .'

'Were you still sleeping with her?'

'No!'

'Then what the hell was it?'

Pressing his eyes shut, he rubbed at them with his thumbs. Perhaps he was on the verge of tears, for when he finally opened them the whites were angry and inflamed.

'She was blackmailing me,' he said heavily. 'Ol stupidly gave her our number and she started ringing up and saying she was going to come over here and give me even more grief. I couldn't stand it. I was feeling completely harassed. So I caved in and went to see her. She promised that all she wanted was to see me one last time, then she'd let me go.'

I folded my arms. I felt as if I were a child and he, the adult, was fobbing me off with fairy stories. 'What was she blackmailing you about?'

'Oh fuck, babe. I don't want to have to go into all that.'

'Just tell me the truth!'

'Okay, if you really insist, then I will.'

Pushing back his chair, he stared into my face. I could feel my muscles tense, in preparation for the blow.

'I slept with her in May,' he said. 'I was confused about you being pregnant, so I went back to her for those few weeks that we were apart. It was completely stupid and I regret it more than anything in the world. I should have told you the truth at the time, but I was terrified of losing you. I'm really, really sorry, okay?'

I gazed back at his exhausted face. In some ways my anticipation of the truth had been worse than the actual fact, and now I felt oddly calm. It was exactly as my girlfriends had warned. Despite his bullshit promises, this stranger who I'd married had been deceiving me from the start.

'So that evening, when you asked me to marry you and promised you hadn't seen Rosa, you were lying?' I said flatly.

'I was desperate not to lose you. Please, babe, say you'll forgive me.'

I shook my head in irritation. Perhaps he had expected tears, or a scene. But now that my fears were, at least partly, confirmed, all I felt was the cold certainty that I no longer loved him. 'So why did you lie about your flat?'

He frowned. 'What do you mean?'

'Your mother says the flat belonged to her, not you.'

His expression suddenly changed. 'What the hell has my mother got to do with it?'

'I went to see her. That was what she told me.'

He glanced over at me in surprise. His eyes had narrowed, and his cheeks had sunk a notch further into his skull.

'You did *what*?'

'I went to see her the day before yesterday. She told me that Rosa owned the flat, not you.'

'She's *lying!*'

Without warning his hand crashed on to the table, spilling my coffee on to Poppy's school bag. I stared at the steaming puddle in shock, hardly daring to breathe.

'So why should I believe you and not her?' I whispered. 'Seems like all you ever do is tell me a big fat pile of lies.'

Grabbing my hand, he gave it a violent squeeze.

'I'm not lying to you! My mother doesn't know a fucking thing! Rosa has her twisted around her little finger! She manipulates her, Mel, like she manipulates everyone else. She'll do anything to keep clinging on!'

'You've never stopped being in love with her,' I whispered. 'You couldn't stand her leaving you, so you went back to her cottage and –'

'Still in love? Jesus! If only you knew!'

'If only I knew what?'

'How much I detest her! Honestly, Mel, I can't stand the sight of her! We were "in lurve",' he wiggled his fingers in the air in a grotesque parody of the phrase, 'for about two or three months and ever since then I've been trying to escape from her. She's completely obsessive. It's like she's smothering me, moving into my flat, taking over my things, even bringing my bloody mother into it!'

I no longer cared about his lies. At that moment, all I was sure about was that our marriage was over. Glancing into his agonized face, I pulled my hand quickly away, rising to my feet. I could not bear to be with him a moment longer. Yet as I started to move past him, he grabbed my wrist.

'Please, Mel! You have to trust me! Rosa's disappearance hasn't got anything to do with me!'

He was gripping my wrist so hard that it hurt. I yanked

it away. I had moved beyond reason, swept into a place where all that mattered was my certainty that he had betrayed me.

'You ask me to trust you, but you've never been honest with me, not once,' I said, my voice rising. 'From the very beginning you've been lying. You lied about Rosa, and you lied about your flat. Even if you wanted to tell the truth, I don't think you'd know where to start. All the time we've been together, you've never once told me about anything that really mattered, just all this bullshit about Spain and this bloody building that we're never, ever going to get finished!'

He opened his mouth, then closed it. His face had assumed the hard, shut-in expression that had become so familiar. No longer caring how he reacted, I charged on. 'I'm sick of your lies!' I spat. 'How can we build a proper marriage when you're always so secretive!'

'I have tried to tell you things . . . I find it hard . . .'

'What about? You won't even discuss when the kitchen's going to be fitted! I mean, why didn't you tell me about your father killing himself? Did you think I wouldn't be interested?'

Folding his arms he stared into space, his eyes blank. 'It's not something I find particularly pleasant to discuss.'

'Particularly pleasant? Jesus! I was such an idiot to . . .'

We both knew what I had been about to say. As I attempted to brush past him and move towards the door, he jumped to his feet and stood before me, blocking my exit. His face seemed to have caved in on itself, his skin sagging, his lips drained of colour.

'Where are you going?'

'I need to get Jo.'

'No you don't, he's fine! Why won't you look at me?'

Slowly I turned my head towards him. For a terrible

moment our eyes met. He was close to tears, his reddened eyes glazed. His mouth was turned down, as if desperately repressing a howl of anguish; his eyelid still twitched. He looked crazed: the kind of person one might cross the road to avoid passing. Yet once I had loved him. Through him, I had imagined that everything might change, our lives transformed into a sunshine-filled idyll of happy-ever-afters. As I stared at him, I knew that those fantasies had finally evaporated, the way that the last furls of mist disperse in the morning sun. He could never save me from myself for he was a stranger, whose stories I no longer believed.

'You don't love me any more, do you?' His voice was soft, but his face was clenched with emotion. His arms went rigid, his fists bunched. Flinching, I moved backwards, bumping into the cooker behind.

'I don't know how I feel about anything any more . . .'

'Please, Mel, don't say that . . . you and the kids mean everything to me!'

Now he was leering over me, his hand on my shoulder as if he were about to push me to the floor. I glared back at him, my palms clammy. I had to get away. As soon as I could, I had to get the children and our bags into the car and accelerate up the lane and away from the warehouse and him as fast as possible. It was exactly as Trish had warned: he was dangerous. And now, as I cowered into the cooker, I knew that he must not guess that I planned to leave.

'I do love you,' I whispered. 'I promise.'

The muscles in his face relaxed. He breathed out, his fingers stroking my freezing cheek. 'I couldn't bear it if you didn't,' he said quietly. 'You're the only person left.'

Forcing myself to smile, I edged away from his taut body. 'I'm just feeling a bit upset,' I muttered. 'And I need the loo.

I'll be back down in a sec. Why don't you have a nice hot bath? We can talk about this more later.'

He nodded, finally releasing me. 'Yeah, that's a good idea.'

I took the stairs two at a time, crashing into the bedroom. Grabbing my half-packed rucksack from the floor, I flung it under the bed. Now I could hear Si's footsteps following me up the stairs. For a moment I froze, desperately scanning the room for evidence of my planned escape. Yet rather than enter the bedroom, I heard his footsteps stop by the bathroom. The door clicked open and then shut. After a second or so, the pipes began to gurgle.

I had five or ten minutes, max. Scurrying around the room, I gathered the few things that I had still to pack: underwear and a change of clothes for me, a handful of Babygros for Jo. Emboldened by the slooshing of water next door, I pushed the clothes inside the rim of the rucksack, hastily zipping it up. My purse was in my bag by the front door. The kids' coats were heaped in the lobby. Forcing myself to move more slowly, I strolled out of the bedroom and pushed open the bathroom door.

Si was immersed in deep, steaming water, his eyes closed. He was going bald, I noticed as I peered down at his head. The little patch of scalp that showed through his thinning hair made my heart dip with unexpected pity.

'All right, love?'

He gave a start, his eyes opening. 'Yeah . . .'

'You look like you're settling in for the morning . . .'

Holding his nose, he slipped under the soapy water, emerging a moment later with a great sigh, like a water buffalo from a pond. Water streamed from his hairy body, his sodden fringe dripping over his eyes. Wiping it away, he gave himself a little shake.

'I'll be a while . . .' he said vaguely.

Nodding, I pretended to saunter from the room, closing the door firmly behind me. Then, diving back into the bedroom, I yanked the rucksack out from under the bed, hauling it on to my back as I leapt down the stairs.

In the living room Poppy was still watching her video. Next to her, Jo had nodded off.

'Quick!' I hissed. 'Get your coat!'

Her face crumpled with bemusement.

'Where are we going?'

'Out!'

Grabbing my bag, which was lying on the floor, I bundled Jo into my arms. 'Please, Pops! We have to move fast!'

'But I don't want to go out . . .'

'We have to!'

Hauling her up, I strode across the room and turned off the TV, ignoring her yelps of protest. Scampering to the front door, I started to rifle through my bag for the car keys. 'Get your coat, honey! And can you get Jo's too?'

'No.'

I felt as if I might burst. 'Poppy, *please*!'

She must have registered the desperation in my voice, for she started to slowly trail across the living room towards the hall.

'Hurry up! Please, darling . . .'

Pressing Jo to my shoulder with one hand and balancing the rucksack and my bag on the other arm, I nudged open the front door with my elbow. Upstairs I could hear water draining from the bath. In a few moments Si would re-appear.

'Come on!' I trilled. 'Everyone in the car!'

But even as I said this, I could see that it was hopeless. I stood despairingly on the doorstep, my useless words fading into the thin winter air. Parked haphazardly by the gate, the battered Volvo that Si had borrowed from Ollie blocked my Fiat in. Even as Poppy pushed past me and skipped over the icy mud towards the passenger seat, I knew that whatever pretext I dreamt up, I could never ask Si to move Ollie's car. I did not have the courage to lie convincingly; the tremor in my voice would give the game away.

'Poppy!' I yelled. 'Run into the kitchen and get Si's car keys from his coat!'

She swerved around, about to head back inside the house, but as she did, I heard the creak of the stairs. Struggling to free myself from the rucksack, I dropped it on the floor and kicked it under a bundle of coats.

'Forget it, honey!' I hissed. 'We'll go out later!'

Turning, I glimpsed Si's legs descending the stairs. For a moment he paused, presumably as he searched the room for us.

'Mel!' he called. 'Where are you?'

'Just here! We thought we'd go for a little walk!'

He had reached us now. Landing a heavy hand on my shoulder, he gave me a small tug, so that I toppled backwards into his arms. Linking his hands around my waist so that I was effectively captured in his grip, he started to nuzzle the top of Jo's head.

'Hello, my gorgeous boy,' he crooned. 'How I love you!'

'We were just wondering if it was going to snow,' I muttered. 'The drive's pretty icy.'

'Yeah, it's foul out there. You'd be mad, going for a walk.'

Reaching for the door with his fingertips, he slammed it shut.

32

That's it. There's nothing more to tell. Shuddering, I look up, taking in the dark, deserted room. The police have gone, emptying the building of their bustling presence. The crackle of radios and stomping of boots on the stairs now seem like a dream, the details of which I can no longer quite recall. A short while ago Trish was here, I seem to remember. She must have retreated to the kitchen with Sandra, for down the corridor I can hear female voices. Outside a few flakes of ice have stuck to the windows. When I stand and press my face to the freezing glass I see that it is snowing.

I feel very calm. Around me, everything has receded. There are no more dancing waves, no rip tides pulling me off course, or flotsam bobbing distractingly in the surf. There's just me and what I remember. And now, as I place my hand flat against the pane, I know that only I can get Poppy back. What I have to do is focus.

*

After a while Si wandered upstairs and from the loft we could hear the rhythmic crash of hammering. The only other disturbance was the phone, which rang once. It was Alicia, sounding tearful.

'I've just heard the news,' she said. 'About poor Rosa . . .'

'Yes . . .'

'The police don't think that Simon's involved, do they?'

I gripped the phone with sticky palms. I did not want to lie, but telling Alicia the truth seemed unbearably cruel.

'They've been questioning him . . . I don't know what they're going to do.'

Down the line I could hear her laboured breathing. She had never meant to be unkind to me, I now understood. She was just a lonely woman, unaccustomed to friendship. And although she had told me to try to love her son, I was about to leave him.

'He wouldn't do something like that, though, would he, Melanie?'

'I don't know . . .'

'Oh, God . . .'

She started to cry. I held the phone to my ear, listening to her sniffs. 'You can talk to him yourself,' I said gently. 'He's here, at home . . .'

'I'd prefer not to. He'll just get irritated with me.' I did not contradict her. 'Will you let me know if anything else happens?'

'Of course I will.'

She rang off. I put the phone down, feeling as if I were filled with lead. Upstairs the noise continued, a furious banging that seemed to reach into the core of my body, reverberating in my throbbing head as if the ceaseless din were coming from inside me and not the gallery. I had no idea what Si was doing; all he told me was that he had some jobs to finish in the storerooms along the gallery. I tried to ignore the racket, concentrating instead on the masquerade that everything was normal: getting the kids their lunch, changing Jo's nappies, playing hide and seek. Now I see that I should have moved the van the moment Si returned to the loft. If I had, we would be with Pat, and Poppy would be safe. But I was afraid that on hearing the engine Si would look out from the dormers and see what I was doing. Fool that I was, I waited until he finally emerged from the loft during the game of hide and seek and I heard him drive away. By then, of course, it was too late.

*

There is no time for regret; blaming myself will not bring my daughter back. What I am thinking is this: whether or not Si killed Rosa and that other woman is immaterial. What matters is whether or not he could hurt Poppy. As I turn away from the windowpane and shuffle slowly towards the stairs, I remain certain that he never would. There is also that other thing, which has been bothering me ever since the police arrived this afternoon, the distant alarm. For a moment I hesitate, trying to bring it into focus, but as before, I am unable to grasp it.

I start to climb the stairs, my mind whirring. Si was upstairs, banging around. Some time, either just before or at the beginning of the game of hide and seek, the noise stopped. I hid and then it was Poppy's turn. I was counting up to twenty, concentrating on feeding Jo. Poppy ran off, and a little while later I heard a door open and close. I had assumed that Si was working in the gallery room because that was where he said he was going to be, but could I have overlooked the most obvious explanation of all? Might he have been not on the gallery, but in the loft? Supposing Poppy crept up the steps whilst he was working, hid in some cubby hole, and then was mistakenly locked in by him? Despite all his talk of love and trust, he's clearly done a runner. Meanwhile Poppy might be stuck in the loft space, the musty Victorian walls blanking out her cries.

Reaching the top of the stairs, I hurry along the gallery to the steep metal steps that lead to the loft. In their haste to find the Volvo, the police haven't even started to search up here; the door remains fastened by the padlock. Now, as

I clamber up the steps, my heart bangs furiously. When I get to the top my shaking fingers twist the lock into the correct alignment until it springs open. There's something dark and sticky smeared over it, and on the wall too: something too unpleasant to countenance. Pulling the padlock off the door and wiping my hands on my jeans, I step inside the room.

'Poppy? Are you here?'

The silence brings a lump to my chest. I step over the threshold, wincing at the cold. The room is in darkness.

'Poppy?'

Now that my eyes have grown accustomed to the gloom I can better make out my surroundings: Si's work bench pushed to the wall, his CD player on the floor and, spreading from the far side, an area of wooden planks hammered into neat lines: the floor he must have been fitting. The image of him placing the planks in order, his face furrowed studiously as he measured the lengths, needles me with doubt. Is such industry really likely from a man who has recently committed a double murder? Through the dormers the clouds pull back to reveal the full moon. I take another step forwards. There is an odd smell in the room.

In the eerie light that has illuminated the loft, I can see almost everything. Stepping carefully around the unfinished floor, I move into the centre of the room, peering around. The smell is stronger here: wood dust, the heavy, earthy stench of damp, and something else which makes the hairs on the back of my arms bristle. It is so powerful that I can almost taste it: a metallic, heavy odour that reminds me of menstruation. My gaze settles on the abandoned winch-house and I freeze. Something – a pile of rags from the decorating, perhaps – seems to have been stuffed into the small space where the goods were once unloaded from the barges below. As if to conceal it, a plywood board barricades the opening. It is from here that the smell comes. I stumble towards it, my legs swaying. There are odd stains smattered over the adjoining walls, I notice now, and some slicks of dark, glistening stuff on the floorboards. As I whisper Poppy's name, I am filled with molten terror.

Grabbing the plywood, I toss it roughly aside, revealing the crumpled dust sheet, squashed into the cubby hole. Something lies underneath it: the shape is horribly bulky, stretching across the entire length of the storage area. In places the fabric is soaked brown. Squatting beside it, I start to pull at the dirty material. The smell is so strong that I almost retch. Tugging harder, I push the sheeting back, coughing at the clouding dust.

My first emotion is relief. Crazily, I almost laugh. This giant dummy, squished into the rotting wooden hole, is not my daughter. It's too big and not wearing her clothes. Instead, it's a joke that someone is playing: a scarecrow, dressed in Si's old clobber, the legs bent back at an unlikely angle, the thick wig clotted with red paint. Extending my hand, I pull at the chilly head, turning it to face me.

For two or three seconds I do not move. I gaze at the face, temporarily paralysed. Why is Si lying here, when he is meant to have taken Poppy? His chalky face stares back, a trail of black blood trickling from his nose. The top of his head appears to have caved in; the bald patch I noticed in the bathroom this morning replaced by a sticky mass of bloodied hair, and some gungy stuff that is making me stagger backwards, fingers splayed across my mouth.

Is it me that's making this keening sound? I must have jerked back some distance from the dust sheets, for I find that I am curled against the wall on the far side of the loft. For some reason I am holding a clump of hair in my glacial fingers. My body is convulsing with violent spasms. I feel as if I am encased in ice.

Other people have joined me. I can hear their footsteps, crashing over the boards. Someone gasps and shrieks Si's name. Then the torchlight that's being waved around sweeps over my face.

'Get her downstairs,' a woman's voice directs.

There's too much noise and commotion. I can't take it all in. I push the hands that come for me fiercely away. I am going to sit quietly inside my glacier, keeping mum. To stop myself from shivering, I hug my knees, curling into a little ball. I'm so cold that I've gone numb. My toes and fingers are tingling; I cannot feel my legs. Is this how it feels to freeze to death? From outside I can hear the singing of sirens and crunch of car doors. Blue lights flash across the darkened space, smothering the moon.

The room fills with police. People barge around with their cameras and white suits like it's a fancy-dress party. Dave Gosforth is back, too. I saw him hurrying in, his peaky face pinched with bad humour. I suppose he thought the case was solved. Didn't I tell him he had the wrong man? Across the room, the rubber gloves are on. I watch as strangers paw my husband over, taking photos and samples, buzzing around his corpse like flies. Someone's fixed up a lamp; its white beam is flashing in my face, blinding me.

If they had forgotten that I was here, now they've remembered. A woman I dimly recognize is walking to my corner, pulling me to my feet.

'Come on, Mel, love. We need to get you downstairs.'

I am being supported back down the steps, my lifeless

legs dragging behind. I stumble on the bottom step, banging my shin, but don't much register the pain. *Si is dead, his head bashed in.* Someone is heaping blankets over my shoulders, I don't know who. All I can think of is Si's face, gazing expressionlessly back. As I hunch over the table where I have been seated, a single phrase is repeating in my mind, over and over like a dirge. *Who has taken Poppy?*

33

I need to pee. I've been ignoring it for hours, but the urge
is increasingly overwhelming. I rise unsteadily to my feet. I
have to get across the kitchen and down the corridor to the
downstairs toilet, but it feels impossible: an endless space
to negotiate. Staring ponderously around the room, I muster
the energy to move. Could this place once have been my
home? As I shuffle past the table, my hands splayed over
the rough breeze-block walls, it feels like the set of a play
I've sat through but failed to understand: emptied of actors,
devoid of meaning.

'Let me help you, Mel.'

It's the woman who helped me down the steps. As I glance
at her tired face I remember that her name is Sandra and
she's an 'F.L.O.', whatever that means. All the time that I
was slumped in the kitchen she was with me. I think she
may have been holding my hand.

'I need the loo,' I mumble.

She follows me along the corridor to the toilet. When I
have finished, she is still standing outside, waiting. Rather
than turn towards the kitchen, I make for the living room,
but she trails behind, watching me thoughtfully. Can't she
see that I need to be alone?

'Why are you following me?'

'I have to stay with you for the time being, I'm afraid.'

I gaze at her, trying to grasp her meaning.

'You mean I'm a *suspect*?'

The concept is so ludicrous that I splutter with dismal

laughter. Sandra stares back, her face apologetic. 'I wouldn't put it quite like that . . .'

My legs can no longer hold me up. Groping for her arm, I sink to my knees. 'I didn't kill him!' I cry. 'Why would I kill him?'

'No one's saying that you did, love.' Bending over, she hooks her hands under my armpits and hauls me up. 'Come on, let's get you comfortable.'

Some time later Dave Gosforth joins us. He's too big for our squashy sofa and balances precariously on the edge, his fat fingers spread over his knees like raw sausages. Like Sandra, his face assumes an anguished, almost tender quality, as if I'm an injured animal he's found lying by the side of the road.

'We need to ask you some questions, Mel,' he says. 'Is that okay?'

'Uhuh.'

He folds and unfolds his arms. I numbly watch his face. Si is dead and Poppy stolen. I feel as if a hole's been blasted through me. Beside that, nothing much computes. Sandra is still holding my limp hand, her eyes imploring.

'Can you tell us again what exactly happened this afternoon?'

'It was like I said. Poppy went upstairs to hide. I was downstairs with Jo, counting. I thought Si was in the room he used for painting. He was putting in some floorboards or something; there was a hell of a noise. Then I heard a door close behind me. After a minute or so I heard a car in the drive . . .'

My voice snags on a shard of pain, an intimation of what will follow. Swallowing hard, I manage to finish. 'I heard someone get in the car and drive it away . . .'

'But you didn't physically see Simon?'

'No.'

'And you didn't hear anything else?'

'No, but it's such a big place. I mean, maybe they went out through the kitchen at the back. And Jo was fussing too. I was concentrating on him . . .'

'And this was what time?'

'Four-fifteen or so. I don't know exactly.'

I glance away. It's amazing that my mouth is still able to form words, yet I sound just like any other woman recounting her afternoon.

'Would you have kept the back door locked, or was it open?'

'It's always locked. We're in the middle of a boatyard, you never know who's wandering around . . .'

'What about the front door?'

'It's a Chubb lock. You couldn't get in without a key.'

Gosforth shuffles a little closer. 'Is there anyone else who has access to your home? Neighbours perhaps? Or friends?'

'Bob and Janice Perkins have a key, in case we get locked out.'

'And they live . . . ?'

'Appledown Cottage. Just up the lane.' I turn hastily to Sandra. I've just remembered something. 'I lost my bag! It had my keys in it!'

'When was that?' Gosforth leans a little closer. If he were the overweight, blonde-haired Labrador that he resembles, his ears would prick up.

'In January. I was in Tesco's. I had it dangling on the handle of the pram.'

'So did you change the locks?' Sandra puts in.

'No . . . I mean I obviously cancelled all my cards and everything, but I didn't think of that.'

295

I stare at Sandra's gently reproachful face. At the time I'd assumed that the bag had dropped off in the supermarket carpark or in the aisles, not that someone had deliberately taken it. And despite it never being handed in, I was so distracted by Jo's colic that I quickly forgot about it.

'Did you report it missing to the police?'

'No.'

'But the bag would have had your address in it, wouldn't it, Mel?'

Now that she's saying it, I realize how stupid I've been.

'I don't know . . .' I shake my head. 'I mean, I didn't really think about it that much. There was so much going on at the time. I suppose I just assumed that whoever had got the bag had taken the cash then chucked it away or something . . .'

Gosforth and Sandra exchange a glance. There's a pause, as if they're about to change tack, but I interrupt them.

'Where's Jo?' I ask querulously.

'It's okay, Mel.' Sandra pats my arm maternally. 'Trish has taken him back to her place for a while. She was planning to give him a bottle. I'm sure he's fine.'

I goggle at her, unable to respond. How can he be fine when his father's stiffening body is squashed into the winch-house, his skull bashed in? For one jolting moment I picture the dust sheet, with its browning stains and grotesquely lumpy form. I'd hurried across the floorboards towards it, unaware of what was waiting . . .

On the other side of me, Gosforth gives a little cough.

'We'll need to come back to these keys,' he says. 'In the meantime, can you tell me if there was anyone who may have had a grudge against your husband? Did he have any enemies?'

Instinctively I shake my head, but my heart jumps. What

was the name of the guy that called? Biz or Baz or something. He had had an unpleasant, insinuating manner. *Tell him I'm getting a teeny bit fed up.* The phrase had stuck in my mind for weeks, like something nasty on the side of the toilet.

'There was a man who called up . . . called Boz? He gave me the creeps.'

There is a significant pause. 'In what way did he give you the creeps?' Gosforth asks, neutrally.

'He wanted Si, and when I told him he was out he was really rude. He said to tell him he was getting fed up.'

'Okay.'

The way Gosforth nods indicates that this information does not surprise him. He's clearly heard of this Boz character before.

'And then a few days later there was this silver transit van . . .' I shudder, remembering the man's almost gleeful expression on catching sight of Poppy and me, and the manner in which he had reversed so quickly backwards, to be swallowed by the fog.

'Go on.'

'I don't know if it was connected. The van was parked right behind my car one day when we came home from school. When we passed it, the driver whizzed off. He gave us this weird smile . . .'

'Can you remember what he looked like?'

'Bald, overweight. He had horrible teeth.'

'We'll arrange a photofit,' says Gosforth. 'It may or may not be significant.'

There is a long silence in which they seem to be waiting for me to remember something else.

'Okay, Mel,' Gosforth says carefully. 'I'm going to show you a transcription of some of the messages we found in the in-box on Simon's mobile. We were wondering if you could throw any light on them.'

Delving into the folder that he's laid on the coffee table, he produces a printed sheet, which he hands to me. For a while I simply gaze at the blur of letters. Gradually the words come into focus, but they still don't make sense.

30/11/04 Meet at Bull 9PM. Need 2CU.
5/12/04 Were RU. Reply on return.
02/01/05 911645123. B.
28/01/05 UR dead.

'I don't understand,' I say faintly. 'What's that number mean?'

'We think it's a bank account. It's possible that Simon owed money and that's what the messages are about.'

When I don't respond, he adds, 'You're in quite a mess financially, aren't you?'

'Are we?'

My voice is as small and pathetic as a child's. The dreadful truth is that I have no ideas about our finances: since moving here Si has managed the bills and the mortgage. In less than a year I have become a dependent woman, with whom her husband does not deem it necessary to share his business affairs.

'Well, for a start the mortgage on this property hasn't been paid for two months.'

'But Si was working in London . . . he was earning four hundred quid a week!'

Gosforth and Sandra regard me with the expression of bystanders at a motorway pile-up. 'I'm afraid he wasn't paying your mortgage, Mel,' Gosforth says with one of his sniffs.

I cannot stand the pitying way they are looking at me. I stare again at the messages. *UR dead*: the threat of a ten-year-old bully, all pumped-up clichés and childish bravado. Would Si have borrowed money from a thug who'd send messages like this? Yet it's true that ever since Christmas we've been floundering in debt, and he had never explained exactly how or why. I'd assumed that the proceeds from the sale of his flat in south London had provided the deposit on the warehouse, but if, as Alicia insisted, it belonged to Rosa and he never actually sold it, then he must have raised the money some other way. Suddenly I picture his face as he tipsily pulled the irises from my hair on our wedding night. They were wilting, sprinkling yellow dust over his fingers. He leaned over and kissed the tip of my nose, just like I was a little girl. After we were married I thought that everything would change, my life start anew. But now I see that even our wedding night rested on these fault lines that have ruptured everything. What did Si say as we'd booked the room? *I've had a windfall. We can afford to splash out.*

'Do you know what Simon was doing in Calais on January 15th?' Gosforth suddenly asks.

'No . . .' I press my fingers against my eyelids, trying to focus. Si went to London immediately after New Year's Day, returning only for Sundays until mid-February. 'I thought he was in London that week, on the build . . .'

'He may have been for some of the time, but not all of it. We can trace his movements from the calls he made from his mobile. He was in France again on the 6th of this month. Any idea what he was up to?'

I shake my head, aghast at how much the police have found out, and how little I know.

'Have you heard of a pub called the Bull?'

'No.'

'And you never met Boz? You just spoke to him the once?'

'Yes, I think so. Si said he was a tiler . . .'

But he was lying.

'And apart from this silver van you never saw anyone else hanging around? I know it's hard after what's happened this evening, Mel, but try to concentrate hard. Even the tiniest little thing may be significant.'

I am attempting to do as he says, but I can't get traction on the question; my mind keeps slipping into a quagmire of images. Si in the bath, a puff of soap on his forehead; Si lying in the muddy grass last spring as the cows looked on; the back of his head, as Gosforth drove him away. He begged me to tell him that I loved him, but I was unable to reply truthfully. Now he is dead, his flesh hardening, his eyes empty. Yet I feel nothing, just this dazed, detached sensation.

'Was there anyone else who seemed to take an interest in Poppy?'

Her name jolts me back to the present. Poppy! I start to stand, thinking that I must *do* something. Somebody has taken Poppy!

'I have to get her . . .'

Sandra's hand is immediately on my arm, guiding me back on to the sofa. 'That's not going to help, Mel. We need you to concentrate on answering the questions. It's very important you remember everything. We still have the sighting of Poppy in what we're pretty certain is Simon's car, remember?'

'Are you saying it was this Boz bloke? That he killed Si and took Poppy because Si owed him money?'

'We're not saying anything. We don't know what's been going on. That's what we're trying to find out.'

'But why would he have killed that Jacqui woman?'

Sandra's mouth twitches. 'Like Dave said, Mel, we can't make any assumptions. What's happened today may not even be connected with Jacqui Jenning.'

'You mean you still think that Si killed her?'

She does not answer, just glances again at Gosforth, who is making unpleasant sucking noises with his teeth.

'What we need,' he says slowly, 'is for you to tell us anything you can think of that may be relevant.'

I stare at him, too paralysed to speak. I have just remembered Poppy's ghost.

34

I buck up and out of the sofa, jerking away from Sandra and Gosforth like a frightened rabbit. Poppy said there was a ghost creeping along the gallery! And then later she saw him in Si's painting room. Yet rather than listening to her, I ticked her off, assuming she was lying. As I recall how impatiently I searched the warehouse that evening, returning in a fury to find Jo squirming on the floor, I want to crash my head against the wall, to punish myself until I'm senseless. I never once listened to Poppy, or took her side. Even when she screamed in the night that she'd seen an intruder I didn't believe her. As I stumble towards the kitchen, the details of her night terrors return with horrible clarity. Every night at 2 a.m. her screeches would yank me upright, my heart pounding. It was the fat ghost she'd seen by the stairs, she'd cried. He had crawled into her head and she couldn't get him out. Along with her increasingly difficult behaviour in the day, I had tucked the nightmares under the convenient heading 'Jealousy of Jo', never bothering to probe further. Yet supposing that the figure she saw on the gallery that night was real?

Lurching towards the kitchen table, I start to search desperately through the detritus, the heaped bills and old newspapers slithering to the floor. When I locate Poppy's picture I clutch it with trembling fingers, tears pouring down my face. Our house: a tall building, crayoned brown, with a pointy roof and lots of little square windows. Amongst the pink daisies stands a stick-figure Poppy, her starfish fingers stretched towards her grinning stick-figure mother. Next to them is a little blob: the baby brother. The stepfather is not depicted. And there, at the top of the building, gawping down with googly eyes, is Poppy's ghost. Could this have been *Boz* or one of his accomplices, who she'd caught creeping around the house?

'Mel?'

Sandra is beside me, standing so close that I can sense her bosomy warmth.

'Look!' I cry, waving the picture in her face. 'Poppy drew it just the other day . . . she said there was a ghost in the house. She saw it in the middle of the night, and then one evening she said it was in the room that Si uses for painting . . .'

She takes the picture from my hands, frowning.

'Like I told you, she was having these nightmares . . .'

'But you never saw anything?'

'I didn't really believe her . . . I mean, I checked the house, but there was no one there.' I stop, remembering my impatient search of the building, ending in the discovery of Si's latest, horrible painting. There couldn't be anyone inside the building, I had concluded, because there was no sign of a break-in. Never did I consider that the intruder might have had a *key*.

'I thought she was making it up, to get attention . . .'

My breath is coming too fast; I can barely speak. I want Sandra to place her plump arm around my back, to coo that there is no ghost, no Boz, no people who wished Si harm. But she stands silently beside me as she looks down at the picture, her lips puckered unhappily. Does she have children? Does she have even the slightest intimation of the panic that now crashes around me, crushing everything?

'Perhaps this Boz person came back to kill Si, and Poppy

got in the way,' I whisper. As I reel backwards, a uniformed officer steps quietly into the kitchen, a sheaf of lined papers in his hands. He looks only at Sandra, his eyes turned away from my face with hushed deference.

'We've just found these,' he says quietly, handing the papers over.

It's a pile of letters, written in a tight, curling script that crawls untidily over the lines: the handwriting of a child, or an illiterate adult. Returning Poppy's drawing carefully to the table, Sandra scrutinizes them, her face unreadable. I watch her in horror. When she has finished, she hands them over.

'Any idea about these?'

Dear Poppy, the first letter reads. *Where watching you. Why dont you say anything. We keep waiting and waiting.*

It breaks off, unsigned. The second is even worse. I scan the few lines, feeling nauseous:

Dont try to get away. We will get you were ever you are.

'We found them in the little girl's bedroom,' the officer is saying. 'They were down the back of the chest of drawers.'

If you tell your mum I will break your neck.

'Someone was sending her letters,' I whisper feebly. 'She wouldn't let me see them . . .'

'I see.'

'I should have insisted she showed them to me . . .'

Sandra gently pulls the letters from my fingers. 'We're obviously going to have to keep these as evidence.'

'I never listened to her,' I breathe. 'I was always too busy . . .'

'It's not your fault, Mel . . .'

'Yes, it is! She never wanted to move from London, but I insisted! Even from the beginning she was scared of the place, but I never bloody listened . . . how can you say it's not my fault?'

'Mel, calm down . . .'

But it's too late. The numbness that was keeping me so pliable has finally worn off. I stand quivering with horror on the cement floor, a hundred images and thoughts hurtling through my mind. Poppy tried to tell me she was being persecuted, but I never listened. All that time, when I had eyes only for Jo, there *was* a ghost. He was sending her letters, too, enacting his revenge on Si by hurting his family. I look around the ugly room: my doomed attempts to cheer it up by taping Poppy's pictures on the walls, the greasy Calor gas stove and wobbly sink. I hate this place, I realize with a stab of anger. I should have followed my instincts that first dingy day in June, when the flapping of the starlings made me feel so sick. All the time that we were trying to make it our home it was seeped in malevolence, sodden with the secrets that Si was hiding from us.

'Where are you going?'

'I can't stay here . . .'

Lumbering across the kitchen, I push roughly past the policeman and make for the door. I need to get away from the warehouse, to splash through the mud towards the creek and the marsh, as far as possible from the evil that now seems to impregnate every brick and every plank of the building. As the door bursts open I gulp at the freezing air, the cold smashing into me like a fist. Stumbling outside, I gaze around the yard in shock.

The world has turned white. In the hours since I climbed the steps to the loft a heavy snow has fallen, crusting the police cars that wait in the drive with a thick white topping. The boatyard and its outbuildings are blanketed; there is even a stack of perilously balanced ice on top of each boat mast, testimony to the glacially still air. Above me the sky has cleared, revealing the studded stars and luminescent moon. Across the creek the newly silvered marshland glints in the light. The scene is hushed, radiant with unfamiliar beauty, and stabs me with icicles of pain. Like Poppy's school books spread over the table, the remainders of our lunch in the kitchen sink or her green froggie wellies plonked by the door, it evokes only her absence. If she were here now, she'd run outside, hooting with excitement as she gathered up the snow, licking it, kicking it, rolling it up for a snowman. But everything has been reversed: the normally blunt artefacts of everyday domesticity lethally sharpened, the unexpected snow making me gasp with pain.

I am wearing only a sweatshirt and jeans with thin baseball boots on my feet, but I hardly feel the cold. I start to plough through the virgin snow, the compacted ice creaking beneath my weight. My only coherent thought is that I must get away from the warehouse, where Si's body lies. As I picture his waxy face, the black blood crusting his lip, I stagger a little, bashing into the side of a police car and causing a wedge of snow to slump from the windscreen. Behind me, somebody is crunching through the snow.

'Mel! Come in, love!' Sandra is tugging at my shoulders, so that I slither backwards, my feet flailing. 'You'll catch your death,' she mutters.

'I don't bloody care! I have to find Poppy!'

'We're doing everything we can . . .'

For a second I hate her for her calm.

'Leave me alone!' I scream, pushing her away. But it's no good. Other hands have grasped me; despite my kicking and squirming I am firmly escorted back into the building, where I stand on the mat in my wet jeans, my teeth chattering.

'We've asked the on-duty doctor to pop in and give you something to help you calm down a little,' Sandra is saying soothingly.

'I don't want anything to –'

She interrupts me, not interested. 'This may be a long haul, Mel. You need to look after yourself. If you have a bit of a sleep now, you'll feel a lot better in the morning –'

'How can I sleep with Poppy missing! I can't sleep!'

I start to howl, snot and tears spurting as I crumple on the floor, all dignity departed.

35

Since I refuse to stay in the warehouse, it's been arranged that Trish will take me in. Sandra gives her a quick call, then goes upstairs to pack my things. The doctor has visited, leaving behind a white plastic pot which rattles with Temazepam. I've promised to take two. Sandra's tucked them in my bag, along with the nightie she's retrieved from under my pillow, a packet of nappies for Jo and a clutch of clothes 'for tomorrow'. The word repels me. After the events of today, how can I wake to tomorrow?

Despite the short distance up the lane to Trish's cottage, it's decided that I should travel there in Dave Gosforth's car. It takes him a while to scrape the snow off the windscreen, but finally, wheels slithering, we move off: me in the front with Gosforth, and Sandra in the back, my overnight bag on her lap. We glide through a transformed world, the track that leads up the lane soft and white, the trees sparkling. It is nearly one in the morning, and no one's around. At the top of the gleaming lane the shining windows of Trish's cottage seem like a cheerful galleon floating in still waters. When the car pulls up outside her gate, we climb out into two or three inches of snow. As we shuffle slowly through her front garden, our footfalls are muffled.

She comes immediately to the door, extending a hand as she helps me inside. She is so heavily pregnant that she waddles rather than walks, her free hand clasped around the bottom of her belly to support the bump.

'My poor darling,' she murmurs as we step over the threshold of the tiny flagstoned hall. I cannot reply. Pulling my hand from hers, I wrap my arms around my middle, as if to protect myself.

'Is Jo okay?'

'Sound asleep in baby's cot upstairs.'

'You must need to sleep, too . . .'

'Nah, I'm fine.'

We step into the snug kitchen, the warm domestic fug of the room feeling like a blanket that's been spread over my shoulders. As before, everything is shining and clean: the floor scrubbed, the stripped wood table cleared, the washing machine humming with activity. Placing my bag on the floor, Sandra hovers for a moment, giving Trish her mobile number, explaining the dose of tranquillizers I'm supposed to take, telling her what time she'll be back in the morning. Gosforth remains by the door, scowling at something. Does he really believe that I'm a suspect?

'If you could persuade Mel to get some sleep, it would be great,' I hear Sandra whisper. 'It's so kind of you to take her in.'

'It's the least I could do.'

I remain standing woodenly in the brightly painted kitchen, staring around. Perhaps it is simply the passage of time, the first layer of shock gradually eroding to reveal the geology of pain beneath, for rather than feeling better at having left the warehouse I feel considerably worse: the dread that's been building inside me somehow thickening. If only I could stop thinking of Si's face, crushed into the winch-house, I might be able to clear my mind.

'You can have the spare room,' Trish says. 'I've made up the bed.'

I nod, allowing her to usher me towards the narrow stairs. Si is dead and Poppy gone, but despite the bluntness of each statement, my mind is unable to encompass what they mean. All I can think of are those nightmarish moments in the loft, when I was curled by the wall and Sandra and Trish came clattering into the room.

I follow Trish up the creaky stairs and into a small bedroom. It's decorated with Trish's usual panache, the floorboards stripped and painted white, the brass bed covered with a large patchwork quilt. On one side of the room an old-fashioned china sink stands on a wooden pedestal; on the other a Victorian dressing table is covered by a pretty length of fringed Chinese silk. Like the rest of the house, the room is spotlessly clean. Where is all the clutter?

My mind does not process the thought: like everything else, my impressions of Trish's cottage float untethered in my brain. I sit wordlessly on the bed, which sags at my weight.

'There's a towel by the washbasin,' Trish is saying.

'Where's Jo?'

'He's next door.'

She pauses by the door, peering anxiously into my face. 'Do you want to talk?'

I shake my head. What I very badly want is to be left alone. But perhaps Trish feels duty-bound to keep watch over me, for she does not move, just leans against the door, her hand slowly circling her belly. She's changed into drawstring trackies and a fluffy red jumper that doesn't wholly cover the solid bump beneath and rises to reveal a fashionable strip of midriff.

'I can't imagine how you must be feeling,' she says.

I shrug. I am willing her to turn and clump back down the stairs. I need silence, so I can trace this prickling thought to its origin. Rosa went missing at Christmas, the police said, just after Si went to see her. They found her blood in her house, and the chisel that killed the prostitute and most likely belonged to Si was buried in her garden. And then there was the passenger seat of his van, which he had so assiduously cleaned. All the evidence points to him, yet now he's dead and something else is forming in my mind. It's so close that it's almost solid.

'I just need to switch off for a while,' I mumble.

'I've got those pills in the kitchen,' she says eagerly 'I'll go and get them . . .'

As I hear her go downstairs, I stand and walk on to the cramped landing, my fingers trailing over the rose-coloured walls. Pushing open the adjacent door, I step inside. The cot stands in the centre of the small room, bright moonlight pouring on to the floor. For a moment I take in the mural of animals that Trish has painted on the walls, the mobile of painted wooden fish that turns slowly above Jo's sleeping head. Moving closer to the cot, I grip the wooden bars with my fingers, gazing down at my baby. He's lying on his back, his arms stretched over his head in blissful repose, his long lashes fluttering on his skin. The sight of his perfectly snubbed nose and Cupid's lips brings tears to my eyes. Wiping my cheeks with my sleeve, I reach over the bars and stroke his smooth cheek. If only he would wake then I would have an excuse to scoop him up and carry him into the brass bed, but he sleeps on, oblivious.

'I've got them.'

Trish's voice makes me jump. I had no idea she was standing behind me. As I turn, she holds out a glass of water and two minuscule yellow eggs.

'You are going to take them, aren't you?'

'Sure.'

Popping the pills into my mouth, I take a sip of the water.

'Night then, my poor darling. Let's just pray that by the time you wake up there'll be some good news . . .'

I nod, giving her a little smile that is supposed to signal that she does not need to worry, and brush past. Once inside the spare room, I push the door closed, sliding shut the old-fashioned latch. Then I spit the bitter-tasting eggs into my hand.

Every nerve of my body tingles, like I've received an electric shock.

36

27 February 2005
3 a.m.

Dave couldn't relax. He knew that there was currently nothing more for him to do: the scene of crime lads were at the warehouse, sifting through every shred of forensic evidence; the Met had arrested Barry 'Boz' Uckfield in a pub in Kennington, and Clive Jenkins had gone up there to interview him. Every force in the damn country was searching for the missing car. He needed to get some kip so he could be fresh for the next day, even if it was only for a handful of hours. But despite having checked into the Travelodge on the Sittingbourne road, sleep eluded him.

He lay on his back, gazing up at the moulded ceiling tiles. It wasn't exactly the Saturday night he'd been expecting. Tonight was their tenth wedding anniversary, and Karen had been planning a special dinner. She'd been cooking most of the morning: chicken kiev, tiramisu, all his favourites. But as soon as he'd got the call telling him that the little girl had gone missing, he'd told her the dinner would have to wait. Giving her a quick peck on the cheek, he grabbed a bottle of cola and a pork pie from the fridge and lumbered towards his car like a bull that'd been shown a red cape. Now he didn't know when he'd next be home. If the little girl wasn't found soon, he'd have to get to used to the Travelodge.

The bed was too narrow for his wide frame, and the room smelt of cleaning fluids. He turned over, huffing. He felt like a pillock, truth be told. For days they'd been edging towards charging Stenning with the murder of Jacqui Jenning and Rosa Montague, but now their prime suspect was dead, the case they'd been so carefully constructing smashed to pulp. From the outset he'd been convinced that Stenning was their man. He'd left his calling card on Jacqui Jenning's sheets the night before she was murdered, was shifty in interviews about both his where-abouts and his relationship with Rosa Montague, and was missing a chisel that matched the one covered in Jacqui's DNA that was discov-ered in Rosa's garden. Even more promising were the stains on the passenger seat of his van. The DNA results had still to come in, but the fabric had been cleaned with bleach in an attempt to remove what Dave was sure would turn out to be Rosa's blood. There'd been a tiny speck by the door handle, and a couple of hairs on the headrest too. Stenning had told them some cock-and-bull story about how Rosa had deliberately cut herself with a knife and he'd driven her to hospital, an event that A & E in Canterbury had denied all knowledge of. Stenning hid it well, but Dave had sensed a repressed violence in the guy, like there was a little chink of normality missing. Despite her stuck-up manner, he felt sorry for the wife. She clearly didn't have a clue.

Yet despite the circumstantial evidence, they still didn't have a sufficient case for the CPS. The forensic evidence was decidedly shaky. Regardless of the stains in Stenning's van, until the DNA results came back there was nothing concrete they could charge him with. The fibres from Rosa's bedcover that they'd retrieved from one of Stenning's sweaters proved only that he'd been in her bedroom, something he'd already admitted. He'd visited her to retrieve some papers, he'd said, and they'd argued. She was 'a nightmare', had caused him more grief than they could possibly imagine, but he hadn't laid a finger on her. On the subject of the redecorated wall and flecks of blood on the window sill, he kept with the same story. There'd been a fight in which she'd ended up plunging a knife into her arm. He'd driven her to Canterbury and left her outside A & E. She was deeply disturbed. All he'd wanted was to get away from her.

There was no direct link to Jacqui Jenning's murder, either. Sure, there was the semen, but the one handprint they'd finally recovered from her kitchen wall didn't match Stenning's. Their only hope, therefore, was the chisel. Whoever had buried the tool in the back garden of Rosa Montague's cottage had done a bad job of wiping off the blood, and within twenty-four hours they had had a DNA match with Jacqui. It was almost certainly part of the set that Stenning still kept in his toolbox, with the same yellow moulded plastic handle as the rest of his tools. They'd even managed to source it: a product sold by B & Q in the late 1990s, now discontinued.

But without better forensics there still wasn't enough to charge him. And now he was dead. Far worse, the little girl was still missing. The thought that he may have made a serious error of judgement made Dave's heart plunge. He had not yet mentioned to Karen that a child was involved in the case, but tomorrow morning it would be all over the papers. He thought of Harvey, snuggled up under his Spider-Man duvet, and his chest went tight. He didn't normally allow his investigations to impinge on his personal life, but he knew that the first thing he'd do when he eventually returned home would be to take his son in his arms and kiss the top of his curly blond head. If it ever came to it, he'd sacrifice everything for Harv or Karen.

Sighing, he turned over. Despite his habitual defences, the case had burrowed into him like worms into mud, and now his mind refused to quieten. Stenning's death was definitely murder, not a chance of suicide. Someone had come up behind him and knifed him in the back. Then, by the look of things, they'd taken his drill and had a little go at his head. It had left a nasty mess. Puddles of blood lay all over the floor; the walls were splattered with the stuff. Whoever had killed him must have got a good soaking.

But the worse thing was the child. They'd gone all out to find Stenning's borrowed Volvo assuming he'd taken her, when all the time he'd been lying murdered upstairs. Bloody fools! Why the hell hadn't they searched the property properly, like they were trained to? Okay, so the loft was a bit out of the way and had been locked, and they'd scaled down the search the moment they thought Stenning had the child in his car. But whatever their excuses, it was a piss-poor mistake to have made, and it meant that they'd lost so much time. Only now, when the girl had been missing for over twelve hours, were they were scrambling around trying to trace Stenning's dodgy business contacts. In sum it was a sodding disaster; no wonder Mel Stenning had been so angry. With a little moan Dave recalled the expression in her eyes when he had questioned her a few hours earlier. He was used to people hating him, but for some reason her fury caused him disproportionate anguish. Despite her disdainful manner, there was something painfully fragile about her, like a pretty vase that had been broken and glued back together many times over. After what had happened today, it was hardly surprising that she'd shattered into a thousand pieces.

He rolled over again, trying to think constructively. If it wasn't Stenning who had taken the girl, who the bloody hell was it? The letters they'd found under the mattress and messages on Stenning's mobile implied that Barry 'Boz' Uckfield might be their man. He'd done five years for fraud in the eighties, eighteen months in the mid-nineties for money laundering, and had only just escaped another sentence in 1999 for GBH when the guy whose arms he'd broken refused to testify. He was currently operating as a property developer on the South Coast, his unsavoury fingers dabbling in a myriad of illegal activities. Yesterday Dave's team had discovered that he'd lent five hundred grand to Stenning back in the summer, possibly with an extra twenty thrown in. They suspected that Stenning's trips to France were connected to this, possibly with a view to working on more of Uckfield's unscrupulous developments in the region. Since then they'd fallen out, and now Uckfield was getting nasty about the money he was owed. They were going to hold him overnight for questioning, but according to Clive Jenkins, who he'd spoken to only twenty minutes earlier, all Uckfield would admit to were the loan and mobile messages. Even if Stenning had seriously pissed him off, why would he kidnap the bloke's stepdaughter? The more Dave thought about it, the less sense it made.

316

There was something else, too. Stretching out his legs, he tweaked the covers another inch over his bulk. It had been bugging him ever since he deposited Mel Stenning at her friend's house and drove out of town over the gritted roads, yet until now he had been unable to put his finger on it. It was something to do with Rosa Montague's place in the woods, but what? Shivering under the thin stretch of duvet, he concentrated hard. There was something wrong about the house, some assumption he had made that only now in the quiet dark was he beginning to unpick. Rosa's blood was sprinkled around her house, yet in contrast to the chaos of Stenning's warehouse the place was as tidy and spruce as a holiday let. Dave lay as stiffly as a pole, vortexed by thought. He had just remembered what he had seen in Rosa Montague's kitchen.

37

For what feels like hours, I lie motionlessly on top of the bed. Across the landing I hear the flush of the toilet and the click of a door, then the building rests back into silence. Only a few yards away Trish and Jo are asleep, but I am more awake than I have ever been since leaving London. Eventually I sit up, swinging my feet on to the floor. Under the burden of snow the rafters of the house creak and shift; from the skirting board comes a tiny scratching sound. I am going to creep down the stairs and into the kitchen. There, I am going to retrieve Sandra's card from the mantlepiece where, a few hours earlier, I saw her rest it against a pewter vase. She said I could call her at any time during the night. When I've got the number I'm going to retrieve the mobile she lent to me from my bag and call her. What I am going to tell her is this: Rosa Montague may have gone missing before Christmas, but she wasn't dead. Instead, she was alive and well and spending Si's money in South Molton Street.

When I reach the bottom of the stairs, I pause for a moment on the freezing flagstones. The kitchen is to my right, the sitting room that Trish has been painting to my left. Through the half-open kitchen door the green light of the washing machine winks encouragingly. I push the door open, wincing at its squeak of complaint. Stepping into the room, I gaze through the dim light at the tidied sink and sturdy table, with its artfully piled pebbles. The clock on the wall shows it is five past three. Almost eleven hours have passed since I last saw Poppy. On the far side of the room, above the empty fireplace, is the mantlepiece. Sandra's card is clearly visible in the slanting moonlight. Tiptoeing across the flagstones, I reach up and retrieve it, peering around the room for my bag.

It's gone. It's not on the floor where Sandra put it as she ushered me into the kitchen. Nor has it been tidied under the table, or balanced on the leather armchair by the Aga. Returning to the hall, I pause for a moment by the sitting-room door, my hand hovering above the latch. I do not understand why, but I am feeling disproportionately afraid. Somewhere inside the room I will either find my bag, or Trish's phone. All I need to do then is call Sandra. Gently lifting the latch with my fingers so that it unhooks sound-lessly, I step over the threshold.

I glance around the room in surprise. I was expecting to see furniture covered in dust sheets, a semi-decorated room that reeked of fresh paint, but there is no sign of Trish's handiwork. I take in the Turkish kilim and heavy Moroccan lamp, an old leather sofa and wooden blinds. As my fingers move across the wall, I notice scuff marks, a faded patch. Despite the cold, my hands are clammy. Why would Trish lie to me about painting the room? Something is very wrong, something to do with that alarm bell. As I peer more intently around, my eyes finally fix upon the wall above the fireplace. For a moment I do not understand. I stare at the wall in confusion. I am meant to be searching for a phone, but what I have seen makes me jerk backwards, gasping.

It's a painting of an angel. Not the demure figure by the chapel that Si sketched for me last winter, but one of the more ostentatious statues at the entrance to the cemetery: stone arms reaching towards heaven, enormous feathered wings stretched wide, as if about to take to the skies. Expressionless eyes gaze blankly from the canvas. Like the painting of the nude that hung in Si's kitchen, half of the face is deliberately obscured, this time by clinging ivy. The creeping vegetation spreads over the crumbling stone torso, climbing up the angel's neck and across her face as it mutates from green to brown to dark red, blotting out her features like smeared blood.

In the two or three seconds that I face the painting, I understand everything. I stand motionlessly in the doorway, staring ahead. I am literally turned to stone. This cannot possibly be a coincidence.

'Mel?'

At the sound of my name I spin around. Trish is standing at the bottom of the stairs, looking at me quizzically. Jo is bundled in her arms.

'What's the matter?' she asks with a smile.

'I couldn't sleep . . .'

She takes a step towards me, her face crumpled with pretend concern. 'Didn't the pills work?'

I slowly shake my head. My hands are so slimy that I have to wipe them on the side of my jeans. I feel as if I might suffocate.

'Can I have Jo?' I whisper.

She does not move, just clutches him a little tighter. 'What's the matter? Why are you looking at me like that?'

'You're Rosa, aren't you?'

She pretends to frown, but her eyes are dancing. 'I don't know what you mean . . .'

'You're Rosa . . .'

She smirks, and my sudden hatred of her lashes me like a whip. How could I have been taken in so easily? She's cut her hair and dyed it blonde, and the baby has added two or three stone to her previously slim frame, but the dark eyes and thin lips, currently curling into a cruel smile, belong to the girl on the boat. *Rosa*. What was it that Si said? *She's a nutcase, she'll do anything.* I gawp at her in horror, fragmented memories hurtling through my mind. That first morning in my kitchen, she'd said her boyfriend had dumped her, gone off with some tart. She was plotting her revenge, she'd added. Innocent that I was, I assumed she was joking!

'What do you mean?' she says, pulling her face into a little frown of perplexity.

'You followed us down here, didn't you? You found out where we lived . . .'

There is a little pause before she replies. 'I really don't know what you're talking about.' Her voice is saccharine sweet, but now that I am finally paying attention I can see the truth in her slim wrists and elegant hands. The fingers that currently encircle my son's head are the same as those in the photo that I identified for the police, carelessly slung over Si's shoulders as if they owned him. She must have deliberately rented this cottage so she could infiltrate our lives, the charm with which she drew me in dipped with poison. And all the time that she was befriending me, coaxing confidences in a masquerade of intimacy, she knew exactly who I was.

I take another step towards her. I have to get Jo.

'Are you feeling all right?'

With huge effort I force my voice to remain steady.

'You've been planning this . . .'

She smiles glassily back at me. I swear she is holding Jo more tightly. And now, finally, the detail that since this afternoon has been scratching at the back of my mind breaks loose. It was when she pretended to comfort me, out in the yard. 'There was no one prowling around the warehouse,' she'd said with breezy confidence. But I am sure I never told her about what Poppy said she had seen.

'You broke into the building and spied on us,' I say slowly. 'It was you who went into Si's painting room . . .'

I am staring at her bump now, making the calculations. He'd slept with her in late May, Si had confessed. But he never had the courage to tell me that she was having his baby. Now, as she stands before me in the flagstoned hall of her cottage, she makes a show of raising her eyebrows, as if in amazement.

'I don't understand what you're going on about . . .'

'How did you know about the prowler?'

'Poppy told me,' she says with a laugh, as if aghast at the implications. 'Or you did. I don't remember.'

She's widening her eyes, still protesting innocence, but her face has turned a fetching shade of pink. I stand before her, my hands clenched. Now that I am no longer confused, I feel very calm. All the time I thought she was my friend, she was my enemy: revelling in my problems as she waited for her moment of triumph.

'It was you who stole my bag, wasn't it?'

She is still doing the amazed thing with her eyebrows, her mouth hanging open in a little charade of innocence. 'Listen, love,' she says slowly. 'Do you want me to get you some more of the Temazepam? You seem ever so het up.'

'I'm not het up. I just want you to give me Jo.'

I step towards her, but she dodges to the left, deftly avoiding my outstretched hands and crossing the threshold of the sitting room. As her eyes alight on the angel she gives a little comedy shriek, like she's just discovered something embarrassing, her skirt tucked into her pants, perhaps, or a blob of sauce on her chin.

'Oops! Looks like you've seen my angel.'

'Looks like I have.'

She doesn't miss a beat, just turns, grinning in a way that tells me she's grown bored of pretending. As she looks me up and down, she chuckles nastily. 'She's a bit more impressive than your tatty little sketch, isn't she?'

The venom in her voice turns my stomach over. She'd do anything to keep clinging on, Si said. But, too consumed by my selfish jealousy, I chose not to believe him.

'What do you want?' I whisper.

'Just to get my revenge.'

She's still smiling: the cold grin of a psychopath. I stare into her pale face, my heart plunging as I recall Si's picture of the woman with the baby. It was never supposed to be of me, but *her*. Poppy saw the 'fat person' up there the evening after I'd told Trish he was painting again. She must have been overcome by curiosity, desperate to see what he was working on.

'You bitch!'

I lunge at her, but she hops out of my way. And she still has Jo. He's been woken by my shouting and is starting to cry. Rosa grips him tighter, his face squashed into her jumper.

'Fair's fair, hon!' she coos. 'If you go around stealing other girls' men, you can't be too upset if they pay you back!'

'I didn't steal Si off you . . .'

'Nah, I know you didn't, not really. It's me he was always passionate about. Poor sod was just too afraid to accept it.'

Barging past me, she moves swiftly down the hall, Jo's screams muffled in her shoulder. For perhaps two seconds I am unable to move. I am thinking about her washing machine, still only halfway through its cycle at three in the morning, the bubbles frothing in the perspex window.

'You killed him, didn't you?' I breathe, but she is already at the front door, pulling her parka over her shoulders, one arm grasping my wriggling baby. She must have changed out of her bloodied clothes before coming to my assistance this afternoon, but forgotten to put them in the wash. Perhaps she bumped into Poppy on her way out of the warehouse and, being literally caught red-handed, bundled her into Ollie's Volvo, where, knowing Si, he'd probably left the keys in the ignition. When she answered my call forty minutes later she wasn't in Tesco's, as she claimed, but here, probably, hiding the car in the garages and erasing all evidence of what she'd done.

For one final moment she turns back to face me. Her face is transformed: drained of colour, her mouth drags down at the edges like she's about to cry.

'The blood made such a horrid mess,' she says mournfully. 'All that sticky stuff going everywhere. But I had to do it, for the sake of our relationship. I mean, he was going around telling you all these lies. He told you he'd never loved me, didn't he? I couldn't have him going around saying things like that.'

Then, before I have time to react, she's opened the front door and is hurrying outside into the blasting cold.

'Where's Poppy?' I scream. 'What have you done with her?'

The door slams behind her. A second later I hear a key turn in the lock.

3.35 a.m.

With a moan of recognition, Dave sat up. He felt as spooked and shocked as if a hand had shot out from under his bed and grabbed his ankle: his spine tingled, the hair on the back of his arms stiffened and his heart pattered wildly. Of course! Now that he had made the connection, it was so bloody obvious! Reaching for his mobile, he leapt out of the Travelodge bed.

They must have finished interviewing Uckfield, for Clive answered the phone immediately.

'Yup?'

Grabbing his trousers from the bedside chair, Dave started to pull them on, wedging the phone between shoulder and jowls. 'Do you remember the tea towels in Rosa Montague's cottage?'

'Not really, no.'

'They were folded up all fancily.'

Now it was Jenkins' turn to play the role of tired cynic. He'd been questioning Uckfield for most of the night, after all. 'Bloody hell, Dave! You're calling me at three-thirty in the morning to discuss tea towels?'

'Yeah, I am actually. I've just remembered. That friend of Mel Stenning, where she's staying the night? In her kitchen they're folded exactly the same way.'

'And?'

'It's obvious, isn't it? I've never seen anything like those towels in my life. She HAS to be Rosa Montague . . . that's why the place was left so neat and tidy. Stenning never killed her. She's packed up her aunt's cottage and followed him and his new wife to their nice new house . . .'

Down the line, Jenkins was very quiet. Dave continued to grapple with his trousers.

'You're saying this is Rosa Montague, all along? And she killed Stenning?'

'Could be . . .'

He'd made it into the boxy bathroom now, and was groping for the shirt that he'd hung on the radiator.

'What about Jacqui Jenning?'

'Maybe she killed her too. She could have taken that chisel from Simon Stenning's toolbox. Remember where we found it?' *When Jenkins did not reply, he added,* 'Did you get anything on Uckfield?'

'Not a twinkle. He's been at a football match all afternoon. Got about a hundred witnesses, and –'

'Call the guys over in Faversham,' Dave interrupted him. He was back in control now, the adrenalin starting to pump. 'Get them to go to the friend's house. Mel Stenning and her little boy aren't safe.'

38

I have to get out. I ram my body into the front door, but all I succeed in doing is bashing my shoulder.

'Open, dammit!'

I hardly notice the smarting pain. Sprinting down the narrow corridor, I dash across the kitchen and rattle the back door. Like the front door, it's locked and there's no key. Screaming with fury I kick it so hard that the wood splinters, but still the door doesn't budge. The shock has sucked the air from my lungs, like I've been struck from behind with a mallet. All the time I thought she was my friend, Trish was planning to destroy me. And now she has Poppy and Jo.

Spinning around, I run back across the kitchen. That I could have ever felt comfortable here is astounding. With her artful decor and homely cosiness she set the scene to beguile me, offering a refuge when in reality the place was a trap. I should have taken one look at the obsessive gleam of her surfaces and guessed that Trish was not what she seemed. What normal person would take such care to keep everything symmetrical? As my eye falls on her tea towels, folded into a psychotically precise fan next to the washing-up, I strike them to the floor with a scream. My hatred for her subsumes everything.

My only hope is the sitting room. Skidding across the tiles, I fling open the door, searching frantically for the phone. It's on its cradle, on a table next to the sofa. Grabbing it, I press the 'on' button and wait for the dial tone, but the line's dead. Either she's deliberately cut me off, or it's the snow. Throwing down the phone, I dart towards the small bay windows, already knowing they'll be locked.

'*Bitch!*'

On the floor by the door is a heavy metal doorstop in the shape of a lion. Scooping it up, I move back to the window, then hurl it as hard as I can at the windows. Terror gives me strength. The glass shatters on impact, pausing intact for a moment, like a cartoon character that, having shot over a cliff, carries on running in mid air, before shuddering to the bottom of the frame.

Cold air gusts in. Using the lion to knock out the jagged glass that remains, I haul myself through the window, landing with a soft thud in deep snow. Now that the blizzard has passed, the moon has reappeared, illuminating every detail of the small garden.

Snow covers everything. Wading through the flurry that the wind has blown into the side of the cottage I reach the thinner crusting of the lawn, my trainers slipping. It is so cold that my cheeks ache; my breath surrounds me in clouds. My heart is pounding so hard that I fear it may explode. Tramping around the side of the cottage, I reach the front. Under its white blanket, the lane is unrecognizable. Rosa's footsteps, left a few minutes earlier, lead across the front garden.

When I reach the gate I pause, trying to clear my head. There is no point in waking Bob and Janice. They don't have a mobile, and from the look of the line that sags heavily against its skewered pole on the other side of the lane, it was the weather and not Rosa that cut the phone. Further down the lane I can make out the distant lights of the warehouse. In these conditions it would take me ten minutes or so to reach it, and another ten for the police to pick up her trail; by then Rosa may have disappeared for good, taking Poppy and Jo with her.

Yet whilst I cannot call for help, the snow gives me the clues I need. Rather than progressing up the lane, the tracks move along a small alley that cuts between Rosa's cottage and the adjacent garages. Stumbling along it, I follow her footsteps around the back of the cottages. Here they join a small path which eventually feeds into the riverside track about quarter of a mile to the north of the warehouse. This was her favourite walk, Trish once told me. Striding towards the estuary, with the peewits fluttering in the reeds and the breezes ruffling her hair, she'd almost forget who she was. I'd nodded empathetically at the time, assuming that she was referring to the need to escape her everyday self, to transcend dreary reality. Now, as I flounder after her, I see that her meaning was so much darker. The woman whose portrait Si tore from his kitchen wall last Christmas is a liar, a mistress of disguises who will stop at nothing to get her revenge. As I recall the times she's looked after Jo for me, I almost retch. I start to jog down the path. I am praying that she has not harmed my children.

The icy marsh stretches before me. In the distance I can see the grey line of water and a low huddle of boats. The track leads towards them. I run faster, the fresh snow crunching beneath my shoes. I have no plan, just the leaden certainty that somewhere in the derelict boats that I am fast approaching I will find Poppy and Jo. I keep repeating their names over and over, as if to ward off evil.

Despite the snow, the terrain is becoming boggy; a little way ahead someone has laid planks across the morass. I start to clank over them, my feet slipping in the muddy ice. I no longer feel afraid. I have become the sum of Poppy and Jo's names, my need to find them erasing all else. If I am cold or tired or my shoulder throbs from Rosa's front door, I am not aware of it. When I reach the water's edge I stop for a moment, peering around. Lying low in the water are two abandoned vessels, one so broken and rotten-looking that it's a miracle that it stays afloat. The second is an old-fashioned fishing boat, its battered hulk green with slime. The wooden cabin is lit up by what looks like a lantern, revealing the silhouette of a hunched adult figure, bent over something. Hearing my footsteps, Rosa glances up and, in the dancing light, appears to smile. I'm praying aloud now, begging God to save my children.

As I reach the water's edge I leap over the rickety jetty, landing with a crash on the deck. 'What have you done with my kids?' I scream. 'Come out and face me!'

There is no response, just the soft splash of water as a clod of snow drops from the side of the boat. Diving towards the cabin, I shake the handle of the rusty door, banging hard against the wood with my fist. I can smell petrol in the air, a thick chemical fug.

The night remains silent. All I can hear is the water, dragging along the silty creek. If they were still alive, surely Poppy or Jo would cry out?

'Fuck you!' I roar, throwing the entire weight of my body against the door. I am so desperate to get inside that, if I could, I would claw the boat apart with my nails. From inside the cabin, I hear a sudden movement. With a click the metal door swings open.

Rosa stands before me. For a second I barely recognize her. Her normally immaculate hair is plastered over her sweaty forehead and her smooth complexion turned red and puffy. Dark bags circle her pink eyes. In a handful of minutes she has turned from pregnant beauty to bedraggled lunatic, her eyes darting from my face to the marshland behind.

Now that the door is open, the smell of petrol is over-powering. I want to lunge at her, to tear her to pieces, but something stops me.

'What have you done to Jo and Poppy?' I say evenly.

She ignores the question; perhaps she doesn't hear it, for her eyes have a strange, disconnected expression. 'Is Si coming?' she whispers. 'I need Si to come and get me.'

She is holding something in her hands. Glancing down, I see the glint of Si's old lighter, the one he claimed to have lost. Her fingers caress it, rubbing it in tiny repetitive circles.

'He's not coming,' I say. 'It's just me.' From behind her, I have just noticed a flicker of movement. Rosa peers dimly at my face, as if she has only just remembered who I am.

'You've ruined everything,' she says softly. 'I was having his baby. You stole him from me.'

'That's bullshit. How do I know the baby's even his?'

She grimaces, throwing back her head and guffawing with deadly laughter as if I have just told a hilarious joke. 'Of course it's his! He was so desperate to fuck me he didn't even bother to ask if I was still on the pill! Who else's would it be?'

I swallow hard. I cannot think about this, not now.

'He adored me,' she continues, seeming to recover her composure. 'It was going to be so perfect. Just him and me and our child. We didn't need to see anyone else or go anywhere. We were soulmates. Why did he have to be so afraid of something so beautiful?'

'You're deluding yourself. He said you were unbalanced. He was desperate to get rid of you –'

'Don't you dare say that . . .'

I don't know whether it's the passion with which she makes this denial or something else, but her face suddenly contorts. For a moment her grip on the lighter loosens, her

331

fingers beginning to unfurl, but before I can snatch it from her, she steps back, grasping it more tightly. She seems to be having trouble controlling her breathing.

'I have to . . . get rid of everything . . . all this is just distracting him . . .'

As she moves aside, my heart jumps. I have just glimpsed Jo, lying in what looks like an old dog basket on the cabin floor. I want to push Rosa roughly aside and grab him, but I do not like the way her thumb keeps fiddling with the lighter, the little flame darting in and out like the tongue of a snake.

'You need help,' I say. 'This isn't going to make anything better.'

She shakes her head, taking another step back. As she moves further into the cabin, I have to stop myself from screeching out loud. What I have just seen in the dingy corner turns me inside out in a heart-plunging mixture of relief and terror. Crouching in the shadows next to Jo's basket, her pale face turned in my direction, is Poppy. She is gazing intently at me but does not utter a sound. Her hair is wet and the blanket that she has wrapped around her shoulders stained with something dark. She is shivering violently. As I gawp at her I suddenly understand why the place reeks of petrol.

'Give me the lighter,' I say.

'I don't think so.'

I am no longer thinking rationally. I've switched on to automatic; only my primal instincts are functioning. All that Rosa has to do now is turn towards Poppy and Jo and make that little flicking gesture with her thumb, and everything will be finished.

'Give me the lighter!'

Swiping at her hand, I barge into her, trying to knock her sideways, but despite her condition she's surprisingly agile.

Hopping to one side, she spins away from me, her hands closing around the lighter. In the second that I stumble into the boat's wheel she darts across the deck towards the corner where Poppy cowers.

'You turned him against me,' she whispers. 'Everything was perfect before he met you!'

I have to get the lighter. Roaring at the top of my voice, I leap on to her back, my fingers scratching her face. 'Get away from there!'

Yanking at her hair with one hand, my fingers grope around her vast belly. She gasps, falling to her knees, but still has the lighter. Now I am punching her face, my past, present and future reduced to the sum of my actions: fist against flesh, wanting to pummel her into oblivion. For a moment my brain short-circuits, producing only the image of Si's dead face, staring up at me from the winch-house. Slapping her as hard as I can, I try to push her down, so that I can sit astride her, but she's heavier and stronger than I could ever have predicted. Rolling around like a playful seal, she disengages herself from my grasp and starts to squirm across the floor, moving ever closer to Poppy and Jo. She's almost there. Flicking at the lighter, she's stretching her arm in their direction, the little blue flame about to make contact with the fumes.

What happens next is so sudden that I am barely able to take it in. As Rosa lurches towards Jo's basket, Poppy leaps from her corner. Her normal seven-year-old clumsiness has disappeared. In the second that she flies through the air towards Rosa, she has the appearance of a tiger, her eyes wild. As I grab Rosa's midriff, dragging her backwards, Poppy's teeth sink into her wrist. Shrieking with pain, Rosa releases the lighter. With one elegant sweep of her arm, Poppy sends it skittering to the other side of the room.

333

It's then that I lose control. As Rosa lies, breathing hard at my feet, I start to kick ferociously at her prostrated legs and buttocks. There's blood on my hands, perhaps from her mouth, which is bubbling with red saliva, and clumps of hair between my fingers. She is a pregnant woman, who only a few hours ago was my only friend. But now I want to kill both her and her unborn child.

'Don't you dare hurt my children!'

She has started to scream, a high-pitched shriek that reminds me of an animal being slaughtered, but I have moved beyond human compassion. Grabbing an oar that's lying on the rusty floor, I lift it high into the air, about to thump her with it. I want to beat her into a pulp, to erase her from the face of the earth.

'Mummy, stop it!'

Turning, I see Poppy, who has jumped to her feet and is frantically trying to grab the oar. 'You're going to kill her!'

Gawping in shock at my daughter, I let the oar fall to the ground. I had almost forgotten where I was. But now, I remember.

'Get out of here!' I yell, gesturing wildly at the metal door. Round-eyed with shock, Poppy scoots across the cabin, the door crashing behind her. Diving across the floor, I scoop Jo into my arms. He's woken now, and is yelling, his arms flung over his head with passion. I am desperate to put him to my sore breasts, but we will have to wait, for any second Rosa will retrieve the lighter.

Yet, as I swing around, I see that rather than scrabbling to reach it, she is hunched in the corner, her hands clutching her knees, as if she's been winded. She is making a low, animal sound: half groan, half piggish grunt. A pool of liquid is gathering at her feet, like she's wet herself.

'Oh God, help me, please . . .'

For a moment I stare at her in silence. She's kneeling over now, her palms flat on the oily floor. Her bloodied face is clenched with pain, sweat beading her forehead. She has just vomited.

'Oh God, I'm going to die . . .'

'You don't need to make such a fuss,' I hear myself say coldly. 'You're not going to die. You're in labour.'

She sighs, falling back on to her bottom as the contraction ends. As she wipes at her mouth, looking blearily around, I see that in the fight she has lost her two front teeth.

'Is it always as bad as this?' she murmurs in a little-girl-lost voice.

'Yes,' I say. 'Always.'

She is seized by another contraction. As she starts to rock to and fro with the pain, I turn and hurry towards the metal door. Bursting through it, I clatter on to the deck, where Poppy is huddled against a snowy coil of rope.

'Mummy!'

From inside the cabin, Rosa produces a ghoulish shriek. Throwing my free arm around Poppy, I pull her towards me. Even if there were time to speak, I would not be able to. Hauling her on to my hip, I clamber with her and Jo on to the icy riverbank. I do not know where I have acquired the strength to carry them like this, but I am jogging over the wooden walkway, moving as fast from Rosa's screams as is humanly possible. Now that I have them back, I never want to let my children go. It is only when Poppy pushes her wet face against mine and kisses me that I realize I am crying.

We do not get far. The children are too heavy, and after a few feet more, my legs buckle. As we sink into the snow, I hold Poppy and Jo tightly against me, small fingers clasped around my arms, legs gripping my waist, faces turned towards my bosom. I have to try to keep them warm, so I pull them as closely as I can against my body, my hands cradling their heads. In those few moments of clarity, before the police torches catch us in their beam and we are surrounded by people and lights, I know that this is all that matters: to be with my children, to love and care for them. Burying my face in her oily hair, I hug Poppy like I'm never going to let her go.

'I'm so sorry, honey . . .'

Putting her arms around my middle, she squeezes me hard. From the top of the lane I can hear the whoop of sirens. The lights move closer, bumping over the shining marsh. In the distance, someone is calling my name.

39

June 2006

The way Dave Gosforth saw it, the world was divided into two cate-gories of people. First were the vast majority: those who were basically good, the ones who were the victims and not the perpetrators of crimes. Sometimes they got into a muddle, or messed up, but basically they were well-behaved, law-abiding citizens, trying to do their best. Into this category he put his family, friends and most of his colleagues. Then there were the others: baddies, as Harvey put it. It was a small but significant minority. Motivated by greed, unable to empathise with the people they hurt and never able to accept responsibility, they were the troublemakers, whose unpleasant activities he had dedicated his career to fighting. He'd been around long enough to know that this nomenclature was sometimes a bit blunt, that circumstances might make good people do terrible things, but basically his beliefs held firm. Okay, so there were the sob stories: the childhood abuse or mental problems that propelled people into going down the wrong track; even though he loathed what he thought of as the 'victim culture', he acknowledged that much. But after twenty years in the game, if there was one thing he'd learned it was that good people, no matter how far they were pushed, did not turn into murderers. In his line of work the basic challenge was to sort the sheep from the goats.

Simon Stenning was not a baddy. During the first stages of their investigation he and Clive Jenkins had suspected he might be, but now it was clear that he was simply a poor sod who, having got into a bit of a mess, was unable to extricate himself without wading ever deeper into the mire. His real mistake was to get involved with Rosa Montague.

He lied to his wife, too, which never helped. Oh yes, and there was the little matter of impregnating Rosa whilst involved with Mel. To that extent, it was his own bloody fault. Personally, Dave had always been one hundred per cent faithful to Karen. To be honest, he despised men who couldn't keep their peckers in their pants.

Rosa Montague, on the other hand, was as evil as they come. She'd killed Jacqui Jenning in a jealous fury after Stenning had picked her up from the Starlite club. It was all Simon's fault, she told the police when the doctors finally allowed them to interview her. He'd been so cruel to her, even threatening to end their relationship. So when he'd gone storming out of her house she'd followed him, just to make sure he wasn't going to do anything silly. Watching him leave the club with that little slut on his arm was just too much she told Dave, her eyelashes batting. She'd thrown up all over the pavement. It was HER he loved, not that tart. They were soulmates, meant always to be together. Just because he was too cowardly to face up to the truth, it didn't mean that she had to give up on what they'd got together. Surely it was only natural that she'd chosen to defend the relationship? So she had waited outside Jacqui's flat all night, until she finally saw her beloved leave. Then she marched into the flat and bludgeoned her rival to death, adding the chisel wounds to the head for extra effect. Her handprint matched the one they'd found in the hall, and, surprise, surprise, she'd left her prints over the chisel.

Dave's team had to cobble the rest of the story together, for after admitting to Jacqui's murder, Rosa refused to make any further comment. Yet despite the defence's attempts to portray Simon Stenning as a lying womanizer who had pushed his emotionally vulnerable girl-friend over the edge, Dave was satisfied that their story held tight. Based on what both Mel and his friend Ollie Dubow had told them, they built up a picture of Rosa Montague as a manipulative obses-sive, who refused to accept that her relationship to Stenning was over. She was an expert in getting people to do what she wanted, Dubow had stated in his testimony. She had even managed to prise Simon and

Mel's new address out of him, calling him late at night and begging for it. She was pregnant, she'd sobbed, she had to see Simon. So he gave her the number and she called Simon, summoning him to her place in the woods. There'd been a terrible scene. According to Dubow, Simon had informed Rosa that since he'd last seen her he'd got married and had a son; even if Rosa's baby was his, he wouldn't be returning. Rosa had punched him in the face, then made a show of cutting her wrists. It was a typical Rosa tactic, histrionics all the way. Simon had driven her to the hospital in his van, dropping her at the entrance to A & E. He'd have to eventually tell Mel the truth, he'd confided to Ollie, but was dreading her response. He had promised he'd never betray her, and now, with his ex-girlfriend pregnant, he was terrified of losing her. As for the credit cards, Dave and Clive decided that Simon must have left them there deliberately, perhaps in the desperate hope that with the use of his money Rosa would leave him alone. After the scene with Simon she must have returned untreated from Canterbury to the cottage. Then she'd cleaned up the mess and, after her shopping spree in London, departed for Kent.

Folding his arms, Dave took a step back from the front door, looking up at the large, dark house. There was money here, however dilapidated the place had become. When you thought of Simon Stenning's posh voice, and the disdainful way he had sneered at the police's questions, it made sense. They should pull that ivy away from the top windows, he was thinking, and give the place a lick of paint. Even in this state it must be worth seven or eight hundred grand.

From behind the door he could hear shrill laughter, the scuffling of little feet, then the sound of a woman's voice. With a click, the door opened.

Mel Stenning stood before him. She had lost weight since the year before and had her hair cropped short so that it clung in feathery wisps around her face, making her look both younger and more vulnerable. Unlike the grimy jeans and jumpers of the winter, or the formal trouser suits she had worn during the trial, she was dressed in a long cotton skirt and a black vest, showing off her Mediterranean skin. The haunted expression that had clouded her pretty features in the days that immediately followed the murder had finally lifted. Her pale face hardly shone with joy, and dark shadows encircled her eyes, but in Dave's view she looked normal again. Now, as she saw him standing on the step, she even smiled.

'Hello there!'

'How are you doing, Mel? Is this a good time?'

'As good as any.'

She stepped back to let him in. Appearing silently at her side, Poppy slipped her hand into her mother's.

'Alicia's out with Jo. She's taken him to a toddler group in the village, can you imagine?'

He smiled, taking in the grand hall and curving staircase. Sandra, who had remained in close touch with her, had told him all about how Mel and her children had moved in with their grandmother. The old girl was a bit batty, she'd said, but the arrangement was surprisingly successful.

'Nice place.'

'Yeah. We've been giving it a bit of a spring-clean. You'll have to excuse the mess.'

She showed him into a huge room, filled with what, to his eyes, looked like a load of posh junk, but was probably worth a bundle.

'Poppy, why don't you go and have a play in the tree house? You can take Ginger up there.'

The little girl nodded. She was about the same age as Harvey, and as she silently stared up at Dave's face, he could not resist giving her a little wink. Blanking him, she turned and skipped out of the room.

'We've bought her a rabbit,' Mel was saying. 'She takes him everywhere.'

'How's she coping?'

She gave a faint shrug, her smile fixed. 'A bit clingy at first, but slowly getting better.'

They sat down. Despite his experience of meetings with bereaved relatives, Dave felt unaccustomedly nervous. He made it a rule never to get personally involved, but something about Mel Stenning had pulled at him. She seemed so alone, perhaps that was it. Her fragility, mixed with her stubborn pride, made him want to take her in his arms and embrace her. He'd never admit it, but a tiny part of him felt responsible for what had happened, too. After all, if he had got the truth earlier, Simon might still be alive.

'She was being bullied at school,' Mel was saying. 'That's what all those letters were about. A horrible little cow called Megan was sending them.'

He nodded. Sandra had mentioned this, too. 'Yes, I heard.'

'Apparently they thought it was hilarious to tease her about having a stepdad. It makes me feel terrible, that I didn't pick up on it.'

'These things happen, I suppose.'

'Only when parents aren't paying attention. I can't believe it was going on so long and I never knew about it.'

'I'm sure it wasn't your fault.'

There was a long silence during which Dave felt unusually awkward. 'So,' he said, squeezing his fleshy palms with his thumbs. The delicate chaise longue on which he was sitting made him feel like an oaf. 'I hope you don't mind me dropping in on you like this. It's a courtesy call, really, just to touch base with you after the trial. We're obviously pleased with the outcome.'

She nodded, her tired eyes fixed on his.

'She's not going to get out, is she?'

'She'll be in prison for the rest of her life.'

'What about the baby?'

'That was partly what I wanted to tell you. I had a nice long chat with Jenny Millburn yesterday. You know, the social worker? He's been adopted by a very nice family in Chelmsford. Rosa won't see him again.'

Mel frowned, picking at the silky threads of the high-backed chair where she was seated. There wasn't a great deal else that Dave could tell her. She had attended the entire trial, sitting quietly at the back of the courtroom, her hands folded in her lap as she listened intently to the proceedings. When the jury had returned a verdict of guilty of the first-degree murder of Jacqui Jenning and Simon Stenning, and of the abduction of Poppy and Jo Stenning, she had nodded with satisfaction, then risen to her feet and left the courtroom. By the time Dave had battled through the media scrum, she was gone.

'How about you?' he asked. 'How are you feeling?'

She did not seem to have been anticipating such a personal question. She looked up at him, her lips silently moving, as if something was about to burst from them that she could no longer contain.

'I . . .'

'You must have found the trial very difficult . . .'

She shook her head, as if it was irrelevant. 'All I can think is that I should have had the guts to trust Si,' she whispered. 'I thought he was lying to me.'

'It's hardly surprising, given what happened . . .'

'We promised we'd trust each other, but from the beginning I'd convinced myself that he couldn't ever love me. Now I know that everything he told me was pretty much true.'

'Come on now, you mustn't blame yourself . . .'

'Why not?' Glancing hastily away from him, she wiped her eyes with the back of her hand. Since that terrible night when she had discovered her husband's body, it was the first time he had seen her cry. 'I'm not very good at relationships, you see. I always mess everything up . . .'

'I'm sure that's not true.'

He wanted to place a comforting hand on her shoulder, but the stiffness of her back made the gesture seem impossible. He was about to make the little speech he sometimes gave to victims about bad things happening to good people, but she interrupted him.

'The thing is, Dave, I've never had any real direction in my life. Before I met Si I was just drifting, waiting for something to happen. That's why I married him, I suppose. I thought he could save me, make everything meaningful.'

Dave nodded, not sure what to say. Mel had risen to her feet and was moving towards the large bay window, through which the summer sun glinted. In the gardens outside they could see Poppy running over the grass.

'It was all bollocks, though, wasn't it? Imagining that all it would take to solve my problems was to meet some new person and be swept off my feet. He thought that all we had to do was wave a magic wand and everything that had happened in the past would disappear. What a load of crap that turned out to be . . .'

'I suppose it's what a lot of people believe.'

'No, they don't.' She turned to face him, her eyes flashing. Crimson spots of anger had appeared on her cheekbones. 'They might say they do, but most people are too busy getting on with their lives to waste them on stupid fantasies. Life isn't about waiting around for someone to save you. It was up to me to make things work, not some knight in shining armour.'

She was glaring at him almost accusingly. Glancing away from her fierce eyes, Dave scrutinized his shoes. He was accustomed to people's emotional outpourings: the grief or anger or raw fear that flooded from them when seated in his interview room. Yet this encounter was different. It was almost as if in the normal course of his work he had cotton wool stuffed in his ears. But for some reason today he'd taken it out and was finally listening.

'I don't think I ever really knew how to love him,' Mel said quietly. 'I thought I did, but when it came to it I wasn't able to. If I'd really loved him I'd have trusted him, wouldn't I? I wouldn't have been so afraid of hearing what it was he needed to tell me.'

'Oh, come on now . . .'

She was not interested in his reassurances. Her eyes flicked away

343

from his, her face clouding with thoughts that she was not prepared to share.

'Mummy!' Poppy was yelling. 'Ginger's eating some dandelions!'

At the sound of her daughter's voice, she straightened up. Her face, which seemed for a moment to have become unbearably hard, softened. 'The point is, I'm not going to drift any more,' she said, almost smiling. 'The kids are all that matter now. I should have realized that from the start. That's why I'm going to stay here with Alicia and try to build some kind of normal life for them . . . Okay, honey! I'm coming!'

Standing, she started to move across the battered drawing room, towards the garden doors.

It was after three. He decided not to go back to the station and his paperwork, but to slip off early. The morning had been humid and cloudy, but now the sky had cleared to brilliant blue. When he reached the dual carriageway he opened the car windows and pressed his foot down hard, enjoying the feel of warm air rushing at him, the bright summer light burning into his face. During his brief discussion with Mel he had felt gloomy and oppressed. He did not like to think that lying behind the comfortable homilies with which he padded his life were darker, more complex realities, but that was what she'd implied. Now that he was outside, however, the impression lifted off him, like mist evaporating. Perhaps they'd go to the beach, picking up a supermarket barbecue along the way. Or he and Karen could crack open a bottle of wine in the garden, watching and chatting as Harvey bounced his ball against the wall.

He was not a drifter, had never struggled for meaning. Mel Stenning had made life sound so impossible, but in his view you didn't need a degree in philosophy to work out the root of happiness: steady work, accomplishable goals, the love of a wife and children. How difficult was that? In a different life he could have fallen for someone like Mel, with her sad eyes and the gentle, wounded manner in which she spoke.

344

But he had his Karen, and his professionalism, and he would probably never see her again.

He was approaching Herne Bay. In the distance he could see the flashing strip of sea, the glint of car bonnets parked by the beach. He drove a couple of miles through the centre of town, then turned into a suburban road. Around the corner, past the postbox: acres of neat, 1960s houses, with their tidy front gardens and manageable lawns. Past kids' bikes and gleaming saloons, shimmering in the sun. In less than a minute he'd be home. He slowed down, clicking on his indicator. Some of his neighbours had climbing frames and slides for their children, others had tubs of cheerful flowers by the front step. Finally he turned into the drive, noting the colourful front gardens with pleasure. Geraniums, delphiniums, peonies: the kinds of flowers you knew where you were with.

Acknowledgements

Many thanks to the following, for their advice, support and encouragement: Clare Conville, Louise Moore, Beverley Cousins, Reg Hooke and Graham Alborough.